THE
✠ LINZ ✠
TATTOO

Nicholas Guild

THE LINZ TATTOO

McGraw-Hill Book Company

New York St. Louis San Francisco Bogotá Guatemala Hamburg Lisbon Madrid Mexico Montreal Panama Paris San Juan São Paulo Tokyo Toronto

1 2 3 4 5 6 7 8 9 A G A G 8 7 6

First paperback edition, 1986

ISBN 0-07-025112-6 {H.C.}
ISBN 0-07-025113-4 {PBK.}

LIBRARY OF CONGRESS CATALOGING IN PUBLICATION DATA

Guild, Nicholas.
The Linz Tattoo.
I. Title.
PS3557.U357T3 1986   813'.54   85-10499
ISBN 0-07-025112-6
0-07-025113-4 (pbk.)

BOOK DESIGN BY PATRICE FODERO

This book is for my friends
Mort and Kay Podolsky,
who know why

❖ 1 ❖

"I'm quite sure it's him, even without his uniform. It hasn't even been half a year, and that isn't the sort of face one forgets."

"I think he's really quite good looking."

Major Robert Briggs, late of His Majesty's XXIst Army Group, glanced across the narrow cabaret table at his new wife and felt a sharp pang of something like jealousy—they weren't very encouraging words to hear a mere four days after one's wedding night.

But she was right, of course. The man he had pointed out to her, standing at the back of the tiny smoke-curtained stage, almost hidden behind six or seven other musicians and a huge double bass, was tall and strikingly handsome. His shoulders could have been a yard and a half wide, and his tarnished blond hair, which he wore rather long, made him look like every schoolgirl's notion of a Viking prince.

It was his face, however, which had struck the chord in Briggs' memory, the pitiless blue eyes—

1

even at this distance one could see that they were a deep blue, like precious stones—and the hard, sharp, impassive features, as if the bones underneath were made of iron.

And, of course, across the back of the left hand, catching a gleam from the footlights as the fingers moved back and forth over the strings of his double bass, was a wide, flat scar. Briggs had noticed the scar the first time they had met, in a prison yard in Germany. There couldn't be any doubt it was the same chap.

"I stood right next to him that god-awful morning at Rebdorf. Seven big bloody Nazi generals took the drop in less than forty minutes, and he never even raised an eyebrow. I felt rather sick, I don't mind telling you—no one looks his best after he's been hanged, and a couple of them had bitten clean through their tongues at the last second, making quite a mess of themselves. It was a pretty horrible thing to watch, but he might as well have been waiting in line for his tea."

"What was he doing there?"

Thelma smiled with interest. He had learned early that, like a lot of American girls, she rather liked gamy stories about the war. She was really quite a blood-thirsty little bitch, which was one of the reasons he had decided to marry her. But just at that moment he found himself wishing she would exhibit a little decent feminine squeamishness.

"Same as my sweet self, I suppose," he said finally, making sure to look away as he spoke. "We were 'official witnesses' if you will, he for the Norwegians and me for the British. There were five or six of us. Yes, six. They served us coffee in tin cups while we waited for sunrise, and there were introductions all round. Probably we were all a bit nervous; the Russian, a great big cad of a fellow with a face as red as a radish, actually started to giggle, I remember. And then, after an hour, the executions began. I'm not likely to forget anything connected with that affair."

The music from what presumably was supposed to be a jazz combo was as bad as any Briggs had ever heard, even in his own country, which over the last several months he had come to regard with a certain distaste. Since moving to New York, where, on the strength of his war record and the profound respect every former colonial feels toward the British upper classes, he had gotten himself a very soft job as a sales representative for one of the big Manhattan advertising agencies, he had become a connoisseur of all things American. American music was louder and better to dance to, American women were more amusing in bed, and American food . . . well, there was simply no comparison. He was acclimatized and happy and on his honeymoon, so there was little enough to complain about. He simply wished Thelma hadn't insisted on this absurd package cruise, and that the rum didn't always taste like diesel fuel, and that sometime or other they could stumble across a band that didn't make "Tea for Two" sound like the Guatemalan national anthem.

He was also rather beginning to wish that he hadn't run into Christiansen—he was almost positive that had been the fellow's name. Or at least that he had kept his mouth shut about it. Thelma was watching the stage with an attention in no way justified by the music being produced there.

"Ask him to come and have a drink with us," she

said, turning toward her husband and smiling as she brushed back a wisp of pale brown hair. It was an astonishingly seductive gesture. "Perhaps he's noticed you too—it wouldn't be very nice to let him think you were trying to snub him, would it?"

Briggs didn't even allow himself time to hesitate. "All right. If you like."

He pinched back the sleeve of his coat to have a look at his watch. It was a quarter after two in the morning—in a few minutes they would be starting back to their ship where, if he hadn't drunk too much, perhaps Thelma's enthusiasm could be channeled into some more useful direction. It wouldn't hurt anything if she ended the evening a bit spiky. Perhaps it wouldn't hurt anything.

"They seem to be taking a break. Shall I just pop over there and renew acquaintance?"

By the time he reached the bandstand, most of the musicians had already left it and were making their way among the closely packed tables to the bar. But Christiansen hadn't stirred; his attention was absorbed by one of the strings of his gigantic instrument, which he seemed to be attempting to tune. He appeared even larger up close, his white dinner jacket stretched across his massive chest, and the expression on his face registered a sullen concentration.

When he noticed Briggs moving around the edge of the stage, his blue eyes narrowed, reminding one of a wary animal.

"I suppose you don't recall me," Briggs began, allowing his mouth to stretch into what he realized had to be a not-terribly-dignified grin. He extended his hand up toward the double bassist, who stared down with what amounted to open hostility. "We met that day at Rebdorf. The name is 'Briggs.' I was the British officer—I stood right next to you."

There was no response. The man appeared not to know what he was talking about. The hand remained suspended in mid air until finally Briggs started to feel just a trifle foolish and allowed it to drop back down to his side.

"I remember you very well—Captain Christiansen, wasn't it? Surely you can't have forgotten the prison."

"My name isn't Christiansen, and I've never been in prison. What would I have been doing in prison?"

The voice was expressionless and rather gravelly, as if from disuse, but the accent was American. It had been American at Rebdorf as well—Briggs had wondered how a Norwegian could have learned to speak such perfect Yankee English. The startingly blue eyes never wavered as the man who claimed not to be Captain Christiansen seemed to wait with patient resignation for whatever might come next.

Briggs hardly knew what to say—could he have been mistaken? No. There was still the scar. Everything, even the voice, could be explained away, but not the scar. It covered the back of Christiansen's left hand like a bandage, the sort of scar that suggested a deep, crippling wound. This was Christiansen.

"We were there to witness the execution of some German war criminals," he answered, with somewhat greater confidence. "You were the Norwegian representative. Surely you don't deny it, old man."

"My name is 'Barrows.' I've never been to Germany."

One finger of the scarred hand glided slowly and delicately up a string of the double bass, as if meas-

uring its tension. The action seemed completely unconscious; the man "Barrows," who had never been
to Germany, regarded the veteran of His Majesty's
XXIst Army Group with the closed expression of
someone who expected that his answer would be taken
as definitive.

"Well then, I'm sorry to have troubled you."

What else was there to say? Briggs turned and
started making his way back to the table where Thelma
was waiting with what struck him as unseemly eagerness.

"It appears I dialed a wrong number," he said,
suddenly not very keen on explanations. It was late
at night, he was tired, and, yes, he *had* drunk too
much. By the time he sat down again he could see
that most of the musicians had returned to the bandstand and the entertainment was about to resume. It
was an appalling prospect.

"I thought you were so positive." Thelma smiled.
There was something just faintly contemptuous in her
smile, as if he had displayed some sort of weakness.
Briggs found himself wondering what she was going
to be like to live with in another ten or fifteen years.

"Well, I still think it was him. Probably he was
just embarrassed. It must be a bit of a comedown,
after all, from officer and gentleman to playing backup
in a cheesebox like this place. The man's entitled to
his feelings— By God, he's gone, isn't he."

Yes, he was. The double bass was resting quietly
on its side, like a fat woman asleep in the sun, and
the wall behind it was empty.

Christiansen had walked no more than a few blocks
when the rain started. At that time of year it came

down in torrents, as rhythmic as the beating of a heart. It was impossible to go on; one simply had to run for cover and wait until the downpour ended.

He stood under the tin awning of an empty grocery store and lit a cigarette. First that damn fool Briggs and now this rain. It just didn't seem to be his night.

Of course he remembered. Briggs had been within arm's length of him there in the prison yard, quietly going green. Imagine anyone who had been through the war sicking up at the sight of a few men being hanged—one would have thought that by then everyone would have seen enough death and horror to render them immune for life, but maybe Briggs had been a clerk or something.

It had rained that night too. There had still been pools of water in the prison yard, and he remembered how in the hour before dawn, in the light from the guard towers, a team of German POWs had swept the walkways so their generals wouldn't get wet feet walking to the gallows. He remembered how von Goltz had stood up there on the narrow wooden stage, his face expressionless, almost frozen, as they slipped the hood over his head. There had been no last words, just a kind of thud as the rope jerked tight. All things considered, it would hardly seem to have been enough.

Anyway, tonight wasn't the occasion for talking over old times. The last thing in the world Christiansen needed was to get entangled with some nostalgic former comrade-in-arms—the fighting hadn't been over even three years, but everyone seemed to have forgotten what it had been like. It was astonishing how sentimental some men seemed to have become about the lost opportunities of carnage.

But tonight there was only time for business. The

business the war had left unsettled. Briggs and his reminiscences and his whiskey and his lady friend could wait.

After about twenty minutes the rain started to slacken and then, quite suddenly, it was just gone. Christiansen ground out his second cigarette under the toe of his shoe and started on again.

The note left at his hotel that afternoon had been as explicit as it needed to be: *"If the man with the strings wishes to hear of mutual friends, he may join me for breakfast tomorrow morning at my house. Gerhart."*

Gerhart Becker lived above his tobacco shop on the Calle de Machado under the name of "Bauer." He had moved to Havana in 1946, coming from Argentina, and had paid to establish his new business enterprise with seventy-five hundred dollars in cash. Christiansen knew all about Gerhart Becker. The information had cost him most of his savings, two years of his life, and three murders. And now Herr Becker was offering a deal to avoid becoming Number Four.

Or perhaps he was merely interested in tricking Christiansen into some foolish mistake so he could eliminate that threat once and for all.

Christiansen had no trouble finding the tobacco shop. It took up the first floor of a two-story building between a luggage store and a small hotel. There was a taxi stand on the other side of the street, at the end of the block, and even at a quarter to three in the morning there were still a couple of cabs about, the interior lights on to show their drivers asleep behind the steering wheel. Perhaps there was a cabaret or a brothel somewhere about—Havana was like that— little clusters of nightlife hiding out in what appeared to be the most respectable of middle-class business districts.

The upper story, where, to all appearances, Becker was sleeping quietly, was curtained and dark. But Christiansen was putting little faith in appearances, so he found himself a convenient shadow to hide in and settled down to wait.

The rain had left the air feeling slightly clammy, and Christiansen kept his hands in the pockets of the blue overcoat he wore over his dinner jacket. He wished he could have had another cigarette, but of course that was imposssible under the circumstances. He was watching the windows across the street.

A man walked by on the sidewalk in front of where Christiansen was standing. It wasn't Becker, who had reddish hair and a round, rather Slavic face, but one of the natives, out, from the looks of him, for a little catting around. Under the wide brim of a light-colored felt hat, Christiansen could see a pencil-thin moustache, a narrow jaw, and two rather frightened-looking eyes. Perhaps he was aware that someone was there in the shadow of the archway that marked the entrance to a darkened restaurant, because his pace seemed to quicken slightly as he passed.

Christiansen was tired. He had been awake for something like twenty hours, and it seemed like a good deal longer than that since anything had passed his lips but cold coffee and cigarette smoke. And on top of everything else his hand felt as if it were stuffed with broken glass. It always throbbed after a night of playing, even the thump-thump-thump of a bass fiddle, but tonight it was worse. The surgeon had told him he would always have trouble with it. Anyway, there wasn't any point in complaining—he should

probably count himself lucky it was still attached to
his wrist.

It was about ten minutes before four when he
noticed that the inside edge of one of the curtains
behind the middle window upstairs was no longer
hanging quite straight. Someone had pulled it a little
to one side in order to see out onto the street.

So, Herr Bauer—the former Herr Becker, the former Sergeant Becker, Ninth Occupation Division, Fifth
Brigade, Waffen-SS, Norway—Herr Bauer was at
home, and just as restless as everyone else. It would
appear he wasn't looking forward to the morning very
much.

Or perhaps he was. From his point of view the
strategy made a certain amount of sense. If he knew
he was being hunted, why shouldn't he take the opportunity of choosing the time and place for an encounter he probably realized was inevitable? Didn't
he have a life here, something worth defending? If he
was sufficiently sure of himself—and this, after all,
was his warren, not Christiansen's—why should he
run?

And when were the SS ever unsure of themselves?

And, of course, Becker was perfectly aware that
he was being hunted. Christiansen had been no more
than a little surprised that morning when he had returned from breakfast and the man at the desk had
handed him a small buff-colored envelope in exchange
for his room key.

*"This was left for you a few minutes ago, Sēnor
Barrows,"* he had murmured, smiling his polite, in-
offensive Latin smile. *"The gentleman said he did not
wish to disturb your meal."*

Becker wasn't even bothering to be coy—the address of his shop was printed right on the flap. It was the sort of envelope that might accompany a box of gift cigars, and even in Cuba it paid to advertise.

And why should it be so surprising that Becker would know he was being hunted? These men were all condemned, convicted *in absentia* for crimes against humanity and sentenced to death by a Norwegian court. But more than that, the old boys' network the SS maintained was probably humming with word that somebody was killing off the alumni of Colonel Hagemann's command. People tend to get nervous and efficient after three of their own have been found hanged in lengths of catgut. Probably by now they knew all about Inar Christiansen, even down to the name on his forged American passport.

The slight hitch in the curtain disappeared. Christiansen waited for perhaps a quarter of a minute and then stepped quickly across the street to the hotel that stood pressed up against the tobacco shop like the next book on the shelf. He wanted to look at Becker's garden.

It was astonishing how no one ever questioned the presence of a strange man in a hotel lobby at four in the morning—provided, of course, that he appeared to know what he was about and didn't loiter. The night porter merely glanced up from his newspaper, perhaps wondering for an instant which of the resident ladies would still be receiving callers at such an hour. He had lost interest by the time Christiansen disappeared up the stairway.

The roof, of course, was deserted.

The hotel had only three stories, but Havana was a city of low buildings so it was possible to stand there on the parapet and look out over the whole broad tangle of streets, smeared here and there with colored light, all the way to the harbor. Above, the stars twinkled as brightly as if it had never rained, mocking in their indifference. If all this ceased in the next instant, they seemed to affirm, who would care? It was a strangely comforting idea.

Christiansen stared down into the tobacco shop's back yard, which was partially illuminated by a light over the hotel's rear entrance. Still, he wouldn't have cared to walk around in it, since its owner had done a thorough job of booby-trapping almost the whole area.

Old paint cans were stacked up precariously at intervals along the gravel pathway that led to the rear entrance. There were boards and tangles of wire. In that semidarkness, no one could have crossed the twenty or so yards of open ground without stumbling over something. And making an unholy racket in the process.

That was undoubtedly the plan. Should he knock at the front door, Christiansen would be invited inside and promptly shot; should he try to sneak in the rear, he would trip the alarm and meet the same fate. In either case, Becker would tell the police he had surprised an intruder, a few pesos would change hands, and that would be that.

As he peered down into the shrouded garden, Christiansen couldn't help but marvel at the Teutonic tidymindedness of the scheme. The SS were such careful, planning bastards. They had murdered people in their millions and laid waste to most of Europe, and all with the precision of an army of file clerks. Everything was always thought through in advance—one arrived at a plan and then followed it to the letter.

Anyone who approached either of the tobacco shop's two doors was as good as dead.

Becker had learned his villainy at a good school. He was down there now, prowling around the rooms of his little house, wound up like a mechanical toy, but he suffered from the same weakness as all the rest of them: he simply couldn't deal with the unexpected. The Germanic soul had no powers of improvisation.

So the attack would come from the one place Becker hadn't troubled to fortify. His own roof.

There had been a couple of straight-backed wooden chairs leaning against the wall in the hotel's third-floor hallway. Christiansen decided he would also see if he couldn't steal fifty or sixty feet of clothesline—if there was a utility closet around anywhere, he should be able to find something.

There wasn't any clothesline, so he had to break into an empty room and make off with the drapery cord, which was only about two thirds the length he would have liked, but he thought he might be able to get by with it.

Like all the establishments around it, Becker's had a flat roof—Latin architects always seemed to ignore the fact that it rains sometimes, even in Havana—and it was about a fifteen-foot drop down from the hotel parapet. The great thing was to get down there without making any detectable noise, since Becker was playing this game for his life and that was enough to make any man preternaturally alert.

Christiansen set the two chairs together on the parapet ledge, seat down, balancing them so that it wouldn't take more than a breath to make either one fall over. Then he took out his pocketknife and cut off about fifteen feet of drapery cord, tied one end to a leg of each chair, and let the loop drop down over the side of the building. From Becker's roof he would only have to give a little tug and they would topple into his arms, one after the other. It was getting himself down that was going to present the problem.

There was a curved drainpipe near that edge of the roof. He could tie the rest of his drapery cord to that and then lower himself over the side—except that he wasn't at all confident the cord would hold his weight unless he used a double length, and that would leave him hanging against the outside wall of the hotel with about a seven-foot fall to the edge of Becker's roof. Christiansen weighed close to two hundred and twenty pounds; dropping from that height, he would make enough of a bang to wake up all the sweating former SS men who had ever lived.

He took off his overcoat and tied the sleeves together through the circle of drapery cord around the hotel drainpipe, wondering the whole time if the thing wouldn't simply pull to pieces the instant it had to bear the full load—he didn't even know if it would reach far enough. He threw it over the edge and watched it as it fluttered to rest against the wall, and he still didn't know. The bottom was lost in darkness.

But at least he could console himself with the thought that he wasn't encumbered with an impossible number of alternatives. He could climb down on his coat—and trust that the Portuguese tailor who had made it for him hadn't economized on the stitching—or he could take the stairs back to the lobby and forget the whole thing. There simply wasn't a third choice.

And so it was that with a thousand misgivings Inar

Christiansen found himself clinging in the black of night to the back of a dress overcoat, working his way down handful by handful as he felt for something solid under his feet and listened with expectant dread for the sound of tearing fabric. As he changed his hold from one hand to the other, he could feel himself swinging against the hotel wall. There was nothing down there, it seemed, except air. His left hand was aching until he could hardly feel his fingers—possibly he wouldn't even know he had lost his grip until he started to fall. And still the edge of Becker's roof seemed no closer.

He changed hands one last time—they were both so slippery with sweat that it hardly seemed to make any difference—and felt again for something solid under him. Nothing. It was all up with him. In another second he would come down with a crash, and then where was he supposed to go? Becker would be able to kill him at his leisure.

He tried once more—nothing. And then once more, stretching down so far that the shoulder joint in his right arm felt as if it might be ready to pull loose.

And then, there it was. The point of his shoe scraped against what felt like a flat surface. Possibly he might have caught on nothing more than a protruding piece of brickwork, but right at that moment it hardly mattered. The hem of his coat was greasy with sweat and slipping between his fingers. He was going down, whether he liked it or not.

And then, as if by some miracle, he found himself clinging to the hotel wall, his feet pressing against something that felt solid enough to convince anybody it was the cinder-block edge of Gerhart Becker's roof.

It was several seconds before Christiansen could

bring himself to breathe, let alone try to move. He was afflicted with a terrible fear that he was about to topple over backward, that there was really nothing there beneath him but perhaps an inch or two of shelf, but finally, after what felt like an eternity, he nerved himself up to let his eyes follow the line of the brick wall down to where he could see that it joined the flat, granite-colored plane of the next building. So far, so good.

Moving his feet slowly and carefully, and staying flush against the hotel wall, he made his way to the rear, where he could see the whole of Becker's little garden and could put his hand on the loop of drapery cord that ran up to his two chairs. One after the other, he pulled them down and set them to rest on the roof beside him. Near the seam where the two buildings joined at right angles there was a downspout running from the hotel gutters. It was round and made of cast iron and seemed well anchored. It would do for the descent.

Finally, he leaned his shoulder against the wall and began to collect himself. His little plan, such as it was, was ready to be put into execution. Everything was assembled. It would have been nice to have had some idea where Becker was hiding himself, but one couldn't ask for the moon. It was time to start. That was the problem.

It was four-thirty in the morning. In three quarters of an hour, sooner perhaps, certainly well before first light, the rubbish carts would start on their rounds and everywhere the city would begin stirring into sullen life. There was simply no space left for the luxury of weariness—or fear, or scruples, or whatever it was—but Christiansen could hardly bring himself to keep his eyes open. His head touched the cool bricks of the hotel, and he found himself wondering why he wasn't home in bed.

Except that there was no longer anywhere on earth he could rightfully call home, something that Becker and his friends had seen to on that second Sunday in June, 1942. Something they had seen to with amazing thoroughness.

No one wears his past comfortably. Christiansen realized he was probably no worse than anyone else— after all, his parents had sent him away. He hadn't asked them to; it had all seemed so natural at the time. He hadn't even wanted it, not at first. But at that age one learns new ways fast, forgetting the old. The two of them had stood together on the dock at Oslo and waved goodbye. He hadn't been any more than a kid, so how could he have known what it cost them, what was in their hearts? He was their pride, and he had watched them growing smaller and smaller as the ship pulled away and left them behind. And now he couldn't ever go back.

There was always so much that had been left undone and unsaid. All the small sins of a thoughtless, selfish childhood accumulate like dust in an unused room.

No, he wasn't any worse than anyone else. He was merely an exile. The fourteenth day in June, 1942— it was as if they had cut something away with a sharp knife, burning the wound closed so it wouldn't bleed. Not flesh and bone, just a part of his life.

A slight tremor went through Christiansen's body, like a reproach, and he pushed himself disdainfully away from the wall. He was finished with being human.

Because somewhere under his feet Gerhart Becker

was waiting with a gun and a mighty fear of death,
and it was time to settle old scores. Christiansen picked
up one of the chairs, holding it by the back like a club,
and pitched it as far out into the darkness as he could
manage. It came down with a great crash against the
wooden gate that separated the garden from the alley
behind. The gate was left standing partially open and
the lights from the house clicked on, staining the ground
a lurid electric yellow.

Come on out, you bastard. The words formed in
Christiansen's mind, and his lips moved soundlessly.
Otherwise he was still as marble. Ten seconds, then
fifteen . . . Nothing. Then the garden fell into darkness again, as if the light had shrunk back into its
source out of simple dread.

Becker wasn't as stupid as all that. He would be
expecting some sort of trap—he would have to have
his look around first.

Christiansen listened with almost painful attention, but he couldn't hear the sound of footsteps inside
the house. He tried to visualize the man's movements—was he still on the second floor, or had he
gone downstairs? It was an awkward business, shooting at someone from above, so Becker would want to
be right there in the doorway when the moment came.
He would check the front first, just to be sure no one
was trying to come at him from behind, and then he
would be back. There was nothing in the garden—he
had seen that with his own eyes—and pretty soon he
would begin wondering what had made all the noise.
An animal, maybe? Havana was full of stray dogs. He
would want to know. He wouldn't be able to stand
not knowing. And the continuing quiet would make

him bolder. He would come back. It only needed a little patience.

Below a certain latitude there is no such thing as silence, and that subtropical night was filled with tiny sounds. Splashes of rainwater were still falling from tree branches and telephone lines, and the dull, scraping noises of insects rose and fell like a bad radio signal. It was a question of listening for the one slight suggestion of a human presence in all the chaos of overlapping, patternless murmurs.

Christiansen tried not to move. He didn't want to create any distractions, not even so much as the whisper of his coat sleeve as it brushed against the side of his dinner jacket. He would have liked to stop breathing.

And then, there it was. Some twenty feet below him, the screen door strained slightly on its hinges. Becker was standing there behind it, his hand pressing against the wire mesh, wondering if he had the nerve to step outside and check to make sure there were no unpleasant surprises waiting for him in his back yard.

When the lights went back on, Christiansen could hardly keep himself from starting. But he was patient. He almost didn't breathe as, slowly, the screen door opened and Becker stepped out from the protecting walls of his house.

What can you tell about a man from looking down at the top of his head? Becker's hair was thinning— that was about all. The light shone against his scalp as he stood with his left arm akimbo. For the rest, he was simply a blank.

He was still too close to the house. He was waiting—he wanted to feel safe before he began moving

out into the garden. Christiansen could see the pistol
in his right hand.

And then, one pace. And then, two. The screen
door closed quietly behind him. He was out now,
looking around. In another second he would turn back
to the house. There was no time to lose.

Christiansen picked up the second chair, lifting it
all the way up over his head. He had only the one
chance to make good.

Perhaps Becker heard something, because at the
last instant he glanced up. The chair caught him across
the face and shoulders, knocking him to the ground,
but Christiansen didn't wait to see—he was already
over the side of the building, his hands clamped around
the metal downspout as he began sliding to the ground.
He hit the earth with a thump, the impact almost
making him lose his balance. As he turned around,
he saw Becker trying to push himself up with his
hands. He was looking at Christiansen with eyes that
flickered fearfully in the yellow light. The gun he had
dropped in falling wasn't more than a foot from his
right elbow. It would have been little enough trouble
to pick it up again.

But Christiansen didn't give him a chance to remember about weapons. He covered the distance between them in a few quick strides and, with a kick
like the stroke of a piston, caught Becker precisely on
the side of the head.

The basement was small, square, astonishingly
deep, and permeated with the smell of tobacco. There
were a few packing crates around made of dark rough
wood with what might have been the names of plan-
tations burned into the slats, so perhaps Becker stored
his wares down here.

Becker was still unconscious, hanging from a sewer pipe by a rope that looped around his chest and under his arms. His hands were tied behind his back and his head was drooping down forlornly. He would twist clockwise through a slow quarter of a turn and then gradually stop and then begin slowly twisting counterclockwise. He looked like a corpse on a gibbet.

There was a double strand of heavy catgut around his neck, knotted just behind his left ear. It was hanging loose for the moment; as gradually Becker began to come back to himself, he seemed not even to know it was there. He shook his head and looked down at the chair that had been placed about six inches beneath the points of his toes. He stretched out one foot, trying to touch the flat seat, but he couldn't quite reach it.

Christiansen, who was sitting on an old steamer trunk only a few yards away, watched unsympathetically.

"Let me down from here," Becker whispered hoarsely. He had probably been a strong man once, but in his middle thirties, and after only a few years of peace, his face had begun to take on a doughy appearance. The color in his cheeks and across the bridge of his nose was blotchy, and his small, close-set brown eyes seemed wet and nearsighted. He was streaming with sweat; it collected in the creases around his mouth and made the bald crown of his head gleam like a polished window.

"For God's sake, let me down."

"All right."

Christiansen got up slowly and took the pocket-knife from his trousers. He smiled as he opened it, as if he were looking forward to drawing the blade

across Becker's throat. He wanted Becker to be afraid.
A frightened man was easier to manipulate.

Becker's eyes widened as he watched—the knife
blade held them as if by some enchantment.

"If you want down, you can come down," Christiansen said, stepping up beside Becker and resting
a hand delicately on his shoulder. With a slight pressure he set him rocking back clockwise at the end of
his rope, which creaked against the sewer pipe as
Becker swayed back and forth and then came to rest.
Christiansen reached up and cut the knot.

Becker's heels hit the chair's wooden seat with a
loud smack, and a panicky gurgle escaped him as the
catgut noose tightened on his windpipe. He lost his
balance almost at once, and, as his knees buckled, he
tried to scream for help, but the sound was cut short.
His face went a deep purplish red as slowly he began
to strangle.

For a moment Christiansen merely watched. The
faint smile had never left his face and his cold, pitiless
eyes narrowed slightly, as if he found the spectacle
amusing. Then, finally, he grabbed Becker by the
arms and helped him to regain his footing. For the
moment, Becker was worth more alive.

"Stand up straight—that's it." Christiansen sat down
again on the steamer trunk and crossed his legs. He
took a half-empty packet of cigarettes from the pocket
of his dinner jacket and lit one. "The noose will slacken
of its own so long as you keep the pressure off. But,
of course, if you relax a little . . ."

He made a vague gesture with his right hand, as
if to suggest that he couldn't be held responsible for
the inevitable, and the smoke from his cigarette drifted
through the air in a ragged line. Becker, who was

filling his lungs in quick, heavy gasps, watched him with an expression of undisguised horror.

"Of course, it's only a matter of time until you grow tired, isn't it. One can't keep at attention forever. You could try switching your weight from one leg to the other—you might last a little longer that way— but it'll all come out the same in the end. You've been a soldier. You've seen men faint on parade, just keel over from one minute to the next. Or your muscles will cramp up and you'll lose your balance again. Only next time I won't come to your aid. I'll merely sit here and watch."

The two men understood each other perfectly. Becker knew that no one was kidding, and that was fine. Christiansen allowed himself the luxury of a shrug.

"How long do you think you can last?" he went on, flicking the ash from his cigarette onto the basement's cement floor. "A few hours? More? I can wait— I don't begrudge you the time."

"What do you want? I'll give you anything you want!" Becker's head squirmed pleadingly in the noose, and the white catgut disappeared into the folds of his neck. His eyes seemed ready to start out of their sockets. "What is this about?"

Christiansen frowned suddenly and threw his cigarette to the floor. "You shouldn't have tried to trick me. You should have known it wouldn't work. I don't make deals with members of the Fifth Brigade."

"I don't know what you're talking about."

"Don't lie to me, Sergeant. Don't compound your mistake. There's no limit to how hard I can make it for you to die."

"What do you want?"

For a moment Christiansen seemed to have lost

the power of movement. And then, as if something
had just occurred to him, he shook his head and
laughed—or, at least, made a sound that was something like laughter.

"Do you remember Kirstenstad, Sergeant? And
you can ask me what it is I want."

"I wasn't there. I thought you were . . . Oh my
God, you have to believe me—I wasn't there!"

"You were there."

Christiansen lit another cigarette and waited. He
had been through it all before. Three times in the
last two years he had looked into a man's face, pro-
nounced the name "Kirstenstad," and been witness
to the change that was like a fall from grace. And it
was never simply a matter of some poor hunted wretch
realizing that his time had come, that he was finally
in the power of his deadliest enemy—that was a part,
of course, but not the whole. It was a kind of moral
terror. No one who had been at Kirstenstad that Sunday morning, who had had eyes to see what had happened there, could fail to know that he had been
delivered over to the purest evil. Christiansen had
learned as much as that.

"I want Colonel Hagemann, Sergeant. And you
can tell me where to find him."

"I was only his orderly—I was . . ."

"Then you would have been standing beside him
that morning, wouldn't you, Sergeant." Christiansen's
face was without expression. Only his eyes, cold and
blue, like ice in the sun, showed that he was still a
man, with a man's hatred. "You would have seen the
mayor of Kirstenstad, wouldn't you, Sergeant. He was
a tall man, in late middle age, with a white mous-

tache—quite a dignified figure, Sergeant. Surely you must remember him. As the trucks rolled up, he came out of his house to see what the disturbance was, to see what the Waffen-SS could possibly want with his little village, and your Colonel Hagemann had him shot down on his own doorstep. It was one of those heroic moments destined to live forever in the myths of the German people, Sergeant, so surely you must recall the scene.

"And perhaps you remember his wife as well, how she knelt in her husband's blood, unable to understand what had happened, and how the Colonel, that fearless paragon, doubtless to set an example for his men, himself put a pistol to the back of her neck and pulled the trigger. Did you clean the pistol for him that night, Sergeant? Wouldn't that have fallen within the scope of your duties?"

The muscles in Christiansen's jaw were working rhythmically as he stared at his captive, precisely as if he had never seen such an exotic creature before. For all its calm, there had been something wild in his voice as he talked about that morning in 1942. But when he spoke again, his tone was once more empty, without inflection, almost dead.

"You soldiers of the Fifth Brigade, you killed nearly everyone in the village that day," he went on, like a man reciting a story learned by heart. "Hardly a soul escaped. I wish I could claim that I wanted to avenge them all, but I can't. I just want the man who murdered my parents."

The cigarette in Christiansen's hand had burned down almost to his fingers—he seemed to have forgotten it was there. Finally he put it out, grinding out the ember under the point of his shoe. Becker watched the whole performance with a kind of morbid fascination.

The strain was beginning to tell on him. It had been three years since Becker had worn a uniform. He had lost his soldier's bearing. He looked faintly ridiculous standing there at attention on top of a kitchen chair. His nose was beginning to run, although he hardly seemed to notice it, and every so often, to keep from falling, he would have to catch himself as he swayed a few degrees to one side or the other. And now he was trembling—just slightly, just enough that he couldn't keep his shoulders still.

"I can tell you how to find him," he said finally, his voice thick, as if the noose were choking him already. His eyes cast about the room; he seemed to be looking for a way to escape. "Why shouldn't I? I don't owe him anything—I thought you were from him, come to clean me away. Maybe if you kill him, I can start to sleep at night."

"Then tell me where to find him."

"Not where—I have not seen the Colonel in a long time and he keeps his movements a secret. But I can tell you *how* to find him."

He forced himself to smile. His lips drew back from his teeth in a grotesque manner. They were in each other's confidence, he seemed to be suggesting. Hagemann was the common enemy.

It was a lie, of course. There was a network that kept the survivors of the Fifth Brigade safe and solvent. There was money to procure new identities for men still hunted by the Allied War Crimes Commission, money to finance new lives—how else had "Herr Bauer" come by his tobacco shop?

But what difference did any of that make? Gerhart Becker wanted to live.

"What can you tell me, Sergeant?"

"There is a girl . . ."

His sentence trailed off as he heard Christiansen's dry, mocking laughter.

"No—really—there is a girl I've heard he's looking for. He—"

"Half the men in the world are looking for a girl, Sergeant. And you know as well as I that the Colonel's is not precisely a romantic disposition. I've heard all the stories. There were probably hundreds of girls."

But something in the way Becker kept twisting his head from side to side, as if he were trying to saw through his neck with the catgut noose, made him stop laughing.

"Go on then, if you must. Tell me about this girl."

"She is a Jewess. She was his mistress—in the camp."

"Waldenburg?"

"Yes. She was the General's before that. The General gave her to him. My colonel was obsessed by her."

"If she was at Waldenburg, she's probably dead."

"No." Becker swallowed hard. He seemed to be telling the truth. He wanted to be believed. "The General made sure she got away alive. She is alive somewhere—you have only to find her and Hagemann will come to you. Even if he has to follow you into hell itself."

"Why? What's so special about her?"

"I don't know."

Egon Hagemann in love? Christiansen didn't believe it. But he believed Becker's story. A girl. A girl who had probably lost herself somewhere in Europe, who could be anywhere. Who could be dead, for all Becker knew.

Still, it was more than he had had that morning. He was perhaps a step or two closer to the Colonel Hagemann who had butchered his family, who had . . .

"What is her name, this girl?"

"Esther . . . Rosensaft, I think. Esther Rosensaft."

"You *think*?"

"That was her name. Esther Rosensaft. He called her 'Saftig,' though she was a little stick of a thing. It was his joke."

"I will strip the flesh from your bones, Sergeant— a piece at a time if you lie to me." Christiansen showed his strong white teeth in a fierce grin, although he never moved from the steamer trunk. "Nothing in the world will be as hard as your death if you don't tell me everything you know. Believe me, Sergeant, I would enjoy making you die by inches."

"There is nothing else!" Becker gasped and sweated and told the truth. He was just a little man after all— he wouldn't have had the courage to lie in the extremity of his life.

"I've told you everything. God, don't do it to me— please let me down. I'm no one. I never killed anyone."

"You were there. You let it happen without a word. You helped your colonel—you're helping him still. Don't plead your innocence to me." Christiansen stood up slowly, giving the impression that his legs had grown stiff from disuse. "But I won't make it too bad for you—I won't leave you here to linger in agony. I'll merely carry out the sentence of the court."

When Becker saw what was coming, his chest heaved wildly and his neck seemed to swell as he rocked his head back and forth. He tried to speak, but at first only a strange gurgling sound came out.

"No!" he screamed—the tiny basement vibrated with the word. "No! You can't—I thought you were from Hagemann! Hagemann was going to—"

But the words stopped with a jerk as Becker kicked his legs in the empty air. His back arched and the catgut ground against the sewer pipe as he trembled and twitched and tried to open his mouth wide enough to let in a breath.

Christiansen had pulled the chair from under him.

2

Vienna, Austria: February 24, 1948

Esther woke up with a start, followed at once, even before the first surprise had worn off, by a wormy feeling of anxiety. It was happening more and more, almost every night now. She had been dreaming about the guard.

The wooden bunks in Cell Block West were four tiers high and as narrow as coffins. A prisoner lying in her bed could hardly see two meters in any direction—one closed one's eyes and the thought came of its own bidding: this is what it will be like in the grave.

The prison lights were never turned out, and the windows were too small and too high up to make a difference. So inside it was always the same murky gray, in which even the guards—even the guard who haunted her, who was sometimes one man and sometimes another, who was real even when she was awake—even the guards hardly seemed to cast a shadow.

It was like being dead. They were shadows themselves.

She had been inside only four months, and already Esther was quite sure she would go mad if she had to stay locked up here much longer. There wasn't even the fear of death to remind one that there might be some value in living. There was only poor food and cold and not enough sleep—never enough sleep—and the terrible grayness of everything. It was worse than the ghetto at Lodz, where she had still had her family, or even the camps. In the camps she had been alternately pampered and terrorized. Everything a human being can lose, she had lost there—parents, innocence, belief in God, the right to think of herself as a human being. Everything except life and the will to keep it. But now she was at the end of her strength. She was no longer afraid of death. That was what made this place so terrible.

For two years and eight months, she had been free. She couldn't face going back behind locked doors—not now, not after relearning that there was such a thing as freedom. She had been eleven when they walled up the ghetto, and then it had been five years of scratching out enough to stay alive and trying to keep from being swept into oblivion when the Germans came looking for people to work to death or shoot in batches or send to the ovens. For five years she had prayed for the war to end, but this time there would be no American soldiers in strange uniforms to hand out rice and milk and tell everyone it was safe to think of going home. No one was going to drive the Russians out.

But perhaps it was only her own wickedness that

made prison so impossible to bear—it was wicked to think that anything could be worse than the camps. At Chelmno her mother and father had been gassed, and at Waldenburg there had been Hagemann.

Esther lay in her bunk, her eyes closed, waiting for the sound of footsteps. One never knew the time here except by the orders one heard—five-thirty a.m., wake up and wash; ten a.m., assemble for first meal; six p.m., assemble for second meal; sometime between eleven and midnight, go to bed. The rest was filled with roll calls, work, punishment, roll calls, interrogations, roll calls . . . It was an endless treadmill.

And always there was the guard. Sometimes he was gone for hours, even days at a time, but always he came back. Sometimes he would merely watch her—she could feel his eyes on her everywhere—and sometimes, quite suddenly, he would be beside her, talking in that low, insinuating, faintly threatening voice of his. And sometimes he was not content merely to talk. She could put up with being mauled, but of course it wouldn't end there. He was just nerving himself up for the inevitable. She knew perfectly well where it would end.

But at least this one was no Hagemann to strip her clothes off in handfuls and shoot at her with his pistol as she tried to run away. She could still hear the smack of the bullets hitting the trees, spattering her with pieces of pitchy bark. Once he had found an abandoned quarry and she had cut and bruised her feet until she could hardly stand, but each time she stopped scrambling over the broken stone Hagemann would open fire, the bullets burying themselves in the ground between her legs or ricocheting off unpredictably. And finally, when none of that mattered anymore, when she was too exhausted even to be afraid, when she would have liked to die, she would look up and there he would be, standing over her, laughing.

"*I love to see you willing to be reasonable, Esther,*" he would say. And, with the pistol still in his hand, he would begin unbuttoning his trousers.

And when he was finished, and she was allowed to limp back to the camp, she would wonder why it had to be this way. Why did she have to be hunted down and shot at and frightened to the verge of madness before he would allow her to yield to him?

Nothing could be worse than that. This was like death, this prison, but death must be worse. And the discovery that one is capable of anything if only it will keep death off, that was the worst of all. The Russians could turn life into death, but nothing they would do could match the horror of what Hagemann had made of her at Waldenburg.

But now the morning was close at hand—or what passed for morning in this place. The guards would come soon. A shout and the sound of a truncheon banging against the door frame, and everyone would scramble numbly to attention in their cotton night-dresses. They would stand there like that, half awake, blinking stupidly, their feet bare against the icy floor, for perhaps three quarters of an hour while the roll was taken and retaken. It was the invariable routine of the place, its purpose unknown, it having perhaps become a purpose in itself.

If one listened, it was possible to hear the guards' boots outside on the tile corridor. It was better to be awake and listen, so as not to be caught completely by surprise. It was horrible to be jarred out of sleep by the barking guards—it was like awakening into a nightmare.

All the guards here were men. It was a women's prison, but the guards were men. The first officer of her cellblock was named Filatov.

Sometimes, while she stood at attention beside her bunk, Filatov would walk by, stop, take off his glove, and run his hand over her body, slipping it inside the neckline of her nightdress or along the sides of her flanks, touching her with his hard fingers in all her private places—if a prisoner could be said to have any private places. If she, Esther Rosensaft, Jewess and harlot, hadn't lost all right to think of this body as belonging to herself.

In her dreams sometimes she would become confused and Filatov would become Hagemann, or the two would blend together. She would be standing at attention and all at once it would be Hagemann there beside her and the finger that was running over the curve of her breast would become the muzzle of a pistol. It was because of this, more than anything he had done to her himself, that she hated Filatov.

But, of course, that was ridiculous because Filatov was merely a man taking advantage of his position, and Hagemann had been something altogether different. Filatov might have a wife who was a shrew, or perhaps no wife at all. All he wanted was a little sex—and not to sacrifice his position of authority. So he threatened, in a way that was almost like pleading, and watched her, and, sometimes, took off his glove. The day would come when he would feel that he was powerful enough—or she sufficiently overawed—to claim more, but for the moment he was content merely to slip his hand inside her dress.

It was best not to look at him, not to smile, but to stand quietly like a shadow, not to resist or yield, and finally he would lose interest and pass by. She had not been raped yet—it happened sometimes here, so she had been told, but so far not to her. She had been here four months, and she had not been raped. If she ever was, she would not resist—it was pointless to resist. She would not weep or even cry out. She would keep the rage inside, where it would not show. She would hate Filatov in the privacy of her heart, and for the rest pretend she was made of marble. It was easier that way, as she had learned from the Germans.

But four months were four months, and still Filatov had not summoned up the slight courage it would require to do as he liked. So perhaps the Russians were better than the Germans.

But it was better to let them do as they wished— no matter what it was—better than to starve and die.

At Chelmno she had dug potatoes—that was the work that permitted her to live while others died. Every morning, through the summer mud, in the icy, lightless winter, they would march out to the fields— five kilometers in each direction—and work for fourteen hours. Some girls had to carry stones until they dropped to the ground and the blood bubbled at their lips as they tried to catch their breath. Those died quickly. The others were worn down, month after month.

And one day, on the march back to the barracks, she had dropped her hoe and, when she reached over to pick it up, had fallen down herself. She couldn't get up. She tried and tried, but she couldn't. She had been at the camp long enough to know what that meant. A couple of her friends managed to drag her back in time for the evening roll call, but the next morning she was part of a line of women threading their way to the gas chambers. In the morning they called your number, and you were condemned.

It had been that way with her parents—one, after the other, they had disappeared into the shuffling columns of the doomed. She would hear about it a week, two weeks later. So now it was her turn.

She was so weak she hardly cared. She could remember some of how she had felt that morning, too dumb with hunger and exhaustion to have much room for fear. Just once every so often the idea would flicker through her mind, *I will be dead soon. They will lock us up in a shed until our turn comes, and then they will herd us inside one of the death chambers. A day from now, or an hour, and the* Sonderkommando *will be hauling my corpse around with hooks, looking for gold in my teeth and washing the filth off my legs with a hose.* But in order to be afraid one needed some imaginative grasp, and suffering was a great killer of the imagination. She could see herself dead, but the picture in her brain seemed to be about nothing. She merely stumbled forward with the others, dully aware that soon this would stop and something else would begin.

In the train, coming from Lodz, she had been afraid. They had been packed tightly together in the darkness of the cattle car, and she had huddled in her mother's arms and wept for fear. And when the doors had sprung open, and she had seen the Germans with their machine guns lined up outside, she had been afraid.

"Don't worry," her mother had said. *"No one will hurt us."* And her father had stroked her hair. After that day, she had never seen him again.

It was a Saturday. The woman in front of her in line turned around and smiled and whispered. "I hope they take us today. It will be a blessing to die on the Sabbath." The woman looked in her sixties but probably wasn't more than thirty-five. The dirt was etched deep into the lines of her face and her teeth were discolored and broken. She looked half mad.

She's going mad, Esther thought to herself. *She's crazed with the fear of death.* She put her hand on the woman's arm and murmured, "It's all right—they won't hurt us."

And then the line had shuddered to a stop. That meant that the pens were full and they would have to wait in the freezing, ankle-deep mud. Here and there one could hear sobbing, quiet and furtive, as if even grief here had to be shabby.

And while the women waited to die, a cluster of German officers had walked around the corner of the building. She heard their conversation—loud, confident voices such as no one used at Chelmno. They seemed different creatures, really like a separate race. Not human because not suffering.

Their uniforms stood out in the drab, colorless landscape. They were real and everything else—this camp, this gray mud, these doomed women—were hardly as substantial as smoke. For a moment they stopped. Someone was speaking. Here and there a few of them lit cigarettes. That moment seemed to last forever.

One of them was looking at her. He was short and fat, and the face above his stiff military collar was a mass of creased flesh, pink as the sun. His eyes were lost in the shadow of his cap bill.

Smile at him, she told herself. *What have you got to lose? Grasp any chance that offers itself. To live is a moral duty. Smile.*

Finally he raised his arm, pointed to her. His lips moved. He turned away and walked on.

I will die, it seems, she thought. *Why should I have thought it could be otherwise? What could anyone want of me now?*

The next thing she knew, two soldiers in light green uniforms had taken her by the arms and were dragging her out of the line.

"She stinks," one of them said. "They all stink," the other one answered.

And for the first time, really, Esther was seized with the terrible dread of death.

Today was her sentencing day. She lay in her bed on the lowest tier of the bunk, listening to the boards over her head creaking as the woman above moved in her sleep, wondering what would happen. Vienna was all around them—sometimes, in the exercise yard, she could hear the noise from the traffic outside—but she was quite sure she would never return to Vienna. This prison was like a separate world. There was a stone wall all the way around the building; she had seen it for the first and last time the day she had been brought here. The Russians had erected another inside it, perhaps twenty feet higher, so that even from the windows on the third floor, perhaps even from the roof, it was impossible to see outside to the street. They meant one to forget there was anywhere else.

She was not guilty of a political crime—except to

the degree that these people regarded all crime as
political. She would be tried for smuggling. They had
stopped her at the checkpoint in the British Zone,
had confiscated her papers—in any case, those were
forged—and had had her strip-searched by a matron.
She had been betrayed, of course. They had found
four hundred pounds' worth of Russian rubles sewn
into the clothes around her waist. The trafficking in
currency was a profitable business, but dangerous.
She was only a courier, of course. She would have
taken a small commission.

The Russians were strict about their money. They
might decide to make an example of her. They might
give her five years.

She would die if she had to stay in this place for
five years.

No, she would not die. One does not die after
having learned that there were no limits to what one
was prepared to do to stay alive.

The Germans had hoisted her up into the back of
a half-empty truck, and she had curled up there under
a pile of empty sacking and listened as the truck lurched
forward and started bouncing along the dirt road that
led out through the camp gates and into the trees.
She could see the trees through a narrow rent in the
canvas flap that closed off the back of the truck, but
she made no effort to discover where they were taking
her. How would she have known, anyway? One direction was the same as another, so long as it was away
from Chelmno.

And before long she was too blinded by her own
tears to see at all. Relief and shame and a sickening
fear of death hardly left room in her chest for a breath

of air. Already, while she lay there, swaying back and forth as the truck stammered along, the gas chambers were probably filling with carbon monoxide. They had a big diesel engine that pumped the gas into four chambers at a time, and sometimes it would start right away and sometimes not. People could wait there, huddled together so tightly they couldn't even fall down, sometimes for an hour or two, waiting to die.

But she wasn't going to die. Not today, not yet.

They drove on for two days, stopping to pull off to the side of the road a few times every day to eat and rest. They never drove at night—perhaps they were afraid to use their headlights, afraid of becoming a target for the Allied bombers. Perhaps they had some other reason. When they stopped, someone would come, pick up the flap covering the back of the truck, and give her something to eat. She was not allowed to come down from the truck except to relieve herself, and then always under the eyes of a guard, but what did she care? She wasn't modest—one lost one's sense of shame very quickly at Chelmno—and the truck was world enough for her. She would sit there, dangling her legs over the edge of the bed, feeling the bright winter sun on her face, listening to the scrape of the spoon against the tin dish as she ate.

She ate and ate during those two days; her stomach was too shrunken to hold very much and a few times she became sick. It didn't matter. It was wonderful to have more to eat than she could hold. What did she care how sick she made herself?

Finally, they arrived at Waldenburg.

For the first several hours, the Germans seemed to have forgotten her existence. She sat on the back of the truck, watching them unload and wondering what was to become of her. The problems of this world had narrowed themselves down to just one: will I live today, or will they finally decide to kill me? She looked around her, sick with dread.

Because Waldenburg was another camp—she had seen the barbed wire fences and the watchtowers as they drove up, and although there didn't seem to be any prisoners about, the barracks and work sheds were clustered together on the other side of a muddy ribbon of roadway.

The camp was divided, like Chelmno. On one side of the road there was grass and neat gravel walkways and painted buildings, and on the other only mud and horror waiting to be. Over there, even the wood of the barracks walls had that gray, lifeless look, and there was a halo of darkness around everything. The road was the dividing line between the human and the non-human, between the masters of the earth and their slaves.

What am I doing on this side? she kept asking herself. *What do they want with me?* She had just turned fifteen that year, and her mother had been a woman of strict principles, so certain possible answers did not occur to her.

A little after noon a soldier brought her a tin plate of stew. There were chunks of meat in it and it was so hot that at first she could barely eat any; she couldn't remember when anything had ever tasted so delicious. The soldier was young, hardly older than herself, and skinny enough that his uniform was noticeably too large for him. The hair on the sides of his head was cut so short that one could see the scalp through it. At first he stood with his back to her and wouldn't answer any of her questions, but after a bit he forgot himself enough to be human.

"It's to be a labor camp," he said, pointing to the bare wooden buildings across the road. "The main body of prisoners hasn't arrived yet, only the construction gangs. They will be assembling bomb fuses."

"And the SS has assigned a general to run this place?" she asked, a little startled at her own temerity—it wasn't safe to question such things. "Even the commandant at Chelmno was only a colonel."

"I can't talk about that." The soldier shifted his weight uncomfortably from one foot to the other and then turned his back again for a moment and then stared hard at Esther's nearly empty plate. "You've eaten enough, I think."

So there was some secret about their presence here. It had struck her from the beginning—these were combat troops. They didn't behave like camp guards; even their uniforms were different.

The young soldier took her by the arm and led her to a small outbuilding that might have been a garage. He unlocked the double doors and thrust her inside. There were no windows and no light, so she had only an instant in which to look around her. There was nothing to see; even the cement floor had been swept clean.

"You'll stay here until you hear different," he said, and padlocked the doors shut behind him.

She stayed in there for a week. After the first night they brought her a blanket, and once a doctor visited her. Twice a day someone came to bring her food and a large canteen of water, but they never spoke.

It wasn't so bad. Every time the doors opened and

the sunlight streamed in on her, her heart began beating wildly and she wondered if they were coming to take her away to be executed, but otherwise she was almost happy. Death was always near, but she had learned at Chelmno that it was foolish to think more than a few hours ahead. For the rest, she could sleep as much as she wanted, and in spite of her confinement, she wasn't bored. The absence of hunger and physical suffering was too much of a novelty for her to be bored. At Chelmno she had felt weak and slightly sick to her stomach, all the time. Her legs had always felt heavy and strengthless, so that walking more than a few yards had been like balancing on a wire. But that was gone now. She felt as if she would be willing to stay just like this, curled up on an army blanket, thinking about fresh bread and the taste of cooked carrots, for the rest of her life.

But finally they did come for her.

There were two of them. In the blinding light of midafternoon, she recognized the general who had pointed her out at Chelmno. He was standing with his tunic unbuttoned, the white undershirt showing beneath it, and his cap was held in his right hand. The man beside him had a corporal's stripes on his arm; there was a rifle slung from his shoulder.

"I think we have fattened her up enough," the general said, gesturing at her with his cap. "Take her with you, but see that they don't do any real damage."

He laughed, as if he had made a little joke, but the other man stared at her with cold, hostile eyes. And then the general walked away.

Finally, when they were alone together, the corporal looked around, shaking his head in disgust. He wouldn't come in but stood outside in the sunshine.

"You have made your mess in here, eh, Jewess?" he said. It wasn't really a question.

Esther kept her eyes on the ground. There was nothing to be gained from answering back, except a beating. She would say nothing—she would not even weep. These people allowed one nothing, not even the luxury of a little shame.

She would be silent . . .

"Come along, then."

The distant sound of boot heels told her that she had about ten seconds before the Russian guards would bang open the dormitory door to proclaim the beginning of her one hundred and eleventh day of imprisonment. She let her feet slide over the edge of the bunk bed and began feeling for her clogs—otherwise there would be no time to put them on, not unless one was willing to risk punishment for tardiness at morning inspection, and today of all days Esther wished not to incur any official displeasure.

"STAHYAT SMEERNO!"

Awake or asleep, it made no difference. Women threw themselves out of their bunks, dropping down to attention so that they seemed to have gone rigid at the precise instant of impact with the cement floor. Half of them, as they stood there with their arms pressed against their sides, hadn't even opened their eyes yet.

The guards walked along the rows checking not so much that everyone was there—why should anyone not be there? where would they have gone?—but simply as an exercise of authority. A woman discovered without her shoulders properly squared or who looked as if she might have just stopped whispering, or simply someone of whom, for some mysterious reason of their own, they had decided to make an example, would find herself on report and sentenced to spend the rest of the month in the laundry room, where the temperature never dropped below sixty degrees and the air was filled with unbreathable, lye-saturated steam.

There were always three of them. They would fan out through the dormitory and then collect together again at the door, where they would shout out the orders of the day—in Russian first, and then with a German translation. They seemed to think they were making some enormous concession to admit that such a language as German even existed.

Esther didn't look at them as they made their way down the aisles of bunk beds; she kept her eyes focused on nothing, staring straight ahead without, apparently, seeing anything. It had been the rule at Chelmno that a prisoner could be beaten simply for looking at one of the SS guards, and something of the same attitude applied here too. Attention was attention. You weren't even supposed to be alive, merely erect.

Filatov stopped directly in front of her. He smiled, and she knew what to expect. It was his day to frighten little girls.

"You have business with the tribunal this morning, eh?" he murmured, in his hideous, undulating, Russianized German. His face was no more than a few inches from her own, and she could smell his breath, like stale cooking grease. He was short, with wide, doughy features and heavy ears, and every word he spoke somehow seemed to convey a shrouded menace. "I wonder what you will get. How would you like to stay here with us until you are an old lady, eh?"

Esther never moved. She never glanced at him. He wasn't there, and she was made of cold, white marble.

After a while he tired of the game, straightened up, and drew a long strip of paper from the inside of his overcoat.

"You will report to the guardroom at once after showering," he barked. It was as if he were addressing the entire room. "You will hear the sentence of the court at nine."

It seemed to give him enormous satisfaction.

"Come along, then," the corporal had said. "It's time to clean you up. If you want to make an impression here you'll have to be presentable. We soldiers of the Waffen-SS are a very fastidious lot."

It was a joke. He threw back his head and laughed. At intervals, as he marched her along, he would laugh to himself, enjoying his witticism all over again.

Her first bath at Waldenburg came out of a garden hose. The corporal held it for her, and she scrubbed herself off with clumps of withered grass because, of course, there was no soap.

During the time she was the General's pet she had a steel tub and lavender-scented crystals that foamed in the hot water. The general had a sensitive nose and even gave her a bottle of cologne. She had three changes of underwear and a pair of patent-leather shoes.

The General sometimes said that he had never been cut out to be a soldier, that actually he disliked the company of men, which was the one absolute condition of the military life. That would be on rare evenings when the General felt disposed to give himself a little treat and they would spend the whole night together and he would drink wine and play the violin. He liked to be told that he played well—it was a vanity of his that he could have been a great virtuoso, or perhaps, even better, a conductor, even another Furt-wängler. *"I gave up all thought of leading orchestras to lead my division,"* he would say, smiling sadly. *"And now, as you see, I don't even have most of my division."* So he would play Bach and Paganini on his fiddle and get quietly drunk. He was not a very active lover; he preferred to lie quietly and have everything done for him. And then he would sleep, never stirring until nearly noon.

And in the stillness of night Esther would listen to the faint sound of his breathing and wonder how she could stand to live.

"The General likes his women well broken in," the corporal had told her as he led her away. She was still shivering from the cold water, but he had given her a soldier's tunic to wrap around her. "You'll spend a little time with the men first, and then you'll get the idea."

He opened the door to one of the barracks and dragged her inside by the arm, shouting, "Here she is, lads! Remember we want her back in good repair." And then he laughed, and shut the door behind him.

She would always remember the way their faces had looked in those first few seconds. There were seven men in the barracks that particular afternoon, and they stared at her, grinning hungrily. They were like animals; she thought at first they might tear her to pieces with their teeth.

There were four barracks. For the next three weeks

she was passed from one to the next. She was the
evening entertainment. She learned everything there
was to know about men.

No, perhaps the Russians weren't as bad as that.

Filatov took her to the doorway of the hearing
room and waited with her outside in the corridor—
personally, so that they were alone together. He seemed
to think he was conferring some great distinction on
her.

"You must look nice for the judges," he said, pushing a loose strand of hair back from her face. "You
want to make a good impression." He kept glancing
around, as if afraid of being overheard.

When the door opened, he took her roughly by
the arm and marched her through it. Suddenly she
was standing in the center of the floor, facing a long
table behind which sat three men in uniform and a
woman in a khaki blouse. The woman was taking notes,
which seemed odd because for a long time no one
spoke so much as a word.

The presiding officer, who sat in the center, directly in front of her, was a captain of artillery—she
could tell that from the cannons on his collar patches.
He seemed about fifty, hard-faced and completely bald.
He didn't even look up from the papers on his desk
when Filatov saluted crisply and stepped back to stand
at parade rest by the door.

"You are Polish?" he asked finally. He was holding
a typed sheet in his hand, as if he wanted to make
certain that he had the right prisoner. After a few
seconds his eyebrows lowered into a frown. "We are
informed you were born in Kaliningrad—is that not
correct?"

"I was born in Königsberg, sir. In East Prussia. I don't know what it is called now. I was a German until 1935, and after that I was a Jew."

"Then you are Polish. All of that is Poland now. You will be repatriated to Poland when your sentence is completed, where you can work to build socialism and make amends for your crime. What is that on your arm?"

He pointed with his pencil and, without thinking, Esther brought her hand up to cover the tattoo just under the curve of her right elbow.

"Is that a number? Where did you get it?"

"At Waldenburg, sir," she answered, her voice hardly above a whisper.

"Waldenburg, eh? Then you are lucky to be alive." His expression betrayed no sympathy, nothing beyond a mild, disinterested curiosity.

And then, suddenly, something seemed to occur to him.

"Isn't it on the wrong arm? I always thought the Germans tattooed the left arm."

When she didn't answer he appeared to lose interest. His eyes fell as if by gravity to the papers on the desk in front of him.

"You are accused of currency smuggling," he said after a long silence, just managing to glance up at her as he finished the sentence. "You were arrested trying to pass the checkpoint into the International Zone with twenty thousand rubles sewn into your clothes. How do you answer the charge, innocent or guilty?"

He had already made up his mind, of course. Esther had been told during her first week in prison that if one tried to plead innocent they merely doubled the sentence. She kept her eyes on the floor.

"Guilty, sir."

"Fifteen years. Take her away."

The floor outside in the corridor was smooth hard-wood, but she would stumble. If Filatov had let go of her arm she probably would have forgotten to keep walking.

"Now, you see?" he whispered. "This is what you get for being so regal with everyone. You made a bad impression. You will have to learn to be a nicer girl."

But she could hardly make out what he was saying. She was too stunned. She had no will for anything. Fifteen years.

She would be an old woman by the time they let her out, dried up and good for nothing. No, she would never be able to live through fifteen years. She would die. One day she would run her head against a stone wall and crack it open like an eggshell. She would die or go mad.

They came to a plain wooden door with a number painted on it in white at eye level. The number was "263." The paint was chipped away with age along the bottom. She had assumed she was being taken to an isolation cell—that was what happened here after sentencing; perhaps they were afraid a prisoner might kick and scream or try to harm herself—but the cell doors down here were all made of iron. She merely noted the neutral fact. It didn't mean anything to her. She had stopped caring about things like that.

Fifteen years. She wished they would kill her instead.

Filatov took a bundle of keys out of his pocket and began fumbling with them until he found the right one. His fingers closed over her shoulder and he pushed her inside.

When the light clicked on she saw at once that this was a broom closet. There were shelves overhead and in one corner a collection of shiny zinc buckets. What was she doing here?

Then she noticed that someone had spread a blanket out on the floor beside the rear wall. There was even a pillow.

Esther turned around as she heard the door slam shut behind them. There was a brassy taste in her mouth and she felt as if she were being smothered, but she told herself not to scream. It would do no good to scream. It would only make it worse.

Filatov was grinning at her, no longer afraid of anything. He was already undoing the buttons of his coat.

✠ 3 ✠

Munich, Germany: February 26, 1948

From the window of his hotel room, Inar Christiansen could look out on an undulating sea of rubble. Here and there part of a broken wall would rise a foot or so out of the piles of shattered brick, like the crest of a wave, but for the most part the devastation was so complete that you might have imagined you were looking at some harsh, stony landscape where no man had ever lived. The bombing planes had done a pretty good job.

But then there was the hotel itself, which had come through without even a broken windowpane. The lobby was filled with potted palms and red velvet love seats, and if you ordered a drink a waiter in morning coat and white gloves would bring it to you on a silver tray. Before the war, when it was still safe, the place had been very popular with middle-level Nazis in town for November Putsch anniversaries or a little patronage for the wife's brother—Party headquarters had been just a few streets away. Now the paying guests all seemed to be the families of American military officers. You hardly saw a German who wasn't in livery.

That, at least, hadn't changed. Germany was still a country where you had to be wearing a uniform if you wanted people to believe you weren't just hanging around to see what you could scrounge. That was why Christiansen had packed his army greens.

He had worn them only one other time since demobilization, to watch General von Goltz hanged at Rebdorf. Now he needed information, and information was always easier to obtain if people imagined you had some official reason for wanting it.

There were certain facts he had had to face about himself, and one of them was that appearances were against him. Big Nordic men weren't terribly popular in Europe just at present. Everyone had spent the last fifteen years listening to Nazi propaganda about the Master Race, and they had a natural tendency to jump to conclusions.

It had happened to him before. *"I'm looking for information about possible survivors of the Waldenburg concentration camp,"* says the blond-haired, blue-eyed civilian with what is obviously a shrapnel scar across the back of his left hand, and the little clerk at the U.N. Relief and Rehabilitation Office is already thinking, *Sure. You want to finish the job you started on them there?* Suddenly no one knows anything about anyone.

But in a Norwegian army uniform you were Norwegian, and it was all right to be Norwegian. Why shouldn't a Norwegian be blond? What else should he be?

When he had been hunting down Colonel Hage-

mann's loyal subordinates from the Fifth Brigade, he
hadn't minded looking like someone who still carried
his NSDAP membership card next to his heart—it
had worked to his advantage, more than once. But he
wasn't trying to win over old Party boys anymore; he
wanted to find one of the victims now, if she was still
alive, and he needed to appear trustworthy to people
who had spent the last couple of years listening to
horror stories. He would wear his uniform.

In the first few months after the war, while everything was still a chaos, men and women who were
fresh out of Auschwitz and Mauthausen had been
moving back and forth across Germany in great un-
organized herds. They would trudge along the roads,
from one Displaced Persons camp to another, hoping
for word of some relative or friend who might also
have survived. They would hitch rides with soldiers
when they could, or else just drag themselves over
the ground, sometimes so sick and frail that you wondered they could manage a hundred yards, and they
would leave little penciled messages on bulletin boards
or the sides of buildings: *"If anyone knows the whereabouts of Cyla Rawicz, wife of Dr. Henryk Rawicz of
Bielsko, Poland, please leave word with the Jewish
Committee in Linz."* It was all most of them had.

Europe had been a madhouse in those days. Nobody was where he belonged, and the DPs, for the
most part, had little enough reason to want to return
to the places that had once been their homes. *"I don't
want to live under the Russians—they're as bad as
the Nazis, almost." "Everybody I knew in Lodz went
up the smokestacks at Treblinka. Why should I care
anything about Lodz?"* People had to be clothed and
fed and housed. Something had to be done about

them. It was a long time before any coherent, organized attempt was underway to find out who had lived and who had gone into the incinerators.

It wasn't as bad as that now, but it was bad. Finding Esther Rosensaft wasn't going to be easy.

Because a lot of peculiar things were happening. People were disappearing into Russia without leaving a ripple, a lucky soul here and there had relatives in England or the United States who were willing to take them in, and the Jewish organizations were running a regular underground railroad for illegal immigrants to Palestine. The fact that Miss Rosensaft was Jewish complicated things considerably. It meant she could decide to go almost anywhere. And it meant that she might simply have vanished into the *Bricha* escape pipeline. Christiansen could talk to the U.N. people or the Quaker relief organizations, but the Jews had their problems running the British blockade and weren't disposed to be trusting. If she had gone that route, it might even be necessary to travel to Palestine and look for her there.

But first things first. There were still a lot of rocks to be turned over in Europe.

As he buttoned the tunic of his uniform, Christiansen's eyes settled on the black leather cello case that was resting on its side next to the closet door. He had sold his double bass in Havana to help pay for the ship tickets to Le Havre. That part of his life was over—he was through playing in fifth-rate jazz groups just to make enough money to keep moving— but nothing on God's earth would get him to part with his cello, even if he didn't have the fingers to do it justice anymore. If there was anything worth saving left in him, it had something to do with that cello.

Perhaps he should have checked it with the concierge, just to make sure no one nipped in and stole it while he was gone. Perhaps he would yet. Yes, safe was safe.

"Your honor is a musician?"

Plump, well-cared-for hands reached out to take the case from him and set it down beside the great grid of key boxes that took up most of the wall behind the front desk. There was something reassuring, almost caressing, about the way the man allowed his fingers to slide over the shoulder of the lid, as if he understood all about the romance between owner and instrument.

"I try." Christiansen lit a cigarette, more out of nerves than anything else. He felt as if he were in disguise. "Could you just put it somewhere out of the way, so nobody will bump into it?"

"Certainly. Of course. The walls here, by the way, are very thick, so your honor would be disturbing no one if you wished to practice later in your room. Is your honor, by the way, familiar with the Saint-Saëns concerto? A beautiful piece, very moving."

Christiansen smiled—the man hardly even expected an answer—and started on his way across the lobby to the big revolving front door. Saint-Saëns. The Germans always assumed they were being excessively diplomatic and cosmopolitan to admit that any foreigner, let alone a Frenchman, was fit to write anything except exercise pieces for children.

With his hands in his pockets and the cigarette pushed into the corner of his mouth, Christiansen began making his way along the side of the street— only the streets were clear, the sidewalks were still covered with rubble—in the general direction of the

Marienplatz. It was a cold morning. The sky was the color of lead and patches of frost sheltered against the broken stone. It must have rained the night before, because pools of dirty water had collected between the cobblestones. Almost no one else was out.

The great square of the Marienplatz was now simply a cleared space surrounded by ruins. Only the church and the Rathaus had survived total destruction; everything else had been bulldozed. Life, however, was beginning to return to normal. Around three sides men and women were doing a brisk business from stalls and pushcarts. There were even a few tourists standing about to watch the reconstruction of the clock tower. For almost the first time since he had arrived yesterday morning from Nuremberg, Christiansen had the sense that he was in a city instead of a wasteland of shattered buildings.

In five or six years, he thought to himself, this will all be back the way it was. And that was all right. He harbored no ill will toward the Germans. The score he had to settle didn't take on such grandiose proportions as that.

"You can't bring either of them back," his aunt had told him. "Your father and mother at Kirstenstad, my son Carl at Iwo Jima—the family has been thinned out enough by this war. Let it rest, Inar. Men with nothing to lose are more dangerous than all the armies in the world. Your parents wouldn't have wanted you to risk getting killed in this vendetta. You don't owe this to them."

"I think maybe I do."

Auntie Inger, who was almost his mother, already getting old, her blond hair turning whiter almost from month to month. To her the war had been like a natural disaster, just something that had happened, terrible and guiltless. All she wanted was to go back to the way things had been—or as close as three deaths in the family would allow. After von Goltz's arrest, Christiansen had come home to the little house in White Plains where he had grown to manhood, expecting to be understood.

"This isn't right, what you want to do. Even if you succeed, you'll never be the same again."

"I'll never be the same again anyway." He smiled and got up from the overstuffed living-room chair. He loved his old Auntie, who had raised him up like her own son, but it had been a mistake to come back here. The life he had lived within these walls had nothing to do with him anymore. He was a stranger now. It was time to leave.

"I'll keep in touch."

"No, don't do that," she had said, shaking her head sadly. "I don't want to wait for the letters to stop coming. If you come back and the thing is finished, fine. If not, then you will have died for me right here, now."

And that was how he had severed his last contact with the past, so he would be free to settle his score. No, he didn't have anything against the Germans. He just wanted to kill Egon Hagemann.

He bought a plate of sausage from a formidable gray-haired old woman with the neck and jowls of a bulldog.

"*Amerikanishes Geld, bitte?*" she asked, in a surprisingly sweet voice. Christiansen fished around in his pocket until he found a fifty-cent piece and when she began to make change for him he waved his hand and smiled. They were good sausage, worth the money, and he too wasn't interested in collecting pocketfuls of the cheap little aluminum coins the new German government in Bonn was trying to convince everybody were legal tender. The woman offered him a fork, and he stood beside her portable charcoal grill eating and watching the crowd.

He had the uncomfortable feeling that somewhere or other he had attracted somebody's notice.

It wasn't much more than an impression, a discordance so close to the limits of his senses that it would have been the easiest thing to talk himself out of believing it was there at all. He just felt edgy without knowing quite why.

Back before the war, when he had been just a kid in New York City with nothing more on his mind than learning the Bach C-minor Courante and how to speak English like an American, he used to walk the twenty-six blocks between his boarding house and Juilliard twice a day, listening to the traffic noises and trying to arrange them into sequences so they would sound like twelve-tone or Haydn's *Creation* or the corridor outside the practice rooms, where, if you stopped to notice, little wisps of what everyone was playing would squeeze out under the doorways and blend together into a chaotic but somehow strangely integrated and comforting symphony. It was a kind of game that had something to do with the scribbled-over sheets of music paper he kept in his desk, with those first hesitant steps toward learning how to write something that didn't sound like a bad parody of Brahms, and also with learning to be in this strange city, so far from home, and to think of it as his own place.

Anyway, he had come to recognize, on some level or other, when the harmony had been broken. Sometimes, for no reason he could have explained to anyone, he would know that something was wrong, turn around, and see a fistfight starting under the shadow of a restaurant awning, or a woman lying on the sidewalk where she had fainted of sunstroke. Once, when some drunk in a taxicab had come lurching right up over the curb at him, it had probably saved his life.

He had listened even harder all during the war, and it had saved his life more than just once.

And now, in the Year of our Lord nineteen hundred and forty-eight, standing in the Marienplatz, eating a sausage amidst the ruins of conquered Germany seven years and ten months after the whole wonderful experience of his student days in New York had suddenly become as remote and unreal as the court life of ninth-century Japan, Inar Christiansen, late of the Juilliard Symphony Orchestra, the Royal Norwegian Army, and the human race, was wondering where he had heard the sinister little grace note that quavered out its warning.

Well, he decided, all things would be revealed at the proper time.

The man at the United Nations office was very cordial, asked no probing questions, and conducted Christiansen back to a file room where the case histories of several thousand Displaced Persons filled up shelf after shelf of file boxes. There were six or seven other people looking through the same material, and tables had been set aside for the sleek, complacent-looking lawyers who were researching reparations claims and the anxious men and women who still, after all this time, were trying to track down the mother or husband or daughter they fancied might still be alive somewhere. This office, and all the other places just like it Christiansen had been to, seemed haunted by ghosts.

He dropped his hat on the table in front of an empty chair and started in. It was going to be a long day.

Just after noon he broke off for a while and went around the corner to a tavern where, for the equivalent of about thirty cents, you could buy a glass of beer and a plate of stew made with stolen U.S. Army Spam. The walls were whitewashed and decorated with posters for soccer matches and bicycle races, and most of the other men there were wearing work clothes. The patroness was about fifty, with a big bosom and reddish hair cut long in the style of American bobby soxers; the metal bracelets around her wrists tinkled with every movement. She seemed to know everybody, even Christiansen, whom she had never seen before in her life.

Christiansen took his plate of stew and looked around for a quiet corner where he could sit down and eat it. His fellow patrons had stared at him for a few sullen seconds when he came in, as if they were prepared to take offense at having lost the war, and then lost interest.

When he was finished he went outside into the fresh air for a cigarette. There was a vacant lot in the next block where the rubble had been cleared away enough to allow the grass to grow, and some children were playing a noisy and incomprehensible game that was rather like hockey except that, as far as Christiansen could make out, there was no ball. He watched for a while, sitting on part of a ruined brick staircase that led up to nothing, nursing his cigarette and won-

dering if he was ever going to get anywhere checking
file folders full of names. It didn't seem very likely.

The records of Displaced Persons were incomplete
at best and were scattered all over the Western Occupation Zones into the bargain. They also had the
disadvantage of being more or less voluntary. It had
been easy enough to get everyone's name and city of
origin in 1945, when these people were all still pretty
startled to discover themselves alive and were completely dependent on the occupying armies for just
day-to-day survival, and some of them, hoping to make
contact again with their families, had continued to
keep a current address on file. But if finally they had
given up hope that there was anyone left from home
to look for them, or if for some reason they didn't want
to be found—and if Becker had been telling the truth
and his Colonel Hagemann was looking for her as well,
it wasn't so unreasonable that Esther Rosensaft might
just decide she wanted to stay lost—then they just
dropped from sight.

Right now, however, Christiansen would settle for
some evidence that, as advertised, Esther Rosensaft
had lived through the war. If he could just establish
that, then there might be other ways of digging her
out.

A car went by on the street, a prewar sedan, dark
blue or black under its winter dirtiness. It had a tendency to grind between second and third gears. There
was a man on the back seat trying not to be seen as
he watched Christiansen through the rear window.
His arm was extended along the top of the backrest
and he was pressed so deeply into the corner that his
head must have been touching the doorpost. That
made the third time today.

It wasn't a bad choice for a surveillance car if you discounted the rattle, and a little oil probably would have fixed that. But people had learned to live with their infirmities since 1939—probably they didn't even hear it anymore. So much the worse for them.

Christiansen didn't try to decide who was trailing him around town. That was one of those questions which had a way of answering themselves after a while, and a couple of shadowy figures in an old roadster didn't provide many clues. If they were the police, which was possible, they didn't present any problem because Christiansen hadn't broken any laws except the statutes against murder, which hardly even counted these days, and if they were friends of Colonel Hagemann, which was also possible, that only meant he was getting close enough to make the Great Man nervous. That Hagemann would eventually try to have him put out of his misery was something he took so completely for granted that he had almost ceased to worry about it. Almost.

He had spent the whole morning looking for a "Rosensaft" on one of the hundreds of lists that were kept in no particular order in files of everything from transportation vouchers to military police reports. He hadn't found one. Perhaps General von Goltz hadn't been quite so successful in ensuring her safety as Becker had imagined.

He had tried every variation in spelling he could think of: "Rosenzap" and "Rothensapf" and "Roterschatt" and even "Saft, Rosa." It wasn't as if clerks with probably only a crash-course knowledge of German didn't make mistakes like that—but everywhere he drew a blank. Perhaps, if the Nazis hadn't destroyed them, there might still be some record at

Waldenburg, but that was in the Russian Zone and they weren't sharing any secrets. Finding Esther Rosensaft was proving as difficult as finding her boyfriend the Colonel. Perhaps he should just forget about this particular hot tip and go back to tracking down Hagemann's old men-at-arms.

But there was still Linz and Vienna and Stuttgart and—perish the thought—even Palestine before he ran out of file folders to look through. He would be very scrupulous. The nature of his task demanded it.

On the eighth of June, 1945, the day after he had formed part of the honor guard for King Haakon's return to his capital, Christiansen had borrowed a car from a friend and had driven north to Kirstenstad. He knew all about what had happened there; intelligence on the incident had been very complete, and he had even managed to interview a couple of the survivors after they were smuggled over to England. He just wanted to have a look for himself.

The only part of his parents' house one could see from a distance was a piece of broken chimney. Otherwise, there was only the doorstep, upon which his father and mother had died, and the outline of the exterior wall. Even the cellar was filled in with rubble, and grass grew where his mother had had her sitting room.

Everywhere else it was just the same. Nobody lived in Kirstenstad now. Nobody could. Nobody ever would again.

Christiansen had stopped his car at the ruins of the post office—in a tiny hamlet like Kirstenstad, only a crossroad in the middle of farmlands, the post office was a kind of boundary, a line drawn in the dirt to say "here is where we begin"—and walked the rest of the way, listening to his bootsoles crunch against the gravel roadbed. He kept thinking, "All of the people who lived here are dead now. It's all gone." He hadn't really believed it could have happened, not until that moment, as he looked at the weeds bowing gracefully in the wind where the blacksmith's house had been, where Madame Koht, the rector's widow, had taught him to read music and to play the wooden flute, where the store had stood that had been successively a bakery, a haberdasher's, and a second-hand bookshop before standing idle for the last two years prior to his departure for America. He hadn't really believed it, but he believed it now. As he stood on the threshold of his home, where the snows of three winters had cleaned away the traces of his parents' blood, something seemed to freeze shut inside him. He turned around and started walking back to the car, faster and faster, until he was nearly running. It seemed as if he couldn't breathe until he got away.

A week later, when he knew what he had to do, he wrote a letter to the King asking to be allowed to resign his commission. There was no difficulty, since he was officially invalided anyway, and he didn't want to be anybody's agent now except his own. He was going to find General von Goltz.

"You'll end up just like all the other vigilantes," a friend had told him. Nils Rynning was his brother officer, his roommate for the two years prior to Normandy, and the only person to whom he had confided his intentions. Nils had pale, almost whitish hair and no taste for revenge. For him, the war was over.

"They aren't masters of Europe anymore, remember? They're on the run. I just want to give them something to run from."

Captain Rynning, who still wore his army greens and had spent every day since liberation taking advantage of the patriotic fervor of Oslo's female inhabitants, leaned across the table toward him and frowned. He was a thin, wiry man, given to sudden movements that those who didn't know him might have ascribed to nerves. They would have been mistaken. Captain Rynning had made thirty-six crossings as a commando and had taken part in the Finnmark operation. Captain Rynning didn't have any nerves.

"Yes," he said, tapping rapidly at the rim of his glass with the nail of his middle finger, as if the sound it made fascinated him. "We have driven the dog back into its hole, where it will lick its wounds and whine. Perhaps, eventually, it will even die there. But still it would be just as well not to stretch one's arms down into the darkness after it. Its jaws are still filled with perfectly serviceable teeth."

Of course. Everyone he knew offered the same warning, as if it had never occurred to Christiansen that the men who had razed Kirstenstad still knew how to defend themselves.

Which brought him back to the problem of the muddy roadster.

Christiansen ground out his cigarette against the shattered brick staircase and, without bothering to look around, started back to his table in the record room. If these people who were keeping such careful track of his movements were Hagemann's men, there was little enough he could do about it. Let them roam about the streets waiting for him to come out again—it would do them no harm to spend the rest of the afternoon growing restless and apprehensive. He would know how to deal with them when the moment came.

Upon his return he discovered that the tables were less crowded. The lawyers were gone and those few souls left, the dogged and determined remnant, were turning the pages of the files with a melancholy fatalism, as if they had lost all real expectation of finding whatever names they were looking for.

And they were probably right. By a quarter after four, Christiansen had satisfied himself that Esther Rosensaft had never registered with the United Nations office in Munich. There was nothing left to do except to return to his hotel.

The U.N. building had a back entrance, but there seemed no good reason why his shadows should have it pointed out to them that they had been detected. They would merely find themselves another car or, if they had the resources, put a different team on him. He went down the stairs into the bleak winter sun and started back the way he had come.

Sure enough, within four blocks the roadster had pulled up behind him and driven past. Christiansen could hear the rattle of the gearbox as it shot ahead. He was careful not to look after it.

What did they want? To kill him probably, but then what were they waiting for? And why suddenly now?

Had Becker been one too many for them? It seemed unlikely—he was a small fish. Had they picked up on him already in Nuremberg? In Havana?

There was a string quartet playing in the lounge that evening; it was a regular Wednesday feature at the hotel, something straight out of Edwardian times.

The notice on the bulletin board had mentioned Debussy—obviously the management was making a concerted effort to let bygones be bygones—and Christiansen had busted his tail on that piece for his first group recital at Juilliard. So he had rather thought that after dinner he would carry his coffee with him and join the eight or ten other people who usually put in an appearance at these sorts of affairs, to have a listen and see if the fourth movement was really the bitch he remembered. He could use the distraction.

But first he had to make it back in one more-or-less contiguous piece.

Because, you see, the car had dropped back and there was a man on foot behind him now. Either they entertained some suspicions that he had tumbled to them and had decided on that account on a change in tactics, or they were moving in for the kill. It didn't matter—Christiansen had made up his mind it was time to force the issue with these jokers, so if they weren't ready to go to extremes now they would be soon enough. One can't allow oneself to be followed all over Europe by such people. Eventually they would start to get in the way.

By the time he reached the Marienplatz the sun had already disappeared behind the half-ruined Rathaus, and with it had gone the tourists and the hucksters and even the police. The pushcarts had vanished and the wooden doors of the stalls were locked tight. There was nothing left but the emptiness and the ruins and the shadowed darkness. As he walked across that vast, hollow plaza, listening to the echoes of his footfalls against the paving stones, Christiansen was painfully aware how easy it would have been for someone with a rifle, or even a decently accurate pistol, to . . .

Or perhaps they were waiting. Doubtless they knew he was on his way back to the hotel—they could anticipate his route. Perhaps they would catch him on some narrow sidewalk, step out from behind the corner of a building, and then, when they were close enough to make quite sure . . .

But this wasn't the first time he had had to face the prospect of a man with a gun waiting to kill him. That was what the war had been all about. And that had been the daily possibility ever since he had set himself the task of squaring things for Kirstenstad.

Still, nothing prevented him from admitting to himself that he didn't like it. The war had taught him the stupidity of imagining that you weren't afraid.

The Marienplatz was no more dangerous than any other hundred or so meters between here and his hotel. He kept going, resisting the temptation to slow down, listening all the time for any sound that kept pace with his own footsteps.

When he reached the other side, he ducked into a shadow and waited.

There was nothing. He had imagined the whole business—the car with the bad gears, the man behind him, the whole sorry spectacle. He was getting paranoid; it happened to people with bad consciences. He felt in his shirt pocket for his pack of cigarettes.

He already had the book of matches in his hand when he saw a gray shape, a man in a dark overcoat, come onto the plaza, hesitate for an instant, and then go to the left and disappear around the side of the Rathaus. Apparently Christiansen wasn't the only one with a bad conscience.

So. That much he hadn't imagined—he was being followed. Nice people with no malice in their hearts didn't find it necessary to be so furtive. The son of a bitch was taking the long way around because he couldn't work up the nerve to expose himself. He liked shadows, this boy did. He liked narrow streets and the shelter of crowds. He wasn't going to walk straight across the Marienplatz, not all by himself, not on your life.

Christiansen lit his cigarette and glanced around him, wondering what he was supposed to do. The enemy had no face—he could be anyone. He probably had a gun, and Christiansen wasn't carrying anything except the coiled length of catgut that went with him everywhere. The odds were decidedly uneven.

It was necessary to find out what this one looked like. He would have to be forced into showing himself.

There was a half-destroyed row of shop buildings across the street from Christiansen's hotel. A few had survived the war without enough damage to force them into closing down, but most were just shells, walls of dead brick that broke off in a ragged line in the middle of the window frames, waiting to be bulldozed. One of them had been a cinema and still contained the ruin of a second story where doubtless the manager had had his office. There was a small window facing out onto the street where perhaps he had stood and watched the patrons queuing up to buy tickets. Christiansen would wait there to see who came to wait for him.

Which meant he had to get there first. He threw his cigarette down on the paving stones—they were a nasty habit he had picked up during the war, and he kept intending to give them up—and broke into a run. He had a head start. He wouldn't try to be devious—he would leave that to the man behind him. That was the great disadvantage to shadowing people; you always had to take the long way around and you couldn't afford to crowd. Christiansen didn't have those problems. He intended to be there waiting when the other guy started to panic that he had dropped out on him.

The distance was probably a shade over half a mile. Christiansen made it in under four minutes and slowed down only as he crossed the Odeonplatz and rounded the corner to his hotel. The front door to the cinema was padlocked, but that meant remarkably little since the whole back of the building was blown out. He climbed over the rubble and up the rickety stairway that led to the deserted office. No one had troubled to lock that door.

The little room was hardly fifteen feet square. There were pieces of the ceiling on the floor and very little else. Except for a calendar on one wall—giving the date as August 22, 1944—and an empty packing case by the little window, everything had been taken away by scavengers. Christiansen picked his careful way through the chunks of plaster and the shattered two-by-fours and sat down on the packing case. The window was broken in two of its four panes and caked with dust, but it provided an excellent view of the whole length of the street.

The hotel had its lights on. It looked quite festive, or would have if the structures around it hadn't been uninhabited, ruined, lurching to this side and that as if time had stopped for them the instant prior to collapse. Munich had been gutted as badly as any city in Europe. It was a metropolis of corpses where anything like celebration was not only in poor taste but almost heartless. Christiansen decided he didn't like his hotel, that he was looking forward to moving on.

The packing case was not terribly comfortable, and it was a cold night. Fortunately the Norwegian army knew all about cold nights, and his greatcoat was proof against freezing to death anytime soon. Still, he would have preferred to be back in his own room, smoking a cigarette and changing for dinner.

It was about a quarter to seven when he noticed the man in the charcoal gray overcoat standing nervously in the shadow of what had once been a furniture store. Christiansen might never have seen him at all, it was so dark, except that the fellow kept shifting his weight from one leg to the other with an impatient movement that reminded one of a child who needed to go to the bathroom. It was a cold night.

Christiansen sat at his window, waiting, suddenly grown very calm, almost disappointed. It was only a man after all, like himself. Perhaps this wasn't even the one.

But then the man in the shadow seemed to make up his mind about something and with a kind of shudder started toward the hotel. Or perhaps he hadn't made up his mind; perhaps it had only been an impulse, one he didn't know whether or not to regret. He walked slowly, as if he hardly knew himself where he was going, and then all at once, when he had come level with the polished revolving glass doors of the hotel's main entrance, a few quick steps carried him through and out of sight.

If this is the one, Christiansen thought, if this is the one he will only stop long enough to check behind the porter's desk to see if my key is in its box. He knows the hotel, so he will know the room number. And he won't wait around. As soon as he is sure that I've not returned he'll come back outside and find himself a place from which to keep watch. If this is the one.

And there he was. He stepped out into the circle of light from the hotel's entrance and stood there on the sidewalk for a moment, looking as if he expected to see his worst enemy. Maybe he did.

It was the first chance Christiansen had had for anything like a good look at him, and he was surprised to see that the man who had been tailing him hardly seemed old enough to have heard of Kirstenstad. He wasn't wearing a hat; his hair was black and curly, like a poodle's, and in need of cutting. It was a thin face, handsome and dark but suggesting a certain lack of decision. Long, rather delicate hands dangled from the sleeves of his overcoat. In a few years, if he was lucky, he might grow into a real fanatic, but nobody believes in much of anything at twenty.

And he was looking straight up at Christiansen's little second-story window.

Christiansen remained sitting on his packing case, as immobile as if he were part of the building. He was intellectually convinced that there was no way anyone could see him from across the street—he told himself that it was impossible, and he nearly even believed it—but he was not foolish enough to move. He would wait and see what happened next.

Nothing. The boy with the curly hair continued to stare up at his window, and then he glanced back inside the lobby of the hotel, and then down at the sleeve of his overcoat. He was a long time deciding.

But in the end he walked across the street. Christiansen knew, with an instinct he couldn't have explained, that in another two minutes this guy would be coming up those shaky, dust-covered stairs and through the door. And Christiansen had nothing in his pocket except a coil of fiddle string.

Could he have seen him through the window? Perhaps, if he knew what he was looking for. But how could the kid have known, when Christiansen himself hadn't known until perhaps half an hour ago? It wasn't as if this ruined movie house were somewhere he haunted like a shadow.

Christiansen could hear him now. The office door was open about an inch, and he was down below, in what had once been the lobby, climbing over fallen pieces of timber. He wasn't exactly being quiet about it, so perhaps he didn't know that Christiansen was upstairs. Or perhaps he realized the futility of trying to make one's way through such a place in silence. Or perhaps he just didn't care whether Christiansen heard him or not.

There was no time to waste—he was on the stairway. Christiansen rose from the packing case and stepped lightly across to the doorway. It was almost completely dark now. He waited by the door, hardly daring to breathe.

All at once he stopped hearing the sound of footsteps on the stairs. For perhaps as long as fifteen seconds there was perfect quiet and then, finally, a slow, cautious creak of dry wood as the man outside resumed his climb. Only now he was being very careful.

The door swung open. He didn't come in, not right away. And then a half step—one foot over the sill, and a huge revolver in his right hand swept over the room like a searchlight.

There wasn't time to think. The two men were hardly more than half a yard apart, and in a fraction of a second he would see Christiansen and fire the revolver. He had only to turn his head.

Christiansen made a grab. His fingers snapped shut over the cylinder just as the revolver stopped in its arc. It was pointed straight at his belly. He didn't know—if the thing was already cocked, he was dead.

They stood there like that for what seemed most of the night, looking directly into each other's eyes. There was surprise; there was fear. Neither of them moved.

And then Christiansen felt the revolver twisting in his grasp. The fellow was trying to pull the trigger, but it wouldn't fire because the cylinder couldn't turn. The gamble had paid off.

With a short, deft movement, Christiansen brought up the heel of his left hand and snapped it into the man's face. There was a sound like a lock clicking shut as the nose broke, and then there was a great deal of blood. It streamed out of the nostrils and the man clapped his free hand across his mouth and nose as though he wanted to keep himself from screaming.

Still keeping his hold on the revolver, Christiansen threw his weight against him, sending him sprawling into the door. In an instant he was down; Christiansen kicked him once in the pit of the stomach, and all resistance was at an end. The man had even let go of his gun.

Christiansen put it in the pocket of his greatcoat and began searching for papers and additional weapons. There was no hurry now—whoever he was, he had other things to think about than fighting back. He lay there on the floor, groaning quietly, as helpless as a baby. Christiansen found a wallet and a pass-port.

The wallet was full of British pound notes, and the passport, which was registered to the British mandate in Palestine, was filled out in the name of one Itzhak Dessauer, resident at 276B Hagesher Street, Tel Aviv.

Terrific. It would be worth something to know what he had done to bring that crowd down on his back.

But there were consolations. Unless things had changed a great deal since the last time he had checked, at least he didn't have to worry that anyone with a name like "Itzhak Dessauer" was working for Hagemann.

✠ 4 ✠

When Itzhak came back that night, the first thing Mordecai Leivick did was send for a doctor—a Jewish doctor, who could be trusted to keep his mouth shut—and the second thing he did was to inquire, in the politest possible way, how little Itzikel, who was such a tough guy that it was all his mother could do to keep him from running off to join the Stern Gang, how a formidable fellow like that had managed to lose his gun and get his nose broken for him on a simple shadowing job. He was a regular miracle was this boy, a real demon.

After the doctor, that good man, had finally left, Mrs. Dessauer's little son sat on a wooden chair in the center of their rented room, slumped slightly forward and resting the points of his elbows on his thighs, looking like a battle casualty with his two black eyes and the dried blood around the nostrils of his puffy, bandaged nose. But his distress was more likely mental than physical. He had made a first-class fool out of himself and, for once, he had the good sense to know it.

"I saw the footprints in the dust on the stairs," he said morosely. He drew himself up straight and then subsided again into a dejected slouch, as if he was beginning to realize the futility of striking attitudes. "I had my gun out, but he jumped me."

"And how did he contrive to do that?"

Leivick, who was leaning against the door with his arms folded across his chest, smiled kindly. His eldest boy, had he lived through Treblinka, would have been just about Itzhak's age, and he liked the little *pisher*, but there was no room in this for sentiment.

The expression in the boy's blackened eyes was genuinely pathetic.

"He just reached out and grabbed the gun," he said finally. "I didn't come through the door right away. I'm sorry, Mordecai."

"And what were you doing going after the man with a gun in the first place—you want to tell me that? If you knew he was up there, why didn't you just tiptoe back down the stairs and leave him in peace, eh? You had orders maybe to shoot him? We don't have enough troubles with the local authorities, is that it?"

"I thought maybe I could pull him in and we could squeeze him a little. I thought I could . . ."

"You *thought*?" Leivick scratched his heavy forearm through the shirt sleeve, wondering if miracles would ever cease. "You were supposed to follow the man and report, Itzhak, not to think. Leave the thinking to me—the Mossad doesn't pay a squirt like you to think."

"The Mossad doesn't pay me at all."

"My very words."

For a moment neither of them spoke. They didn't need to—Itzhak knew the rules now. He would keep his creative outbursts in check.

It was almost possible to feel sorry for him. After all, his heart was in the right place.

"I still think he's one of Hagemann's thugs," he said, shrugging his shoulders as he stared down at his hands with sullen concentration. "God knows, he looks the part."

Leivick ran a hand over his scalp, which was perfectly bald, and sighed. He had already missed dinner by about two hours, something that couldn't help but add to his impatience, and now it seemed that he had a congenital idiot to deal with. He wished the other fellows would hurry up and come back; the strain of listening to such rubbish was beginning to get him down.

"Itzikel, please allow me to remind you of something. The SS don't like Jewish people, not even nice boys like you. If that had been one of Hagemann's men you would not be sitting here feeling your nose throb. You would be dead, probably with embellishments. Okay? We made a mistake—the man isn't a Nazi assassin. He's something else, so live with it."

Dessauer looked less than convinced, but Mordecai Leivick had almost ceased to care. These young *Sabras*, they seemed to live in a dream world where every Gentile who wasn't an Arab had to be Martin Bormann.

As soon as he heard footsteps in the hallway outside, Leivick reached into the top drawer of the room's battered old dresser and pulled out a duplicate of the British army revolver which earlier that evening Itzhak Dessauer had so ignominiously lost. He was reasonably certain who it was, but there were such things as necessary precautions.

"Mordecai, it's us" was followed by two sharp raps on the door. The pistol went back inside the dresser drawer, and Leivick walked over and threw the catch on the door lock.

The two men who came inside were both in their middle thirties and carried with them that indefinable suggestion of having seen it all. They were old campaigners: Jerry Hirsch, who had grown up in America and emigrated to Palestine with his parents in 1929, had joined the Haganah in 1934, at the age of twenty, and served with the Palmach in Syria during the war. Since the truce with the British authorities had lapsed he had been spending most of his time in Italy, getting survivors of the Final Solution past the blockade—that was where he had met Mordecai, in June of 1945. He was a short, compact man and tended to sway at the shoulders when he walked, like an American. He looked like no one in particular and had participated in the *Exodus* affair. The current reward for his capture was fifteen hundred pounds, which made him the sixth most wanted man on the British Army Authority lists.

Amos Faglin, who closed the door behind them, was taller and thin to the point of uneasiness. His face was crowded with difficult angles—the cheekbones and the shelf over his eyes seemed to jut out like the corners of carved stone blocks, and his jaw could have been drafted with a straightedge and a pair of calipers. He had blue eyes that never seemed to rest. His wife and two daughters lived in Haifa, but he hadn't seen them in nearly a year. Like Hirsch, he had fought in

Syria with the Palmach and, like Hirsch, he was a smuggler. His specialty, however, was weaponry—he was an expert in small arms and explosives, which he regularly shipped in boxes marked *Agricultural Implements* to his father-in-law's warehouses in Jaffa. Unlike Hirsch, he was not a celebrity. The British, so far as was known, remained unaware of his existence.

"Did you have your look?"

"Yes, and so did he."

Jerry Hirsch was standing beside a small table beneath the room's only window; his hand rested on the lid of the portable coffee pot that was kept there, as if he were testing to see if it could still be warm. It wasn't—nobody had made any coffee since that morning, and it was a quarter to ten at night—so he lifted his fingers away with great delicacy.

"He was sitting out in the lounge in his dinner jacket, listening to a crowd of fiddle players. He had us spotted the second we came into the room. He seemed to know all about us; we might as well have had *Haganah* printed in white letters down the lapels of our jackets. He watched us watching him for a minute or so, and then he seemed to get bored and turned back to his concert. I'll give him that—he doesn't rattle easy."

Dessauer visibly brightened. It seemed to make him feel better that Hirsch had been impressed by the man who had taken away his gun and broken his nose. He was about to say something when a glance from Leivick made him close his mouth with a snap.

"He is not small," Faglin added as he sat down on the bed. He took off his hat and set it beside him on the coverlet, quite as if he hoped to stay there forever.

"I would hate to feel those hands around my neck. Shall we kill him?"

The expression on his face suggested it was not something to which he looked forward.

"We are not murderers, Amos. We don't even know if this man poses a threat to us."

"He certainly posed a threat to Gerhart Becker." Jerry Hirsch laughed soundlessly at his own joke. He was crouched on the floor, pawing through the contents of his suitcase until he came up with a carton of American cigarettes. "What a way to kill a man—do you suppose he was trying to make it look like a suicide?"

Mordecai shook his head. He had been giving the matter a good deal of thought since Itzhak had come back with his broken nose.

"No—a man who hangs himself isn't found with his hands tied behind his back. Is it your impression our friend would be careless enough to overlook a detail like that?"

Now it was Hirsch's turn to shake his head.

"Precisely. And I have trouble with the idea that Hagemann would order one of his old subordinates— his personal servant, in fact—killed in such a manner. SS men deserve the courtesy of a bullet, and Hagemann is the type to be very scrupulous about observing such little niceties."

"Also there is the fact that he saw fit to spare our Itzikel." Faglin treated the young man to a weary contemptuous smile. There was nothing personal in it. Like Leivick, he understood that Dessauer had to be impressed with the magnitude of his failure if there was to be any hope of his developing into a dependable operative.

"Yes, there is that."

Mordecai pushed himself away from the dresser and began measuring out teaspoons of coffee into the pot. He was dreadfully hungry. Except for the war years, he had always been a heavy man, and it might be tomorrow morning before any one of this crew thought about food. Coffee was better than nothing.

"Which leaves us with the question, what does he want? Hagemann is murdering his old associates, but this one doesn't seem to be part of that. And now we find him dressed up as a Norwegian army officer and checking into the records of Displaced Persons. What name, by the way, is he using at the hotel?"

"Christiansen." Faglin, who was watching with more than routine interest as Leivick made the coffee, glanced down at his hand, just as if he were checking a memorandum written across the back of his thumb. "Inar Christiansen."

"Good God! Well, what would you expect?"

They all turned to look at Itzhak Dessauer, the source of this odd interjection. He was smiling behind his bandages, apparently quite proud of himself.

"It may even be his real name," Faglin went on, as if determined to ignore the interruption. "This is the first time we have been this near to him—perhaps we could manage a set of fingerprints." He shrugged his shoulders wearily, as if he really couldn't imagine why they should bother.

"Perhaps we could even ask him to pose for a portrait," Jerry Hirsch added. His eyebrows were working up and down *à la* Groucho Marx—it was his method of signaling irony.

"Jerry's right. He's been one step ahead of us ever since we first became aware of him last April in Brazil.

He doesn't bear toying with. Do you want some of this?"

Leivick held out a coffee cup to Amos Faglin, grasping it by the rim with his middle finger and thumb. Faglin accepted it somewhat grudgingly.

"Then what do you have in mind we should do about him, Mordecai? If he isn't one of Hagemann's thugs, then why does he do their work for them? He's killed two members of the Fifth Brigade that we know of—he's practically making a career of it."

"A man does not have to be working for Hagemann to have good reason for killing former SS men." Leivick smiled and shrugged, as if admitting to some ludicrous family infirmity. "Who should know that better than us?"

Faglin tasted his coffee and made a face as if either he didn't like it or the subject of Inar Christiansen was beginning to bore him.

"Then if he wants Hagemann himself, he's competition. It could be we should kill him after all."

This was not a line of argument which Leivick wished to encourage, so he smiled.

"As you said yourself, that might not be easy. Since the indications are he's no amateur, anything of the kind could turn into an expensive proposition, and I'd hate to lose any of you boys."

"Then what?"

Faglin and Hirsch, the men of action, exchanged an impatient glance. They shared the soldier's view of things. They had little tolerance for dilemmas.

Mordecai Leivick's smile began to take on a fixed quality.

"Then what, Mordecai?" Hirsch also accepted a cup of coffee, but set it down on the dresser while he finished his first cigarette. He wasn't an absent-minded smoker; he seemed to prefer savoring his vices in isolation. "He isn't likely to go away, and we can't ignore the man forever. What are we supposed to do about him?"

Leivick didn't like the way they were all staring at him. It was on occasions like this that he wished he had emigrated to America and gone into the jewelry business with his late wife's cousin. But no, he had to be a nation builder—and now they were all expecting an answer.

Well, they were right to expect it. After all, he took his orders from Tel Aviv, but they took theirs from him.

"Maybe we should ask him," he said finally, wondering if he hadn't taken leave of his senses.

Having allowed himself to be captured by the wild hope that there might be someplace along his route where he could buy something to eat, Leivick was crushed with disappointment to find that, for the most part, the street lights hadn't been turned on. But what should he expect in a city under military occupation? Most of the buildings had been gutted by the Allied bombing—people had other things to think about besides nightlife.

Leivick had seen ruined cities before. They gave him no feeling of satisfaction, even when they were German. He wasn't awed, or even oppressed. He was merely hungry.

Perhaps Christiansen, if he didn't kill him or call the porter to have him thrown out of that fancy hotel where he was staying, could be prevailed upon to order up a couple of sandwiches from room service.

Would Christiansen kill him? He thought not. Itzhak Dessauer had gone after the man with a gun and
hadn't suffered anything worse than a broken nose—
and richly deserved, too. And less than three hours
later, Hirsch and Faglin had seen him quietly sipping
his coffee and listening to the hotel's evening entertainment. He hadn't spared Itzhak because he was
afraid of retribution—according to Hirsch, he didn't
seem the type to be afraid of anything. He just wasn't
a homicidal maniac.

So Leivick wasn't worried about his life, he was
merely worried. Mr. Christiansen, if that was really
his name, was an imponderable.

It was over an hour's walk to the hotel, and as he
pushed through the revolving door Leivick was glad
to be in out of the wind.

It was like a different world inside. The carpets
were clean and the brass polished; there was an air
of prosperity and fashion such as Leivick had almost
forgotten was possible. He crossed the lobby—glad,
under the watchful eye of the concierge, that he had
thought to wear his best suit—and began his assault
on the stairway. Christiansen's room, as they had already established, was on the fourth floor.

In Prague, before the war, when he had been an
attorney for the Ministry of Public Works, sometimes
he and his wife would come to a hotel like this for
dinner. Life had been comfortable in Prague, very
agreeable, right up to 1938. Right up to Treblinka.

Now he wondered how he could ever have been
so naive.

He was tired by the time he reached the final flight
of stairs, tired in both flesh and spirit. It had been a
long day, and he was fifty, and everything seemed a

trifle unreal. Perhaps he simply disliked being reminded that there were places where the old life still
continued. Perhaps, finally, that was why he had turned
down his wife's cousin's offer and had gone instead to
Israel, where they were building a whole new order
of existence, where there were no ghosts except among
the living.

And then, suddenly, he felt better. He stood there
with his hand on the balustrade, and a strange, sad,
somehow comforting emotion took possession of him,
and he lost the sense of wandering through emptiness.
It was several seconds before his conscious mind took
note of the music.

No more than a wisp of sound, it floated through
the still corridor, hanging in the air like smoke. A
cello, full of melancholy dignity. Someone was playing
the radio.

And then suddenly the melody broke off in the
middle of a phrase, and the phrase was repeated,
shaped just a little differently. It wasn't a radio—one
of the guests was playing to himself, and not at all
badly either.

Leivick listened, hardly breathing, entranced. The
grandeur of the prelude, full of double stops and qua-
vering trills, gave way to a jolly, dancelike tune that
transformed itself, without so much as a pause for
breath, into a sinuous aria executed at blinding speed,
the notes slipping eerily into one another as if all
played on a single string.

I wonder how he manages it, Leivick thought. And
then it occurred to him that the music was coming
from behind Christiansen's door. It had stopped even
before he raised his hand to knock.

"Come in—it isn't locked."

Leivick tried the knob, which turned easily in his hand. Hotels always kept their doors locked, simply as a matter of habit; one had to press the button on the mortise plate or the door would lock automatically as soon as it had swung shut. Therefore, he had been expected. He pushed the door open, but didn't cross the threshold. He would wait and see.

What he saw was a man sitting in a chair—and, yes, he was every bit as big as Faglin had claimed. His sleeves were rolled up over arms matted with blond hair, and his left hand held both the neck of the cello that rested against his knees and, between the first and middle fingers, the bow. In his right hand was a British army revolver of familiar pattern. It was pointed straight at Leivick's chest.

"You play very beautifully, Mr. Christiansen. Shall I come inside, or do you plan to shoot me from this distance?"

"I said, 'Come in.' "

With some misgivings, Leivick stepped forward a few paces and allowed the door to close behind him. Christiansen didn't move; the pistol continued to line up on Leivick's chest. Nothing had changed, except that now he was firmly inside the trap. He held on to his hat brim with both hands, as if to give assurance of his good behavior.

"Mr. Christiansen," he said finally, "do you suppose I could prevail upon you to put that thing away? If I had meant you any harm I would hardly have come here alone."

"Are you alone?"

Even sitting, Christiansen managed to convey the

impression of being extremely tall. There was something intimidating about his very stillness—he hardly seemed even to be breathing. The eyes in his hard, handsome face were as impassive as ice.

"Yes, I'm alone. Quite alone. Do you imagine, Mr. Christiansen, that we would storm you in your hotel room?"

"I haven't any idea."

The muzzle of the pistol came up a fraction of an inch, as if he were correcting his aim—now, Leivick concluded, the bullet would probably catch him square in the throat.

"All I know is that suddenly you people are crawling all over me. The kid I took this off of didn't give the impression he wanted my autograph."

Now the pistol wasn't pointing at anything. It was simply lying in the palm of his hand, an exhibit. He set it down on a small table beside his chair.

"Perhaps you'd like to tell me what I've done that I've got a Palestinian Jew following me around with a gun in his pocket."

"Perhaps you'd like to explain to us your sudden interest in Displaced Persons."

"I asked first."

It was hot in the room. Leivick began unbuttoning his overcoat. Finally he found himself a small, rather ornate chair that had been hiding out of sight behind a dresser, moved it to the center of the room, and sat down. The two men were facing each other directly, across perhaps seven feet of rather fanciful Persian carpet.

"You were in Havana ten days ago," he said, as if stating a neutral fact. "You murdered a former SS sergeant named Gerhart Becker, living in that city under the alias of 'Bauer.' "

Astonishingly, there was no reaction. Christiansen never so much as blinked—they might as well have been discussing the railway schedule. It seemed that nothing about this man, absolutely nothing, was going to be easy.

"Three months before that, in São Paulo, one Dieter Kurtz, also formerly of the SS, was found in a closet by his Brazilian girlfriend, hanging from one of the hooks. He had been strangled with a length of very heavy catgut, the E-string from a double bass to be precise."

He glanced at the cello which Christiansen was still holding delicately by the neck, but once again, the man might as well not have been listening.

"I happened to be in São Paulo just then," Leivick went on. He had decided not to be impressed with this display of unnatural calm. After all, as Christiansen must have realized perfectly well, the Mossad was not exactly a police organization. "I was negotiating with Kurtz over a piece of information. He was badly frightened and, as it turned out, he had reason to be. If you had waited just one or two more days, Mr. Christiansen, you would have saved me a great deal of trouble."

"What makes you so positive any of this is my business?"

"That was a double bass you were playing ten nights ago in Havana, wasn't it, Mr. Christiansen? I was sitting rather far from the stage, but I don't think I could have been mistaken."

The cold blue eyes narrowed slightly—the man

was actually amused. Of course he had killed Gerhart Becker and Dieter Kurtz—and, could it be, one or two others about which even the Mossad remained ignorant?—and clearly he didn't give a damn who knew it. All at once Leivick felt a certain helplessness.

"It would seem that we've been following the same trail now for some time." Leivick shrugged his shoulders, as much out of resignation as anything else. There was no point in threatening such a man. "We watched from a window across the street while you climbed down onto Becker's roof. We watched you leave an hour and a half later. As a matter of fact, it was Becker who alerted us to you, when he delivered that note to your hotel."

"Had you been trying to make a deal with him too? I'm surprised you didn't call the police the minute you were aware of his danger."

The very blandness of the remark carried a certain contemptuous irony—what business had anyone to hold commerce with vermin like Gerhart Becker? Christiansen rose suddenly from his chair, strode across the room to where his cello case was lying on the floor like an empty coffin, and, with touching delicacy, slid the instrument inside, like a father lowering his favorite child into the grave.

"We had made a decision by then that you were the more promising lead. Did you know that for over a year now Colonel Egon Hagemann has been having his former associates from the Fifth Brigade assassinated? Under the circumstances, it was a natural enough mistake. We thought you might lead us back to him."

That, at least, elicited a reaction. As he stood up from buckling the case lid closed, the muscles in

Christiansen's jaw were working as rhythmically as a heartbeat. The unreachable man had at last been reached.

Yes, this one too knew what it was to hate with soul-killing intensity. He was human after all, and a casualty.

"Is all of this about Hagemann? Is that it?" Christiansen leaned back against the dresser, his arms folded across his chest, making him look even more massive. "Because if you have some private arrangement with Hagemann, you can just forget it. As soon as I find him, he's a dead man."

Leivick, who had remained seated, threw himself back into his chair until it creaked distressedly. He was hungry past imagining; he felt as if the walls of his stomach would begin caving in on him at any moment.

"Mr. Christiansen," he said at last, glancing up at that enormous and angry man with an expression of great self-pity. "Mr. Christiansen, finding the Colonel is not the problem. If you would be so kind as to inquire if the kitchen would still be willing to send up something in the way of dinner, I will tell you precisely where you can find him. Nothing would give me greater pleasure."

A quarter of an hour later a waiter arrived, pushing a wing table covered with an immaculate white cloth. When he had left there was a place setting for one, complete with a crystal water glass and a small arrangement of flowers. The meal consisted of melon, cold roast lamb, fennel hearts, sautéed potatoes, apricot mousse, and coffee. Leivick hadn't seen anything quite like it in nearly ten years.

"I trust you weren't kidding about Hagemann," Christiansen said as he sat down in his chair to watch Leivick eat.

"No, I wasn't kidding."

"Then?"

Having killed the first big urge, Leivick felt able to pause for a moment and pour himself a cup of coffee.

"He's in Syria just now." He looked up, smiling kindly at Christiansen, for whom at that particular moment he harbored only the warmest feelings. "He stays at the Hotel President Kuwatly in Damascus, in a suite on the top floor. In another week he will travel to Spain, where he owns a house, but in either case you would merely be throwing your life away if you attempted to kill him. He's very well guarded by his own people and in both countries he enjoys the protection of the government—informally, but none the less impenetrably. As you see, however, locating him hasn't been our difficulty."

It was encouraging, if perhaps a trifle uncomfortable, to know that at least he had managed to secure Christiansen's undivided attention. In his vast, almost morbid stillness, the man had a way of concentrating himself, of seeming to focus his will like sunlight through a lens, so that one had the sense that every corner of one's mind was being opened to that merciless white glare.

But Leivick wasn't really bothered. Within limits, he was prepared to be candid—he would have to be, or they could end by having to fight Christiansen as well as the Nazis and the Syrians. He was not the sort of man anyone wanted for an enemy.

"What we need to do is to lure him out," Leivick

went on slowly, filtering a teaspoon of sugar into his coffee. "I have one or two pointed questions I should like to put to the Colonel, and if he could be gotten away from his bodyguard for a while he might be persuaded to answer them. After that, you could kill him with my blessing. My government—when, in a few months, we have a government, and when the Arabs give us a moment in which to catch our breath— my government would probably give you a medal for killing Hagemann. He is more our enemy now than ever, and he has had a long and gaudy career as an anti-Semite."

"You can keep your medal, but maybe you'd better tell me why it's so important to keep Hagemann alive long enough to answer questions. What questions?"

Christiansen closed and opened his eyes with almost deathlike slowness. His enormous hands were folded together in his lap—he seemed indifferent to everything. It suddenly occurred to Leivick that this was a man who understood he was acting out his part in a tragedy.

"Mr. Christiansen, fair is fair." Leivick smiled wearily. The rest seemed to him inevitable, words rehearsed many times already. He wondered why Christiansen didn't see even then that the thing was settled. "I have answered your first question—you know now why we've taken such an interest in you. Now you answer mine. What have you been looking for in the case histories of our surviving remnant? What do you expect to find among the DPs?"

The silence was almost a third presence in the room. Life, hope, even the small, still hum of one's own mind seemed to have stopped for good and all. And then, for no apparent reason, Christiansen turned his staring gaze to the wall behind Leivick's head. His voice was empty, almost toneless.

"The bait for your lure," he said, and Leivick knew they were within striking distance of a bargain.

"Mr. Christiansen, perhaps the time has come for me to tell you a story."

"You seem a clever young man; you must have picked up all sorts of information about the Fifth Brigade while you were hunting down its old membership. Did you know they were garrisoned in Poland for a time?"

"Yes." Christiansen nodded solemnly. "During the second half of 1943, after their year of combat duty in Russia. It was the nadir of von Goltz's career, that eastern period, a disciplinary bloodletting after . . . after Norway, and before the establishment of the concentration camp at Waldenburg. They lost about seventy percent of their numbers, without being permitted replacements. I don't suppose they enjoyed themselves."

Leivick found himself studying the hard, impassive face, pondering the significance of what he had just witnessed there. Norway—yes, of course. He wondered why that had never occurred to him before.

"Precisely. After Norway." He smiled faintly and shrugged his shoulders, doing his best not to imply that he was presuming to understand anything. "One gathers that the thoroughness and zeal with which they carried out their assignments in that country were a bit much even for the SS. After all, Norway is 'Aryan.' In Russia, on the other hand, they could behave any way they liked.

"And, of course, that was even more the case in Poland. In Poland they didn't even have to worry about the Red Army, only the old rag-bag band of partisans."

He paused for a moment to give Christiansen a chance to say something, but that proved a fruitless occupation.

"Colonel Hagemann and I have never met," he went on finally. "I hope and pray he's never heard of me, and during that part of the war I never troubled much with names. What did I care about the identity of the Regional Deputy Commander, SS? He was a German—that was the point. And the Germans were as impersonal as demons. Nevertheless, that was where we had our first contacts, in Poland.

"He was a famous man in that sector. I had not the honor of being one of his victims, but I don't feel slighted. The Fifth Brigade did its very best in the time given them. It has nothing to do with my current interest in him, but he has much innocent blood on his hands.

"It was an accident of timing, really. The day we broke out of Treblinka, I had been there ten months. General von Goltz and his men were only recently posted to the region, so perhaps, if we do them justice, they had never even heard of the place. Even so, our paths crossed soon enough.

"We made our escape in August, 1943. Six hundred

men, more or less, out of the thousand or so still alive by that time. We knew we were slated to be killed within a matter of days; we were absolutely the last in line. The trains had stopped coming—there were other, newer camps by then, where the process of extermination was more efficient and, besides, Treblinka was not equipped to make use of slave labor for the armaments industry. We were burning the last of the bodies. We had ten thousand corpses to go, and in the arithmetic of that place ten thousand corpses meant a little less than two weeks. After that the Ukrainians would massacre us, to be massacred in their turn by the Germans. So we had to get out. It was a clear choice: escape or die.

"We had stolen a case of hand grenades, and someone had managed to buy half a dozen rifles from somewhere—probably from the Ukrainians, who were running a black market in food and could be counted on to do anything for the right price. I was one of those who broke into the storage hut where the petrol was kept. The plan was to burn the whole camp down, kill as many of the Germans as possible, and then scatter before reinforcements arrived.

"I will never forget the moment I heard the first series of explosions. I expected to die in the next few seconds, but I have never known such joy. And then, all at once, the southern watchtowers shot up in flames, and I was part of a mob running for the antitank barriers. We didn't think—we ran. To stand still was to die, so we ran, not looking to the right or left, not caring that the bullets were as thick as hornets and that men were dropping all around us, merely running. Our very souls were in our legs.

"The antitank barriers were simply low concrete pylons with tangles of barbed wire strung between them. Our masters hadn't seriously considered the possibility of a mass escape attempt; once in a while some poor devil, driven most of the way out of his mind by despair, would make a rush for the fence, but usually the Ukrainians with their machine guns would cut him down before he had covered thirty meters. The defenses were deemed adequate.

"But not on that day. The watchtowers were burning, there were snipers in the windows of the barracks and the kitchen, and hand grenades seemed to be going off everywhere. The Ukrainians had other things to think about. I don't suppose they managed to kill more than one in seven of us before we reached the outer barrier.

"Of course, the first ones there became hopelessly tangled in the wire. They didn't have to wait to be shot; those of us behind simply trampled them to death. We clambered over the bodies of our comrades, living and dead, just as if they were blocks of wood. The momentum was irresistible. Nothing could have stopped us—we hardly knew where we were or what we were doing. We were mad with desperation.

"And when we were outside the camp—'outside the camp'; the words themselves, had we breath to say them, would have sounded as unreal as 'flying to heaven'—when we were outside, we ran. There were woods two, three hundred meters ahead, so we ran for them. No one stopped until a bullet found him or he dropped with exhaustion. The Germans would bring in reinforcements soon enough—we knew that. The Germans had dogs and flamethrowers, and the strength of men who had not had their lives bled away from them a drop at a time. So we ran for the covering darkness, scattering in as many directions as we could.

"Perhaps six hundred out of a thousand lived to be free that first day and night. A year later, when the Russians finally came, I don't suppose there were more than forty of us left. The winter, starvation, and Polish peasants who would sell a Jew to the Germans for ten zlotys and the satisfaction of doing God's work—they saw to it that not many survived. And the soldiers, who would hunt us the way they might have hunted grouse, for the sport of the thing. And finally, and worst of all, Colonel Hagemann. We were among his first assignments in Poland, and within his limits he was a very effective officer.

"But, as I have said, I was in Treblinka for ten months."

Leivick glanced down at the plate bearing his half-eaten dinner—the sight of it made him feel faintly sick. He picked up the napkin and used it to wipe his face, wondering why he was talking like this. The story had laid buried deep inside him all these years—what could he possibly gain by telling it now, and to Christiansen?

"Would you have a cigarette?"

Christiansen dug a pack out of his shirt pocket, shook out one cigarette for Leivick and then one for himself, and then lit them both with a paper match. His handsome, rather brutal face revealed nothing, neither sympathy nor distaste, not even annoyance—nothing except the simple fact that he understood what was being said to him. But he did, in fact, understand. That in itself was rare enough. That perhaps was reason enough.

The cigarette was stronger than Leivick had expected and seemed to burn his tongue. He was even beginning to feel slightly dizzy. It was just that he was out of practice, of course; he had lost the habit during the war years, when tobacco had been an unimaginable luxury—it might as well have been ambergris. But this seemed the night for returning to old patterns.

"I won't impose on you by describing my experiences in that place," he said, breathing out the stale white smoke, perfectly conscious that he was being less than fair. "Suffice it to say that I arrived at the railway siding with my whole family and the full moral burden of civilized Europe. When I crawled out, over the corpses and barbed wire, I took nothing with me except my life. I was psychologically equipped to survive—in that respect, I was more than a match for Hagemann. So, I survived.

"That first night I found a great thicket of blackberries. It was too heavy to see into, so I crawled inside and slept on the muddy ground. I waited there all night. I didn't care how badly I got scratched up. Sometimes I could hear a faint scream in the distance, more often the sound of rifle fire.

"With the dawn, after I had eaten a few handfuls of berries—they weren't quite ripe and by the end of the day I was doubled up with cramp, but they got me through and that was enough—I decided I couldn't risk staying any longer in one place, so I was on the move again. I headed straight into the sun—I couldn't think of anything to do except to try reaching the Russian lines. They were over six hundred kilometers east at that time, but there was no way I could have known. One direction was as good as another.

"It was about seven-thirty that morning when I realized I was square in the middle of a German patrol area. The first time I heard a twig snap I threw myself to the ground in some high weeds and waited, my heart pounding inside my chest so that I thought I might die from the pain of it. *They'll kill me now,* I thought to myself. *In twenty minutes I'll be dead,* When I finally saw one of them, I had to stuff my hand into my mouth to keep from crying out.

"He was alone, and he didn't seem to like being outside on a steamy August morning. He held his rifle by the strap, letting the butt drag along in the soft earth. He was weary and bored and obviously thought the whole affair was a waste of time. Why should anyone be out in the woods chasing after a gang of runaway Jews? Why should anyone care?

"Finally—and who would have believed such a thing could happen in the German army?—he sat down on the ground with his back against a tree, set his helmet down beside him, and lit a cigarette." Leivick flourished his own, leaving a narrow circle of smoke hanging in the air. "He was—what is the expression the Americans use?—he was 'goofing off.'

"How long does it take someone to finish a cigarette? Three minutes? Four? I had exactly that much time to cross perhaps thirty meters of ground on my hands and knees. If I made a sound, if my sleeve brushed against a dead leaf, I was dead. If this man's sergeant or one of his comrades came along, I was dead. If for any reason at all the poor devil turned his head, I was a corpse. On my hands and knees I crawled, like an animal. I think I must have been half mad, because I wasn't afraid. I was going to kill this man— that was all I could think about.

"When I was five meters away, I could smell the tobacco smoke. When I was three, I could hear him breathing. When my shoulder was almost touching the bark of the tree, I reached around, locked my hands together over his throat, and started to pull.

"You, of course, know all about what it is like to strangle a man, don't you, Mr. Christiansen. I suppose, like everything else, it loses some of its terror with repetition, but that was my first time. I leaned into that tree so that my arms held it and the German's throat both, and I tried to squeeze them both down to nothing. I think I may actually have heard his neck break, but after all these years I can't be sure. If I did, that was the only sound he made, but you should have seen his face when finally I could bring myself to let go. There was a little trickle of blood running down from his left ear. But, of course, I'm not forgetting you know all about that sort of thing."

He smiled, not at all unkindly, and ground out the cigarette, which had burned its way down almost to his fingers. Christiansen offered him another, simply by holding out the pack, but he shook his head. They might have been strangers, waiting together for the rain to stop.

"He was only a boy. I don't imagine he could have been more than seventeen. That fact registered itself on my brain, but it meant nothing. Years passed before I felt even a twinge of regret, or remembered that quite possibly he had known nothing of what was being done in his name. I stole his uniform—it was loose on me, can you imagine? and he was a slender lad. I stole his rifle, his boots, even his cigarettes. I left him where he was, dressed in my camp clothes, and I started to march east.

"I passed two or three more soldiers—at a distance, fortunately—and I waved to them and went straight on. I never stopped until late that afternoon, by which time my guts felt as if they might burst, but by then the Germans were far behind me.

"For a month I lived on what I could steal. The Poles were used to renegade Germans, and little disposed to argue with the barrel of an infantryman's rifle. If I found a soldier alone, I killed him and took his ammunition and his hand grenades if he had any. Finally I crossed paths with the Resistance.

"You had to buy your way in. I had a rifle, two hand grenades, and four boxes of cartridges—the Resistance was glad to have me. That was my introduction to the art of war, that autumn and winter with the partisans. In the spring, just as the weather began to turn hot, the Russians crossed the border into Poland. In June I was sitting in the field tent of a Major Govorov, drinking what passed for coffee and listening to the shortwave for news of the British and American landings at Normandy. We kissed each other and cried. We were as happy as children."

"And how does this bring us to Hagemann?"

In the moment of silence that followed, Christiansen rose from his chair, as quietly as a specter, and took a fresh pack of cigarettes from the carton that was lying open on the chest of drawers. Leivick watched the massive shoulders hunch as the soft explosion of the match lighting glowed behind his cupped hands, and he found himself thinking, *No one will ever catch this one with his back comfortably against a tree. Faglin was right to counsel discretion, and Faglin is not a timid soul. Some men are harder to kill than others.*

Because those were the choices. If Christiansen could not be persuaded to throw in his lot with them, they would have to kill him. For one thing, he would know too much.

Because he would have to be told the truth about Hagemann. After all, they were asking him to restrain himself, to resist the temptation to take the next plane to Damascus—where, after all, Christiansen might fancy his chances of survival a shade more than the Mossad did; or his chances of survival might interest him less than his chances of success. He had to be persuaded that something of importance might be gained by waiting.

And that object would never be achieved with a few short declarative sentences: *"Hagemann presents a threat to us for this-and-this reason, and we need him alive because of these-and-these political and military considerations."* What would keep him from answering, *"Why should I care about that? My business with Hagemann is personal—why should anything else matter to me? I won't give up my revenge for an abstraction."*

No, it couldn't be managed that way. The reasons were good ones, good enough to satisfy any decent man, but they had to be made real to him. So he had to know everything.

And on that, perhaps, might hang more lives than just his own.

"I was in a position to discover a great many things while I was with the Russians," Leivick said finally, when Christiansen had sat down again. Somehow it was impossible to talk to the man while he was towering over one like a patriotic monument. "I could speak German and English, a good bit of soldier's

Polish, and even a little French, and they had need of interpreters. Beyond that, the regimental political officer had sent a full report on me to Moscow, and it would seem I fit into certain plans for the future that were being concocted there. I was a Czech, and a lawyer with government experience. The Russians knew they were about to fall heir to the whole of Central Europe, and they were going to need collaborators to help them rule it. They had an interest in effecting my conversion.

"Need I say more? I had no objections to calling myself a Dialectical Materialist, and I wanted to stay alive. The central thing to remember about the Communists is that they think anyone who isn't for them is automatically against them and a fascist into the bargain. I had not the slightest inclination to end up lying in a ditch with a bullet through my head. I learned to speak Marxist jargon and let them believe anything they liked. The result was that I was trusted, up to a point.

"I began to see that point on the horizon the day I let it be known that I had served with a partisan group which had come in contact with elements of the Fifth Brigade, Waffen-SS. Suddenly I found myself being interviewed in a farmhouse outside Lublin by a pair of grim-faced hoodlums from the NKVD who had been flown in from Moscow for no other purpose. We talked for three days. During the whole time I had no idea whether I was under arrest or not.

" '*Did you ever capture any of them?*' they asked. '*No, of course not,*' I lied. '*The Resistance didn't take prisoners. What could the Germans have told us that we didn't already know better ourselves? The only time I ever saw a German soldier in custody was once*

*after we had ambushed a small patrol outside of Czy-
zew, and he only lasted an hour. A farmboy with a
personal grievance to settle cut his throat.' 'Are they
still deployed in that sector?' 'No.' 'How do you know?'
'We stopped seeing that particular sleeve patch on the
tunics of dead infantrymen.' 'When did they with-
draw?' 'It's difficult to say. Sometime after the winter,
I should think.'*

"Three days they kept me at it. I never knew there
were so many ways of asking the same set of questions.
We would sit around a kitchen table, and they would
scribble little notes back and forth to each other. Once
I summoned up enough courage to ask them why they
were so curious about this one unit. *'Merely routine
intelligence reconstruction, comrade. We like to know
the terrain.'* And then the two of them exchanged a
look that would have peeled paint. After that I left
the questions to them.

"One of the greatest gifts a man can possess is a
capacity for telling convincing lies. If a lie is to hold
up it has to be both detailed and consistent. It is not
enough if it is like the truth—it must be the truth,
only slightly deflected. One has to be able to believe
it oneself.

"I will never be sure, but I think during those
three days I came several times within an eyelash of
disappearing into some NKVD dungeon. I think perhaps the only reason I am alive today is because I
managed to convince my inquisitors not only that I
knew nothing worth knowing but that I hadn't a suspicion that there was anything to know.

" *'Did you ever hear anything concerning the Fifth
Brigade's activities after leaving your sector? Any gos-
sip in camp—that sort of thing?' 'No.' 'Don't you find*

that a little strange? How do you explain such un-
characteristic silence?' 'I am a Czech Jew. Need I say
more?' I remember I grinned defiantly into the brute's
face. The Russians are very touchy about anti-Semi-
tism—on the one hand they think we're all Trot-
skyites, and on the other they think they are being
anti-Party if they show it. *'I speak a little Polish, enough*
for work purposes but not enough to make listening
to long personal reminiscences very comfortable. Be-
sides, the Poles would never entirely trust me.' That
half-lie probably saved my life.

"Because, as it happens, I had heard a few ru-
mors—nothing very specific. But how was it to my
advantage to confess knowledge of such things? In
wartime it is dangerous to be the bearer of secrets.

"I am not now laying claim to more than the casual
fund of speculation that is any fighting unit's common
property in wartime. We too wondered what had happened to the Fifth Brigade. They were exhausted, of
course, and down to a shadow of their full operational
strength. But it was not the usual practice to reinforce
such units; generally they were simply allowed to bleed
to death. So we were surprised when suddenly this
one unit was withdrawn instead.

"The most popular theory—and the one, as it happened, closest to the truth—was that their commander, your General von Goltz of blessed memory,
had somehow wangled his way back into Himmler's
good graces and was happily out of the combat area.
The hot topic of speculation was what the General had
done to earn his ticket to safety.

"The one thing we did know, although its significance escaped us at the time, was that von Goltz's
departure from Poland was preceded by a rash of ar-

rests. The northwestern part of the country was virtually cleared of certain categories of technical personnel—chemists, pharmacists, brewers, the entire surviving faculty of the medical college at Gialystok."

"Brewers?" Christiansen raised his eyebrows, which had the effect of making him seem to come awake with a start. "What would the SS want with brewers. Were they thirsty?"

It was impossible to tell from his expression whether he was making a joke or not.

"Brewers know about mixing vats and steam pipes and cooling chambers—the whole apparatus of high-temperature chemistry on an industrial scale. And the SS was in the manufacturing business, and they needed slave labor with the proper qualifications. What they had in mind was a trifle more complicated than beer, but the principle was much the same."

Knitting his hands together tightly across his stomach, Leivick wished he had another cigarette. He was conscious of a certain excitement, even a certain pleasure in his grotesque narrative, and it made him feel uneasy. He did not like reducing any part of that vast collective suffering to the neat rhetoric of a detective story, but somehow it seemed unavoidable, as if to understand the thing and to trivialize it were indistinguishable acts.

"But the important thing," he went on, breaking his sentence with a sharp intake of breath, "the important thing is that none of those men were ever heard from again."

He made a dismissing gesture with his left hand.

"Of course, in those days that was not an uncommon fate. The number of people who disappeared from Europe between 1939 and 1945 runs into the millions, and I don't suppose there is any great mystery about what happened to our brewers and professors of anatomy. There is a trench, about fifty meters long, just inside the eastern perimeter of Waldenburg concentration camp; the Russians dug it to bury the corpses of the inmates, who had been machine-gunned to the last man just two days before they would have been liberated. Doubtless that is where one would search for them."

For an instant Christiansen looked as if someone had struck him. His eyes widened suddenly and he actually flinched—one could have imagined he felt the ghosts of those machine-gun bullets passing through his own body. The hand lying on his left thigh clenched and then relaxed, as if of its own accord. For the first time Leivick noticed the broad, flat scar and wondered how it had come to be there.

And it came to him with the force of a revelation that even in this short time he had grown quite fond of Christiansen, that, if it came to that, it would cost him no small amount of pain to order his death.

"So perhaps now the connection becomes clear to you?" he said, smiling coldly, a little astonished at the tone his voice had assumed. "The SS were in the game for high stakes—they couldn't afford any witnesses. But there was one, of course. There always is at least one."

"But not among the camp inmates?"

"No, not among them. They had all been silenced."

There was a clock ticking somewhere. Leivick resisted the temptation of looking for it—probably Christiansen had some sort of alarm on his night table, and, in any case, it wasn't important. By now, Faglin and Hirsch were probably wondering what had happened to him. In a while he would have to telephone them, or they might come to break down the door.

"No, but there were the soldiers themselves, the men-at-arms of the Fifth Brigade. And soldiers of a routed army have a way of being captured by the enemy. It was from one of these that I learned what had happened to General von Goltz and his men—and got my first inkling of how they had been occupying themselves at Waldenburg.

"It was early April of 1945. The Russians were already in possession of the Berlin suburbs, and the German defenses had nearly evaporated. I was with an armored unit about twenty miles from Dresden. I had the job of interrogating prisoners. The poor little fool was trying to make his way home to Görlitz and his mother when we nabbed him. He had gotten rid of his uniform right enough but had carelessly retained his SS identity papers—Private Hugo Scheidemann, Fifth Brigade. He was as good as dead as soon as he fell into our hands.

"But you know the SS—at every level, they always think they can arrange something for themselves. *What will happen to me?*' he asked. '*I expect you'll be shot in an hour or two,*' I told him pleasantly. '*We don't mean to be rude, but we're in a hurry.*'

"I remember he grabbed my sleeve with a kind of spasm. It made me look at him, actually look at him, for the first time. I suppose he was about twenty-one or -two, with silvery brown hair and the face of a schoolboy.

" '*I know a secret,*' he told me, in a stifled, panting voice, and I thought to myself, *Yes, I'll bet you do.*

The SS had turned them into passing fair butchers sometimes even before they had learned to shave. Yes, I had no doubt he knew more secrets than just one.

" *'Why don't you keep your secret,'* I told him. *'Carry it with you to the grave, where it will be safe.'* I couldn't help myself. I kept wondering if he could have been one of those who had made such sport of hunting down my comrades from Treblinka, God forgive me.

" *'But I know about Waldenburg,'* he answered, his eyes pleading. *'Surely you must have heard of Waldenburg—they were up to something important there. I could tell you. Surely the Russians will be interested enough to . . .'*

"He couldn't finish his sentence, of course. He hung his head, as if suddenly grown ashamed. I said nothing. I merely waited in silence, thinking of those two stony interrogators from the NKVD, wondering if I was about to learn why they had been so concerned with everything I could tell them about the Fifth Brigade.

" *'I saw people killed there,'* he went on, and then paused again, perhaps this time for dramatic effect.

"I don't suppose I looked terribly surprised—why should I have been? Why should anyone have been surprised at anything in those days, let alone that the SS had killed people at a place called 'Waldenburg'? I should have been surprised to hear the name of yet one more death camp to add to so many others? No, it was a trifle late for that. At any rate, whatever reaction he had been waiting for, he didn't get it.

" *'But not in the ordinary way—not with bullets, or anything like that.'* He shook his head. Clearly he put great importance on this one point. I was beginning to entertain the idea that perhaps his wits were turned. *'They had a special chamber—it was an experiment, do you see? They would do people in batches of five.'*

" 'Do' people. That was just the way he expressed it.

" *'A friend of mine took me to see one day. I didn't know anything about it before that. I only found out by accident.'* Yes, of course. The poor boy, how could I have imagined anything else?

" *'But the way they looked when they came out . . .'*

"A tremor seemed to pass over him. I don't believe he was acting. I don't believe he was that clever. The memory seemed to rise up before his eyes like Banquo's ghost, so perhaps he did have a conscience, although, finally, it seemed to have made very little difference.

" *'You and I have seen enough dead bodies,'* he said, taking me into his confidence. It was a delicious moment if one had a taste for farce. *'The corpses came out stiff, like iron pokers—just rigid, and with their arms and legs all twisted.'* He paused for a moment and caught his breath, and suddenly, at that moment, I knew I wouldn't even try to save him. I didn't want to. His confidence in my influence was misplaced, so it made no difference, but in an instant I had come to hate him for the way he seemed to be trying to number himself among the victims—for that, and for burdening me with his horror.

" *'And their eyes—yes, their eyes.'* His hand was still resting on my sleeve, and he began, in the most tentative way possible, to pull me toward him, as if he wished to whisper this last and most significant detail directly into my ear. '*A dead man's eyes get large—the black part in the middle, I mean—but not these. Their eyes were shrunk to nothing, as if they had been staring into the sun for hours. As if their eyes had clouded over altogether.*'

" '*Yes. That's very interesting,*' I said—or something like it I suppose. '*I'll see the division commander hears of it right away.*' It did no harm to let him live in hope for another hour.

"I think he was proud of himself, in some perverse way. As if he had demonstrated that his powers of observation were of a very high order and therefore he deserved to live. I felt rather differently about the matter. You see, he had just imparted to me a secret that would, if I was less than careful, end my life as well as his.

"The soldier who was standing beside me spoke no German, for which I was suddenly grateful. I smiled at the promising youth, turned to my companion, and said to him in my villainous Russian, '*See to it that this one is shot with the first batch. There's nothing to be learned from him.*'

"Are you surprised, Mr. Christiansen? No, I don't suppose you are. War makes us all very practical. Still, I wasn't taking any chances.

"That night I borrowed a car. No one minded—the fighting was winding down almost to nothing. I told the duty officer I had business in Dresden and would take my chances going through the lines. I was very mysterious about it. He merely shrugged his shoulders. I was associated in his mind with Intelligence, and hence the NKVD, so he wasn't interested in asking questions. I went straight down the main road, dodging around the bomb craters. I never encountered a single German soldier who thought fit to challenge me, not once, all the way to Bayreuth. As soon as I got there I changed out of the Russian uniform I had been wearing and became, once more, a refugee. The truck had enough petrol to take me to Würzburg, where I knew I would be safely inside the American zone. I was not interested in taking risks."

Leivick stood up—his knees felt as if they might crack under the strain, but he couldn't have sat still another moment. It had been a long and anxious day and he was tired, tired and frightened. Because now the moment was upon him when he would have to tell the final, terrible secret. He wondered where they would all be in an hour's time.

"We have kept very complete records of the various camps," he said, standing beside the window and looking out on the undulating sea of rubble that was just visible in the broken, piecemeal light that seemed to seep from the hotel like sap from a wounded tree. It was not a view he much admired. "We have our refugees, and friendly sources among the Americans, even the British—even, come to speak of it, among the Russians. We know what they were doing at Waldenburg. We know the whole history of the work carried on there.

"It began in 1936. A German chemist named Schrader was trying to develop a new insecticide from organic phosphorus compounds. He found one that worked beyond his wildest dreams—so well, in fact, that it couldn't possibly have been used in agriculture. In a solution of just one part per two hundred thousand, it was deadly. When he and his assistant began trying to produce the substance in quantity, they became ill themselves: they found they had difficulty breathing, and their eyesight became so poor that they couldn't see at all by artificial light. Finally they had to abandon their research to save their lives.

"There was a law in Germany then that any discovery with potential military applications had to be reported to the government. Schrader found himself on a train to Berlin. He had discovered, poor man, the very first nerve gas. He called it Tabun.

"The Wehrmacht, of course, fell in love with it. It was odorless, colorless, and lethal. The pupils of test animals' eyes shrank down to nothing—hence the night blindness Schrader had experienced. They foamed at the mouth and vomited. They developed debilitating diarrhea. Finally, after five or six minutes, they went into convulsions and died in extreme agony. It worked on some chemical in the muscles, you see, throwing them into violent and uncontrollable contractions. Nothing, no treatment known to medicine, could save them. One perished from asphyxiation, strangled to death from the inside.

"The substance could be absorbed through the skin, so gas masks were no protection, and it killed in very small concentrations. Tabun was the perfect, the ultimate weapon in the arsenal of gas warfare. Schrader got a new factory, all his own, in Elberfeld, and within a year he had developed a new compound, ten times as powerful, which he called Sarin.

"Of course, by then the Nazis knew they would be precipitating a European war within a year or two, so they poured vast amounts of money into developing these two gases—hundreds of millions of reichsmarks. When the war did begin, huge factories were built in Poland. Even by 1943 the Germans had stockpiled enormous quantities of Tabun and Sarin, enough certainly to have convinced England to drop out of the war if they had used them in bombing raids over London and a few other major cities. Probably enough to end Russia's resistance. The German General Staff were cradling the fate of Europe in the hollow of their hand.

"You are perhaps wondering how, then, the Germans were ever restrained, why it was that they are not now masters of the earth and we grinning corpses? You may wonder indeed."

He glanced back from the window, over his shoulder to where Christiansen was sitting motionless on a small gilt chair. He could feel the corners of his mouth twitching and wondered how he must look. *Oh, Mordecai*, a voice said inside his brain, *Oh, little brother, how did it ever come down to this for you? Have you gone mad to be speaking of these things?*

"The fact is, they lost their courage." Leivick shrugged his shoulders, as if refusing to take responsibility for such foolishness, and moved away from the window. He could feel Christiansen's eyes on him, like gun sights, as he paced off the distance from one wall to the other. "That, and a certain fastidiousness on Hitler's part, are the only reasons anyone can imagine.

"Their Führer, you see, had been gassed in the First War. He was blinded for a time and was in a military hospital recovering when the Fatherland surrendered. His memories of the experience, it seems, were vivid and unpleasant. He never favored the use of gas in warfare.

"And then there was the question of what the Allies were doing. Nothing, not a thing, as it turned out, but the silence in American scientific periodicals concerning certain substances convinced some key German scientists that the Allies must be pursuing research on their own—actually, they were merely developing DDT—and they, in turn, convinced Hitler. Work continued in the secret factories, but plans to deploy the new weapon were quietly dropped.

"By 1945, of course, the whole idea of chemical warfare was also militarily unfeasible. There simply weren't any planes—the cities of the enemy had become forever out of reach. When they knew the war was lost, the Germans tried to destroy all trace of the whole research effort, but the factories in Poland, by the sheerest chance, fell into Russian hands almost intact. Our information is that they were dismantled and shipped home. Probably, at this very moment, they are in full production somewhere in the Urals.

"The end of the story? Not quite. Because, you see, there was a third gas, many times more powerful even than Sarin, described in the few surviving records as Trilon 238. The substance was being mass-produced at Waldenburg, almost up to the hour of its capture."

"And Colonel Hagemann walked away with that secret under his hat."

It was the first time Christiansen had spoken in almost half an hour. Leivick was startled by the sound, almost as if someone had fired a pistol in the room.

"Not quite, God be praised." Leivick smiled thinly. "But he seems to believe he can put his hands on it. He seems to have the Syrians pretty well convinced that he can.

"There is going to be a war in the Middle East, Mr. Christiansen. That much is obvious. The United Nations has voted that Palestine shall be partitioned into Arab and Jewish states, and that partition, as the Arab leaders have so noisily declared, will be resisted. Israel will be born—we Jews will have our homeland, provided we can hold it.

"Try to imagine, if you can, the applications of such a toxic nerve gas in the sort of war our Arab brothers are preparing to unleash on us. The distances that restrained Hitler in 1945 will not apply in Palestine. One doesn't have to drop Trilon 238 from a plane—one can just as easily charge artillery shells with it, and artillery shells are delightfully selective. The Jewish sections of, say, Haifa could be saturated, killing probably eighty or ninety percent of the population, and Arab families living five or ten blocks away would hardly be inconvenienced at all. Our troops might suffer similar losses long before they ever had a chance to engage the enemy. What is to save us then? We are discussing the final annihilation of a people here, Mr. Christiansen. What Chelmno and Auschwitz and Treblinka failed to accomplish will be brought to perfection in the streets of Jerusalem."

"Don't trouble yourself about it. In a week you can read about Hagemann's death in the newspapers—with my compliments."

"It isn't enough, Mr. Christiansen. I'm genuinely sorry."

"It'll just god damned well have to be."

Leivick wrapped his arms together, suddenly cold. He understood exactly how the man felt. The sense of his own powerlessness overwhelmed him.

"We must have not only Hagemann but his secret, Mr. Christiansen. That terrible weapon must be buried forever, or we will never be safe. After all we have suffered, have we no right to live? This is our last

chance. The few of us who remain, some of whom
have never known anything except war and fear and
the threat of extinction, we have one last opportunity.
That is why we must lay our hands on your Colonel
Hagemann. That is why, before he dies, we must find
out from him what has become of his terrible weapon.
Will you help us, Mr. Christiansen, or does your revenge take precedence even over this?"

For a moment there was only silence. There was
nothing to suggest that Christiansen had been moved
by anything Leivick had said. Then he picked up the
pack of cigarettes from where it was resting on the
arm of his chair, extracted one with his fingernails,
put it in his mouth, and lit it. When finally he did
glance in Leivick's direction, his face wore an expression of scarcely contained anger.

"No, it doesn't," he said finally, as the smoke
wreathed around his head like a halo. "But when I've
helped you get what you want, Hagemann is mine.
You people aren't the only ones he's wronged."

Leivick allowed the air to escape from his lungs—
slowly with almost sensual pleasure. He hadn't realized that he had been holding his breath.

"Of course, Mr. Christiansen—that goes without
saying. Now. You had mentioned something about
'bait'?"

✠ **6** ✠

Vienna, Austria: March 1, 1948

The second great disappointment after their arrival was the Danube, which was neither beautiful nor blue but a chocolate brown, flecked here and there with garbage and rainbow patches of floating oil. Christiansen had asked for a room with a river view—which, not entirely coincidentally, meant that he had only to look out his window for the best prospect of the Russian Zone money could buy—but after all he decided that, except for purposes of business, he would be just as happy to keep the blinds drawn.

"It was just the same in Franz Josef's day," Mordecai told him, shrugging his shoulders with amused sympathy. "My father brought me here in 1912, and the river was just as dirty then. I liked the giant ferris wheel at the Prater much better."

The first great disappointment was word that Esther Rosensaft was going to spend the next decade or so in a Russian slammer.

It was all there in the dossier which through some

121

mysterious agency was waiting for them when they arrived from Munich. Mordecai bought a magazine at the newsstand in the railway station, and the dossier was inside. There was even a photograph.

"She looks like she could use a little feeding up," Christiansen had said, holding the photograph by a corner. "Where did you get all this?"

"My dear Inar, you've been fighting the Nazis all these years and you've never heard them mention the International Jewish Conspiracy? I'm surprised at you."

It was simply that he hadn't yet gotten over the first sharpness of his disappointment. Christiansen found it easy not to take offense.

They sat in silence as the taxi drove them to their hotel. It was rather as if a practical joke had been played on them, and they had come all that way for nothing. No, Christiansen didn't take offense.

Mordecai had phoned the Jewish Agency's central office in Geneva, and they had been able to report only that Esther Rosensaft had been alive as of July, 1947, and had given Vienna as her permanent address. There was also a suggestion—just a suggestion—that the lady had led a checkered life since the war's end and that perhaps inquiries would most fruitfully be addressed to the Viennese police.

Which, by some labyrinthine indirection, was naturally the source of the dossier.

And it was all there, of course. Esther was your typical black market small-timer—one previous arrest, no conviction (had she sweet-talked somebody, or perhaps traded a little information?). She had held jobs as a bar girl, a waitress, even a letter carrier for a private mail service. She seemed to have a lot of unsavory friends. This was someone who had learned to get by in the big world.

Until four months ago, when she had been arrested at a checkpoint on the Wallenstein Bridge with twenty thousand rubles in her corset. Fifteen years was a longish stretch, and the Russians didn't believe in time off for good behavior.

"The boys will be arriving tonight," Mordecai announced quietly. "Perhaps they can think of something. This is more their line of country than mine."

Christiansen stared out of the hotel window, watching the Russian guards on the Gürtelbrücke as they searched the back of a dark green delivery truck, and wondered if he hadn't led them all on a wild goose chase. The Russians controlled every stinking foot of ground east of the Danube and, barring a skyhook, there was no way to cross except over the heavily patrolled bridges. Esther Rosensaft, if they wanted to keep her, would be hard to smuggle out. And they wanted to keep her. Hell, they were holding her under lock and key.

"*Seien Sie doch mit meinem Cello vorsichtig,*" he barked at the porter, who was about to hit the case against the door frame. "*Ich verdiene damit meinen Unterhalt.*"

The poor man set the luggage down gingerly, leaning the cello against the bed and whimpering an apology. Christiansen, to salve his conscience, gave him a larger than usual tip and, as the porter was backing out of the room, began unstrapping the case to see how his darling had made the journey. It was his own fault—he shouldn't have lost his temper. Usually he didn't allow anyone to carry it except himself.

"You shouldn't shout at people like that, Inar," Mordecai said quietly, with an amused expression playing over his face.

"It's a Guarnerius," Christiansen answered, his voice hardly above a murmur. His hand slipped down the neck with a caressing gesture. "It's an inheritance from my first teacher at Juilliard; when he died he passed over his own son to give this to me. God knows, it's worth more than I am."

"But still, you shouldn't shout at people. A man your size—you frightened that poor man half to death."

Christiansen didn't answer. Mordecai was right of course, but the dumb bastard might have cracked the varnish.

He would have liked to take it out and play for a while. He just wanted to hear the sound of it. But he felt embarrassed in front of Mordecai, who would probably have thought he was showing off or something. That was what he had always hated about recitals. If you loved, really loved the thing, then it shouldn't be just a "performance." He hated even the sound of the word.

"And you weren't being entirely truthful, were you. You don't earn your living with your cello, although there isn't any question you could. I wonder why it is you don't."

It wasn't an innocent question. Mordecai had a way of probing, of gently turning over the earth until all the roots were exposed. He seemed to think it important to understand everything—and, just possibly, he was right.

"A concussion grenade tore open my hand," Christiansen answered, holding it up so that the light from the window glistened against the scar. "It broke all the bones, every damn one of them. I still have tiny pieces of shrapnel embedded in the muscles—there was no way they could get them all out and leave me with enough finger control to unzip my fly. I cramp up if I play longer than fifteen or twenty minutes."

"But you can manage the double bass for hours, it would seem." Mordecai smiled, as if slightly ashamed. "I've seen you."

"That's jazz—big sloppy chords you change every half hour. I could play that crap with my elbow."

Christiansen reclosed the lid and grabbed his coat from where it was lying across the back of a chair. Suddenly the room seemed too small for him.

"I won't be back for dinner," he said, keeping his voice featureless. "I figure somebody should have a look at this prison of theirs."

Just to be on the safe side, he took a taxi to the International Zone and walked across at the Salztorbrücke. He had a Norwegian passport, and the guard apparently hadn't been instructed to regard all Norwegians as spies. Christiansen explained that he was a tourist and that he wanted to see the Augarten. The guard shook his head, but not in disbelief.

"Is very no good," he said, in probably the most appalling German Christiansen had ever heard. "*Fräuleins* very no nice, and very too . . ."

He groped for the word, swinging his hand about in a tight little circle. It seemed to irritate him vastly.

"*Kostspielig?*" Christiansen ventured helpfully. Anything to end the suspense.

"*Da . . . Ja.*" The Russian nodded vigorously, four

or five times. "Too very much money. And like pigs—fat. Stink too. Americans and British get all very good ones. Very most Americans . . . capitalist bastards."

He looked as if he would have liked to spit on the pavement for emphasis, but just then his officer came up. The officer, who looked like a provincial schoolmaster and was probably all of twenty-five, stood just out of effective reach, frowning like a deacon while Christiansen had his papers returned to him with all the hasty rudeness anyone could have expected. You didn't have to be in occupied Europe very long to figure out that the Russians really weren't such bad fellows. It was simply that they were more frightened than anyone else.

It was late afternoon and cold. A damp, faintly unpleasant smell hung in the air, a little reminder that this was an island between the made-man canal and a narrow, wandering branch of the Danube.

Several of the trees lining the Augarten were nothing more than dead logs sticking out of the ground. Russian fire on the city had been particularly intense during the last few days of the war, but it hadn't been flattened like Munich. Still, the trees had been burned up. The grass looked scorched too, but that was probably just the time of year. It all made a dismal impression.

Even in their short acquaintance, Christiansen had decided that he liked Mordecai Leivick a good deal. They had gone to first names almost at once, almost the way the Americans did. They got along well; perhaps someday they might even become friends, if they had the chance and it didn't get in the way.

Still, he wished Mordecai would stop asking him

personal questions. For one thing, he knew perfectly well that it was all going into a dossier in Tel Aviv or Jerusalem or wherever the Jews would make their capital after partition. He didn't think it was any government agency's goddam business how he felt about having his hand shattered and not being able to tour the world as the Norwegian Casals. He didn't think it was anybody's goddam business. He was all kinds of things now, some of which he didn't like very much, but at least he wasn't a child prodigy anymore.

"You must send him abroad," Professor Skram had told his father. *"He knows everything I can teach him. You must send him to one of the great maestros—in Germany perhaps, or France. He has a duty to his genius, and so do you."*

For three years, twice every week, his father had driven him into Oslo for private lessons with the first cellist of the Royal Symphony Orchestra, the dean of the conservatory. It was a two-hour journey in each direction, and while the instruction was taking place the mayor of Kirstenstad would sit out in the entrance hall on a hard wooden chair. He was a busy man with no great passion for music, but Inar was his only child and would one day astonish the world.

So on the way home from that last lesson, father and son sat together in the car without a word.

For three days the subject was never once raised, but the atmosphere in their little home was heavy with this unsettled question. Inar knew that at night, alone in their bedroom, his parents were trying to decide what they should do—he knew from the anguished way his mother looked at him, as if she feared for his life. And finally, at Sunday dinner, his father told him he was to go to America, to live with the family of his younger sister in a place called "White Plains, New York."

"I have written to her," he said, in his calm magistrate's voice. *"We will of course compensate her for your maintenance, and you will study in New York City, where, I am assured by your professor, there are many fine opportunities for a young man who wishes to improve himself. It must be New York I'm afraid, and not Berlin or Paris as perhaps you had hoped. You are still very young and must have someone responsible to look after you."*

Yes, of course. He was just thirteen years old. He loved them both, but from that moment on they almost ceased to be his parents. They must have realized that was what it would mean.

So he had gone off to live with Auntie Inger, to attend American high school and study at Juilliard and run around with his teen-aged cousins. God, how he had loved America. And how bored he had been the three times he had gone back to Norway to spend a month with his mother and father in Kirstenstad. His life was simply elsewhere—in his music and in the excitement of New York—and he couldn't wait to get back to it. He wondered now if his parents had guessed, and what they must have thought then of the sacrifice they had made to his "genius."

And then they had died without him, shot to death at their own front door, and his hand had been ripped open by a piece of shrapnel from a concussion grenade, and that had been the end of that. There was a kind of retributive justice in those two transactions which he couldn't quite define but which was there just the same.

It would have been even tidier if he had honestly staked his heart on a concert career, but he hadn't. His parents, it seemed, had given him up for nothing because by the time he was in his third year at Juilliard he had decided that he didn't want to be a virtuoso—he just wanted to compose. He would hole up somewhere, he had decided, in some little college maybe, and write music that didn't sound like film scores or twelve-tone squeaks, music that had a life both on and off the page. Perhaps he could have learned everything he needed for that at the Conservatory in Oslo—he didn't know.

What would his parents have thought? He didn't know because he had never asked them. It had never occurred to him to ask them.

His teachers, of course, had believed he was demented. "You go on the concert circuit and in fifteen years you can retire to a house on Lake Lucerne and write all the music you like. You have the gift, boy, but give yourself a chance to grow up first. At twenty, everyone thinks he wants to be Stravinsky."

Well, he sure as hell had grown up, and now he didn't have to worry. His future was Colonel Egon Hagemann. Everything after that was a blank.

Anyway, he just wished Mordecai would stop worrying about his sensitive artistic nature and keep to business.

The prison faced onto the Heine Strasse, but you couldn't tell much about the building from the pavement. There were a couple of uniformed goons with automatic weapons posted at the entrance in a high stone wall, and behind that the Russians had built another wall, just boards nailed end to end up to a height of about eight yards, apparently with no other purpose than destroying the view. Possibly at one time the place had been a ladies' academy or a post office or even a private home for someone with a lot of money and a taste for fortress architecture. The point was that nobody just passing by was about to find out.

The wall—both walls, to be precise—ran all the way around the block. Christiansen took the long way around to the back for a look. There were no adjoining buildings, just the prison complex itself, so everyone could just forget about moving in next door and punching through with a few dozen sticks of dynamite. There wasn't going to be any easy way. Nobody was getting in there with anything less than an artillery company.

Christiansen hunched his shoulders inside his heavy civilian overcoat, but the sensation of cold that had settled in his throat and chest had little enough to do with the temperature. Despair was beginning to cling to him like sodden wool. He could almost smell it.

There was simply no way anyone was going to spring Esther Rosensaft from her cell and then make a dash for the American Zone. It would take an army, and the Russians were the ones with the army. It was hopeless.

He stood under the awning of what looked like a ladies' hairdresser—it was closed, of course; what the hell kind of business was a ladies' hairdresser going to do in the Russian Zone?—wondering if there wasn't somewhere he could get a cup of coffee and something to eat. He was hungry and he needed to sit down and do some thinking. If there was no way of reaching the girl his deal with Mordecai would come unstuck and it would be every man for himself again. He didn't want that. He didn't want the Syrians bombarding the

Jews with Hagemann's nerve gas, but he also wasn't about to go quietly home to Norway with his parents' murderer living in luxury in Damascus. He wasn't going to depend on the Mossad to do the right thing. The Mossad might cut some deal of their own, even with Hagemann. He couldn't blame them; God knows, no one had a right to blame them for looking out for their own survival. But he had to see Hagemann with the blood pouring out of his nostrils. He just had to, or he would never draw another easy breath. So there had to be some way of getting that goddamn girl.

Christiansen was on the other side of the street from the guarded entrance, on the next block, a distance of perhaps sixty-five or seventy yards. At first, when they snapped to attention, he thought the soldiers were just being relieved, but when the barren metal gate opened one of the two people coming out was a woman.

The man who was holding her by the arm was wearing his greatcoat, and therefore it was possible to tell only from the pistol on his uniform belt that he was an officer. He shook her a couple of times, like a storekeeper with a kid caught stealing apples, and then pushed her out onto the sidewalk. It made sense. People did get released from prisons, even Russian prisons, and the Army of the Proletariat wasn't likely to give them a hero's send-off, complete with flowers and a military band. The lady was getting kicked out.

She staggered for a few seconds and then, when she had found her feet, yelled at her tormenter, using an expression that was presumably local and definitely outside Christiansen's vocabulary of German curse words. Even at that distance he could hear the guards laughing.

When she started on her way she came in Christiansen's direction, so all he had to do to get a good look at her was to wait quietly in the shadow of his awning. She was wearing a flowered summer dress, probably the clothes in which she had been arrested—leave it to the Russians to turn out their prisoners without proper clothes, probably without the price of a *Kaffee mit Schlag,* and in the late afternoon so they wouldn't have a day to find themselves a place in out of the night cold. She walked along with her arms wrapped around her slender body, hunched over like an old woman, although probably she wasn't more than twenty-nine or thirty. When she passed in front of him on the other side of the street he decided to give her a bit of a lead, just in case any interested parties back at the slammer were still watching, and then catch up with her. You never knew.

He followed for perhaps a quarter of a mile, with the wind picking up from minute to minute. She didn't seem to be heading in any particular direction—she was just trying to keep the blood pumping, hunting at random for somewhere warm. They were well out of sight of the prison when Christiansen noticed that he seemed to be part of a parade. There seemed to be someone else interested in tracking the lady down.

Men betrayed themselves even through their tastes in overcoats. This specimen favored navy blue, with wide, pointed shoulders and a pinched-in waist. Christiansen was well behind, but he would have bet anything the lapels were as pointed as foxes' ears. Nationality didn't seem to matter—a certain class of hoodlum always gave the impression their notions of sartorial splendor came straight out of old Edward G. Robinson movies.

He was a big man, and he was in a hurry. His hands were jammed deep into his pockets and he kept glancing around as long strides carried him nearer and nearer to his quarry. Finally he was almost running.

The woman turned her head. She must have heard something, the sound of footsteps, but it was too late. A gloved hand locked on her arm, just above the elbow, and pushed her forward. A few more paces and they reached the mouth of a narrow alley; a sharp tug and they disappeared inside. Christiansen had never had a chance to see her face, but this wasn't anybody she was looking forward to meeting.

He didn't wait for the screaming to start. In his pocket was a coil of catgut—he never went anywhere without it. The ends were knotted into handles. He took it out, holding it in his left hand as he ran.

The first thing he heard was the soft, muffled sound that fists make when they strike the body—not the face, the body, where they don't leave any marks. Then, as he stepped inside, he could see them—or at least the man as he huddled over his victim—and the sounds changed. It was the face now, and the curses were well within Christiansen's working knowledge. "You little whore. You bitch, so you thought you could hold out, did you? You worthless, ugly old tramp . . ."

It was just as well. The stupid bastard was too busy with his righteous wrath to notice anyone coming up behind him. The shadows of the surrounding buildings closed over all three of them as Christiansen moved in, the coil held in both hands now, with a big double loop, like a halo he was about to try on, grasped delicately with the tips of his fingers.

He wasn't more than five or six feet behind the

man when suddenly both the beating and the curses
stopped. A hand went into the overcoat pocket, but
Christiansen didn't wait to see what it would bring
out. He stepped forward, dropped the loop over the
man's head, and pulled.

He pulled hard—he wasn't fooling around with
this one. A sharp backward yank and the noose went
tight, cutting off a sound that might have been anything, perhaps just a grunt of surprise. A knife clattered against the stones.

He pulled again, even harder, and the man jerked
backward, just as if his legs had been pushed out from
underneath him. With the ends of the coil held in
both hands, Christiansen started dragging the man
along the pavement, back into the darkness.

*"I suppose, like everything else, it loses some of
its terror with repetition,"* Mordecai had said, but that
was eyewash. Killing was killing, and it never got any
easier.

It takes very little time for a man to die like that.
For a few seconds, as the noose pulls him, he kicks
and tries to scream, and his hands claw at his neck so
that they draw blood, but only for a few seconds.
Unconsciousness comes quickly—in a quarter of a
minute he's as good as dead. The hands go limp and
the fighting stops; he's just a weight at the end of a
string. And then, if you don't let go, in another minute
or so he really is dead. Christiansen put his foot on
the back of the man's neck, keeping the catgut taut,
until he was sure.

It had a way of embedding itself in the flesh, so
it wasn't very pleasant to unwind. As he slipped the
coil back into his pocket, he glanced up and saw the

woman, realizing with a shock that he had forgotten all about her.

She hadn't moved. She was still crouched against a wall, staring out over her knees—frightened, of course, but alert and wary. That she had just seen a man garroted was not what was uppermost in her mind. She wanted to know what Christiansen would do next.

The first impression was confirmed—she was about thirty. It was a face that ran a little too heavily to bone to be quite pretty, but she wasn't bad. The eyes that peered up at him from under the heavy brows were intelligent if perhaps a trifle small. Her heavy frame and reddish-brown hair, cut short—after all, she had been in prison—made her look like a farmgirl fallen from grace.

"Would he have killed you?" Christiansen asked, in English. It was a sudden inspiration. It established his credentials as a neutral.

She didn't answer; at first he thought probably she hadn't understood. And then she glanced down at the knife that was still lying on the cobbled pavement next to her left foot. Of course she had understood. It wasn't her fault if strange men asked stupid questions.

"Here, we can't have you freezing to death."

He took off his overcoat—hell, he wouldn't die of exposure—and placed it carefully over her so that she was covered almost up to the mouth. She didn't seem impressed by the kindness.

"What's it to you?" she asked.

The room was too large to be heated efficiently by the tiny coal-burning fireplace, and dinner consisted of bread, boiled ham, a little cheese, and coffee liberally adulterated with chicory. Because she liked being paid in American money, the landlady wasn't asking any awkward questions. In fact, Christiansen had the distinct impression that she and Sonya had done business before. Sonya seemed to know her way around.

"Eight months I was in that stinking place," she said, to no one in particular as she lay on her side in front of the fireplace. She had taken a bath as the absolute first thing; she had said she wanted to rid herself of the smell of disinfectant. And now, she said, she wanted to get roasted, like a joint of meat. "And all because I gave a Russian major a bad time when he wanted to cheat me on the price. These people give you eight months for spitting on the sidewalk. I started studying English in 1942, just in case things went the wrong way, and then I get caught in the stinking Russian sector."

One injustice seemed to rankle as much as the other. She turned over, so that her back was to Christiansen, who was sitting in a massive chair that could have been the throne of the Hapsburgs. She wasn't the modest type; she wasn't wearing anything except a huge white towel tucked in under her arms, and it was plain how pink the fire had made her bony shoulders and the backs of her legs. She wanted to be warm and comfortable, and to let her dinner digest. And she wanted to complain about the Russians.

"Christ, what pigs. I was lucky not to catch the clap in there." She sat up, wrapping her arms around her legs so that her head rested on her knees. She had hardly even looked at Christiansen.

"I thought it was a woman's prison," he said, aware that he sounded like a chump. What did he care? The point was to keep her talking.

She let her head roll a little to one side and then, quite suddenly, gave him a knowing smile, as if they shared some secret.

"The guards never let that stop them." A short, bitter laugh escaped her lips. "Christ, they must cut each other's throats to be posted to that stinking place. For them it's just the biggest cat house in Vienna."

Christiansen still had half a cup of coffee balanced carefully on his thigh; he picked it up and allowed himself a sip. It was something to do, since she seemed to be waiting for some response. He just wanted her to go on. He wanted to hear about the inside of Mühl-feld Prison.

"I guess it must have been a pretty bleak time for you," he said quietly, as if stating the obvious. The coffee was extremely bitter and, of course, there was no sugar. He must have made a peculiar face because the woman smiled.

"Is that how you usually pick up girls?" she asked. "Hanging around prisons, waiting for the garbage to be thrown out?"

"Not as a rule, no."

The smile kept tugging at the corners of her mouth as she studied his face with an almost embarrassing frankness. It was impossible to tell whether she liked what she saw there or not, and probably it made very little difference, even to her. Christiansen decided he really wasn't interested in a professional opinion.

"Do you want to sleep with me?" It was just a question, on the order of "Would you like a cigarette?"

"No."

"Then what do you want? Or did you just kill Otto for the fun of it?"

"Was that his name?"

"Yes, but don't feel sorry—he was no loss. He wanted me to come back to work for him. He would have carved me up good, except for you."

Her eyes narrowed with what was probably supposed to be smoldering seductiveness—she seemed to imagine he was about sixteen. It was almost funny. When she saw it wasn't working, she stopped.

"A pity," she said. It was almost possible to believe her. "You know, you really are a nice-looking man. I don't get one like you every day. So tell me, what is it you do want?"

The silence was awkward, almost dangerous. It was the last question Christiansen felt inclined to answer, partly because this was not anyone he could trust and partly because he hardly knew himself.

"Perhaps I'm just a good Samaritan."

"Yes, sure. And I'm the Virgin Mary." She laughed—it was a delicious joke, apparently. And then suddenly the joke was over and her face tightened.

"I've seen men killed before, you know." With a quick movement of her hand she brushed a strand of hair back from her face. The gesture carried a certain brutal authority. "We've had the war and the Russians, and I haven't lived with my eyes closed. You're no tourist. That was a very professional job you did on Otto—he never even made a sound."

Then, with a kind of pleasant sigh, she stretched out full length on the rag rug in front of the fire. She covered her eyes with the back of her right hand, and her stomach rose and fell slowly with every breath. Christiansen was a very dangerous man, she had decided, someone who murdered as if he had been born to it, but what was that to her?

The towel around her slipped open a little—perhaps she had intended it to—uncovering her right side, all the way up to the rib cage. There was a scar, about four inches long, running down her belly just inside the soft mound made by her hip bone. It was still fresh, angry and red at the edges. After a moment she pulled the towel back into place.

"You don't like it, do you," she said, slipping her fingers in under the fringed edge. "I don't like it either—a scar like that is bad for business. Christ, what a mess they made of me in that place."

"Where? The prison?"

"No, the hospital. I had to wait two hours for the ambulance, damn them. I thought my guts would pop open."

"There isn't a hospital in the prison?" Christiansen tried to keep the excitement out of his voice. The chair creaked beneath him as he moved.

"No, just an infirmary. They have a big, smelly Russian nurse there who couldn't cut a splinter out of your finger. I think she's queer for the girls, you know? You don't go near the place unless you're really sick, and then they have to send you to the hospital."

Christiansen smiled at her, perhaps a little uncertainly. He didn't want her to say anything more. He didn't want to look at her. All he wanted to see was the image in his mind, an ambulance pulling out through the prison gates.

✠ 7 ✠

It was a few minutes to ten when Christiansen crossed the Salztorbrücke back into the International Zone. Sonya was probably asleep. He had given her enough money to keep herself for at least a week and she had told him everything she knew, content not to ask why he was interested. She would stay there in the room. Where else would she go? she had asked. He had a key. He had a feeling she would be useful later on.

Apparently the shift had changed, because the guard on the Russian side of the bridge wasn't the same one who had warned him about the whores in the Augarten. This time it was a kid of perhaps seventeen, who went over every page of Christiansen's passport as if he imagined it to be forged and was looking for a mistake. He seemed to resent his failure when he handed the passport back and waved Christiansen across.

Christiansen decided he would walk back to the hotel.

They had agreed before leaving Munich that it was best to find rooms in the American sector. They had made their bookings in advance, with Hirsch, Faglin and Dessauer in a hotel in the next block. There was no point in looking like a convention.

He anticipated no problems with either Hirsch or Faglin—they were both basically technicians, willing to take Mordecai's word for it that he was someone they could work with. But Dessauer, whom the others treated like the baby of the family, couldn't seem to forgive him for having broken his nose. Finally, as if it was the most devastating insult he could think of, he had called Christiansen a *goy*, a word Christiansen had had to think about for perhaps a quarter of a minute before he could even remember what it meant. Everyone learns a little Yiddish in New York, but that had been a long time ago. The outburst had been followed by an embarrassed silence.

There were lights everywhere in the International Zone. Christiansen remembered Emperor Franz Josef's remark about putting a tent over Vienna to make the biggest brothel in the world, and then he remembered Sonya and decided to put the subject out of his mind.

When he got back to the room he found that everyone had arrived. Hirsch had brought sandwiches and bottles of beer with him from the train station, and they were all having a late-night picnic. Christiansen accepted a bottle of the beer and told them about Mühlfeld Prison.

"It's a real bank vault," he said sullenly, holding the bottle by the neck. "We'll never crack her out of there. We might as well try knocking over the Kremlin."

"It's still just a prison." Jerry Hirsch sat staring at his sandwich, as if he rather expected it to bite him.

"We have people who practically specialize in stuff like that," he went on. "Acre Fortress wasn't exactly a cracker box, you know. We could bring in a few demolition experts. We could be in and out before they knew we were there."

Christiansen shook his head, frowning.

"It won't do—I read about Acre. We don't have an adjoining bath house here so that all we would have to do is punch through a wall. We don't have a ready-made army waiting for us on the inside. This is Austria, not Palestine. We don't have a friendly local population ready to hide us until the Russians get tired of searching for us."

"He's right, Jerry." Mordecai smiled glumly from where he stood by the huge rosewood wardrobe that separated the room's two beds. "And there is the political side of things to be considered. The Haganah gets a fair share of its arms from Czechoslovakia, so we don't want to antagonize the Russians. It would be better from several points of view if this operation could look like some quite ordinary criminal matter—the local underworld retrieving one of its own."

"No one will believe that. This woman isn't important. Who would go to the trouble?"

It was Faglin who had spoken. He was lying full length on one of the beds, staring at the ceiling through exhausted-looking eyes. He seemed already to have made up his mind that they were doomed to failure, but he had been like that even before they had left Munich. Mordecai claimed he was merely homesick.

"It is important, however, that we give them no reason to believe anything else. Inar, my young friend, have you any ideas? Perhaps more important, have you any cigarettes?"

It had become a ritual by now. Christiansen took the pack from his shirt pocket, shook out two cigarettes, one for himself and one for Mordecai.

"There are no medical facilities inside the walls," he said, feeling a curious sense of relief. He turned his hand so that the smoke crept across the ball of his thumb before snaking upward into the air. "If she were to become suddenly ill—if she had an attack of appendicitis, for instance—they would have to send her to one of the civilian hospitals in an ambulance. She'd be within reach then."

The stillness was almost palpable, as if they suddenly had found themselves in the presence of a miracle and were afraid to mention it for fear it might vanish. Dessauer, who was sitting on the second bed, close enough to Mordecai that he could have touched him, looked as if he would have liked to say something but didn't know what.

"We could slip her something," he whispered finally, his throat working nervously. "They must have visiting hours. We could pretend we were relatives or something . . ."

There was an odd clicking sound in the room, which Christiansen at last determined was coming from the other bed. Faglin was laughing.

"Such a sheltered life you've led, Itzikel. Don't you know what Russian prisons are like?" Slowly, with an appearance of great effort, he turned his head the few degrees that allowed him to look in that direction. "If they have a visiting room, they make the prisoner sit in a steel mesh cage with a guard right behind the chair. There will be one window into the room where the visitor sits, and the visitor will have a guard too. Sometimes there's glass in the window and you talk through a microphone, but even if there's only more steel mesh you're not allowed to touch. You have to keep your hands in plain view, all the time—it's the rule. Nobody *slips* anyone anything."

Dessauer was silenced. They were all silenced. It seemed to be the moment of defeat.

And then Mordecai smiled his sad, ironic smile.

"We don't have an army inside," he said finally. He took the cigarette out of his mouth and looked at it as if he wondered why it kept burning. "This isn't Acre—Inar is right about that. But people go into prisons as well as out. Perhaps we could smuggle in just one little soldier."

The plan was straightforward enough. Faglin and Hirsch would take responsibility for getting the girl out of Mühlfeld Prison and, while they served as a distraction for the police, Christiansen would smuggle her back to the American Zone. The three of them would rendezvous the day of the escape, but until then they would keep clear of each other—it was safer that way. Mordecai and Itzhak, thank God, would stay behind and out of harm's way.

The only thing was that while Christiansen, the lucky devil, had a passport that allowed him to pass the Russian checkpoints without challenge, Faglin and Hirsch had to smuggle themselves in.

They would use the sewers, since the plans were available at any of the city's libraries and not even the Russians could guard every manhole cover in the Brigittenau. The water, which smelled bad but not as bad as they had expected, was up to their calves and lumpy with ice. Even with rubber boots on, Faglin could hardly feel his feet at all.

Faglin had been born on a kibbutz just south of Caesarea. The sea was only half an hour's walk away, and it was never cold. Faglin, who hadn't been home in eleven months, and then only for a brief visit, hated the winters in Europe.

By three-fifteen in the morning they had traveled just a little under two kilometers. They had been at it for over an hour. They had only their small electric torches, so it was necessary to move with some care in order to avoid making too much noise. They had crossed beneath the Danube some time back, so they could come up to the street whenever they wished. All they had to do was to find a storm drain with a grating that would yield without waking up the whole city.

There were rats down here. One could hear them scurrying off and, from time to time, the torchlight would catch them basking on the filthy banks of the sewer main. They would blink and scratch themselves and nose casually into the water. It was a peculiarly disagreeable sight. Faglin would be glad to be back up at street level, where the danger would be greater but at least they would be men once more.

For the hundredth time he readjusted his shoulder pack. He was carrying a change of clothes, some tools, his revolver wrapped up in an old pair of pajama bottoms, about seven pounds of plastic explosives, and various other odds and ends. He was tired and it had been a long time since dinner. Hirsch was carrying some sandwiches, but of course it was impossible in a sewer to think of eating. He could hear him walking about four meters behind. Hirsch never seemed to get tired.

At twenty after, his torchlight fell across a line of steel rungs leading up the side of the sewer wall. They had found an exit.

Hirsch took off his shoulder pack and handed it to Faglin, and then, while Faglin held the light, he made his way up the rungs to the storm drain cover. Soon only his feet were visible below the narrow gully.

"Pass up the torch," he murmured. A hand came down to accept it. Faglin stood below in the near-total darkness, trying to fight off the sensation of being at the bottom of a well.

When Hirsch came down again his face was streaked but he was grinning with pleasure. He took a moment to catch his breath.

"It's bolted in place," he said finally. "From the inside—the damn Russians don't trust anybody. A couple of wrenches and a few drops of cable oil, then give me fifteen minutes and we'll be out of here."

It took him less time than that. One by one, the loosened bolts dropped down and embedded themselves in the muddy sewer bank, each time just missing Faglin, who stood below holding the light.

"Can you see anything?" Faglin asked, straining his voice into a tense whisper. The only answer was the scrape of the drain cover as Hirsch lifted it out of his way. A moment later a hand came down again, and Faglin brought up Hirsch's shoulder pack until the fingers closed around its strap. They were on their way up.

When Faglin clambered to the mouth of the open storm drain, the first thing he saw in the light from the street lamps was Hirsch's face. He looked demonic crouched there at the gutter's edge. A line of filth ran across his nose and jaw and he was glistening with sweat; he might have been staring straight into his own death from the expression of half-crazed anxiety in his eyes. As soon as he had his shoulders out of the sewer pipe and was able to turn around and see behind him, Faglin could understand why. They had come out directly across the street from a police barracks. The lights behind the second-floor windows were on.

"Let's get out of here."

The drain cover slid back into place with a noise that seemed loud enough to be heard by all the policemen in Vienna, but as the two men hurried away down the street no one shouted after them to halt. There were no shots fired. There was no sound at all except the slap of their shoe soles against the walkway.

"I think we've just used up all our good luck," Hirsch murmured tensely as they rounded the corner. "Let's look for somewhere out of the cold where we can hole up until after curfew lifts."

They found a factory building with a basement door that would open to some slight persuasion. They were able to light the boiler, and within two or three minutes the whole room was deliciously warm. Hirsch took the sandwiches from his shoulder pack, where they had been cushioning a small, flat wooden box that held the detonators. Provided no watchman came to chase them off, they would stay right there until six in the morning, when they would no longer be subject to arbitrary arrest. There was a small cupboard containing a few cups without handles, a spoon, a metal pot, and a small canister of tea; they were able to brew some with the water from the boiler's runoff valve. It tasted rusty, but it was tea.

"All the comforts of home," Hirsch announced, making a gesture with his arm that took in the whole room.

Faglin merely shrugged. To his mind, Hirsch had a way of enjoying these little adventures that was almost indecent.

"Come on, Amos—cheer up. We've got two whole hours ahead of us with nothing to do but relax. That's as good as a lifetime."

"Sure. It's the Ritz bar."

"You just miss that little wife of yours back in Haifa." Hirsch laughed and clapped him on the back. "You family types, all very admirable but no thanks. For me, now, women are like marzipan—a piece now and again is tasty, but they cloy. That's the best way to feel if you're a soldier."

"You'll marry, just like everybody else. Just wait until the war is over, then you'll see things the other way."

But Hirsch merely shook his head, as if a child had said something foolish. He took a sip of his tea, made a face, and pitched the rest onto the basement floor, where it made a fan-shaped pattern on the cement.

"This war won't ever be over," he said finally, setting the empty cup down beside his right foot. "Not for us, anyway. We'll still be fighting the Arabs fifty years from now. If we live, you and I will be at this until we're old men."

"If we live. If Hagemann can be stopped, and we aren't all peppered with nerve gas in the first artillery barrage."

They allowed the subject to drop.

After about twenty minutes, Hirsch drew a pack of cigarettes from his trousers pocket and lit one. The match popped into life with a kind of scratching cough, filling the air with the smell of sulfur.

"I think Mordecai must be losing his grip to trust this big Swede as far as he seems to." The basement room was gloomy enough to be an antechamber to Hell, so the end of Hirsch's cigarette threw an oddly sinister glow over the lower part of his face as he spoke. "I think it would be better if we tried to smuggle her out ourselves. He has his own game to play—what's to keep him from simply disappearing with her after we've delivered her to him like a bouquet of roses?"

"You sound like you think he's a goddam Nazi. You saw the report—the man's got more battle ribbons than teeth. He's a hero. Besides, he's not a Swede, he's a Norwegian."

"He's a *goy.*"

"You sound like Itzikel."

"Well, Itzikel was right. The only difference is that I'm not dumb enough to call the man names to his face. If there's anything Jews should have learned since 1933, it's the difference between us and them. And Christiansen is definitely one of them."

"I had the impression you kind of liked him."

"Who said I didn't like him?" Hirsch asked irritatedly, picking a loose piece of tobacco from the end of his tongue. "I just don't trust him, that's all."

At the first hint of gray light through the basement windows, the two men washed their faces and hands in the water from the boiler tap and changed their clothes—one felt better and was considerably less conspicuous for not smelling of three hours in the Viennese sewers. They waited until they had heard three or four sets of footfalls before they ventured outside, where there was a cold, persistent wind and the clouds that hung low in the sky were tarnished to a flat gray.

"Let's check Weber Strasse first," Faglin murmured tensely. He felt dreadfully exposed; he was carrying a revolver tucked under his belt and there were still fifteen pounds of explosives in his shoulder pack. It seemed the most logical thing imaginable that either the police or one or another of the omnipresent Russian patrols would any second now come rushing in at them, shouting *"Jew terrorist!"* at the tops of their lungs. What could be more reasonable?

"All right. It'll be a damn nuisance if there turns out to be anything there."

It was the sort of thing one couldn't tell from the street map they had purchased the afternoon before— in the whole district there were only two small red crosses to indicate the presence of a hospital. The one on Weber Strasse was nearly twice the distance from the prison, but they had to be sure. They had to know where the Russians would call for an ambulance if they had an emergency with one of their convicts.

It was a small brick building taking up only one corner of the block. They went all the way around. The rear entrance was just that, a doorway in the back. There were no special provisions for emergency care. The sign in front read: *"Frauenklinik."* Faglin swallowed hard and made his decision. The Russians weren't going to bring anyone here, and there had to be a limit even to Mossad thoroughness. The Jewish State would not make war on newborn babies. They were not going to blow the place up.

"It would only have been the gas main or something," Hirsch announced consolingly, "just enough to put them out of operation for a while."

"And maybe twenty or thirty of the weaker ones would have frozen to death in their cribs. I'm glad— I wouldn't have wanted it on my conscience."

"Besides, it leaves us with that much more for our big bang."

Faglin once more adjusted the straps of his shoulder pack, wishing as he did it that Hirsch wouldn't talk that way. He started to say something but saw that Hirsch was grinning at him.

"Come on, Amos. Relax," he said. "Time for lunch."

The Russian Zone was not very accommodating to the casual tourist—there were hardly any restaurants at all, and the few food stalls were almost empty of goods and jammed with customers trying to barter furniture and old clothes for a few ounces of coffee or half a dozen shrunken little apples. Everyone seemed to have plenty of money; it just didn't seem to be worth very much.

But Faglin's parents had come from Vilna, so he had grown up speaking good enough Russian to convince any Austrian that he was probably a plainclothesman in the NKVD. Added to that, he had British money. The combination proved irresistible to a grocer on the Blumauergasse who, after a few minutes of hectoring, disappeared into his back room and returned with a paper bag containing several large hard rolls, lemonade in an old wine bottle, and a sausage that must have weighed close to four pounds, and all for the ridiculously low figure of two pounds ten—enough to buy dinner for four in almost any restaurant in London. The grocer was frightened of Faglin, so he only robbed him a little.

"Can we steal an ambulance?" Hirsch asked, using his American jackknife to carve off a large piece of the sausage as they walked along.

"Yes, that will be easy. We know approximately when the call will be coming in, so we can wait outside near the loading dock. Perhaps, if the ambulances have radios, all we'll need to do is listen. If not, we'll know when the stretcher bearers come running. In either case, we stop them—quietly—and take their places. Surely there will be someplace in the ambulance to hide the bodies; we want the police to find the correct number of corpses, so we'll have to take them along."

"Then it's a good thing the weather is cold."

"You have a twisted sense of humor, Jerry."

"If you think so, then let's sit down here and eat. You worry too much about corpses, my friend. They have too much reality for you."

They sat with their legs over the edge of the canal embankment, the bottle of lemonade between them as Hirsch hacked away at bread and sausage with the rough efficiency of a stonecutter. It was almost ten in the morning, and the milky sunlight hardly seemed to warm them at all. Now and again they saw Russian soldiers patrolling in twos along the Handels-Kai or over the bridges, but this deep inside the Zone no one was interested.

"Then let's go to the prison first," Faglin said abruptly, as if announcing the results of some inner dialogue. "We can leave the hospital until later. The less we show ourselves around there the better."

"But first finish eating, Amos. You look like a scarecrow. Didn't your mama ever tell you to eat?"

"She hardly ever told me anything else."

Mühlfeld Prison was as forbidding as Christiansen had led them to expect. The back gate was massive, even taller than the surrounding stone wall, and behind it there was a chain and behind that a parked troop carrier. No one was coming in or out without the Russians' approval.

But at least now they knew where to bring the ambulance.

"They will send a guard with her," Hirsch said. They were walking by on the opposite side of the street, hunched inside their overcoats like men who were in a hurry to be someplace warm. The soldiers, of course, paid no attention. "It will be a problem if they send more than one."

Faglin laughed out loud. A gray squirrel, startled by the sound, glared at them from the safety of a tree as they passed.

"And why should they do that, do you suppose?" The laughter subsided into a cough as he shook his head at the absurdity of the idea. "A girl doubled up with stomach pains, who doesn't weigh fifty kilos to start with—what do they need, an army?"

"You know how they are about security. Every prisoner is a counterrevolutionary, and every counterrevolutionary is either Trotsky or the Czar. It's a matter of prestige, I suppose. We have to make plans for a second guard."

"All right. One will go in the back with the girl, right? I'll take care of him. If there's another, we'll say it's too crowded and have him sit up front with you. Have a pistol taped under the dashboard. Just give me a chance to take care of mine first. I don't want him jumping out of his skin at the sound of gunfire."

"How will you do it?"

"How do I always do it?"

That seemed answer enough. Hirsch nodded soberly and they continued along their walk. It amused Faglin to think that even twenty years ago they might have been a pair of rabbis out to take the air and dispute a point of theology. Now they were soldiers, plotting a raid on a Russian prison. It constituted progress of a sort.

They took the long route, going several blocks out of their way in order to approach the prison from a different direction, so they could have a look at the front entrance.

"We'll drive around this way to the Heine Strasse," Faglin said, looking out at the broad, almost empty boulevard. Petrol was difficult to find in the Russian sector. "It's quicker to the hospital, so it'll be what they expect. After you've turned the corner onto Tabor Strasse, I'll kill my guard. I forgot to ask— will you have any trouble shooting with your left hand?"

"I am left-handed."

"Oh, that's right. I had forgotten."

"Will you look at that?"

They were at the corner, some thirty meters from the checkpoint at the prison's main gate. A rather pudgy man in a green suit, carrying his overcoat across his arm, was having his briefcase searched as he came out. He looked nervous, although obviously there was nothing for the guards to find; he kept running the flat of his hand across his thin, rather oily-looking hair, glancing around as if he would have liked to take flight but didn't quite have the courage. It was impossible to tell whether he had seen them or not.

"You recognize the face, of course," Hirsch said, putting his hand on Faglin's arm and gently pulling him around so that their backs were toward the checkpoint.

"Of course. It's Plessen."

It was a terrible thing to have happen, worse even than putting the Russians on the alert. The Russians, after all, were not very active antagonists, but Plessen was the enemy incarnate. Faglin struggled to regain his composure, cursing himself for being surprised. After all, what could be more natural than for Hagemann to have tracked Esther Rosensaft to the gates of Mühlfeld Prison and then send his tame lawyer sniffing around?

"Perhaps he didn't recognize us."

"Don't be daft." Hirsch tightened his grip as they walked slowly back to the shadow of the building. "He's not a fool. Besides, I had a little run-in with him in Naples once—he tried to denounce me to the police. We can't take the chance. We have to kill him."

Yes, they would have to kill him.

They split up at the next corner, where they were well out of sight of the prison, and Faglin set off down the street at a dead run. Plessen was heading back toward the Augarten, where he might have a car parked, so they had to intercept him before then. Hirsch would go back to the Heine Strasse and follow him from the opposite side of the street, making himself suitably conspicuous—the idea was to herd him straight into Faglin's waiting arms. But first Faglin had to be there, so he had to hurry.

One thing, at least, they didn't have to worry about. Plessen, no matter how scared he was, wouldn't go rushing back to Mühlfeld to throw himself on the protection of the Russians. His had not been a blameless life. One word would be enough to ensure that Plessen disappeared into a Soviet labor camp forever, and he knew it.

As soon as he reached Tabor Strasse, Faglin started north. His way was parallel to the Augarten, and if he looked to his left he could see the bare back of one of the old palace buildings. By the time he crossed the Heine Strasse his breathing was nearly normal again. Plessen was nowhere in sight.

Plessen wouldn't get away—Hirsch was right behind him, and Hirsch had a pistol. If he met anyone, or tried to enter a car or board a bus, Hirsch would shoot him dead. It would be noisy and dangerous, but that wouldn't do Plessen any good. Hirsch was an excellent shot.

Still, the Russians weren't going to be lulled to sleep by having people murdered on the streets of their sector. It wouldn't make anything any easier.

Faglin glanced around nervously, resting his head on the back of a bench where, possibly right up to the final bombardment of the city, people had sat waiting for the bus to come. The green wooden slats on one side had been torn to splinters, probably by a piece of shrapnel, and the absence of legs on that side made the whole structure tilt like a gangplank.

Plessen was nowhere in sight. It was all very disheartening.

Faglin slipped his hand inside his pocket, and the fingers automatically closed around his knife. He had only to squeeze the sides and the blade would spring straight from the hilt, like a snake sticking out its tongue. Just hold it against a man's heart and squeeze; the point would go through anything, even leather. It was a remarkable weapon. He had taken it off a dead Syrian in 1943. He wondered if he would ever have a chance to use it.

He saw Hirsch first, and then, about three quarters of a block in the lead, pushing along as fast as discretion and his stumpy little legs would allow, Plessen. It was only necessary to wait.

And then, as luck would have it, a pair of Russian soldiers turned up, out on their evening patrol. They were coming straight down the Tabor Strasse, their machine guns, hanging from shoulder straps like a couple of ladies' handbags, swinging in a little arc with every step, from right to left and back again. Faglin lifted one foot up to the seat of the crumbling bench and began to make a great display of retying his shoelace.

Plessen would reach the corner first. The question was, what would he do when he saw the two soldiers? Hirsch was only ten or twelve meters behind him, and he would have to assume that Hirsch was armed and hostile. After all, he knew Hirsch well enough to have made trouble for him with the Neapolitan police, so he knew what kind of man he had to deal with.

Hirsch was not the timid type. A couple of Russian peasants in infantryman uniforms weren't going to stop him if he felt like killing Plessen. He would simply kill them first, one shot apiece, before they ever had a chance to raise their weapons. Plessen wouldn't have any illusions about that.

And, besides, one word in that quarter and he was on a prison train for the Arctic Circle. Hirsch didn't have anything to hide, but Plessen did.

Hence there was no chance that he would want to do anything but avoid the Russians. After all, he didn't know for certain that Hirsch wasn't just going to scold him for being a bad sport about the Italian business. So he would sheer off, trying to avoid them both.

But which way? Across the street? No, there was too much traffic—he wouldn't much fancy waiting at the intersection for a break, not with Hirsch at his back. So he would go up Tabor Strasse. He would turn the corner, walk straight past the two Russian soldiers, and keep going.

And that was where Faglin would intercept him. He took his foot down from the bench and began making his leisurely way up the sidewalk.

He passed the two Russians; they never so much as glanced at him. They were too busy talking about the cheapest places to buy cigarettes. He heard the sound of their boot heels dying away behind him.

He stayed back from the curb. He wanted Plessen to walk by him on the left side. His right hand went into his overcoat pocket. He didn't look behind him.

One, two, one, two, quick march. Not running, not seeming to hurry very much, but eager to be on his way—Plessen's footsteps clicked against the pavement with the regularity of a metronome. Faglin allowed himself to slow down to a stroll. The Russians, by now, were probably twenty-five or thirty meters behind them.

As Plessen tried to move around him on the sidewalk, Faglin reached out and took him by the right arm, just as if they had been friends all their lives.

"I hope you are not carrying a gun," he said in English—Nazis always found the sound of English so reassuring, and he didn't want Plessen to bolt on him. He tightened his grip. "But you wouldn't have been stupid enough to carry a gun into a Russian prison, now would you. After all, they let you come back out."

"What is it you . . ."

Plessen's eyes bulged out of his thick, cunning face. He was frightened, but he had the composure not to raise his voice—that was something.

"A word with you, *Herr Doktor*—nothing more. We'd like to know what brings you back to historic Vienna."

They kept pace together at a slow walk, arm in arm for all the world could have seen. In another quarter of a minute they would reach the next corner. It seemed an immense distance.

"Are you one of the Jews? Are you with—? I never—"

"Yes, Herr Plessen. I am one of the Jews." Faglin allowed his left hand to run slowly up and across the back of Plessen's overcoat, until his arm was resting in the friendliest manner possible on the other man's shoulders. The fingers of his other hand curled around the hilt of his knife. "But all of that was a long time ago, and all of us are here on other business. Tell me, what do you hear these days from Colonel Hagemann?"

There was no sound now except the wind, high up, pushing against the naked branches of the trees that stood beside the sidewalk. A scrap of paper floated by on the street, settling quietly to the stones every few yards, like an exhausted ghost.

"Hagemann? You said, Hagemann? I—"

"Don't lie to me, Herr Plessen." With the pressure of his arm, Faglin guided him around the corner. They were safe now, quite away from everyone. "I'm not from the War Crimes Tribunal, but I know what I know. So don't take the trouble to make up pretty stories. What does Hagemann want inside Mühlfeld Prison that he sends you all this way?"

"Well, I don't know. That is . . . He seems to have friends . . ."

Faglin wasn't even really listening. Nothing that Plessen could tell him would be of the slightest interest, not compared with the mere fact of his being in this place at this moment. Actually, he was looking for a nice private place to get rid of the body.

". . . you know, I have my standards. I'm a Doctor of Jurisprudence, you know. It's a question of a client's . . ."

God, the man was such a fool—he probably even believed some of it. About five meters in front of them, there was the shell of a house. The walls of the surrounding buildings were gouged by shrapnel holes, but this one seemed to have taken a direct hit. There was a stairwell down to what had probably been the servants' entrance. It would do.

There was no one else on the street. Perhaps people lived in some of these houses—people lived wherever they could. Perhaps someone would chance to be glancing out his window, but that wouldn't matter. Sensible people did not report crimes to the Russian authorities. If anyone saw, they would let the patrols find the body tomorrow morning.

Plessen was still talking. ".   . It seems a romantic interest . . ." He didn't appear to notice when Faglin took his right hand out of his pocket. He didn't seem to hear the hard, cruel snap as the blade shot out from Faglin's gloved fist.

Faglin let his arm swing across, and the blade caught Plessen just at the edge of his overcoat lapel. There was a dull sound, like a cough, as it buried itself up to the hilt.

People always acted so surprised when they were stabbed. As Faglin took his hand away, Plessen stared down at the knife that was sticking out of his chest like a coat peg and the expression on his face changed, his eyes widening as if he just couldn't believe that it was there. The blade was buried deep into his heart, so he was already dead—he simply didn't know it yet. He looked up at Faglin, who was still standing right beside him, and he opened his mouth to say something, and that was when it happened. He just died, from one instant to the next. His knees started to fold under him, and even as Faglin was shoving him down the basement stairway, even as his arm shot out as if under its own power to grab for the iron railing, he was already a corpse.

At the bottom, perhaps three, perhaps four meters below the level of the street, the body lay in a crumpled pile. Faglin went down, pulled his knife loose, and wiped the blade off on Plessen's coat sleeve. He took the wallet from the breast pocket. Let the police believe this was a simple robbery if they liked—in any case, let them work a few days before they made an identification. He took the briefcase as well.

By the time he had finished, Hirsch was already at the top of the stairs waiting for him.

"You do nice work," he said, smiling coldly. "Now let's get out of here. Christiansen will be waiting."

❖ *8* ❖

It was the rule at Mühlfeld Prison that any inmate receiving a visitor was confined in an isolation cell for the twenty-four hours following. No one pretended there was any reason for this, since no secrets or contraband could be passed between people separated by heavy mesh screens, and certainly not in the presence of two Russian guards, and it didn't seem to make any difference who the visitor was. Mother, lawyer, husband, NKVD interrogator, agent of the International Red Cross—twenty minutes of conversation in the reception room meant a day and a night in solitary. It was the rule, that was all.

The cells were in the basement. They had concrete walls and were very cold. There was one blanket. Esther wrapped herself in it as many times as she could and lay down on the plank bed. It was the first time she had ever been here because it was the first time she had ever had a visitor.

Every ten or twenty minutes the eye slit in her door would darken, which meant that someone was outside looking in. Sometimes it was the guard on duty—she could hear the regular click of his boot heels as he paced up and down the corridor—but sometimes, probably, it was Filatov. For over a week now, he had been watching her constantly. He never seemed to go off duty; she could feel his eyes on her wherever she went. It was as if he hated her, or was afraid she might find some means of running away, or both. Perhaps he was simply waiting for another chance to shove her into another empty room.

She had let him push her down onto the blanket, had turned her face to the empty wall, and had tried, with all the energy she could command from her giddy, half-paralyzed mind, to force herself into being somewhere else. She couldn't fight him. She didn't try. But she didn't want to feel his clammy hands on her face and shoulders; she didn't want to hear the way he grunted over her. She thought perhaps, if she willed it with enough conviction, if just this once there was no part of her to say, *No, live!* then perhaps she might die. Could anyone just die like that? Yes, she believed they could.

But she couldn't. It must have been that somewhere inside her, hiding where she couldn't find it, a piece of her had still been clinging shamefully to life. *"To live is a moral duty,"* her father had told her in Lodz, when a chunk of mold-covered bread the size of one's fist was something to fight over, when every morning clean-up crews found more and more wasted bodies in the streets. *"Every Jew knows that his only victory can be to survive."* So she had made it her business to survive, and had learned there was no victory in it. There was only remorse.

Afterwards Filatov had petted her and told her

about all the favors that would come to her now, all the gifts and privileges. They always did that. She waited, looking away, with all the apparent stupidity of an animal, trying not even to exist as she kept her rage and self-loathing buried deep within her. At last, when he had grown weary of her silence, he led her back to her barracks.

And now she was lying in an isolation cell, trying to keep warm, and Filatov was on the other side of the locked door. It was almost a relief.

But she had had a visitor today, for the first time in her four months at Mühlfeld. Why should anyone come to visit her here? So she was now an object of interest to more than just Filatov.

And then there had been that strange encounter in the recreation yard this morning, that woman with her hard, passionate face. That had been perhaps even a little more unexpected.

It was all very disquieting, and at the moment all Esther wanted was to be quiet. What only twenty-four hours before had seemed the most monotonously predictable, the most hopeless, the most solitary of existences was now crowded with unfamiliar voices speaking of the mysterious future. She was glad to be locked away. She was desperate for time to think.

The ceiling of her cell was nearly four meters high, and in the center there was a single light bulb in a metal cage. It flickered and made faint popping sounds, as if at any second it might die away and leave her in darkness. She was not frightened of the dark, but she hoped the light would stay on. It was too cold to sleep and soon it would be time for the evening meal. She was hungry, but she didn't want them to have to leave the door open so she could see to eat. She hoped

Filatov hadn't made some sort of arrangement with the guard on duty.

They had told her after the two o'clock roll call: "Someone has made an appointment to see you this afternoon." There were no details. She was told to go to the matron for a clean dress, and to wait.

At a few minutes after three, a guard came to the barracks to fetch her. He was someone she had never seen before, so perhaps his duties were restricted to the reception room—the Russians were great believers in specialization. He took her to a tiny room, no larger than a broom closet, and directed her to sit down on a wooden chair in front of a window that looked into another room and was covered with a heavy wire screen.

"You will not touch the wire," he told her, in German—possibly he wished her to understand from the outset that there were to be no private communications, that every word spoken would be noted. "You will leave your hands in your lap. If you attempt to touch the wire, the interview will be broken off at once and you will be severely punished."

And then they waited, she sitting in her chair and he standing beside the only door, in unbroken silence.

And then, in the other room, a door opened—at least, she heard the sound when it closed again—and a man in a green suit sat down in a chair on the opposite side of the screen.

It was difficult to see him through the wire, which was thick and so closely woven that even Esther's fingers could hardly have gone through the mesh, but he seemed a dapper little figure, pink and fleshy with thinning hair. He had a way of folding his hands together over his chest that somehow emphasized their softness, suggesting that he took an almost feminine pride in them. He smiled at her, his eyes glittering sympathetically.

"Fräulein Rosensaft?" he asked, allowing the tips of his fingers to press together. "Fräulein Esther Rosensaft, born in Königsberg in 1928? Your father was Julius Rosensaft, a civil engineer in that city?"

She was so astonished that for an instant she thought he must be talking about someone else. But, yes, that was her name—she had almost forgotten it. Finally she could bring herself to nod.

"Good. It would have been a pity to come all this way and find myself talking to the wrong young lady." The smile broadened slightly, as if to emphasize that he was making a small joke. He opened the briefcase he had been holding on his lap and took out a file folder crammed with papers that rustled noisily as he sorted through them.

"You seem to have gotten yourself into a certain amount of trouble, my dear. Still, no one is blaming you." He was careful not to glance up from the long, official-looking document he held clutched in his right hand. "I'm sure life hasn't been easy for you since the war, and your family is sparing no expense to procure your release."

"My—?"

It became impossible to finish the question. Her face grew hot, and for an instant she forgot herself enough to begin bringing her hands up to her mouth. And then she remembered the guard standing behind her and pushed them back down against her thighs. Those few seconds, staring through the wire barrier at this blandly smiling man, were an agony.

"Yes, my dear. But allow me to introduce myself.

My name is Gustav Plessen. I am an attorney in Heilbronn retained by your aunt, a Mrs. Erica Adler,
living at present in Trenton, New Jersey, in the United
States. She is your father's sister and is very anxious
to do what she can for you. We have filed a petition
for clemency with the military governor. We have
every hope."

"Is my aunt here? Is she—"

Esther shook her head; she could hardly see through
her tears.

"No." Plessen, the attorney from Heilbronn,
seemed to regard the question as a trifle foolish. He
cocked his head a little to one side, the way one does
when in conversation with an engaging child. "Your
aunt has young children and was thus unable to come.
She only heard you were alive a few months ago,
apparently from one of the Jewish agencies. I'm sure
you can appreciate her surprise when she subse-
quently learned that you were incarcerated."

He smiled again. He had established his client's
perfect right to remain with her family in Trenton,
New Jersey. He was obviously a man for whom the
world organized itself into conveniently intelligible
moral categories. It seemed clear that there were to
be no more troublesome questions. Esther could feel
her bowels shriveling with mortification.

"But we'll have you out soon enough, my dear.
The authorities are sympathetic. These things take
time and money, but I think another few weeks should
see you free of this place."

As the guard led her away, Esther Rosensaft, niece
of an American lady named Adler, kept wondering

why she couldn't seem to feel anything except dread. She was happy, of course—that she was happy she knew as an objective fact, the way she knew her age and the color of the linoleum in her barracks—but she couldn't seem to make that translate into something besides a cold, sickened sensation all through her neck and chest. It was as if she had received a warning and couldn't make out when or about what. There had simply been too much for one day—that was it. Her nerves had been stretched too tight, and now they were having their revenge. In a few hours she would be all right again.

She wondered what America could be like, and what part of it was Trenton, New Jersey. Right after the war, in the refugee camps, everyone had been dying to go to America. To have relatives willing to sponsor you was to belong to a kind of aristocracy. It meant that you were going to return, almost from one day to the next, to normal life, the way it had been before 1933.

Esther could hardly remember what "normal life" had been like. In 1933 she had been five years old. The world had been mad for as long as she could remember.

There had been three places everyone hoped to go—America, England, or Palestine. Hardly anyone had any hope of going anywhere, but the general consensus, unless you were a Zionist, was that America was best.

And now, it seemed, she had an aunt in America.

Every year at Passover dinner, her father would make the same toast: *"Next year, in Jerusalem."* Had he meant it? Perhaps, toward the end, when "next

year" had begun to seem as unreachable as the ful-
fillment of prophecy. It was a tradition and, after a
while, something of a dare. *"Next year, in Jerusalem."*

*"The secret government of Israel reaches out its
hand to you,"* the woman had said. *"You are a Jew.
We are Jews, working for a Jewish state. There is
nothing else."*

And she had meant it, standing there beside her
in the recreation yard, her burning eyes looking past
Esther toward some distant prospect only she could
see. She had been a Zionist, this one—Esther had
known a few others like her. They all believed in a
future.

Lately, because the weather had turned slightly
warmer, everyone who was regarded as medically fit
spent the hour between noon and one in the tiny
exercise yard that was enclosed by the prison building
on all four sides. The prisoners tramped around in
circles for twenty minutes, one line inside another,
moving in opposite directions, and then, for the re-
mainder of the time, they stood together in little groups,
talking quietly and trying to keep warm. The guards
watched nervously from the doorways, but they did
not interfere. Even Russians knew that there was
nothing to fear from the conspiracies of a crowd of
underfed women convicts.

People tended to cluster according to barracks assignments; the prison was wormy with informers and
everyone was frightened except among familiar faces.
As a Jew, an enemy of the state that had vanished,
Esther had few friends—the Viennese ladies, residents of Mühlfeld, had little enough reason to regret
the good old days of Nazi rule—and the constant at-
tentions of Filatov hadn't made her any more popular.

Almost everyone, probably, assumed she was a spy
for the guards. So it was something of a surprise,
almost a pleasure, when the tall woman with the heavy,
muscular arms and the zealot's eyes—a new prisoner,
since her fingernails still looked freshly cut and filed—
came to stand beside her, asked her when they were
likely to be let back indoors, and glared up into the
pale winter sun as if it were her mortal enemy. For
perhaps a minute they stood together like that, sharing the square meter or so of cobblestone between
them just like people who did not have to answer roll
calls six or seven times a day.

"I don't think there will be another opportunity,"
she said suddenly, turning her shoulder toward Esther, throwing her into shadow. She was close enough
that Esther could smell the carbolic soap in her newly
issued prison dress. "I think there is something you
ought to know."

She turned her left hand so that the little finger
was pressed against her thigh, exposing the inside of
her forearm. There, just under the elbow, in blue ink,
was tattooed a worn-looking five-digit number: 39789.
The hand closed into a fist.

"Auschwitz, class of 1943. Perhaps I look a little
strange to you? A little unfeminine? I have Doctor
Mengele to thank for that. He was experimenting with
hormones for his race of supermen. I haven't had a
period since my twenty-first birthday."

"I'm sorry," Esther said, the tears glistening in
her eyes. It all came back in that moment—Chelmno,
the deaths of her parents, Hagemann, everything. She
couldn't tell what she felt, whether pity or shame. She
didn't know what to say, except to repeat, "I'm sorry."

"Don't be sorry about me, Esther Rosensaft—my

business here isn't about me. And don't look so startled either. You can't tell if the guards might not be watching."

It took no more than a few seconds. Two or three slow, deep breaths and she was all right again. She glanced around, looking for Filatov, but he wasn't there. It was all right.

"What do you want with me?" she asked, surprised at the sound of her own voice. "Leave me alone. There's nothing I can do for you here."

"Which is why we are getting you out. This is no health spa—you think I checked in here just because I like prisons? You're leaving. Tonight."

"You're insane!" Esther began to edge away from the other woman, who took her arm, just above the wrist, in a grip that felt as if it might crush the bones. "Let go of me. You talk like that and you'll have both of us in trouble. What do you think, that people can just walk out of here?"

"Listen, you little guttersnipe. Haven't you heard of the Mossad? Yes, I rather thought so. Then pay attention. The day before yesterday I was in Istanbul. They flew me here so that yesterday morning I could buy a bowl of onion soup at the Kaffeehaus Franz Josef and spill it all over a Russian sergeant, telling him in the ensuing argument that, since all Russians were pigs anyway, he shouldn't even notice the difference. I'll probably get eighteen months for it, but who cares? When I come out, if everyone does their part, I'll have a country to come home to. Israel. You've heard of it. I may hardly be a woman anymore, but I'm still a Jew. They can't rob me of that. And so are you, whether you like it or not."

She had never let go of Esther's arm, and the

passionate murmur of her voice was almost hypnotic.
She made it sound—yes, almost believable.

"Why me?" she asked finally, shaking her head.
"It's not . . ."

"Why not you? I don't know the reasons. I was
told, 'Do this.' I do it—I don't ask questions. I don't
know why they want you, but they do. So here I am,
and tonight you will be going out."

"You came *here*? You consented to it? Here?"

"Yes, why not?" The woman actually smiled, but
even that seemed a kind of defiance. "After what you
and I have been through, what difference can it make?
If I can't be in Israel, why should I care where I am?
And I can't be in Israel, at least not until after we've
gained our independence. Two weeks ago some of us
blew up a police station, and I was recognized. This,
I expect, will be almost restful."

A guard standing at the entrance to the western
cell blocks glanced at his watch. There probably weren't
more than two or three minutes left before they would
all be herded inside and this opportunity would be
lost forever. Esther could feel the blood throbbing in
her neck. It was as if a hand were trying to squeeze
the windpipe shut.

"How will you get me out?"

"There is a capsule," the woman said calmly. She
seemed almost bored. "Dinner last night was at six
o'clock—take it with dinner tonight. The timing is
important. Shortly after midnight you will become
very sick, so sick you and everyone else will think you
must be dying, but don't worry. Just let things take
their natural course. By tomorrow morning you'll be
out of this place. You'll probably be having buttered
toast and coffee in the American Zone."

"A capsule? How did you get it inside? They strip-search all the new prisoners."

"You are young, aren't you. Tell me, when you were brought in did they bother to check the inside of your mouth? I didn't think so. It was fastened to the gums behind my lower set of front teeth with a dab of flesh-colored putty. Nothing could have been easier."

The guard carried a whistle to his mouth and blew it. The hour was over. Everyone began shuffling toward the doors, to get inside where it would be warm. In this cold, if they lingered even a few more seconds she would attract attention.

"Where is it? Give it to me, quick!" Esther whispered fiercely.

The woman was already turning away. And then, for just an instant, she looked back, smiling contemptuously.

"When you have a few seconds alone," she said, "you might look in your dress pocket."

Lying on her plank bed in the flickering light, she reached into her pocket for perhaps the tenth time to make certain it was still there. It was a flat little pill about the size of a drop of water.

"You will become very sick, so sick you will think you must be dying." It had, of course, occurred to her that should she take it she might really die. Perhaps someone was trying to poison her—how could she possibly know? Of course, there was no reason why anyone should wish her dead, but there was also no reason why anyone should go to so much trouble to help her escape from Mühlfeld. It was necessary, for

the moment, to leave the whole question of motives aside.

Of course, her aunt in America . . .

The lawyer had said all she needed to do was to remain patient. He was petitioning the military governor and, as everyone knew, Russian clemency was as much a commodity to be bought and sold as cheese. If her aunt was rich enough . . . And the Americans were all supposed to be fabulously rich.

It was almost too good to believe. In Trenton, New Jersey, she could begin life all over again. Perhaps her aunt would pay for a surgeon to remove the number from her arm—no one would ever have to know that she had been in the camps. She would take the past, everything that had been done to her and everything that she had done, and bury it all somewhere deep inside her, where it would never find its way out again. Perhaps she could even get married someday. Why not? If she herself could start believing she was once again a nice girl—not the sort of girl who lets herself be used by soldiers because she wants to be sure she will be alive and have something to eat when it's over— then perhaps some man might. She could . . .

"Is my aunt here?"

"No. Your aunt has young children."

It really was too good to believe.

Julius Rosensaft had been the only child born to Immanuel Rosensaft and his second wife, Sophie, née Charmi. There had been an earlier marriage, producing two daughters. Anything could have happened to them; one of them might even have survived to have a husband in Trenton, New Jersey.

But Esther's father, had he lived, would have been

forty-seven years old, and the youngest of his half-sisters would still have been ten years older. Even in Trenton, New Jersey, it was a rare woman who, leaning hard on sixty, had children young enough to keep her at home. The attorney Plessen had made an error. There was no aunt in America, no infant cousins. He had made the lie just a shade too elaborate.

And this man had been no Zionist missionary, trying to save her from going mad in a prison cell. If she left Mühlfeld in his custody, she realized at once, with a clarity that astonished her, no one would ever hear from her again.

As she lay there, listening to the light bulb click, her eyes misted over and she felt curiously lethargic. She wanted to stay where she was, forever and ever. At least here, at Mühlfeld, no one was trying to kill her. She was safe, if for no other reason than because to be here was to be dead already.

"Oh, God," she whispered, hardly even forming the words with her lips. "Oh, God, will I really have to stay here forever?"

And then a voice inside her answered, *No. Take the capsule.*

Why not? It was a chance—she had no right to ask for more than that. By morning she would be either free or dead. At that moment it hardly seemed to make any difference which. She would take the risk that that strange, distorted woman had been telling her the truth.

By the time the guard unlocked the door and brought in her tiny tin tray with a piece of gray bread and a bowl of thin, dust-colored soup, she had regained her composure and was sitting up. It was all very simple once one had made up one's mind. After that, everything was easy.

"Citizen guard," she asked, making her voice softly timorous—she was begging a great favor and wanted him to know it. "Citizen guard, could you please tell me the time?"

"Why? You afraid you might be late for an important appointment? Hah, hah, hah!" He was a big man, in his middle forties, his crinkly hair turning white at the edges, and his laughter made the cell vibrate like the inside of a drum.

"Please, citizen guard, I only want to know because—"

"Be quiet, girl," he answered, with a casual wave of his enormous hand. "I don't care why you want to know. The time isn't a state secret. It's five minutes after six."

"Thank you, citizen guard."

After the door slammed shut behind him, she waited another minute, counting off the seconds to herself—it was perhaps the longest minute of her life. And then, with a deft movement, she tore the soft center out of her piece of bread, wrapped it around the capsule, and swallowed it. She drank off the soup as fast as she could, before she lost her nerve. It tasted faintly of iodine.

In six hours it would begin to work. In seven, or perhaps eight, she would know the worst. She lay down again on the plank bed to await her deliverance.

9

It was dark, everywhere dark. No sound except the guns, miles away, murmuring like sullen old women. But they would come closer. By first light, certainly by seven or eight tomorrow morning, the Russians would come—that was what Hagemann had said. All the morning she had crouched in her room, behind the locked door, listening to the crackle of machine guns. They were liquidating the prisoners in the other camp, in batches from the sound of it. It seemed to take forever. And then, of course, Hagemann would come back, unlock the door, and shoot her too. The Germans were making preparations for their retreat, and they intended to leave no witnesses.

But Hagemann had never come back. Trucks had driven up and down along the gravel roads, and now and then there had been another short burst of rifle fire, and then silence. Esther waited a long time—hours, it seemed—and then tried to break open the door. There was no window, only the door, and she couldn't . . .

It was too strong. She was trapped inside.

Her shoulder ached from throwing herself against the door, and she had skinned her hands on the rough wood. She sat down on the edge of the iron bedstead, thinking she was about to cry, but she didn't cry. All she could remember was that soon it would be over— either the Russians would burn down the camp, and she would die inside this room, or they would find her and kill her as a collaborator, or they would set her free. One way or the other, it would all be finished in a few hours.

She had no idea of how long she had been sitting there when suddenly there was the sound of boot heels on the floor outside.

The Russians? It couldn't be the Russians, not so soon. Esther could still hear their guns firing in the distance, louder now but still far away. The Russians were still far off.

It was Hagemann. He had remembered and was coming back to kill her. It would be like him to leave it to the last, to let her begin almost to believe that he was gone forever and then to come back so he could make a slow job of her death.

He would cut her throat—he had threatened to often enough. He would grab her by the hair, pull back her head, and push the point of the knife across from one side to the other, taking his time. He would want to enjoy himself.

She tried not to make a sound, to pretend she didn't exist. It was no good thinking she could fight him off—she had never been able to resist him. She had always been too frightened of him for that. And now the doorknob rattled, and the key turned in the lock with a snap . . .

"Esther, I'm surprised to find you here. Didn't he take you with him?"

It was not Hagemann. It was the General.

He was carrying a gas lantern that threw a thick, yellowish halo of light across the floor and made his pink, heavy, utterly familiar face look cavernous and deathlike. He set the lantern down on a table and pulled up its shade, flooding the room with light.

"I didn't want to give the Russian spotters something to shoot at," he said. "They're only about six hours away. I was just having a final look around before I left."

"Is . . . Is Hagemann—?"

"No. No, my dear." The General shook his head sadly, as if he were beginning to realize that the joke was on him. "They've all gone, some time ago. You and I, I'm afraid, are the only ones still here. Come along—I expect you must be hungry."

It was a cool April night as they walked through the deserted camp. In the east, the horizon was a burning red. The flashes from the Russian artillery provided almost the only light, throwing the guard towers and garrison buildings into sudden relief against the flaming night sky. The General carried his lantern and moved with long strides, hardly seeming to notice.

Finally they came to the officers' mess. Esther found some bread and a plate of cold ham, and they sat down at one of the large tables.

"We'll leave in a few minutes," he said. He wasn't eating. He didn't seem to be hungry. "The British have reached the Elbe, so we'll head for them. You'll come with me, Esther. I don't like to think what the Russians would do with a pretty child like you."

"And what of you, *Herr General?*"

"Me?" The question seemed genuinely to surprise him. "I should, on the whole, prefer to be hanged by the British rather than by the Russians, but that aside, it makes remarkably little difference. I'm afraid I have been a very wicked man, my dear. I'm on the lists, so certainly they will hang me."

He closed his eyes for a moment, as if dying already in imagination.

"You are wondering, perhaps, why I don't simply shoot myself? It is a fair question. I am a Catholic. I should like to die in a state of grace."

There had been over fifteen hundred prisoners at the Waldenburg camp. They were all dead now, shot on the General's orders, and their bodies lay not two hundred meters from where the General was commenting on the state of his soul. Esther put down her sandwich—she too had lost her appetite.

"But don't be too scornful of me, Esther dear. One's duty sometimes takes strange forms."

"You are a butcher. I heard the firing squads this afternoon—you murdered all of them." She could hardly believe that she was saying such a thing. It was like asking to be killed.

"Yes, my dear, I did." He made a gesture with his gloved hand, a vague pass through the air as if wiping something away. "But I haven't had you killed."

"You gave me to Hagemann."

For an instant he looked as if she had struck him— yes, the accusation had gone home. And then, just as quickly, he recovered himself and smiled.

"I did do that. But you see, my dear, he needed distracting. It gave him something else to think about while I . . . I suppose you are alive now only because in the confusion he forgot your existence, and now you will live, the only witness, because of my caprice. I'm sorry about Hagemann, Esther, but that's not why I've saved you. You see, I discover I have a use for you."

Half an hour later they left in the General's car— his driver, apparently, had fled with the others. Esther sat on the front seat, the case containing the General's violin resting on her lap. "I will spend my remaining days of freedom practicing the Mendelssohn F Minor," he had said, "now that it will no longer be proscribed."

They didn't dare use the headlights, but there was a moon and the night sky was like glass. She didn't want to look at anything anyway; her arm burned where he had tattooed on the number.

They had had to go over to the prisoners' side of the camp to find the instruments, and she had seen the open parade ground where fifteen hundred corpses were stacked together like cordwood. She had heard the shooting. She had known all afternoon what they were doing, and she still couldn't believe it. All those men, some of them still bleeding through the bullet holes in the backs of their necks. The General hadn't even glanced at them.

"It is your authentication," he had said. "This way, no one will ever be able to say you were anything here except a prisoner. I will drop you off at Bamburg—when the war is over, you will be well inside the American occupation zone. I myself plan to go on to Ulm. My mother lives in Ulm, and it is as good a place as any. It will be interesting to see how long the Allies take to arrest me."

What had he been talking about? The words had buzzed in her head like flies, just an empty noise. She didn't understand anything anymore. She had imagined she understood, but she had been mistaken. It was impossible, even indecent. There were no reasons. There was only death—and the terrible emptiness of the living.

And why had he branded her? He had the number on a slip of paper—he had taken it from his wallet, even as they sat in the officers' mess, staring at each other over their broken meal. This had been no inspiration of the moment.

She could wonder, but she found it impossible to care.

"I was very fond of you, Esther. You must always remember that." As the car lurched over the pockmarked road, unrepaired since the winter because there hadn't been time for anything except the suspense of fear, he spoke as if he were already dead. "I saved you from the gas chambers and kept you alive. Think of me with some kindness, since I don't imagine this chapter of your life will ever quite close."

They had hardly escaped the perimeter of the camp when the first artillery shell exploded behind them. The sound was like nothing she could have imagined. The air seemed dyed red with noise. And then the cold, numbing silence afterward . . .

Have I been hit? she wondered. *This pain in my belly—I think . . .*

Oh, God, she would die. Now she would. Now . . .

She opened her eyes with a start. It was like catching herself in a fall, only she hadn't been falling. There was no cannon fire now, only blackness. Where was the—? Gone—dead for years now. Even in the darkness, the prison walls closed around her. She had been dreaming.

And then the pain came again, shooting straight through like a ragged piece of metal. That was real.

She rolled over on the plank bed—why had they switched off the light?—and found its edge with the palm of her hand. She wanted to get up, to reach the door, to cry out that she needed help. If she could just . . .

When it came again—like something twisting, cutting at her bowels—she screamed. It made the pain worse, but she couldn't help herself. The scream came of its own accord, pushing the sharp point in deeper. It wore her out so that she couldn't breathe; she tried, but it was agony. The pain came in surges now, tearing at her. She screamed again, but there was no air.

When the door opened, all she could think about was how the light hurt, how it seemed to be part of the pain. Someone was kneeling beside her, speaking to her, but she couldn't hear the words.

How had she gotten onto the floor? She couldn't remember.

"Fräulein. Fräulein . . ." It was the guard, the one who had brought her supper. The voice faded away sometimes. He tried to roll her over onto her back, but she clutched at her legs, keeping herself wrapped up in a ball. Each time he touched her she thought she would die of the pain.

Finally the door closed again. She was alone for a long time in the cool darkness. As long as she was alone she found she could just bear it.

It was only then, as she lay on the cold cement floor—she wished the cold would go right through her; she wanted it to turn her to ice—that she remembered the capsule. They were killing her, and she had helped them. She would be dead now, just like General von Goltz, and it was all right because she had lived a pointless, worthless life. She should have died at Chelmno, to be turned into ashes that could shame no one. She had been dead since that day when she had lifted her eyes and smiled at the German officer, hoping he would save her. She hoped it really was the Jews who were killing her now. They had a right to their revenge. The bodies, stacked so neatly at Waldenburg . . .

Slowly, gradually, she began to straighten her legs. If she took her time, the pain wasn't too bad. It wasn't any worse when she lay on her back, if she kept her knees up. Her belly felt tight and angry and she held it gently between her hands, pushing in at the sides.

And then it went through her again, the stabbing pain. She held her breath, waiting for it to pass off, fighting hard not to scream again. She felt sick with pain—oh, God, if she became sick; she felt it would split her apart.

When the door opened again, Esther put her hand over her eyes to keep out the light. She heard voices—there were two of them now.

The nurse—yes, the nurse. She could tell from the smell of carbolic soap. She had heard terrible things about the nurse. Hard, blunt fingers probed at her belly and now she couldn't help herself, but her voice was only a thin wail.

Everything that happened after that was vague, shadowy, like the flicker of pale light. People took her by the arms and legs and lifted her up, but they weren't real people. Only pain was real and it filled her, as if her skin were only a membrane to hold it. Once she opened her eyes and saw Filatov—always Filatov, even now he wouldn't leave her be—his face only a few inches from her own. He looked demonic, like a monster in a dream, as if even now he would have liked to . . . As if he enjoyed this, even more.

And then everything was quiet. She was lying on a stretcher and they were outside—she could feel the cold night air, a little trembling breeze against her bare arms. She felt better. She couldn't move, but the pain was almost gone and there was only a terrible weakness. They were on a loading dock; people were standing around, the nurse and Filatov and another guard, as if they were waiting for something.

Filatov and the other guard were speaking in low voices. She couldn't understand what they were saying; she only knew a little prison Russian. Filatov nodded. The thing seemed to be settled.

Was she going to be all right now? As if the same question had occurred to her, the nurse came over, slipped a hand under the blanket, and pressed her fingers against Esther's belly, just a little below and to one side of the navel.

God, there it was again! She couldn't scream. She tried, but she could only cough. And the coughing made it worse, like fingers, like the nurse's thick fingers, tearing her open to see what was inside.

They left her alone until the ambulance came.

The man who came out through the rear doors was wearing a white hospital jacket—she was going to the hospital? Yes, of course, why hadn't she guessed, except that her mind wouldn't work beyond the immediate present. He was very thin, and his wrists came a long way out of his sleeves. His face looked as if it had been cut from wood with a sharp knife, all lines and edges. She saw it all, everything, with astonishing clarity. It all seemed to be happening to someone else.

The stretcher had short wooden legs. There was a metal ring bolted to the one nearest Esther's left foot, and Filatov was busy threading a chain through it which he cuffed on her leg just above the ankle. When he had finished, he dropped the key into his pocket, grinning at her, showing his teeth. You will find anywhere we take you is a prison, he seemed to be saying, and I am the guard.

There were negotiations going on, all in Russian. It seemed that the nurse thought she should come along too, but she was only a civilian and was therefore in no position to insist. The man in the white hospital jacket kept shaking his head, and neither of the guards seemed to care.

All Esther could do was to lie quiet, trying not to take a deep breath. Her pain left her no time to think, or even to feel afraid. It occupied her attention completely, becoming the frame of reference for everything else. She dreaded the moment when they would begin to carry her to the ambulance because the slightest movement would make the pain move too, stabbing into her, twisting. *Let them keep talking*, she thought; *let me lie still here.*

She was afraid of the nurse and of Filatov. They might touch her. They might do anything. She watched them, waiting, dreading.

Finally the man in the white jacket took the upper end of the stretcher, letting Filatov take the foot, and they began the slow, careful process of moving her. They lifted her up, trying to keep her level, and then

the attendant backed her through the open doors of
his ambulance. They set her down, fixing the legs into
slots, and Filatov jumped inside and closed the doors.
It seemed a long time before they began to move.

The inside of the cabin was cramped; no one, not
even Esther, who was small, could have stood up.
Filatov sat crowded into a rear corner, bracing himself
against the walls with his arms, watching with evident
suspicion as the attendant, who was kneeling beside
the stretcher, sorted through the contents of a small,
flat black bag no larger than a woman's purse. Perhaps
he simply didn't like leaving the security of Mühlfeld
Prison.

"You mustn't be frightened," the attendant said,
in German. It was not very good German. Esther
realized with a slight shock that the man could not
possibly be an Austrian, but she was unable to carry
the idea any further because the ambulance's side-to-
side movement as they made their slow progress over
the cobblestones of the prison courtyard was a tor-
ment. She opened her mouth, but it was only to moisten her lips with the tip of her tongue.

"I'm going to give you an injection. In a few minutes, you will feel much better."

He had a nice face, with kind eyes. The eyes of a
married man who still loves his wife, Esther thought.
She wanted, more than anything, to believe in this
man's kindness.

The man with the kind eyes brought a hypodermic
needle out of his bag. It had been prepared in advance—the tip was buried in a ball of cotton about
the size of a cherry. It was very large; she couldn't
remember ever having seen a needle so long. The
liquid inside the glass shaft was a smoky yellow. He

tied a piece of rubber tubing around the upper part
of her arm and dug the needle into a vein on the
inside of her elbow. She could feel something coursing
up her arm, cold and burning at the same moment.
It reached her armpit and then poured into her body.
It made the inside of her mouth feel pasty and dry,
but the pain was beginning, very slowly, to die away.

Filatov didn't like it. He shouted something in
Russian, loud enough in that narrow space to be ac-
tively painful, and made a gesture with his arm as if
warning the attendant away from her. Even though
he was sitting behind her, Esther could still see the
arc his hand made through the air. They were all close
enough to touch each other.

"Calm down, you bastard," the attendant murmured, again in the German which he must have
guessed Filatov would not understand. He took a
handkerchief from his pocket and wiped the haze from
the ambulance's rear window, peering outside. "We
haven't reached Tabor Strasse yet."

What was he talking about? As her mind cleared,
Esther began to remember about the rescue—that
was why she was so sick, wasn't it? *"Just let things
take their natural course,"* the woman with the burning eyes had said. *"By tomorrow morning you'll be
out of this place."* All right, Esther would stick by her
bargain. She would simply lie back and let everything
happen. After all, she was outside the prison walls,
wasn't she? She didn't care what the man with the
kind eyes meant, if he meant anything.

The ambulance turned a corner—she could feel
the swaying of her own body, and Filatov pressed the
tips of his fingers against the wall just above her head
to balance himself. The attendant pushed himself back

from the rear window and Esther saw his hand slide guiltily into the pocket of his coat. He twisted around a few degrees, looking back over his left shoulder at Filatov. It was impossible to read his face.

"Eedeletyeh syoodah," he said, looking at Filatov. His hand came out of his pocket, but there didn't seem to be anything in it. *"Skawruh!"*

Filatov's eyes widened, as if he felt he wasn't being shown proper respect. For an instant he didn't seem to know what he should do—he might have been getting ready to say something—but then he began to rise up to a half crouch. He was frowning; he seemed to feel it was all a great imposition. But the fool was still too completely wrapped up in his prison guard's sense of invulnerability even to begin to be afraid.

Didn't he see? Wasn't it obvious? Esther could almost smell the menace in that tiny enclosure. It was like a fourth person in the compartment with them, sitting there between the two men, turning his eyes from one to the other, smiling like an idiot.

The attendant reached out and took Filatov by the lapel of his heavy double-breasted overcoat, as if to help him up. The right hand went back a few inches and, yes, there was something in it. With an ugly snap, like the sound of a hammer glancing off rock, a bright tapering blade, only a little longer than a man's finger, shot out from the attendant's clenched fist. Filatov seemed to fall forward to meet the thrust, and the blade disappeared into his chest, cutting through the overcoat just inside the left-hand row of shiny metal buttons.

It was over in a moment. The attendant pulled his knife free and stabbed again, in almost the same spot, but he was only making sure. Filatov stared at him helplessly, his arms hanging limp. He seemed not so much surprised as ashamed and a little insulted—he hadn't expected anything like this. He must have died in that instant, his lips seeming to form some sound of reproach.

He sank down to his knees and then collapsed forward, brushing the attendant's shoulder as he fell. The expression on his face never changed. He lay there, his head just to one side; he seemed to be staring at her. Even now, even in death . . . Suddenly Esther felt she was about to scream.

But the attendant clamped his hand over her mouth. There was blood on his fingers; she could smell it. She began to struggle, trying to push his arms away from her, when all at once she realized what she was doing and that the pain was gone. She wouldn't scream now. She would be very calm.

"Are you all right now?" he said to her, holding her hands together above her lap. "No—don't look at him. Are you all right?"

She nodded slowly, trying to remember when she had sat up, wondering if it was true. Yes, she seemed to be fine. No, she wouldn't look at Filatov. Why did she feel sorry for him? She didn't know.

"We'll stop in a minute. When we do, I'll open the back of the ambulance and help you down. Then I'm going to point a direction, and you're going to run. Run as if your life depends on it, because it does."

He let go of her hands—tentatively, surprised perhaps when she didn't fall over—and then he looked at her feet and his eyes tightened.

"You can't run anywhere in those. Kick them off."

Her wooden clogs fell to the floor, one, two, and

then she remembered the chain around her leg. It pulled tight with a rattle.

"We'll get you out of that," he said, and his hand disappeared into Filatov's overcoat pocket. In a second the chain was coiled up on the stretcher like a snake.

"That stuff I gave you won't last forever. You'll have about five more minutes before it quits on you. Get as far away as you can."

As he spoke, the ambulance glided to a stop. He picked Filatov up by the lapels and dumped him back away from the doors, face down. And then he pushed open the doors and everything turned dark, cold, and silent. Before she knew she had done it, she was down and standing beside him in the street. There was no traffic—why had she expected there would be? The pavement felt wet under her bare feet.

"Are you one of the Jews?" she asked. It sounded such a stupid way to phrase it.

"No questions now. You see that?"

He raised his arm and pointed to what looked like a vast emptiness. It took a second or two before she realized it was a park and the blackness was threaded through with the trunks of leafless trees. There was nothing else there, just an empty park in the middle of the cold night.

"Yes."

"Good, then run. Run!"

She didn't wait, she ran. Across the pavement and into the darkness, feeling the air sweeping around her legs, not caring about anything except that she was free. She was really free! If she died in the next moment, it would have been worth it. Nothing could hold her. She ran as fast as she could, her foot splashing into a puddle of water she hadn't seen, free as air.

And then she stopped—she didn't know why. Perhaps she had heard something. She looked back over her shoulder; she saw the ambulance.

And then, an instant later, it wasn't there. It was gone, lost inside a smear of smoky orange light. A flash like the end of everything. Nothing moved.

Her chest tightened as she braced against the concussion, but there was no shock. The air seemed to die around her. It was the sound, the angry, strangely hollow rumble that did it. She felt the hem of her dress whipping around her legs, and her own scream was lost in the roar of the explosion.

Waldenburg. That last night, with the Russian artillery banging around them. It was back. They . . .

This time there was no joy in her flight. Her lungs ached with panic as she ran into the darkness. She saw the line of trees in front of her, crooked silver lines cutting through the black, and they filled her mind. Escape—she couldn't even think it. There were no words, there was only the jolt of her feet striking the ground and the inferno behind her.

As she passed, the naked branch of a tree cut at her face. She knew it had happened, knew precisely what it was, but felt nothing. There was no room.

And suddenly she stopped—or something had stopped her. Her legs gave way beneath her, she could feel the thing that had hit her all along her chest, but she didn't fall. She hung there suspended. It wouldn't let her fall.

It was an arm. She could feel the fingers clutching at her rib cage, digging into the flesh. A great black arm.

A gloved hand came around and clamped over her mouth, and she twisted her head to see. His face was almost white in the moonlight, and his eyes glittered hard and blue. He was huge—she kicked her legs and found she wasn't even touching the ground. He picked her up as if she were no more than a child's doll. He didn't speak at first; his face was like a cruel mask.

"Quiet," he said. "Not a word."

There was nothing left. Fear had pushed out everything else. She couldn't even try to fight him. She let the cold darkness close in on her brain.

✠ *10* ✠

Vienna, Austria: March 5, 1948

It was daylight. Motes of dust floated on the sunshine that came slanting in through the curtained window. There was a carpet on the floor, with spots where the pattern had been almost worn away, and the air carried the smells of cigarette smoke and cooking. Esther was lying in a bed. It had sheets and a down comforter and she felt buried in it.

She turned her head a few degrees and counted the people in the room. There were two of them: a woman, sitting on the edge of the bed, cradling a coffee cup in her hands—Esther could feel the pressure of her body pulling on the blankets—and a man. The man was standing in the doorway. His arms were crossed over his chest and he looked ángry. He was the same man who had caught her running through the trees.

"You want something to drink, *Liebling?*" the woman asked, putting a hand behind Esther's head and bringing the cup to her lips. "You had us worried there for a few hours."

Esther drank the coffee, which had grown quite cold, and tried to remember. There wasn't much, just a few vague impressions—the inside of a car, part of a stairway, almost nothing else. She remembered being carried some of the way, and telling herself not to struggle, that to struggle was to invite death. She looked at the man in the doorway again and, curiously, discovered that she was no longer afraid of him, not the way she had been afraid of Filatov. He was not vicious. She just knew that; she couldn't have said how. The coffee made her feel better. It cleared her mind, and she no longer felt so strangled.

The woman took the cup away and set it on a small table beside the bed. Esther had the impression she had seen her somewhere before. The woman smiled, as if she could read her thoughts.

"I saw you a couple of times in the yard," she said. "You were Filatov's little bird, somebody told me. I'll bet right now he's—"

"He's dead."

Esther's voice sounded raspy with disuse. She was surprised it worked at all.

"I'm glad to hear it. He'll be no loss to the world."

"Why don't you take a walk, Sonya. See if we've attracted any police."

The man's voice was deep and quiet and gave the impression he meant to have his way. He uncrossed his arms and buried his hands in the pockets of an old pair of blue wool trousers. He was waiting.

Sonya, who was so kind and who knew all about the life inside Mühlfeld, rose from the bed without turning to look behind her. Her expression, as she glanced down at Esther, seemed to counsel submission: *Learn from my example to do as he says, and everything will turn out all right. We both know what men are like.*

When she was gone, and what sounded heavy enough to be an outside door had slammed shut behind her, the man who meant to have his way pulled a tiny wooden chair up to the side of the bed and sat down. For a long moment he was silent as he studied her face. It never seemed to occur to him that she might be just as curious.

There had been a Ukrainian guard at Chelmno whom everyone called "Goliath"—he stood out in Esther's memory as the biggest man she had ever seen. This man must have been just as big, perhaps even a shade taller, but strong and graceful-looking where Goliath had been merely heavy with huge, clumsy lumps of muscle. This man seemed all chest and shoulders inside his white shirt, and his enormous hands, one of which was covered across the back with a flat scar, were almost beautiful.

He was handsome in a brutal sort of way, but the brutality seemed to be more something that life had done to him than part of his own nature. It was a strong face—that was the word that kept coming into her mind as she looked at him. His hair was golden and a little too long, as if he had forgotten for some time to have it cut, and his cold blue eyes were at once fierce and quiet. His face was like a mask behind which he was waiting for the treachery of strangers.

It occurred to Esther that this was the first time in many years she had been alone with a man inside

the four walls of a room and did not feel herself to be
in danger. It was as if he belonged to some different
order of creation and had never learned to . . .

"You had a visitor yesterday," he said suddenly,
in a voice that suggested nothing. "A lawyer named
'Plessen.' What did you have to say to each other?"

Perhaps he didn't mean to, but he made it sound
as if he were accusing her of something. But of course
the attorney Plessen had told lies, and perhaps not to
her alone.

"He said he was from my aunt in America—Trenton, New Jersey. He said he was appealing my case
to the military governor."

"He was not from your aunt. He was from Egon
Hagemann."

At first all she felt was the surprise—just a kind
of stunned sensation, passionless, crowding out everything else like the noiseless white flash of an explosion.
For an instant she couldn't even grasp why she was
so astonished. Even the name, at first, seemed connected to nothing.

And then this cooled into fear and then, that almost
forgotten emotion, shame.

Yes, of course he was accusing her of something.
She could feel her face going hot with shame as she
realized that he must know all about Hagemann, all
about the things that had happened at Waldenburg.
She could see it in his eyes that were so careful to
remain impassive as they searched her face. Of course
he knew. Who could help knowing about Esther Rosensaft, the little whore who had stayed alive by letting the officers and men of the Waffen-SS do whatever
they liked with her?

"I didn't know. I didn't . . ."

"Did he ask you anything? More important, did you tell him anything?"

"No—I mean, yes." Her voice was thickening and she felt an almost irresistible urge to begin sobbing. Why did this man, this particular man, have to know about Waldenburg? "I mean, what was there to tell him? He wanted to be sure I was the right Esther Rosensaft. There was a guard standing behind me the whole time. What could he have asked me?"

"That's a good question."

He rose from the chair—he just seemed to go up and up—and stepped over to the window and glanced outside, as if he were expecting someone. The sun caught the planes of his face so that the cheekbones seemed to gleam.

"I'm told Hagemann was pretty fond of you," he said finally, not moving from the window. He seemed to be looking at nothing. "Is that why he wanted to get you out of Mühlfeld?"

"Colonel Hagemann used to tell me about his other women—the ones he'd had in Russia and Poland before it became my turn. He liked to . . . They all died."

She sat up in bed and let her legs swing over the edge until she could touch the floor. It was something of an experiment; she would be glad to find she could get up. She didn't want to talk to this man about these things while lying back against a feather pillow.

"He was going to kill me. He told me often enough—we would have little 'rehearsals,' except that I never knew if . . . I'm sure I would be dead now if the General had not intervened. No—" She shook her head bitterly, wishing she could find a way for once to hurt a man back. "I don't imagine Colonel Hagemann would rescue me from prison for sentimental reasons."

She would not cry. She had been through far worse moments than this, and she was weary of always giving men the satisfaction of their little victories over her, as if the only pleasure life held for them was to humiliate Esther Rosensaft. She would not cry.

And when she was quite satisfied that she would not, she looked up and saw that this man was once again studying the view through the room's only window. He hadn't been watching. He had afforded her a moment of decent privacy, just as if she had a right to it. It was like a revelation.

"What do you mean when you say the General 'intervened'? Do you mean von Goltz?"

"Yes, von Goltz—General von Goltz. He was not as bad as Hagemann."

"He gave the orders." He was looking at her now, and the muscles in his jaw were visible under the skin.

"Did you know him?"

"I arrested him. I watched him hang."

His blue eyes were no longer so cold now. Now they seemed to want to burn through her, as if he had hated her all his life.

"I—he saved me. Twice. What you say is true, but he is dead now and I have no right to kill him all over again."

"You were his mistress."

"Yes. I had no choice about that either, except between that and death."

She looked into his face, his hard, implacable face, and felt a strange kind of grief, as if this were the first time she had been brought to see everything she had

forfeited by allowing herself to be taken out of that
winding column of the condemned at Chelmno. He
was no one to her, but she had lost him—that day,
now. She had traded her decency for her life, and
now she felt sick with remorse.

"I'm sorry—I wasn't there, so I have no business
passing judgment on you. Probably no one does."

"Are you one of the Jews?" she asked. Suddenly
it seemed the most important question in the world.

"No."

Esther had just finished her bath and was drying
herself with a large white towel—it was one of the
most voluptuous experiences of her life—when a clock
tower that must have been several blocks away struck
twelve. She could only just hear it. It made a little
puffing sound, like someone hitting the soft earth with
his fist.

When she came back out into the bedroom, she
found that Sonya had brought her some clean underwear and was sitting on the chair, doing her nails with
a file.

"You want to borrow it later?" she asked, flour-
ishing the thing in the air. "Inar brought it to me
yesterday from the International Zone. It's such a fight
to put oneself back in order after a stretch in jail. I
still haven't got the smell of that prison soap out of
my skin."

"Inar?"

Sonya held the nail file level about a foot above
her head and scowled to indicate whom she meant.
It was enough—Esther nodded and murmured a little
assenting sound.

"And, no, he's not my boyfriend, so you don't have

to look so miserable. He was just being considerate. He's actually a very kind man, although you'd never believe it to look at him." Sonya laughed as she blew on the nail of her little finger. "Don't worry, he'll get around to you when he's had a chance to relax a little. I'd give another five months in Mühlfeld—well, at least another three—if he'd show half as much interest in me."

"He wants me for something else. He doesn't even know I'm alive, not in that way."

"Oh yes he does."

Esther couldn't have brought herself to make a reply. She had imagined the capacity for simple embarrassment, that mingling of confusion and something almost like pleasure, was a thing that had died in her a long time ago, but it seemed not.

"You just give him a little time to breathe," Sonya went on, her attention complacently absorbed with the details of her manicure. "He doesn't think there's enough of him left for all that now, but he's as human as any other man. I saw the way he sat watching by your bed last night, looking down at you as if into a mirror. Maybe he doesn't know it yet, but it wasn't all just revenge or politics or whatever in hell he thinks he wants. There was something else too. But take my advice and let him figure it out for himself before you set the hook in him."

"I'm sorry." It was all that Esther could think to say. "I didn't mean . . ." She sat down on the edge of the bed and picked up a piece of the clean underwear, looking at it as if she had never seen its like before. She let it slide over her fingers and into her lap.

Sonya seemed to think she was being very comical.

"Don't worry about it," she said, trying not to smile too widely. "He's not really my type. Not that I'd turn him down—I wouldn't say no to having those hands sliding up my dress one time. But you could say he doesn't fit into my plans. I want a man who's close to forty and about ten pounds overweight, a man who makes a salary and likes to garden. If he's been married before and has a couple of children, that would be another point in his favor—I'm not sure I'm still young enough to have any children of my own. I've got to look out for my retirement. I'm too old to have time for white knights like Inar."

The hardest part was maneuvering the casket down the stairwell. Christiansen had carried it up on his back, but there hadn't been a body in it then.

"You're going to be Sonya's mother, all packed up for burial in the family plot in Konstanz. I have the death certificate, the export license, even a receipt from the cemetery for a down payment on the grave site. If they've been told to look out for a woman, they'll have Sonya to look at."

Esther had taken it all in, saying nothing, solemnly working away at the carton of ice cream he had brought her—she needed a little spoiling after four months in the slammer, and the poor little chit looked like she could also use the calories. Her eyes were large and full of misgivings.

"What if they want to look inside?" she asked finally, pointing with her spoon at the black wooden casket that lay on the hearth rug like a corpse in its own right.

"You'll be made up to look old—I have a rubber mask and coverings to make your neck and the backs of your hands convincingly withered. You'll be deep asleep, so deep they won't even be able to see you breathing. We're going through the checkpoint at night, so they'll only have klieg lights. Everyone looks dead under klieg lights. You'll make a very plausible cadaver."

He tried to smile, probably without much success. She was right to think it was a screwy idea—more right than she could ever imagine.

"Will they be looking for me?"

"Difficult to say." Christiansen shrugged and began to light a cigarette. "They will have found three bodies in that burnt-out ambulance but, between twenty-five pounds of plastic explosives and a full gas tank, those three will probably be a little difficult to identify, even as to sex. We're hoping the Russians will be a few days figuring out that you weren't incinerated too. We're hoping that for now they won't have any clear idea what last night's explosion was all about."

That line of conversation didn't seem to be making her any happier. Apparently, in spite of everything, Esther Rosensaft hadn't yet learned to be indifferent to killing. It was probably a point in her favor. Christiansen decided to change the subject.

"You haven't finished your ice cream," he said. "What's the matter, didn't you like it?"

"It was fine. I just seem to have lost my appetite. I'm sorry—it was very kind of you."

It was late afternoon, and she had been up and walking around for hours. Now she looked tired. She sat in the chair, her shoulders slumped, her skinny little arms dangling in her lap. She was like a weary child—the short black hair, the eyes, the whole bit. It took an effort to remember that she was not a child, that she knew her way around men and a good deal else, that she was probably perfectly aware of the sort of impression she could make on a big, dumb Norwegian by playing cute and helpless and full of finer feelings. It was worth reminding oneself that getting sentimental about Esther Rosensaft wasn't going to help trap Colonel Egon Hagemann. Esther Rosensaft, after all, was supposed to be the bait.

"Finish it anyway. I don't want your stomach to start growling at the wrong moment."

He spent what was left of the daylight attending to the lady's makeup.

Mordecai had found the mask and all the rest of it. Mordecai was better at finding things than anyone Christiansen had ever known, even in the army. All that was left was to fix the hair and blend in the edges.

It was decided not to use a wig. A wig was too easily detected and, besides, they only wanted to make her look around sixty. Christiansen decided to strip some of the color out with lye and leave the rest.

"Where did you learn to do this?" she asked. She was in her slip, sitting between his knees while he worked on her hair. She kept glancing up at him, which didn't make the work any easier.

"In New York, playing the theaters. I was a musician, but you learned to do a little of everything."

"The theaters? Are they nice?"

"They're not bad—hold still."

"You were a musician? What did you play?"

"Just hold still. We'll save the confessions for another day."

The mask was very good. A little spirit gum, a little grease pencil, and Esther looked wrinkled and ravaged. When she closed her eyes, she looked dead.

"I'm going to give you a shot," he told her. "You'll feel a trifle cold just at first, and then you'll just drift off—there's no pain. When you come around, you'll be in the American Zone."

Without a word, and as obediently as a child, she lay down in the casket. Her eyes never left his face, as if the sight of him was all that gave her the courage to be silent. Christiansen inserted the needle in a vein on the inside of her upper arm, where the sleeve of her dress would cover it. After a few seconds, she closed her eyes. In less than a minute her hands were white and cold. It gave him a peculiar feeling to look at her.

"I've got a couple of packer's straps here somewhere," he said to Sonya, as soon as he had screwed the lid on the casket. "You'll have to help me get her down to the van. I'll go first down the stairway, and you take the foot end. Let's go. We haven't got a lot of time."

It was twenty minutes after nine. Outside there was a wind blowing, and the night air was stinging with ice. Christiansen swung open the rear door of the van, and they pushed the casket inside.

"I almost forgot. Give me your hand—no, the left one."

He took a gold ring out of his trouser pocket and slipped it onto her finger. She looked a trifle surprised, which was probably natural. There was no point in making a big personal issue of the thing, however.

"We're supposed to be married. It's on your passport, and they look for mistakes like that. And try to remember this is your dead mother we've got back here. It would be nice if you were clutching a suitably damp handkerchief as we rolled up to the checkpoint."

The Russian Zone had its speed laws, of course, but the curfew had cut the normally thin traffic down to almost nothing. They made good time as they plunged along toward the Dresdner Strasse.

"We'll cross at the Gürtelbrücke," he said, shifting up with a grind that told him he was going to have to watch himself. For some reason he was unusually tense tonight, almost as if he hadn't been doing things like this more or less regularly for years. "There'll be less of a lineup, and it crosses straight into the American Zone."

"Will she be able to breathe in that box?"

"Sure. It doesn't show, but the lid is a little warped— enough to let in some air. Besides, right now she's hardly breathing at all anyway."

"But can she stay alive like that?"

"No." He turned and grinned at her, feeling like a character in a Poe story. "That's why there's a bit of a rush on. If we don't bring her around inside of two hours we might as well just leave her in that casket, because it'll be all she needs."

Within six minutes they had made it to the checkpoint. They joined a queue in which they were the eighth vehicle. Christiansen turned off his ignition and his lights and settled down to wait.

At twenty-seven minutes before ten, they were the seventh in line. The Russians seemed to be making a very thorough job of their searches tonight, which wasn't particularly encouraging.

"Do you want a cigarette?" he asked, holding out the pack. There were only four left, hardly enough.

"No, thanks. They're bad for the smile."

She gave him a sample, with plenty of white, even teeth. The lady was clearly counting her assets. Christiansen struck a match, cupped his hands around it, and lit up, all the time watching how the checkpoint guards were crawling over the lead truck like ants.

"What'll you do when we get out of here, Sonya? Will you be all right?" One had to say something—they couldn't just wait in silence or they would be as jumpy as cats when the time came to look like an old married couple. It was nineteen minutes before ten.

"Don't you worry about me," she said, smiling all over again. But this time not quite so much like the lady in the Pepsodent ads. "Give me three weeks and I'll have an American boyfriend. In five months I'll be a housewife in Topeka, Kansas. I like the sound of it—'Top-EE-ka.' Have you ever been to the American Midwest?"

"Never. They tell me it gets cold out there, though."

"That shouldn't bother a Norwegian."

"You're not a Norwegian."

By the time the Russians had finished their search, it was eleven minutes to ten.

"Sixteen minutes. At that rate, by the time we're through our passenger will have been dead for ten minutes."

"But the others are all cars—perhaps they won't take as long with them. Could we pull out of line and try again tomorrow?"

"No. They've already seen us. They'd be on us before we got two blocks."

"Could I have that cigarette now?"

"Sure."

She held it uncertainly between two rather bony fingers, taking short little drags now and again as if she were trying to remember how it was done. She was a brick, was Sonya. She wasn't thinking about getting caught and spending the rest of her life in Mühlfeld—she was thinking about those ten minutes.

The next two cars were waved through—they hardly even had to roll down their windows. There was hope yet.

The lead car was now an ordinary enough sedan that looked brown under the harsh white light but could have been any dark color. When the driver opened the trunk, the guards started carrying suitcases over to the side of the checkpoint—there seemed to be half a dozen of them. The driver produced a ring of keys, and each suitcase in turn was carefully searched.

"They've got a live one," Christiansen murmured. "We could be here all night."

After twenty-three minutes, one of the guards climbed into the driver's seat and wheeled the car back and out of view. The driver was nowhere to be seen, but it didn't take a miracle of imagination to figure out what was probably happening to him.

"Let's hope they're happy now."

It was fourteen minutes before eleven when the van was permitted to pull up under the klieg lights and Christiansen handed his and Sonya's passports, the export license, and a death certificate made out in the name of Frieda Schratt to a guard who stared up at him with evident suspicion through spectacle lenses as thick as biscuits. The guard took these documents with him when he vanished into the station house. There was nothing to do but sit and wait. Christiansen rolled up his window. Esther Rosensaft had now been in her trance for slightly more than an hour and a half.

"Inar, do you see that man over there? The one with the shoulder boards on his greatcoat?"

Christiansen didn't make an issue of looking. He just let his eyes drift by, the way a man does when he's bored from waiting in line.

"He's a lieutenant, and he's got campaign ribbons from Leningrad and Brest-Litovsk. What about him?"

"I think he's an old client of mine, from before I went inside."

"Good Jesus, that's all we need. Has he recognized you?"

"I don't know."

The lieutenant was obviously the officer in charge—he had that jaded look of someone who knows that he must be pleased. He was perhaps thirty-five and had the sort of wide, Slavic face that made you think it must have been molded in wax and then left in the hot sun just a few seconds too long. He wasn't looking at the van—at least, not at that precise moment—and he didn't give the impression he was thinking about women. Maybe it would be all right.

Nine to eleven. Nothing. How long did it take to read a few pages of forged official documents?

Six to eleven. The lieutenant had finally noticed Sonya. He was peering at her in a furtive sort of way—if Christiansen glanced up, he would drop his eyes—but he seemed to be trying to place her.

"Was he a good customer?"

"How should I know? What kind of a question is that, anyway? He came a couple of times. How the hell am I supposed to remember? In that business we don't keep an appointment calendar."

"Sorry. I was just wondering how likely he would be to remember."

"All my boys remember me."

Finally, the guard came back. He handed Christiansen the two passports and the export license. He kept the death certificate.

"I shall have to look at the body," he said, in remarkably clear German. "A formality, you understand."

And he smiled. It was Be Nice to Grieving Norwegians Week.

Christiansen climbed down from the cab and went around to the back. He unlocked the rear doors with his ignition key.

"I hope you won't find it necessary to remove the casket from the van. My wife, you understand . . ."

"Yes, of course."

The guard was carrying a flashlight. They got inside the van, one at a time, and then Christiansen took a screwdriver from his pocket and began unbolting the lid. It was two minutes after eleven.

Esther looked convincingly dead—she might even be dead by now. The guard threw his flashlight beam across her face, but he seemed to have no taste for such things and quickly shut it off.

"Yes, that's fine," he said, his voice just a trifle shaky—maybe he didn't like being closed up in a black metal box with a corpse. "You may close up now."

He hopped down and left Christiansen alone. Christiansen gave each screw about two turns, just enough to make it look right, and came out himself. It was six minutes after eleven.

The lieutenant was standing outside, waiting for him.

"How long have you been married, *Mein Herr*?" he asked. His German was almost unintelligible. He looked angry.

"A couple of months," Christiansen answered, trying to sound as if he were standing on his matrimonial dignity. He wondered how he should play it—would he be expected to know all about his wife's shady past? It was a nice question. "Why?"

"Nothing, *Mein Herr*. My condolences to your wife. I wish you all the best."

And then he grinned, the tasteless bastard. Yes, of course he remembered. What did he want, to compare notes?

Christiansen took the death certificate the guard was holding out to him and walked back to the cab in grim silence. He and Sonya waited, hardly able to breathe, until the barrier was raised and they were waved through. It was eight minutes after eleven.

She's just a little thing, he kept thinking. *What if I got the dosage wrong?*

He raced down the empty street and went around the first corner he could find, pulling the van to a halt with screeching tires.

"I don't want to know how it comes out," Sonya murmured, her hand already on the doorlatch. Her eyes were full of dread. She looked older. "I'm sorry, Inar. I can't . . . Goodbye."

She was gone before he had a chance to answer. The street was dark, and in a few seconds all there was to hear was the tick-tick-tick of her high-heeled shoes against the sidewalk.

But Christiansen wasn't thinking about Sonya. His

hands were shaking as he unlocked the rear doors of the van and climbed inside. There was no time left, no time at all.

The hell with screwdrivers—he slid his fingers in under the casket lid, where there was a gap of perhaps half an inch, and pulled. With a scream as the screws pulled loose, it came away. Her hands folded together at her waist, Esther lay there, just as she had for the last two hours, just as she might for eternity if he hadn't been fast enough. Christiansen took a small, flat leather case from its resting place between her shoulder blades, took out a syringe that was already loaded, and started to look for a vein. There was a nice big one just above the knee—hell, she'd never feel it. He drove the needle home.

Nothing—she was dead. He pressed his ear against her chest, but he couldn't hear anything. He wasn't sure . . .

He stared at the withered mask, hating it. He hated the whole stinking operation—he hated himself for consenting to do something like this. She wasn't even twenty, and now she was dead.

He began to peel the mask away. He couldn't stand it, couldn't stand seeing her look like that. He began pulling away the rubber in great pieces; the spirit gum that had been holding it in place stretched and snapped like taffy. He wanted to see her face.

And then he heard what might have been a soft moan—something must have hurt her. And if she could feel pain, she was alive. He put his face close to her lips to see if he could feel her breath.

Yes, there was something. Christiansen experienced a choking sensation in his throat. He peeled away the last of the mask, and waited.

After a moment, one of her hands moved. The tip of her tongue came out to moisten her lower lip. God damn it, she was alive.

An eye fluttered halfway open, and she moaned again. With the ends of his fingers he brushed a strand of hair away from her face. It was a long time before she was conscious enough to look up into his face and return the pressure of his hand as it held hers.

"Welcome back to earth, kid."

✠ 11 ✠

Vienna, Austria: March 6, 1948

Mordecai Leivick stared out of his hotel room window at the dark pavement three stories below. There was nothing to see; not even the street lamps were lit. No one passed by on the sidewalk. There was no traffic. Life had come to a dead hush, and the moonlight caught nothing but the last flurries of snow, giving them an ashen luminescence as they drifted in damp clumps toward the ground.

"Itzikel, make some coffee like a good boy. They can't be much longer now, and they'll be cold."

Itzhak, who was still wearing a piece of tape across his nose, was already measuring teaspoons into the pot, which was resting on their illegal hot plate like a memorial bust on its pedestal. He had been remarkably talkative and cheerful all night, as he always was when Hirsch and Faglin weren't around—they hadn't a lot of patience with him, but they were out of the city, lying low in case the Russians should launch any inquiries. After all, he was merely a boy.

It was difficult sometimes to be sure of one's own motives. Perhaps it would have been best if Leivick had yielded to his scruples and sent Itzhak home. There were a dozen ways he could justify his decision to himself—after all, everyone has to begin somewhere; every agent has to learn his trade—but he knew that the real reasons were more personal. Itzhak was the grandson of an uncle, one of the earliest Zionists, something of a scandal in that family of German-speaking assimilationists, and, beyond that, there was the fact that he was just the same age as Leivick's own boy, who had disappeared into the gas chamber at Treblinka. There was no resemblance, but the parched heart of a man in his late middle age doesn't require more than a hint. So if it meant so much to Itzhak that he be allowed to prove himself, then so be it.

The coffee had just begun to boil when there was a knock on the door. Not an ordinary knock—someone was kicking it with the point of his shoe. Leivick took his revolver from the dresser drawer.

"Let's not be rude," he said, aiming the pistol at the center of the door. "Let them in."

But it was only Christiansen. Leivick felt a trifle foolish pointing a gun at him, especially since his arms were full of a young woman in a black dress, fast asleep, whom one assumed was Esther Rosensaft. She was cradled against his chest with one arm hooked around his neck like a child being taken upstairs for the night.

Itzhak was staring at the girl's face, which was half hidden against Christiansen's shoulder.

"Get some blankets. She's been having fits of shivering all the way up the stairs."

It was really true. They wrapped her up like an Indian papoose and laid her out on Leivick's bed, and she buried her head in the pillow, trembling with cold. She seemed only half conscious. Christiansen sat beside her, his massive hand covering her eyes as if to shade them.

"Good God! Itzhak, get her some coffee—make it strong."

"No." Christiansen shook his head without turning around. His whole attention seemed absorbed by the girl's fitful, troubled rest. "She's been pumped full of junk for the past thirty-six hours. I think we should just let her sleep it off."

But Itzhak brought the coffee anyway, if only to have an excuse for coming close to the bed. Leivick took the cup from his hands, without tasting it.

"How did you get her through the lobby?" he asked.

"She walked, right past the desk and up the stairs. The clerk might have suspected she was a little the worse for drink, but she did it fine. God alone knows where she found the strength—she collapsed as soon as we turned the first corner."

Christiansen smoothed down the girl's hair, his hand almost covering her head. It seemed to quiet her.

"The van is parked across the street. I think it would be a good idea to lose it somewhere." He was looking straight at Itzhak, and the expression on his face was almost angry. He held out the keys. "Take it into the International Zone. Walk back—no cabs. Don't be seen."

"You ought to be nicer to him," Leivick said after the door had slammed shut. "He's not a bad kid, and you can't possibly hold a grudge over that business in Munich. Feuds are bad for efficiency."

Christiansen looked at him as if he couldn't imagine what he was talking about, and then his blue eyes seemed to cloud over with anguish.

"She hasn't seen or heard from Hagemann since forty-five," he said suddenly, in the voice of a man making his confession. "She doesn't even know what was going on at Waldenburg. Mordecai, I don't think she knows a goddamned thing."

The next morning she was almost as good as new. She sat up in bed, breakfasting on sweetened tea and rolls with orange marmalade, reading with almost feverish excitement a two-day-old newspaper that had happened to be lying around. She seemed to be looking for articles on Palestine.

"Feeling better are we, dear?"

Leivick sat down on the edge of the bed and smiled. At first she seemed frightened and then she glanced up at Christiansen, who was standing in the doorway, and apparently found that reassuring.

"Are you one of the Jews?" she asked.

"Yes, God help us. I'm one of the Jews." Leivick shrugged his shoulders, suggesting that he found it a questionable distinction.

"Were you in the camps?"

"Yes, dear. Treblinka. Like you, I lost everyone."

For an instant she seemed frozen. Only her eyes seemed alive as they filled with tears, and then, on what was obviously a sudden impulse, she threw her arms around Leivick's neck and kissed him on the face.

"That's all right now," he said after a few seconds. He took her wrists and gently pulled her away. He looked up to Christiansen and showed his teeth in a rather sheepish grin, but there was no disguising the fact that this little incident had moved him. Christiansen might as well not have seen; he was actually turned a little to one side, as if trying not to be there at all.

"You mustn't cry, my dear," Leivick went on, holding the girl's hands in his own, almost as if he didn't trust them. "We can't change anything with tears, now can we?"

It seemed to work. Three minutes later, anyone might have supposed that nothing had happened. Esther Rosensaft, still in the long-sleeved black dress because there was nothing else for her to wear, was like a pensive little widow—the strain of the last few days was still etched into her face, but she was perfectly calm.

"Now you must have guessed, Esther—may I call you Esther?—that we didn't go to all the trouble of arranging your escape from Mühlfeld Prison simply from impulses of Jewish solidarity. Do you understand that, Esther? Do you have any idea why you have such importance for us?"

She shook her head. She was silent, weighed down, it seemed, with a sense of futility. She stared down at Leivick's hands, which still held her own.

"Does it have to do with Hagemann?" she asked finally, looking up, her eyes darting between Leivick and Christiansen. "That lawyer—you said he came from . . . Will he tell Hagemann where to find me?"

"He won't tell anyone anything. He's dead."

Christiansen shifted his weight from one foot to the other. He sounded almost bored. "But Hagemann won't have to be told."

"That's quite true, my dear. After all this time, the Colonel seems quite eager to have you back, and you know even better than we do what that probably means."

Leivick squeezed her hands and smiled rather thinly. He found it difficult to remember all this girl had been through, she seemed such a child. But, of course, she realized that to fall into Hagemann's clutches was to die. She knew all about Colonel Egon Hagemann.

"It comes down to this, Esther. We're not keeping you prisoner. You're free to leave when you like and go anywhere you think best. But as long as Hagemann is alive you'll be a hunted animal. He means to find you—we can't even begin to guess why—and if he finds you he'll kill you just as soon as he's got whatever it is he wants. Do you see that?"

The girl took back her hands and hid them under the blanket that was covering her legs. Something in her thin, ravaged face seemed to harden, as if it had just occurred to her that now there was no one she could trust except herself.

"I think you know why Hagemann wants me back," she said, her voice even, almost tranquil. "In forty-five, when the Russians came, he forgot I was even alive. I was nothing. I was not even worth the trouble of shooting. And now I am so important, and I want to know why. Please don't tell me you don't know."

"Be happy in your ignorance, my dear." Mordecai rose from the bed. He felt old and worn through to the bone. "We know what Hagemann wants, but not from you. Your place in this is, believe me, a mystery."

With what seemed a common impulse, they both turned to look at Christiansen, who was still standing in the doorway, which was almost hidden behind his enormous shoulders.

"You can go one of two ways," he said, his cold blue eyes fixed on the girl. "You can help us to get Hagemann, to put him out of business once and for all, or you can spend the rest of your short life wondering when he's going to catch up with you. And Hagemann has a long reach."

It was as if the room had turned suddenly colder. They all felt it, even Christiansen, whom Leivick was beginning to imagine must live in a universe of just that temperature. The girl even drew her arms together over her thin chest.

"I guess that's no choice at all," she said.

The key, of course, was General von Goltz.

"After the trial, he sent a note around to my hotel room saying that he wanted to talk to me," Christiansen said. He was sitting in a comfortable-looking chair covered with gray cloth, and he was smoking a cigarette. He didn't seem so much relaxed as discouraged. "I was all packed and ready to leave. I had had the satisfaction of seeing him sentenced, and he would hang in fifteen days. I would be back for that, but fifteen days was fifteen days, and there didn't seem any point in waiting around in Rebdorf. I wanted to get back to looking for Hagemann."

They were all there, in the little parlor of the suite the Mossad was renting at the rate of twelve marks a day. It was a few minutes after one in the afternoon, and the remains of the lunch they had had sent up were still visible as a pile of dishes stacked up on the writing desk. The girl was on one end of the sofa, her feet tucked up under her so that she looked a little like a nesting bird. Leivick was crouched on the divan, still nursing a last cup of coffee which he held in both hands. Even Itzhak was there, but obviously more interested in looking at the girl from the other end of the sofa than in Christiansen's story. Christiansen, for some reason, had taken to blowing his cigarette smoke out through clenched teeth. It made an odd impression. It was like listening to a story told by a Chinese dragon.

"But it was not something I could just ignore," he went on, the smoke curling around his face. "I had been the arresting officer, and there were other reasons. A relationship had been established. You can't hate a man and hound him to his death without noticing that he is, in fact, a man and entitled to certain decencies.

"The condemned cells at Rebdorf are in a kind of dungeon. The prison used to be a castle, and it was a pretty grim place. Down there, below ground, the walls sweat, and each of the seven men who were awaiting execution was housed in a tiny stone room with a ceiling so low that probably all of them had to be careful about standing up straight. I felt like I was climbing into a packing crate.

"And it was cold. No one was feeling very compassionate toward these fellows—each one of them had done enough to deserve hanging a dozen times over—but those cells . . . Von Goltz and the others must not have been having themselves much of a time down there.

"The guards that morning were French—I was told it rotated every day, and that day it was the French. They're good haters; the officer on duty came with me to the cell door, slid open the eye slit, and, with an expression of intense satisfaction on his face, invited me to look inside. There wasn't anything to see but a middle-aged man in a black uniform sitting on an unmade bed, but he seemed to get quite a kick out of it. It wasn't until he had actually opened the door that von Goltz even bothered to look up. He smiled when he saw me, just the way his jailer had.

" 'Come in,' he said, motioning me toward him with his arm. 'I'm afraid there's not much I can offer you in the way of entertainment, but you are very welcome.' It was strange, but he didn't give the impression he was making a joke."

He glanced around at the three of them, his eyes finally coming to rest on Esther Rosensaft, as if the whole story were being told for her benefit alone. Leivick found himself wondering what was developing between those two, and if it was likely to get in the way. Finally, Christiansen ground out the cigarette in an ashtray he was balancing on his thigh and then went through the ritual of lighting another. He did it with the quiet attention that seemed to characterize all his actions.

"There was no chair, or even another piece of furniture, and it was impossible to stand, so when von Goltz moved over to make room for me on his narrow little bed I sat down beside him. It didn't seem strange at the time, but it does now. Somehow I couldn't feel any hostility toward him at that moment. Perhaps if we had had our meeting in one of the interrogation rooms upstairs—facing each other across a table, like opponents at bridge—it would have had a very different quality. I don't pretend to know.

" 'You are wondering why I asked to see you,' he said finally. He sat with his hands resting on his knees, half twisted around so he wouldn't have to address himself to the cell door. He had lost a lot of weight since his arrest and he looked sickly—it might just have been all that time indoors. I couldn't help thinking that that was probably how some of his prisoners at Waldenburg had looked, but there wasn't any anger in the idea. He was already a dead man. I only hated him abstractly.

"I don't remember what I said—probably I didn't say anything. I was too busy feeling the pressure of those narrow stone walls. It was like one of the tiny domed crypts you see in monasteries, where for centuries layer after layer of monks have been buried against the Second Coming. I couldn't shake the impression that this was a visitation from beyond the grave, that I was holding conversation with a shade.

" 'I wanted you to know that I don't hold anything against you,' he went on. He was rubbing his hands up and down against the fabric of his trousers, probably because he was cold. 'I don't suppose that means very much to you now, but it may someday when this war, like all the others, has found its place in history. You understand, don't you, that I was condemned simply because I was on the losing side?'

"He knew it wasn't true. You could see it in his face—it was just something he would have liked to believe.

" 'What will you do now?'

" 'Find the rest of you,' I said, smiling at him. I wanted him to know. I was enjoying myself. 'With time, I'll work my way up to your second in command. Hagemann isn't making it as easy as you did. He isn't waiting around the house for someone to come and arrest him. But I'll find him.'

" 'You think so, do you?' He was smiling too—he seemed to think I was faintly comical. 'I wish I could be alive to see that, but I don't think Hagemann will have the moral imagination to appreciate someone like you. Hagemann, I'm afraid, thinks in rather more practical terms.

" 'But you had better hurry, my friend. You see, there's a time limit on the Colonel.' "

Christiansen was looking at the glowing tip of his cigarette with evident distaste. After a few seconds of motionless silence, he drew the ball of his thumb across his left eyelid in a way that suggested he was prey to unpleasant recollections.

"I didn't know what he was talking about, of course," he went on. "And it was obviously intended as some kind of riddle, so there wouldn't have been any point in asking for an explanation. He was to mount the gallows in fifteen days; if he wanted to be gnomic there wasn't anything I could do about it.

" 'Someone told me you were a musician.' Von Goltz leaned toward me so that our shoulders were almost touching. 'The cello, isn't it? I play the violin, did you know? Nothing in comparison with yourself of course, but not too badly for a soldier. Hagemann always undervalued the beautiful. Perhaps someday, however, he may come to appreciate his limitations. Do you really think you can catch him? Actually, I rather hope you do. I'll even tell you something that might help you—that'll make two little jokes I've played on him since our parting.'

"And then he reached inside the breast pocket of his tunic—they had removed all the insignia of his rank from the uniform, even the brass buttons—and took out a sheet of paper. It contained the names of fifteen officers and men of the Fifth Brigade, along with their ranks and, in a few cases, cities of origin. He must have copied it out during the trial, since prisoners weren't allowed writing instruments in their cells.

" 'These people were closest to Hagemann,' he said, and put the list into my hand. 'And you are wondering why I would do such a thing to my own subordinate? It's merely a question of evening the odds. The SS does strange things to a man's soul—I suppose I can't break the habit of playing God.'

"He wasn't smiling anymore. He was perfectly serious. I looked at the list, noted that about half the names were of people either in prison already or known to be dead, and put it in my pocket.

" 'Why didn't you run?' I asked him. For some reason the question had never occurred to me before. 'Why didn't you join the others in South America, or wherever the hell they went? You must have known you were on the lists as a war criminal.'

"Do you know what his answer was?" Christiansen leaned toward Leivick as he stabbed out his cigarette and set the ashtray down on the floor. His eyes were wide and rather fierce, almost challenging.

"I wouldn't have any idea."

Christiansen smiled at him—if that was the word for the expression on his face. At any rate, he had the answer he wanted.

" 'I haven't any talent for that sort of thing.' In just those words. I suppose it was a kind of boast."

The story was finished, but it left its residue. Everyone seemed to be waiting, even Christiansen, for General von Goltz, dead and in a grave at the Rebdorf Prison cemetery for half a year, to make his final confession.

"Yes—it is just what he would have said."

They all looked at the girl, as if only just that moment aware of her presence. Her arms were folded across her chest. *Is she cold?* Leivick found himself wondering. The room was quite comfortable, but she appeared to be trembling. Her eyes were wet, and her mouth twitched under the stress of some emotion she probably couldn't have explained even to herself.

"He was always just that way, always charming while he traded people off against each other like chess pieces. He would always insist upon having the final word."

"He certainly seems to have had it this time."

Leivick got up from his divan, listening to his knees crack under him. He wanted another cup of coffee badly enough to kill for it. Of course there was none. They couldn't even make any themselves because they were out of grounds.

Then it occurred to him that this was, after all, a hotel, and that in Vienna anything could be had simply by picking up the telephone.

"They can take the dishes away while they're at it," Christiansen announced gently. Leivick turned around and stared at him, but the mind reader had lost interest in his trick.

"I've often thought that if I'd understood everything von Goltz was trying not to tell me during this interview I'd have Hagemann right where I want him." The fingers of Christiansen's left hand curled uncon-

sciously into a fist. " 'Hagemann always undervalued
the beautiful.' Perhaps by now he's seen his mistake."

He was looking at the girl with a calm, speculative
gaze. Hadn't he said from the beginning that she would
be the bait for their trap? Leivick felt himself going
cold inside.

And the girl, what must she have felt? Christiansen's eyes seemed to hold her, as if she couldn't have
looked away if she wanted to. Yes, in all probability,
if Christiansen were to ask her she would risk putting
herself back within Hagemann's reach.

The poor little creature—she sat there still, in her
shabby, wrinkled black dress, thin-faced and friend-
less. Yes, of course, even if she didn't know it yet
herself, she had fallen in love with that hard-eyed
angel of vengeance, God help her.

Leivick stared at the telephone receiver which he
held in his right hand, wondering what he was doing
with it, and then set it back down on its cradle. His
throat ached with pity and a bad conscience.

"We should get Miss Rosensaft some new clothes,"
he said finally. It was an obvious enough remark, but
having made it gave him a peculiar satisfaction. "Perhaps later this afternoon would not be too early. What
do you think, Christiansen?"

He purposely avoided glancing in Itzhak's direction—he could feel that black look boring through the
back of his head without having to confirm it.

"I suppose so. She can't go around in that." He
shrugged his shoulders, still looking at the girl exactly
as if she were a piece of furniture. The mask was firmly
in place today, Leivick noted to himself. "Is there a
department store or something around here? I don't
think it's worth the risk of taking her into the Inter-

national Zone. You'd better bring your pistol, Dessauer, and we'll give her a proper bodyguard."

The expression on Itzhak's face showed clearly
enough that Christiansen had made precisely the right
move.

"But could I have a bandage or something first?"
the girl asked. She did not seem as pleased as Itzhak
by the prospect of the afternoon's outing. She was
grasping her right arm protectively, just below the
elbow. "I don't want the saleswomen to see my number."

It was one of those moments when the sense of
astonishment comes perhaps two or three seconds ahead
of the idea that prompts it. It was like being startled
from behind. Leivick, who was standing beside the
dresser, found it necessary to wait a little, just to be
sure he was sufficiently in command of himself to
speak at all.

"Surely it isn't on that arm, my dear," he said at
last, a little surprised at the evenness of his own voice.
"It's on the left, isn't it?"

Instead of answering, the girl undid the two little
buttons on her right sleeve and pushed it back. The
number was there, sure enough.

"No—don't cover it up again. Where did you get
that, at Chelmno?"

"At Waldenburg," came the answer. Clearly she
wasn't enjoying the conversation; she wouldn't even
look him full in the face.

"There were no serial numbers at Waldenburg."
Leivick felt almost as if he were passing a death sentence. "If a prisoner was brought in from another
camp, one of the work camps . . . But they didn't
bother at Waldenburg—why should they? There were

too few inmates, and they planned from the beginning
to kill them all in one run when the project was finished. You never got that number at Waldenburg,
Esther."

The girl brushed the sleeve back into place with
a single angry gesture. She looked from Leivick to
Christiansen and then back again, and her little mouth
had compressed into a thin, colorless line.

"You old bastard, what do you know?" she shouted
suddenly. "I was there, not you—me! You think I did
this to myself? General von Goltz himself, that last
night . . ."

And then, all at once, she couldn't speak at all.
She seemed to be choking. She couldn't make a sound,
not even to cry. It took her a long time.

"He did this to me. He took me over to the other
camp, where I could see the bodies, the dead men,
piled up like logs." She took a deep breath, as if she
were breaking through to the surface from deep under
water. "He burned this into my arm, and then he took
me away. I hated him then! I wished he had let me
die there."

It was over. She was quiet again. But you could
read it in her eyes—that terrible, burning sincerity of
youth. Of course she had been telling the truth.

Leivick knelt down beside her, took her right arm
in his hands, and pushed the sleeve back as gently as
if he were uncovering a fresh wound. She didn't try
to resist him.

"I've never seen such a number," he said. " 'G4/
3454641.' There were only a few thousand prisoners
at Waldenburg—even at Auschwitz the numbers didn't
get above five digits. I've never seen one that begins

with a letter, or carries a stroke mark. What does the 'G' stand for? Was the *Herr General* signing his work?"

She glared at him. She hated him at that moment, and why not? Leivick couldn't find it in his heart to blame her.

"He did this to you himself? *He* did it?"

She didn't even have to answer. Leivick let go of her arm, and it dropped back into her lap like something dead.

"Are you thinking what I'm thinking?" It was Christiansen who had spoken. He had risen without being heard and was standing beside the sofa. He put his scarred hand on the girl's shoulder. " 'Hagemann always undervalued the beautiful.' 'That'll make two little jokes I've played on him since our parting.' "

Yes, of course. It was perfectly obvious. That was why Esther Rosensaft hadn't died at Waldenburg—she was the bearer of a message. Leivick stood up and looked at Christiansen, smiling a trifle uncertainly.

"Yes, of course. The number—it's some kind of a code."

12

A message—yes. But to whom, and about what? How much was it possible to know about a cipher tattooed across a girl's arm?

"It may not even be a code," Mordecai said, not looking very happy with his discovery. "It may be nothing more than a number—a safe-deposit box number perhaps. We are talking about how von Goltz decided to transmit the instructions for a technical process—a formula, if you wish. There will be papers—procedural notes, perhaps even blueprints. He had to have stored them somewhere safe. A bank, probably. Somewhere in the western military zone, I should think."

They were alone. Dessauer was on guard duty outside Esther's bedroom door while she took a nap— she was still a trifle punchy from all the narcotics she had had pumped into her—so Christiansen had suggested he and Mordecai step across the street to a *Kaffeehaus* for a quiet word or two. They sat hunched over their cups, on either side of a small table next to a plate-glass window through which the pale sun of a fine, cold late winter's afternoon was shining like a promise. Each of them was smoking one of Christiansen's American cigarettes.

"One thing's for sure—we'll have to have that tattoo removed. We don't know whether Hagemann knows what he's looking for or not, but we can't very well take the chance. We'll have to have it cut out. I think she'll be just as happy about it."

Mordecai nodded in agreement. He probably already had a doctor in mind. Mordecai always seemed to know just the right people for any little thing that needed doing.

"And we shall have to have a watch on her at all times," he said. "She is the key to everything now—well, certainly one of them."

He smiled. He was making a joke. Christiansen, who had had enough riddles for one day, merely waited.

"There is a real key, of course. At least there is if my theory about the safe-deposit box is correct. I should imagine Hagemann has that. How much else he knows we shall have to find out." He shrugged his shoulders; he was not underestimating the difficulty. "We have our piece of the puzzle, and he has his. And, of course, his standing with his Arab backers, perhaps even his life, depends upon his acquiring both."

"She's expecting me to take her shopping this afternoon. You were the one who suggested it—you can be the one to tell her it's too dangerous."

Mordecai shook his head.

"No, we must go ahead with it. I doubt if Hagemann even knows she's out of Mühlfeld yet and, besides, he wouldn't be stupid enough to do anything that might kill the golden goose, if you will pardon the expression. If we begin treating her like a prisoner, she will begin to think like one again—she is accustomed to that role. We can't risk that. We will need her willing cooperation later."

He looked out the window, watching the people crossing back and forth on the sidewalks, and it was almost as if he envied them. He seemed to have aged even in the past few days.

"She likes you," he said, turning back to Christiansen with a smile that no longer had anything of pleasure in it. "I think she has a bit of a . . . *Sie hat sich ganz in Sie vernarrt.* How would you say that in English?"

"She has a crush on me."

"A 'crush'? What a way to put it. But why not? She has spent several months locked away in a woman's prison. She is young, and you have been kind to her. How many men have been kind to her in her life, eh? She probably thinks of you as her savior, as Sir Galahad on his white horse. Why shouldn't she have a 'crush' on you? It would not be the worst thing in the world if you were to cultivate those feelings in her. They may be useful later on."

"Mordecai, you're an even bigger son of a bitch than I am."

"Yes, I know." He took a sip of his coffee and set the cup back down noiselessly on its saucer. "I have chosen to be a nation builder instead of a jeweler or an accountant, and nations are built on the unwilling sacrifices of the innocent. It is a cruel necessity."

And so, at a few minutes before four that afternoon, Christiansen changed into his army uniform and his greatcoat and, with Mordecai's big British service revolver in one pocket, took the little lady out to see about refurbishing her wardrobe. She made a comical sight; she was wearing Dessauer's raincoat over her black dress, and it reached within a few inches of the ground.

Dessauer, like an idiot, was proving how tough he was in nothing but an ancient tweed jacket. Dessauer was being a surly little bastard, but it was possible to feel sorry for him because he had a point. Children should fall in love with other children. What Mordecai had said made Christiansen feel a little ashamed of himself, although he didn't quite know why. It wasn't as if he had done anything.

"You look nice in your uniform," Esther said, putting her hand on his sleeve. "I didn't know you were a soldier."

"I haven't been a soldier since the war's end. I should have thought you had had your fill of soldiers."

What could have made him say a thing like that? She let her hand slip from his arm, and the pleasure died out in her eyes. Christiansen had decided he wouldn't encourage her. There was no place for anything like that in his life right now and, for all the wisdom of Mordecai's sly little suggestion, he didn't want to hurt this girl any more than was necessary for the accomplishment of their business. She had had enough of that in the past several years.

But perhaps there was some less brutal way of putting an end to all these touching symptoms of young love.

They walked down the stairway together, the three of them abreast. Dessauer, like a well-brought-up young man, offered her his arm, and she took it. Perhaps that was the best plan—just stay out of the way and let nature take its course.

"There's a place not three blocks from here that does a good business in secondhand clothes. I'm afraid that's the best we'll do outside of the International Zone, and we can't risk taking you there. The Russians have powers of arrest there."

"I see. Secondhand will do quite well, so long as they are warm."

They exchanged a glance that seemed to settle everything. There would be no more gushes of girlish admiration. Things would stay on a business footing, and she could save herself for someone who had the time.

The weather seemed to be warming up a bit—perhaps they would even have a drop of rain by evening. The clouds overhead were high and sparse but the color of tarnished pewter.

People on the sidewalks, the women with their net shopping bags and the men with their hands buried deep in their overcoat pockets, didn't give the impression they were in any hurry to get back within doors. It was a pleasure to breathe the moist, still air and to feel the sun's soft heat. There was a certain animal comfort to the way the light seemed to blunt the sharp edges of naked tree limbs and the corners of buildings.

Since the walkway was a trifle narrow, Christiansen fell behind a few paces and left Dessauer and Esther to go on together. Dessauer was being very gentlemanly and correct and, aside from the odd polite murmur, they didn't seem to have a lot to say to each other. Christiansen contented himself with keep-

ing a nervous watch on the faces of the other pedes-
trians. He couldn't rid himself of a nagging suspicion
that he was being watched. His hand slipped into the
pocket of his overcoat and closed around the butt of
Mordecai's pistol. It was only a feeling . . .

The proprietress of the secondhand-clothing store
opened the door for them even before Christiansen
had a chance to touch the knob. She was a huge,
withered woman with black eyes that looked as if
someone had pressed them into her face like raisins
into dough—the network of lines over her nose and
cheekbones seemed to suggest something of the sort.
She stood by the door, ducking her head and making
little sighing sounds, all directed at Christiansen whom,
from the fact of his uniform, she must have selected
as the one with the money.

"We need things for the young lady," he said,
taking Esther by the arm and pulling her forward into
everyone's line of sight. "A couple of dresses and a
suit—yes, a suit, one with long sleeves. A good warm
winter coat as well, and underwear. Can you oblige
us with all that? Do you have any shoes that might
fit?"

They both looked down at Esther's feet, which
were still shod in a pair of prison clogs that were too
big for her because she had had to borrow them from
Sonya. The old woman scratched the soft, wrinkled
folds of her thick neck and frowned.

"A small foot," she said, seeming, by the way she
said it, to turn the matter into a philosophical issue.
"She won't be easy. In Vienna, all the women have
big feet—in Vienna, we are all great ones for dancing."

"I haven't danced in a long time."

Esther's serious little face revealed nothing—she

might even have accepted the proprietress's stupid attempt at a joke as literal truth. In the silence created by her innocence, she looked up to Christiansen as if she wanted him to interpret for her.

Well, what was so surprising? She was a child, really. Almost a newborn. She had spent most of her young life under one or another kind of arrest, and prisons weren't the place where one learned how to understand a joke. Or how to dance either.

"See if you can come up with something," he said harshly, wondering why he was so angry with an old woman who obviously hadn't meant any harm. "We aren't looking for dancing shoes."

With hardly more than an uncomprehending shrug, she put her hand on Esther's shoulder and guided her through a curtained doorway into a back room which, apparently, she regarded as a purely feminine sanctuary. Christiansen and Dessauer were left alone together among the dusty counters and the racks of men's suits and overcoats.

Christiansen took out a cigarette and lit it. The smoke felt dry in his lungs and he couldn't taste it at all, but at least it gave him the appearance of an occupation. He had an excuse for not noticing the rather pointed rudeness with which Dessauer was staring at a wall shelf full of men's and women's hats—bowlers, huge Edwardian productions with purple feathers, cloth caps, silk opera hats of both the collapsing and the non-collapsing variety, all promiscuously jumbled up together. But young Itzhak wasn't interested in these little fragments of social history; he seemed to be peering through to something on the wall's other side. That, at least, was probably the impression he wished to convey.

Dessauer didn't like him. Christiansen knew all the reasons: he wasn't Jewish; he had broken the kid's nose for him; he seemed to hold some prior claim to the attention of Esther Rosensaft. There was nothing new about any of this. This was simply the first moment, as Christiansen suddenly realized, when that hostility had caused him any twinge of discomfort.

It had been a long time since he had allowed himself to think in such terms—since that day in June, 1945, when he had stood amidst the ruins of Kirstenstad, looking down at the spot where his parents had died, he had imagined himself as having a human relationship with only two people on earth: Ulrich von Goltz and Egon Hagemann. There had been only the hatred of those two men, with nothing left over for anyone else. Having given himself up to the task of settling his blood debt, he really couldn't bring himself to care what anyone else thought of him.

But now, all at once, he would have been easier in his mind if this boy could have been made to like him. He didn't want any more enemies. Nobody was giving Itzhak Dessauer any trouble over possession of Esther Rosensaft's fair young body, so the rotten little bastard didn't have to be such a hard case all the time.

Outside on the sidewalk, on the other side of the street, a man in a dark tan raincoat hurried by. His hat brim was pulled down, and he was walking with his head cocked to one side, as if the shop windows interested him, so it was impossible to see his face. He was gone in a minute. Christiansen turned away from the big plate-glass window with a feeling of desolation that was beginning to seem almost comfortably familiar.

"When we're finished here, I think it would be

just as well if you took the girl through the back way," he said, not quite looking in Dessauer's direction. "I'll give you about thirty seconds' head start, and then I'll shadow you back to the hotel. We seem to have attracted some attention."

"I've got a gun—I can manage."

Dessauer's voice was tight, as if he were coiled up like a spring inside. Yes, Christiansen could just imagine how he'd manage.

"Nevertheless, we do it my way."

For the first time that day, the two men's eyes met. And no, nobody was going to vote Christiansen Most Popular Man In Vienna.

"How do you like it?"

They both turned toward the curtained doorway. Esther was standing there, smiling, radiant, her arms held out to the sides. She wore a gray wool suit of a type that had probably been fashionable four or five years earlier, with sharp, padded shoulders and a skirt jagged with narrow pleats. She spun around for them, rising up on her toes, making the hem of her skirt flare out; she was obviously intensely pleased with herself. The old woman, who was immediately behind her, her hand resting on the frame of the doorway, smiled in approval. They all smiled. They couldn't have helped themselves.

"Isn't it pretty? Don't you think it's pretty?"

The questions were both directed at Christiansen, who felt something tugging at the inside of his throat and who wished he were somewhere else just at that moment. He didn't want to be reached by this girl— he didn't want to be reached by anyone; that sort of thing just wasn't on the program—but she was reaching him whether he wanted her to or not. When she looked like that, when she was happy and it seemed to light her up from the inside, he just didn't have any way of defending himself.

"Yes. It's very pretty—it makes you look very nice."

That, apparently, was all she needed to hear—or, what was just as likely, she saw more in his face than the bare confirmation of the words—because she danced across the ten or twelve feet of floor separating them and caught his hand. It was a perfectly spontaneous gesture, as automatic as a drowning man's catching at the floating wreckage, but suddenly he found she had him. She tugged at his arm as if she wanted to pull him down so she could see herself reflected in his eyes.

And then something changed. All at once, from one instant to the next, she seemed to have lost interest in him. She wasn't even looking at him; she was looking at something else.

"What is it? What—?"

He never had a chance to finish. She cut him off with a wild scream, the sound of an animal, and threw herself into his arms. He felt the jolt of her tiny body against his own, and then the sound of broken glass coming from behind, from the store window, and then something like a small explosion. Of course he knew almost at once what had happened.

His right hand went into the pocket of his overcoat, and with his left he swept the girl away from him. She was trying to shield him with her body, but in that fraction of a second all he felt was a certain annoyance; she was just something in the way. It wasn't until he tried to move her aside that he noticed the first sharp little twinge of pain in his left shoulder. The gun was in his hand and he was bringing it around to aim when he heard the second shot. He assumed it would kill him.

But it didn't. In fact, it had come from inside the store. As he turned around, the first thing he saw was Itzhak Dessauer standing in the middle of the room, his huge British service revolver held in both hands, firing round after round through the shattered window. No one was outside, but, then, no one would be.

"Dark raincoat? Hat? Itzhak!"

Christiansen thrust his way toward the door, releasing the girl so that she collapsed to the floor in a little heap. Outside on the sidewalk he could see someone running, running because he had missed his chance and now two men with guns would be hot on his ass.

Dessauer was still standing there, holding the revolver in front of him, motionless as stone. Christiansen grabbed his jacket lapel and shook him until he came out of his trance.

"Get her out of here," he shouted. Dessauer stared at him for an instant, and then nodded—he had come back to life. "Use the back way, but watch yourself. They might have someone waiting, so stay off the streets. Steal a car—do anything. Just get her back to the hotel. And thanks for saving my neck."

There wasn't time for anything more. Their eyes met for just a second and then Christiansen hit the door, making the little bell jangle with panicky excitement. When he burst out onto the sidewalk, a couple strolling by turned to stare at him as, gun in hand, he went charging down the street like a hundred-meter runner. There were more people outside; it was the hour when offices began to close for the day.

The man in the raincoat had about a seventy-yard head start and a crowd to hide in. If he had a car anywhere in the neighborhood, Christiansen would never catch him.

But there he was. Christiansen saw him turn around, raise his gun as if he wanted to try a shot, and then, apparently thinking better of it, turn and run. Perhaps he didn't like the distance. Perhaps he had seen the gun in Christiansen's hand and didn't like the odds. Either way, he cut into a side street, nearly knocking down an old woman pushing a shopping cart. They were putting on quite a show for the neighborhood.

"Okay, you son of a bitch."

Christiansen almost laughed. He had forgotten about the wound in his shoulder. He had a long stride, and he knew he was gaining. He would run the bastard into the ground.

But when he reached the corner he knew he had been suckered. Raincoat was waiting for him—he knew that even before he saw him. He was just standing there, the gun held steady in both hands, like a man shooting at targets in his back yard.

Someone yelled. Christiansen didn't let himself slow down; he just made a dive for the front end of a car that was parked by the curb. He heard a shot, then another, and then he hit the pavement and rolled. He didn't have any idea if a bullet had found its mark. A truck swerved to avoid him, tires squealing like a maimed animal.

The impact had nearly kicked the wind out of him and his elbows felt as if they had been broken with hammers, but Christiansen landed right-side up and ready to shoot back. He managed one round—it ricocheted off the stone wall with a whining sound and hit nothing. There was no one there.

Hell, he hadn't missed by much. The son of a bitch was running like a jackrabbit. It seemed he didn't want to die either.

Christiansen got to his feet and discovered, to his intense relief, that everything seemed to work. There were no fresh bullet holes in him, and he wasn't falling flat on his face. He would settle for that. He still had to catch a certain someone; there wasn't time to get killed.

There were little clumps of people standing around on the sidewalk, watching him. They all had the same stunned, uncomprehending expression on their faces— didn't they have sense enough to get out of here? It wasn't hard to get shot in the middle of a war zone.

No one was being clever now. Raincoat was running for his life, pure and simple. Christiansen started after him.

It was a track meet now, and Christiansen had the longer legs. Raincoat must have known that; he was up on his toes like a sprinter, putting everything he had into it. He wouldn't last long that way. They turned another corner, no more than forty yards apart now.

At the next street down, at right angles to them, a trolley car was coming—not very fast, but fast enough. If Raincoat didn't stop, chances were he would go under the car—another gruesome little accident statistic. If he did stop, Christiansen had him.

The trolley driver rang his bell in warning. He must have seen what was happening, although the car didn't seem to slow any.

But Raincoat either didn't hear or didn't care. He wasn't stopping for anybody.

"Hold, dammit!" Christiansen shouted. He let himself slow a little. There was no way . . .

Except that there was. At the last second, Raincoat threw himself over the tracks like a broad jumper—he couldn't have had more than a few inches of clearance, but he made it. He almost deserved to get away.

By the time the trolley had passed, Christiansen was well behind. His quarry had the lead back. He hadn't even broken stride. Christiansen was beginning to feel the wound in his shoulder again.

They kept on for two more blocks. They were both tiring. And then, quite suddenly, Raincoat disappeared through the open gateway in a high board fence. By the time Christiansen caught up with him, he was nowhere to be seen. He had disappeared into what looked like a lumberyard.

There were stacks of finished boards everywhere, set up in rows, turning the place into a warren of narrow, dark little alleys. Except for the gateway, which was wide enough to accommodate the truck traffic, the board fence went all the way around on four sides, so there was no other way out. They would settle their business right here.

Christiansen waited a moment, pressing himself up against the outside of the fence—he had no desire to walk into the same trap twice—and then he hurtled through the gate, aiming for the edge of a pile of uncut logs that could offer some protection.

All he felt was the soles of his shoes touching down on the packed earth. He didn't think he had ever run so fast in his life. All he heard and saw was the pop,

pop, pop of a pistol going off somewhere to the right
and the tiny sprays of dust as the bullets dug into the
ground around him.

But the fourth one caught him. Just as he reached
the log pile he felt the impact an inch or so to the left
of his spine. It was like being smacked with an axe
handle. His legs gave out under him and he hit the
ground face first.

His gun was lying in the dirt just a few feet away—
he had to get to it. Raincoat must have seen him
stumble and guessed the rest. He would be moving
in for the kill. Christiansen began to force himself up
onto his hands and knees. The slightest movement
and his back felt as if someone were trying to tear it
open with a pair of cargo hooks.

But there was no choice. He could hear footsteps
running across the open yard. In another two seconds
he would be either armed or dead.

He threw himself down, clutching at the pistol
and just catching it with the tips of his fingers. He
rolled over—God, he could hardly even breathe—
and brought the pistol down so he could steady it
against his bent knee. There was nothing left to do
except wait and hope.

But Raincoat wasn't that stupid. He wasn't going
to just rush in like the Gadarene Swine—he probably
knew as well as anybody that no one has to be in
perfect health to pull a trigger. He would take his
time, listening for the silence that meant he didn't
have anything more to worry about.

Christiansen dragged himself to the side of the log
pile so he would have something to rest his back against.
Raincoat wasn't more than ten or fifteen feet away—
you could almost hear his heart beating. He was wait-

ing for the right moment. By now, if he had been paying attention, he had to know that Christiansen was hurt bad but still alive. It was a question of who would make the first move.

Because there was a time limit, of course. They hadn't been very private about their little brawl, and by now someone must have called the police. It wouldn't be very long before this yard was crawling with American military police, and they would both want the thing settled before that—Raincoat so he could get out of there and Christiansen because the other man had seen Esther Rosensaft.

Because, of course, Raincoat was Colonel Hagemann's boy. He had been gunning for Christiansen—that was why he had pulled his shot when Esther threw herself in the way—but the girl was the kind of little bonus in which his boss would be very interested. Raincoat had to be put out of his misery.

By sheer force of will, Christiansen managed to push himself up into a standing position. He was reasonably sure now that the bullet had broken a rib. He wasn't sure whether it had touched the lung, but in practical terms it hardly mattered. He couldn't seem to keep any air in his chest.

He was so busy thinking about how much he hurt that it was only by accident he noticed the shadow on the ground, not three yards away.

It was late afternoon. The sun was setting, and the yard was laid out along an east-west axis so that the spot where Christiansen was standing was in deep shade. And just to the front of the log pile was Raincoat, who apparently hadn't thought to look down.

Or perhaps he didn't care. He seemed to be slightly crouched, as if he was about to make a dash across the open space between the log pile and a stack of finished boards not ten feet away. Perhaps he was counting on surprise. Christiansen brought up his revolver, cocking the hammer as soundlessly as he could.

And then, there he was—just a flicker of movement. Christiansen turned his head a little, enough to let him see and also enough to slow him down for just that tenth part of a second, and fired.

Had he got him? He didn't know. And then he noticed a tiny spattering of blood on the ground and knew that the score was now more or less even. Raincoat had a bullet in him too.

Why hadn't he fired? Christiansen had seen the gun. Perhaps he had been hit before he had a chance. And now he was trying to drag himself away. All he had in his mind now was escape. You could tell from the sound of his gasping.

Christiansen forced himself away from the wall of log and discovered that, yes, he could still put one foot in front of the other. The time for being smart and cautious was over. He was going after his man.

Raincoat was waiting for him. He was standing there, leaning against a stack of wooden pallets. He was holding his side, just below the heart, and his left arm was hanging straight down, but he still had his gun in that hand. It was a Luger—standard Wehrmacht issue.

To look at, he was about what you would expect. Average height, close-cropped black hair. The lines around his mouth said he would never see thirty again. His black eyes seemed to burn in their sockets. He looked exhausted. He had come to the end of his tether, and he knew it.

Christiansen walked up on him slowly, but the man made no attempt to raise his weapon. When they were perhaps fifteen feet apart—close enough that there was no chance of missing—he stopped. The big British service revolver was aimed just an inch or so to the left of the man's breastbone.

What the hell. It wasn't written in stone that you couldn't take a prisoner alive—he might even have a few things to say that would make it worth the risk. Why not give the poor bastard a chance for his life?

"Drop the gun. Go ahead—drop it."

But no one was buying. Slowly but deliberately, the man started to bring up his left arm. He wanted it the hard way.

Christiansen fired, once. The impact jerked the man backward, as if he had been pulled from behind. He lay there in the dust with his knees almost touching his chest, as dead as they make them. Christiansen walked over, took the pistol from the lifeless hand, and pulled open the magazine. It was empty. There hadn't been a bullet in the chamber.

"Oh, for Christ's sake."

That was the moment the cavalry arrived.

With much squealing of tires, two U.S. Army jeeps came tearing in through the lumberyard gates and pulled up with a jerk on either side of the spot where Christiansen was standing over the body of the man he had just killed. He turned around to find that, to the right and left both, he was staring down the business end of an M-1 rifle.

Fuck it—he was tired of heroics. He dropped the Luger and the revolver, muzzle first.

The American lieutenant who crawled out of the

passenger seat of the right-hand jeep had a pistol of
his own, a .45 automatic which he insisted on pointing
at Christiansen's head.

"You take it easy, fella," he said. He was a hell of
a lot more nervous than he needed to be. "You got
the whole neighborhood upset. Jesus, what did you
think you was doin'?"

Christiansen decided it was time to stand on his
dignity. Slowly, so that no one got excited, he pulled
his wallet from the inside pocket of his overcoat.

"I'm Captain Inar Christiansen of the Norwegian
Army," he said, giving each word all the weight it
would bear. "This man took a shot at me, and I followed him here."

"Oh, yeah? And who's he—Martin Bormann?"

It was a joke. This boy was one of the smart ones.
Nobody was going to put anything over on him. All
at once, Christiansen discovered that he was fresh out
of patience.

He reached down and grabbed a handful of the
dead man's shirt. He was tired and his back felt like
it was broken, but he didn't care anymore. The fabric
gave way with one great yank—everything just peeled
off, shirt, overcoat, the works.

"Hey, fella, you can't . . ."

"Look for yourself, stupid," Christiansen growled.
The corpse pitched over on its right side, almost naked
from the waist up. With the point of his shoe, Christiansen pushed the arm out of the way.

And there it was, tattooed just under the left armpit, the SS blood-type number.

* 13 *

At a quarter to ten that evening, Christiansen still hadn't returned to the hotel. Esther was desperate enough to suggest phoning the police, but Herr Leivick wouldn't hear of it.

"If he's alive he'll send us word, and if he isn't there is nothing we can do to change that. In either case, we shall have to leave Vienna—our anonymity here is at an end."

He shrugged his shoulders and smiled unhappily. He had liked Inar; anyone could see that. He didn't believe he could still be alive after all this time. Esther wanted to crawl into his arms and cry.

"You should have seen the look on his face," Itzhak kept repeating to Herr Leivick. "A hole in his shoulder big enough to put your hand through, but he didn't care—he didn't even seem to notice. Inar isn't afraid of anything. The way he went charging after that god-damned Nazi, I think he was ready to tear him apart with his teeth."

It was Inar now. Not Christiansen, or that *goy*

bastard, but Inar. And Itzhak was happy because he had found a new hero, and heroes can't be killed. It was like an axiom in geometry. Itzhak was the only one who was happy.

Esther wished he would shut up.

So they waited. Herr Leivick packed his suitcase and made coffee, and they sat around in a silence interrupted only occasionally by Itzhak's assurance that all would be well, that the man who had tried to kill them in the secondhand clothing store was dead in a ditch somewhere and that nothing as insignificant as a bullet could prevail against the House of Israel's new god.

But Esther was not so convinced. She had seen, time and time again, that courage and virtue were helpless against the superior power of evil, and all she could find it in her heart to do was to mourn. She wished she had been left to go mad in Mühlfeld Prison. She wished the shot that had wounded Inar could have killed her first—anything before this. It just wasn't in her to surrender love once more. It didn't matter that he hadn't cared about her, just as long as she could be free to love him in peace. Now, finally, she had found something—someone—to love more than her own life. If he really was dead, then she didn't care what happened to her.

"Have some coffee, my dear." Herr Leivick pressed the cup into her two hands, molding his own around them as if he didn't trust her not to spill it. He knelt beside her chair, his eyes full of kindness. "It's a hard thing, I know, but you and I both have experience of hard things. There's nothing to be done about it, and it's still possible he may be alive. Inar is no sacrificial lamb."

She touched his face with the tips of her fingers, trying to smile. He only wanted to comfort her. How could she possibly explain that there was no comfort for what she felt, that even the sound of his words stabbed her through like a knife with a broken point? She couldn't say any of that, so she said nothing, and tried to smile.

They waited in silence, the coffee untouched. Finally Esther set the cup down on the floor.

That was just before the telephone rang.

"I'm in my room," he said. Yes, it was Inar. She could hear his voice as Herr Leivick tilted the receiver a little away from his ear so that she could listen. It was really he.

"Oh, God," she whispered.

"I've been the guest of the American military police. They've been patching me back together. Come on down, if you like, and I'll tell you all about it."

That was all the invitation they needed. Herr Leivick fished through his jacket pocket until he found the key, and then all three of them went down the back staircase to the room Inar had rented for himself and Itzhak after he and Herr Leivick had decided she needed a room to herself.

Inar was sitting on his bed. His shirt was off, and his whole chest was wrapped in heavy bandages. He looked tired; his skin seemed almost gray. He was drinking a glass of water.

"I killed him—self defense." He showed his teeth in a ferocious, mirthless grin. "Nobody minded. The war crimes office in Nuremberg had him on their lists. His name was Pilsner, just like the beer."

"And he was working for Hagemann? You have no doubts?"

Herr Leivick sagged into a chair. He seemed afflicted, almost as if he had received news of a close friend's death.

"Would I kid you, Mordecai? He was SS, a real hard case. Nobody was going to take that one alive."

"I see."

No one seemed to be paying attention to her, so Esther sat down quietly on the bed beside Inar. She just wanted to be near him. There was a patch of gauze taped onto his rib cage just below the shoulder; the dried blood showed through from underneath like a glowing ember. She would have liked to touch it, but somehow she couldn't summon the courage.

He glanced down at her and smiled.

"It's where they took the bullet out," he said. "It broke the rib, followed it around to the side, and then ran out of steam. It was lying right under the skin."

Herr Leivick made a noise in his throat, as if he wanted to clear it.

"Do the Americans know who you are now?" he asked.

"They know who *I* am, but that's all." Inar shrugged his massive shoulders—his body smelled warm and clean. "They were very friendly once we'd sorted out who had been trying to kill whom. They even drove me back to my hotel. I gave them an address in the International Zone, thanked them very much and waved goodbye, and then took a cab back here. Don't worry about the Americans."

"Does it hurt a great deal?"

"I've felt better. What do you expect, Mordecai? I've got two new bullet wounds, but they've got company—old residents in the neighborhood. I'll mend. But, you know, we have to get her out of here."

He made a curt gesture in Esther's direction. It was like being dismissed from existence.

"Itzikel, why don't you take Esther back upstairs? I want to have a little talk with Inar."

Herr Leivick rose from his chair and slipped his hands into the pockets of his trousers. He seemed to be thinking about something else as he smiled at her, as if she had stirred some memory.

On the stairway and in the two-room suite that Herr Leivick and Esther divided between them, Itzhak was morosely silent. He hardly even looked at her. He seemed angry, or at least resentful. For twenty minutes together he stood leaning back against the dresser, his arms folded across his chest, staring at nothing.

"You should go to bed," he said finally. What could she possibly have done to offend him?

"I don't feel like it." She shook her head. "I'm not tired—I wouldn't be able to sleep."

It was not an answer that pleased. The silence continued until Herr Leivick returned.

"I shouldn't think of going down there just yet," he said, looking at Itzhak and shrugging his shoulders helplessly. "I don't think you'd find it particularly restful—our friend seems to be in something of a mood. He's playing his cello."

"He's what?" Itzhak was frankly incredulous. He seemed on the verge of laughing out loud until he saw the expression on Herr Leivick's face.

"Why not? You've seen the case often enough— did you imagine he carries it around with him merely for the exercise? He's quite good. Besides, music is very soothing to the nerves. He's had a hard day. I'm only telling you because I think it would be wise if you slept up here tonight."

Itzhak's mouth compressed into a thin line.

"I wish you wouldn't talk to me like I was a kid, Mordecai."

"You are a kid."

"I wasn't such a kid this afternoon, with that Nazi."

"I know—Inar told me about it. He said you did very good work. But you still have to learn to be a little tactful, Itzikel. You won't be grown up until you learn that other people have souls as well as you— even overgrown, golden-haired *goyim* like Inar Christiansen."

"Would it be all right if I went?" Esther asked suddenly. It was an impulse—she hardly knew where she found the courage. "I could just sit outside his door and listen. I wouldn't disturb him."

Herr Leivick turned to her with a curious, measuring narrowness of the eyes. He almost seemed to have expected something of the sort. Finally he held out the room key for her, waiting until her fingers closed around it.

"Go ahead," he said, with the deliberateness of a man who has hit upon an idea and isn't sure whether he is pleased with it or not. "Go down and listen, if you want to. Who can say? It might be just the sort of disturbance he needs. Itzhak, just walk her down and make certain there aren't any unfamiliar men loitering around in the halls, would you?"

Itzhak didn't seem at all pleased with the assignment, but he stuck the pistol back into his belt, pulled his sweater back down to cover it, and opened the door for her.

Already, at the foot of the stairwell, one could hear the whisper of music that seemed simply to be part of the atmosphere, like the scent of flowers in an empty room. She sat down on the last step—Inar's door was only a few feet away—and looked up at Itzhak, smiling.

"You'll be safe enough here," he said, looking nervously away. The sound of the cello seemed to upset him, as if it hinted at the existence of things he would just as soon not know about. "Do you want me to come down for you later?"

She shook her head. No, she didn't want that.

When he was gone, and she was alone there in the hallway with that strangely human voice, she was almost a little ashamed of her own sense of relief. Itzhak was a nice boy and, as he had pointed out to her more than once, one of her own kind, but he seemed to be waiting for something—something he almost seemed to demand as a birthright—that she couldn't possibly have brought herself to give him. She didn't love him, could never love him, could never want to love him, even if "love" amounted to no more than giving him freely what she had given to so many men already, and all because they too had demanded it as a birthright. Itzhak wasn't anything like them, but somehow that didn't make any difference. It didn't matter that he was her own kind, because she didn't have a kind anymore. She wasn't a nice Jewish girl whose father could speak for her while she hid in the next room. Her father was dead, and there wasn't anything nice about her. Itzhak would have to look elsewhere.

But with Inar it was different. It wasn't simply that he too had been through the fire, although that was part of it—that he knew the worst of her and could imagine all the rest was a relief to her conscience. It wasn't that he had saved her from dying piece by piece in that Russian prison. She wanted him. It was a new experience for her—she wanted to feel the weight of his body over her. She wanted that helplessness. It would be the first time any man had had her because for that moment and that moment alone she needed it. It didn't make any difference that he didn't care anything about her. Why should anyone care anything about her? She wasn't anybody. He could throw her out tomorrow morning, but she would still have had something she could keep for the rest of her life. It was what she imagined virgins must feel like.

And he played the cello too. The sound of it made her so happy she felt like crying.

General von Goltz had played the violin, keeping time by tapping his foot on the floor. B, D, B, C-sharp, A—just notes. He liked a piece with plenty of double-stops and trills. He would play them over and over, each time exactly the same. He liked an audience. The music that this man was playing in the solitude of his hotel room was nothing like that. It almost wasn't music at all. It was almost like the sound of someone speaking, except that the words were lost. It was like something from childhood. It was like Isaiah prophesying in the wilderness.

And it was beautiful. Unearthly—just a long melodic line that never repeated itself, going on and on, tragic and beautiful. A lament for Israel—for Esther Rosensaft. Except, of course, that Inar Christiansen was not a Jew and hardly knew Esther Rosensaft was alive. Still, it didn't seem to make any difference. There was room in that sadness, even for her.

And then, suddenly, it stopped. A second later the door opened, and Inar was looking out at her with a puzzled expression on his face. It was only then that she realized she really had been crying.

"Have you come down to complain about the noise?" he asked. It was hard to tell whether he was joking or not.

"What was that you were playing?" she asked.

"Nothing. Just doodles. It keeps the shoulder muscles from stiffening up." He glanced up and down the corridor and then back at her, and then smiled. It seemed so strange to see him smiling.

"Come in."

He stood a little aside for her and then closed the door again. She stood in the center of the room, not quite sure what to do with her hands, until he made a curt gesture toward a small wooden chair standing against the wall. His cello rested against the bed.

"Play something else," she said as she sat down. "Something that isn't so sad."

At once she felt like an idiot, but he merely smiled again. He seemed to have taken the attitude that she was a child who must be entertained, so he sat down once more on the bed, hoisted the neck of his instrument up to his shoulder, and began to play.

"What was that?"

" 'Little Brown Jug.' It's an American song."

"Please don't make fun of me."

"I'm not—that's what it's called. I'm sorry."

He looked as if he were about to say something else, but then he stopped, lowered his head, and began to play again. This time he was concentrating, and the tone was caressing and rich. The heavy, strong fingers of his left hand danced back and forth across the strings. He hardly seemed to realize anyone was there.

When he stopped he closed his eyes for a moment and then looked up at her, no longer smiling.

"That was Bach," he said. His hand seemed to pain him; he let it slip down the neck until it rested on the cello's wide, feminine shoulder. "You didn't get your new clothes today, did you. I'm sorry—we'll go back in the morning. Have I thanked you yet for saving my life? I honestly think you did, you know."

"Does it really hurt where he shot you?"

"Yes, it really hurts. That just means it won't kill me."

"I love you."

She could feel her eyes flooding with tears again. She felt humiliated by the way he was looking at her, as if she had admitted to an act of shameful cowardice. No, of course he didn't want to hear. But she couldn't help herself. It seemed as natural to tell him so as to love him, and as natural to love him as to breathe.

"I'm no prize, kid," he said finally, shaking his head in resignation. "All you're going to buy yourself is a bad time."

Was it really possible, after all? She pressed her hands down into her lap—it was the only way she could keep from reaching out to touch him. She wanted to touch him, to be touched by him. To feel his strong fingers pressing against her body.

"I love you."

It seemed all she was able to say.

He got up and carried the cello over to its case.

All the time he was putting it away he never looked at her. He seemed to be waiting for her to disappear.

Finally, after the lid was closed, he turned around.

"I killed a man today." His eyes hardly seemed alive at all. "I seem to be doing that quite a lot lately. I don't much enjoy it. So don't tempt me, Esther. I'd like nothing better than to crawl inside you and hide for a few hours, but it wouldn't work out. I can't give you anything you really need. I've got the mark of Cain on me."

"So have I."

She pushed up her sleeve to show him. At that moment she was almost glad—the numbers seemed to give her a kind of right. They meant she was one of his own kind.

There was just a second when she thought she had won. She could feel his tenderness, like the warmth of his body. Yes, of course; he understood everything.

And then, in an instant, his face changed.

"Go upstairs," he said, almost shouting. His eyes had a cold blue light in them, and he almost seemed to be trembling. "Tell Mordecai to come down here. Wait—just a minute."

He took her by the arm, turning it around so he could look at the tattoo, holding it up to the light. He was tremendously excited; she could feel the tension through his whole body. He had forgotten all about her.

"Damn you. Damn you, you bastard. You . . ."

But she couldn't finish. She could only sob. And he wasn't listening anyway. There was a desk next to his bed. Still holding her by the arm, he dragged her over to it, opened the drawer, took out a piece of paper and a pencil, and copied out the number. G4/

3454641. She wasn't even there for him, only the number.

Finally, he let her go.

"Well, what are you waiting for? Get Mordecai—go on!"

G4/3454641. He wondered how he could have missed it, how he could have been so stupid.

"Hagemann always undervalued the beautiful." Von Goltz's own words—and Christiansen had been dumb enough to think he had been talking about Esther. Perhaps he even had, but not only. The key had been there all the time. *"I play the violin, did you know? Nothing in comparison with yourself of course, but not too badly for a soldier."*

And von Goltz had put those numbers on her arm himself. With the Russians only a few hours away, he had taken the time.

"I play the violin, did you know?"

Well yes, it was all so fucking obvious. The General had made Esther the bearer of his last message to the world, his will and testament. It was a code, just as Mordecai had guessed. But numbers can stand for letters, which can stand for notes. The tattoo stood for a phrase of music—a little joke. *Ein Musikalischer Spass.*

G4/3454641. What was the G for? A treble? Why would von Goltz want to indicate a clef? A key signature? The numbers, obviously, were intervals, but from what? G? Were the intervals chromatic or part of a scale? At least there was a limit on the number of possibilities.

Christiansen picked up his pencil again and sketched

a hasty five-line staff, trying the chromatic intervals from G. G, B, B-flat, B, C, B, C-sharp (call it D-flat and keep it in the family), B, A-flat. Key of A-flat major, more or less. It didn't look very promising, and it would probably sound like shit.

The key of G was no help—it only had one sharp and that an F, so a progression in which the highest interval was a 6 would never reach it. G was the dominant of C, so maybe the key was C.

Chromatic intervals were a washout, so he would try a straight scale. Okay, from G that went G, C, B, C, D, C, E, C, G.

He looked at his little clef full of notes and decided this was a considerable improvement. Now, if those were the pitches, what were the note values? For the moment he would assume they were all equal, so that only left the time signature.

He had his cello out of its case and was just about to begin playing when Mordecai walked through the still-open door.

"What did you do to that poor girl? She's practically hysterical."

"Just listen to this."

Christiansen played his nine notes, and immediately they sounded like something he had heard before—they were even pretty. But the timing was off. What did the stroke mean? A bar line? Okay. Then the rhythm could be either da-da-DUM or Dum-da-Dum-da. He tried the first. No, that wasn't right. DUM-da-DUM-da-DUM-da-DUM-da. Paydirt.

"What we have here is a musical phrase, probably in the key of C, definitely in three-quarter time. Listen again."

It sounded just as right the second time through. Mordecai sat on the chair so lately vacated by Esther Rosensaft, his head cocked a little to one side.

"It's very nice," he said, without giving any indication of being overwhelmed. "What is it?"

Christiansen laughed—he couldn't help himself.

"What is it? You ask, what is it? I'll tell you what it is. It's G-4-3-4-5-4-6-4-1, that's what it is. It's what Goltz put on our Esther's arm. It's your code, you goddamn idiot!"

He swallowed hard, surprised at his own vehemence. He wasn't angry with Mordecai—what the hell was the matter with him?

"It may or may not be my code. You've been able to turn a series of numbers into a little tune, which by itself proves nothing. How does that make it a code?"

Yes, of course he was offended. Mordecai's face was as blank as the wall behind him, but that didn't mean he liked being called names. And now he was demanding some kind of proof.

Christiansen played the phrase again. Nine little notes—one, two, three, four, five, six, seven, eight, nine. He didn't care who he offended. He was right.

"I know this piece," he said, matter-of-factly. "I can hear it in my mind, an oboe solo with the violins playing an octave lower, *sempre piano*. When you play the cello in a student orchestra you have a lot of time to sit on your backside and read the stuff everyone else is playing. If we can track down the score those nine notes came from, we'll know everything von Goltz put into that tattoo. Let's go find ourselves a music store."

Lifting the instrument from his shoulder, Christiansen rose from the bed as if he wanted to leave that minute. He put the cello back into its case, parked the case in the closet, and closed the door. Mordecai hadn't so much as taken his hands from his knees.

"It's one o'clock in the morning," he said finally. "There is a curfew in this city. Where are we supposed to find a music store?"

He smiled, so at least he had forgotten about being insulted. He was a practical man pointing out a practical consideration. The whole business could wait until tomorrow morning.

No, it couldn't. Christiansen began hunting around for a clean shirt big enough to go over his bandages.

"Come on, Mordecai. We're going to need that International Zionist Conspiracy of yours now. We've got to find a music store!"

"You might bear in mind, there are very few Jews left in Vienna these days."

Christiansen stopped with his arm halfway into a shirt sleeve. He turned around to look, just to be sure his ears hadn't been playing tricks on him. Mordecai still hadn't gotten out of his chair. He was very still and serious. Apparently it hadn't occurred to him that Christiansen wasn't kidding either.

"Do I have to remind you what it is we're looking for here? Do you remember the picture you painted for me of what Hagemann and his Syrian friends would be able to do with even a small quantity of von Goltz's precious nerve gas? I'm not indulging a whim, Mordecai. Find me a music store, or in a month's time there may not be very many Jews left in Tel Aviv either."

Ten minutes later they were out on the street, hoping they wouldn't run into one of the American patrols.

"He's not a Jew," Mordecai was saying, almost under his breath. He still didn't like this, but at least he had gotten over the idea that he was being asked to play parlor games. "His name is Merizzi—God knows, probably Austrian for the last four hundred years. I picked him because his home address indicates that he lives above his shop. We'll just have to wake him up and hope he doesn't decide to call the police."

It was very quiet outside, and cold. Christiansen's wounds hurt him, and he would have liked a cup of coffee and a cigarette to steady his nerves—he knew he was still strung out from this afternoon. But one had to bear with one's infirmities. They hadn't passed a car or a lighted window in six blocks.

"I've been thinking—it must be late eighteenth century."

Mordecai turned around to look at him as if he suspected a hint of madness.

"Haydn or Mozart. At Juilliard we played Haydn and Mozart until our hair turned white. It's third movementish—funny how I can almost catch the rest of it, but not quite. I'll know it the minute I see it."

Herr Merizzi's establishment was near the university; they actually had to cross into the International Zone to reach it. The shop was the first floor of a two-story building that looked as if it had been put up in the middle of the last century, in an architectural style that could only be described as Shoddy Imperial Baroque. The windows were separated by twisting pillars of broken, discolored cement. There were no lights on, of course—it was past the bourgeoisie's bedtime. Christiansen pressed the electric doorbell with his thumb, leaning against it. He could stand the noise if the family could.

Within forty-five seconds they could hear footsteps on a hall stairway.

Herr Merizzi opened the door and stuck his head out. He was wearing a dark wool robe over his night-shirt, and he was angry.

"Have you any idea of the hour?" he asked, sputtering. He was thin-faced and small, with a large mustache that somehow gave him a melancholy appearance. "My wife is . . ."

The sentence just died—perhaps whatever his wife was or wasn't seemed somehow less important with Christiansen's pistol pointing at the center of his face.

"We wish to do a little research," Christiansen said softly, pushing his way inside. "There's a point my friend and I wish to settle, and when we've done that we'll leave. And you'll be twenty American dollars richer. Do you understand? You can simply go back to bed when we're finished. There will be no trouble, and tomorrow morning you can buy your wife a nice present."

A door opened at the top of the stairway, and Christiansen saw the murky outline of what must have been a large woman wearing her hair loose so that it looked like a shroud. He put his pistol back into his pocket, where she wouldn't be able to see it.

"Fritz?"

"Nothing, my dear—just business. Go back to bed."

The shape in the doorway disappeared soundlessly and the thin wedge of light collapsed to nothing.

"You did well, *Mein Herr*." It was the first time Mordecai had spoken, and the sound of his voice made Fritz's head twist around on his shoulders with the suddenness of a mechanical toy. "Perhaps we could all go into your shop?"

Merizzi's place of business was a room hardly wider than the hallway that led upstairs to his apartment. The long walls were lined with bookcases, with little brass plates nailed to the shelves indicating the contents. Christiansen took down several boxes, the sides cut at an angle so one could read the spines of the scores they contained.

"Symphonies—and Mozart's piano concerti, just for insurance."

Mordecai nodded without much enthusiasm. He was standing with the proprietor, his back to the door so no one would get any flashes of inspiration. There was a desk in the precise center of the room. Christiansen sat down behind it, snicked on the light, and began sorting out the contents of the boxes. He hadn't realized before how much the Classical masters had liked the key of C. Without half trying he turned up ten Haydn symphonies, four more by Mozart, and four concerti. Fortunately, not every one of them was in three-quarter time.

It took him slightly more than an hour to find what he had been looking for.

"Come take a look at this."

Herr Merizzi was asleep in a chair, his chin resting in the palm of his hand, so Mordecai tiptoed over to see what Christiansen had circled in heavy black ink.

"See the first violins?" he asked, pointing to the top line of the string section. "Just like I remembered, an octave lower than the oboe. And there I was down in the basement, scraping out the tonic. Do you believe me now?"

They both looked at Merizzi, who had probably been disturbed by the sound of Christiansen's voice. He was coming awake again.

"I believe you, but where does it bring us? What does it mean?"

In answer, Christiansen closed the score. The cover read:

WOLFGANG AMADEUS MOZART
SINFONIE IN C
(LINZER SINFONIE)

He rolled up the score and put it under his arm. It was time to leave.

"Thank you, Herr Merizzi. Our apologies to your wife." He took out his wallet and counted two ten-dollar bills into the man's hand. Merizzi gazed up at him, blinking uncomprehendingly. "I'll keep this if I may. Please go back to bed now, and forget any of this ever happened."

They managed to get four blocks without hearing any police sirens, so apparently that was precisely what he did do.

"Does the curfew apply in the International Zone?"

Mordecai shook his head. "No, I don't believe so."

"Good—then let's take the long way home. I need a drink."

The place they found was in a basement, not fifty yards from the Burgtheater; it was like a hundred little joints Christiansen knew in the New York theater district where actors and musicians got together after the shows closed, too keyed up even to think about sleep. It had just that atmosphere—the party that has gone on just a little too long. They were shown to a table by the stairway—the waiter, one gathered, had sized them up as tourists and therefore best kept out of everybody's way—and Christiansen ordered a brandy and hot water. He could use the anesthetic.

"Just coffee for me," Mordecai said. When he had the cup in front of him, he consented to take one of Christiansen's cigarettes.

"So. Now we know where to look. From the whole world, we have narrowed our focus to the city of Linz—and all because Mozart wrote a symphony there. Von Goltz went to all that trouble just to tell us that one thing."

"He's telling us more than that." Christiansen took the cigarette out of his mouth and set it in the huge glass ashtray that took up so much of their tiny table. He unrolled the score and opened it to the place he had marked, putting it beside Mordecai's right hand.

"You see how the section is marked? 'Trio.' Why pick that section unless he wanted us to know we should be looking for three things instead of just one?"

"Three things?"

Mordecai took a pen from his breast pocket and, at the top of the score, directly over the nine notes Christiansen had circled, wrote out the number from Esther Rosensaft's arm: G4/3454641.

"What is the significance, do you suppose, of the line?" he asked finally. As if to emphasize the question, he wrote out the number a second time.

"It's a bar line—look at the score. G, C, then the rest follows in the next measure."

"But it doesn't, don't you see? The final note begins a new measure, so if von Goltz was being consistent he would have put in a second line—here." He drew it between the final two numbers. G4/345464/1. "He must have had a reason. Von Goltz could count just as well as you or I."

Mordecai took a sip of his coffee, set the cup down, and smiled. His discovery seemed to please him very much.

"Perhaps your original thought was correct. Perhaps '3454641' is the number of a safe-deposit box. Then we would have the box number and the city.

"Do you have any idea how many banks there must be in Linz?" Mordecai asked, still smiling through the haze of his cigarette smoke. "We have two things— perhaps we have two things—but we still need the third. What do you suppose 'G4' is intended to tell us?"

Christiansen didn't have the faintest idea. He was tired of being clever. He was tired of guessing games.

His wounds hurt him and the brandy wasn't helping at all. He wanted to go back to the hotel and go to bed. His cigarette tasted like burning newspaper.

He dropped a handful of coins onto the table. One of them rolled over the edge.

"Let's get out of here. We'll have the walk back in which to consider the matter."

Mordecai bent over to pick up the coin from the floor. He set it on the table with the others. Then he began to get up.

"A map," he said suddenly. He had to put his hand down on the table to steady himself—that was how it took him. "Every map I've ever seen has letters along the top and numbers down the side. 'G4' must refer to a square in a map grid. That's our third thing."

"There must be an official map of Linz—the Nazis had an official everything."

"Yes—we'll have it checked. How much will you wager that we'll find only one bank with a street address within those coordinates?"

Neither man spoke as they walked back toward the university. After a few blocks, the only sound was from their footsteps. Beyond the Maria Theresian-Strasse, which marked the northern limit of the International Zone, there weren't even any street lamps.

Von Goltz had deposited his legacy in a bank in Linz. They had the account number, and they knew where to find the bank. But they couldn't claim the inheritance quite yet.

"There will be a key to the safe deposit box." Mordecai spoke so softly that he almost seemed to be talking to himself. "I think we can assume Hagemann will have that. And the box will be in someone's name.

The bank will doubtless require a signature. We have half the pieces."

"And Hagemann has the rest."

"Yes. And whoever finishes the game with them all will be in a position to dictate the history of a nation."

Mordecai stared down at his feet as they walked along, his face tight and frowning.

"There are some things it is better not to know," he said finally, as if announcing some decision. "This is a terrible weapon, the sort of secret that must corrupt anyone to whom it is revealed. I could wish for the sake of my country waiting to be born that neither side might have it. The Jews are as human as anyone else. They will not be improved for possessing so absolutely the power of life and death."

"But better them than the Syrians—isn't that what you think?" Christiansen didn't know himself quite what the question meant.

"What I think is, better no one at all."

There was simply nothing more to say. They parted on the steps of the hotel.

"Aren't you coming inside?" Christiansen asked. But Mordecai shook his head.

"No. I must make a telephone call, and it's better that I don't use the hotel lines. You understand. I shall see you again in the morning."

So Christiansen went inside alone. His room was on the third floor, and the elevator had been out of order since the day of their arrival. He had the stairway all to himself.

He supposed, really, that he ought to be extremely pleased with himself. After all, they had figured everything out. What was left except to get a key and some information from a man who went around with a bodyguard even Stalin might have envied? It should be easy. Sure it should.

And if it wasn't, why should he care? He would kill Hagemann or Hagemann would kill him—it seemed to make remarkably little difference.

He was tired, that was all. You get tired, and it makes you sick of life. He was tired all right. He wished . . .

Oh, the hell with it.

He unlocked his hotel door and let it swing shut behind him before he switched on the light. Esther Rosensaft was sitting up in his bed, naked, resting on one elbow, the sheet covering her up to the arms. She looked at him through dark, serious, unsmiling eyes. The duplicate of his room key was lying on the night table. God damn Mordecai.

"I'm sorry about tonight," he said. "I guess I gave you a pretty rough time. I guess I do that a lot."

"Yes. But I've decided to forgive you."

* 14 *

Barcelona, Spain: March 17, 1948

In an hour they would be in the station. Christiansen took out a cigarette and lit it, using only his right hand because Esther had long since taken possession of the left and was playing absentmindedly with his fingers. The quartet score spread out over his knees, which he had bought during a three-hour stopover in Zürich simply to have something to read, had long since ceased to be very interesting.

Since yesterday morning, Esther had been very quiet. Up until then anyone would have supposed she was having a marvelous time—she was in love, to hear her tell it, and on a kind of honeymoon trip and, barring the locked cattle car that had transported her and her family to the extermination camps, this was the first time she had ever been on a train. Now she just sat there, without speaking, staring out through their compartment window as the scenery slipped by, with Christiansen's left hand held palm up in her lap.

In Barcelona, Christiansen would leave the train and Itzhak Dessauer would take his place.

It was an elaborate plan—too elaborate to Christiansen's way of thinking. They were staging a little domestic drama. Dessauer was to be the bridegroom, taking his new wife on a marriage trip to the Spanish Mediterranean. That was how the bait was to be displayed to Egon Hagemann. The young couple would stay in a hotel in the resort town of Burriana, where Hagemann maintained a villa overlooking the coast. The idea was to make him forget himself long enough that he would risk venturing out beyond the protection of his fortified enclosure and his bodyguards, on the theory that not even Hagemann would think to bring an army into a lady's bedroom. Mordecai and his people were taking a hell of a lot for granted.

"Hagemann will never buy it. He'll know he's being set up. He knows Esther was in Mühlfeld. By now he certainly must have heard that Plessen is dead. And a couple of days after that episode, not half a dozen miles away, I killed one of his soldiers. He's bound to draw the appropriate conclusions."

"Of course, but what choice do we have?" Mordecai had shrugged his shoulders, smiling in a way that suggested he found the whole situation faintly ludicrous. "For that matter, what choice will Hagemann have? His ambitions—his survival, from everything we hear—are all predicated on gaining possession of the girl, so he will have to try for her whether he suspects a trap or not. He will take his precautions, needless to say. Everything will hinge upon which of us has been the cleverer."

Mordecai and his boys had been in Burriana for over a week now, keeping watch to learn how Hagemann spent his time and settling the details. And since everybody seemed to know all about him, Christiansen was supposed to wait until the last possible moment before putting in an appearance. He was intended to serve as the distraction.

But in the meantime there had been the journey, and Esther, and it had been almost possible to forget about Egon Hagemann, Kirstenstad, revenge, and the fate of the Jews. Christiansen had been escorting his new lady on a leisurely tour across southern Europe, learning all over again how to enjoy himself. It wasn't hard.

Esther couldn't seem to get enough of him—she would sit on the other side of the table in restaurants, watching him eat as if the sight of a man shoveling food into his face were somehow the most enchanting spectacle she could ever hope to witness. And bedtime kept getting earlier and earlier.

Women, he had discovered, could be very intimidating—at least, this one could. That first night, in his narrow hotel bed in Vienna, he had kept her cradled in his arms while she wept as if her heart would crack. She would take that comfort from him, even while she begged him to despise her, to remember always and forever that she was no better than a street whore. What had they done to her in those places that love should be such a confession of self-contempt? To kill the body or cripple the soul, if not both then one or the other. To make life a bitterness and a humiliation, in itself a kind of death.

He had been lonely and womanless too long—he knew that—and her warm, soft, hungry young body was pressed up against him as if all she wanted was to disappear inside his flesh, but at that moment, listening to her sobbing confessions, even his lust had given way before an enormous and unmanning pity.

"It's all right," he had whispered, stroking her hair with the palm of his hand, conscious that he was lying but not knowing what else to say. "It's all right. None of that will ever come back."

And then she had dug her fingernails into his chest, to remind him why she was there.

And after that, strangely enough, everything had been fine. She seemed to like it when he made love to her. It seemed to make her happy, even through the tears with which she still regularly wetted his shoulders. But what, finally, it meant to her he couldn't have said. He didn't even know what, if anything, it meant to him.

This is just kind of a vacation, he kept saying to himself. I need it, and she needs it. But pretty soon it will have to stop or it will begin to get in the way. She's a poor little thing and she likes me and she's fun in the sack, but that's all there can ever be for either one of us.

All of which, as he perfectly well knew, had nothing to do with anything. The fact was the little minx had gotten under his skin with more than her fingernails.

"What is this?" she asked, closing the score that lay unattended on his knees so she could read the cover.

"What it says: 'Bartók, String Quartets.'"

"Are they good?"

"Yes. He was a great genuis. My composition teacher introduced me to him when he first came to America in 1940, a frail little man who hardly spoke. It was right after the German invasion of Norway, so all I could think about was getting to England and joining what was left of the army—I'm afraid I didn't pay him much attention. I didn't care so much about genius in those days."

"Could you play them for me?"

"It takes four people to play them. You probably wouldn't like them anyway—they don't sound a thing like 'Little Brown Jug.'"

It was their private joke. They smiled, and she leaned against his shoulder. And then suddenly she was very serious again.

"When will I see you after Barcelona?" She was looking down at his hand, still cradled in her lap, and as she spoke she ran the tip of her little finger across the scar that covered its back.

"I don't know. I'd be around, but people are going to be watching you. Try to remember—you're supposed to be married to Dessauer."

"Will I have to sleep with him?"

"It isn't part of the plan, no." He smiled again, but less easily. The subject made him faintly uncomfortable. "Whether or not it's part of Itzhak's plan, I couldn't say."

"I will do what is necessary—no more. Perhaps he won't even want me. I am a tainted woman, but you are the Righteous Gentile. He will not want to offend you. Would it offend you?"

It was not, he decided, a question he much liked being asked. He wouldn't answer it. Perhaps he couldn't.

"I think just maybe you carry this 'tainted woman' nonsense a little far," he said finally. "Lots of people came out of the war with memories they'd just as soon bury. The war turned everything upside down, so we all had to behave like devils just to stay alive. You never did anyone any harm."

"Didn't I? Not even myself?"

She guided his hand up so that his fingers rested just below the elbow of her right arm. Even through the fairly heavy material of her blouse, he could feel the angry little welt that marked where her tattoo had been. A doctor had removed it in Vienna, but the scar remained. Well, they all had their scars.

She had told him all about the camps, all about von Goltz and Hagemann, much more than he cared to hear. He knew all about her version.

"You were a prisoner, and your jailers were the worst this world has to offer." He could only shrug his shoulders, as if to say, *What can I tell you you don't already know?* "You might try to bear in mind that nobody was giving you any choice."

"Weren't they? Haven't I a choice now?"

Christiansen stood on the platform, watching the train slide away, wondering why he felt so relieved. He was fond of Esther—he wasn't sure how much further than that he was prepared to go, but he was reasonably certain that if he gave himself half a chance he could work up a real sentimental enthusiasm for her. Anyway, he was glad that for a few hours at least he wouldn't be seeing her.

"*Would it offend you?*" She didn't even have to put the question into words. It was always there. It constituted the atmosphere of their relationship. He just didn't have an answer.

But for a while now he was at liberty to think about something else.

Was that why men went off to war, to get away from the ambiguities of their womenfolk? Was that what he was doing? Just then it seemed to him the theory had a lot to recommend it.

Once you got outside the train station, Barcelona looked like a nice enough place. There weren't any bombed-out buildings—that was it. There was plenty of open ground, but it wasn't covered with rubble. Just trees and plastered walls and sidewalks. Ordinary life. Of course, Spain had had nine years to clean up the wreckage from its war; maybe the whole of Europe would look this way before long. Anyway, the city was a pleasant surprise.

Until you noticed the crowds of Civil Guards standing around, with their crisp black uniforms and their lacquered hats. They all carried little pistols in their clipped-up, patent-leather holsters, and they were everywhere. It seemed the current regime wasn't taking any chances.

Like almost everyone else in the civilized world, Christiansen had developed an allergy to snappy tunics and gold braid—he didn't like the fancy-dress ball through which soldiers tried to intimidate the rest of the human race. He didn't like government policemen.

And all these guys standing around with their hands on their belts were friends of Colonel Egon Hagemann. Old-line Nazis were very popular in Franco's Spain—it was a point to remember.

It was cold. There was still a little of winter left, even in Spain, and Christiansen dug the rabbit-fur-lined gloves out of his overcoat pocket as he crossed the plaza in front of a massive Gothic cathedral, its central doors open and gaping like the mouth of a dead monster. A few elderly women were coming down the steps.

Away from the plaza, the buildings crowded together and the streets were not as clean. Carpets and bedsheets hung from the iron balconies on the upper stories. There was hardly any noise—like all northern Europeans, Christiansen somehow expected Latins to conduct affairs at the top of their lungs—and everyone moved quickly and furtively. It was almost like walking through a city under military occupation.

On the other side of the Ramblas was a district known as the "Barrio Chino"—one could only guess why, since there weren't any Chinese anywhere in sight. There also weren't any women leaning suggestively against the lampposts and no one approached him with photographs of his kid sister, but Christiansen didn't have to have it explained to him that he was in what passed locally for the red light district. It was one of those places where you seemed to see only other men on the sidewalks, and everyone was very careful to pretend everyone else was invisible. Even at this hour of the morning, the bars were open. One of them was called the "Hotel Goya." That was what the sign in the window said. It was Jerry Hirsch's idea of a joke.

It was a small, dark room. Just inside the shelter of the doorway, a huge green parrot eyed Christiansen suspiciously through the bars of its cage, twisting its head around as if to whisper over its shoulder. There were no confidences here, it implied, nowhere in out of the storm.

Hirsch was sitting at a table in the rear, nursing a cup of coffee that looked as if it hadn't been touched in a couple of weeks. The women in the tight satin dresses who were taking up space around the bar looked up hopefully as Christiansen pushed aside the beaded curtain that formed a kind of second entrance, but their enthusiasm died almost at once as they saw Hirsch raise his hand in recognition—another damned *inglés* who wasn't interested in girls, it seemed.

"Did Itzikel and the girl get away all right?" Hirsch asked almost before Christiansen had had a chance to sit down. Hirsch had a way of referring to "the girl" as if she were an item you took off the grocery store shelf. Hirsch didn't waste a lot of time cultivating his charm.

"They're fine."

"Good—then that's taken care of."

It was impossible to tell what he might have meant, so Christiansen decided not to try. But he would be just as happy when this business was over, and with it the need to stay on civil terms with Hirsch.

"Do you think it would be possible to get some breakfast in a place like this? I haven't eaten yet."

"Yes. They cater to every appetite here." Hirsch turned and caught the bartender's eye. "I'll join you, if you don't mind. I think my prestige with the management could use the lift."

Five minutes later a fat, breathless little woman with the sleeves of her white blouse rolled up high on her arms had brought them two plates of food so hot the steam rose up and hit them in the face. In Spain, one gathered, they didn't kid around—there was rice, beans in heavy brown sauce, lumps of meat the size of a child's fist. There was coffee sweetened with a local brandy, and a wooden bowl filled with dried apricots.

"Maybe we should have just asked for cornflakes," Hirsch murmured, grinning with a parody of horror as the good lady, who was presumably the bartender's wife, retired back into her kitchen.

"Tell me about Hagemann." Christiansen spoke quietly. Anyone watching would have supposed his attention was entirely absorbed by the food in front of him. "What have you found out? Have you seen him?"

"I've seen him. I've seen him nearly every night for the past week."

Hirsch smiled, lifting a heavy forkful of meat to his mouth. He seemed to be enjoying some private irony, with Christiansen as the principal victim. They weren't really enemies—it was almost as if they understood each other too well.

"There's a club he favors, a kind of cabaret. You know the kind of place—the emcee tells dirty jokes you might have heard from your mother, and the girls up on stage never quite manage to take their clothes off. The band is terrible. Anyway, Hagemann likes it. He goes there every couple of nights and stays until around midnight. The place is run by a fellow named 'Ernesto' Lutz—born 'Ernst,' Tubingen, 1901; also old-school SS, in case you hadn't guessed. The management keeps a table for the exclusive use of our friend and his entourage. Did I mention that? Hagemann never goes anywhere without three or four bodyguards—they wrap him up like a baby with the croup.

"The local authorities act as if he's incognito royalty or something, so we've had to exercise a little discretion. The one place we do have under control is our hotel, the Casa General Moscardó. Faglin and I have both got jobs there. We created a few vacancies." He smiled again. He was just full of good cheer. "We'll nab our friend there, when he comes to relive old times with Mrs. Dessauer."

"You really are an unpleasant son of a bitch, Hirsch."

"I know it."

"What about the house?"

"Oh, that." Hirsch pushed away his half-empty plate with a look of unconquerable distaste. No one, he seemed to imply, could eat that much food. "I think you can just forget about the house. He's got the sea on three sides—the compound is on an out-cropping of rock, with seventy-foot cliffs, straight up and down. You can't even get near it from that direction. For the rest he's got a chain-link fence, and of course it's all patrolled. He's got a regular platoon of bodyguards, and they live on the grounds in a barrack of their own. The regular servants are all Spanish nationals and go home at night, but the boss treats them pretty well and the police have got the hell scared out of the whole town, so we haven't been able to get near any of them. What goes on up there is a closed book to us. Forget the house. We're going to have to put the touch on him in town."

One of the whores was standing by the doorway, trying to feed pieces of bread to the parrot. It was a big bird with a beak that could do a lot of damage to a lady's fingers, so she was a little nervy as she held out the bread through the cage bars. She had a high-pitched giggle and she kept glancing back at her friends for moral support. Apparently it was a slow morning in the Barrio Chino.

When Christiansen decided he had had enough breakfast, he took out a cigarette and lit it with the nickel-plated lighter Esther had bought for him during their one-day stopover in Lyon. He felt uncomfortable, as if he had been awake too long.

"Why don't I just kill him for you?" he asked suddenly. He smiled, but he wasn't kidding. "You people have your side of the code, so Hagemann can't put his hands on his secret weapon—you're safe. All you need to make it all come out right is for me to walk up behind him at that special table of his and put a pill in his ear."

"You'd never get away with it. His boys would cut you down before you had your hand out of your pocket. And even if you succeeded, how would you ever get out of there alive?"

"That would be my problem."

"No it isn't—it's ours." Hirsch glanced nervously toward the doorway as if the parrot worried him. "Nobody is safe until friend von Goltz's recipe book is in the custody of the Mossad. The only way we can guarantee that Hagemann won't get it is if we have it ourselves, and that won't happen unless we take Hagemann alive so we can squeeze him."

"He won't get it if he's dead."

The cigarette had burned down almost to Christiansen's fingers, so he crushed it out against the side of his plate. Hirsch watched him, and finally sighed and shook his head.

"That would settle everything for you, wouldn't it, brother." He laced his hands together over his stomach and leaned back in his chair, frowning like a judge. "That's the difference between us—some Nazi kills a few dozen of your friends and relations and you go all huffy about it. All of a sudden it's a blood feud, just like the Hatfields and the McCoys. All you can think about is how good it's going to feel when you make the son of a bitch start bleeding through his ears. Shit, Hagemann butchered thousands of my people, but when you're a Jew you learn to take a broader view of these matters."

He wasn't finished—he showed his teeth in a joyless grin. He looked relaxed enough, except that the joints of his fingers were slowly turning purple.

"So what if you kill him?" he went on, finally. "What difference will that make? We don't know how much von Goltz may have told him or who else the Colonel may have taken into his confidence. If he doesn't get Esther Rosensaft to tell him he may figure the whole thing out for himself some other way, but at least with Hagemann we know where we are. You kill him and I guarantee another will spring up to take his place. Revenge solves nothing. I don't want to spend the rest of my life wondering when the poison gas canisters will start raining down on my apartment building. I want that formula."

It had started to rain by the time Christiansen left the Hotel Goya. He could hear them pinging against the metal awnings over the shop windows, big wet drops like tears. When he felt the rainwater going down the back of his neck, he turned up his overcoat collar. Norwegians were supposed to be immune to the coldest, wettest weather; they weren't supposed to catch pneumonia on the Spanish Mediterranean—it was a question of national honor. He decided he had better find somewhere in out of the damp before he disgraced himself, but first he wanted to get out of this tangle of cat houses and bars.

Making a dash through the traffic, he crossed the

Ramblas, reaching the curb just ahead of a great sheet of water thrown up by a passing taxi. He waited under the cement balcony of a hotel until the rain subsided. It didn't take long.

Hirsch had offered him a lift into Burriana, but he thought it might be better if he found his own way. After all, Hagemann had the cooperation of the local police, and Hagemann might be halfway expecting the arrival of a large Norwegian with a scarred left hand—he had given plenty of indication that he knew all about Inar Christiansen. There was no percentage in compromising the Mossad's end of things as well. Christiansen would get there by himself.

Besides, Hirsch made him nervous.

"If and when you do get this stuff, what will you do with it?" It hadn't seemed such a naive thing to ask.

"That's a leadership decision," Hirsch had answered, just a little too quickly. He shrugged his shoulders and his face went blank; Christiansen might have been talking to a plaster wall. "I'm just supposed to get it. It's use is a political question."

Sure. Except that to Hirsch a weapon was just that, a weapon. Something to be used against one's enemies. He planned to win this war of his. He didn't care how; he just planned to win. Well, who could blame him? Where would he go—where would any of them go—if they lost?

Talking to Hirsch always gave him a bad conscience. Hirsch had a way of lumping all Gentiles in with the *Einsatzgruppen*—there were only two kinds of people: Jews and people who murdered Jews. Or consented to their murder, or turned away with a shrug. That Inar Christiansen hadn't been the commandant of Auschwitz was merely an accident of history.

But Hirsch was right about one thing—in his heart, all Christiansen cared about was settling up for Kirstenstad. He wanted to kill Colonel Egon Hagemann. That was what was important to him personally, and he could be ashamed of it because he had no business putting one man's death above the survival of thousands.

So he would help them get their fucking formula, and then nothing on God's earth would stop him from pulling Hagemann's guts out an inch at a time.

But first he had to get to Burriana.

* 15 *

Christiansen ran down the sail on the boat he had rented in Castellón de la Plana and tied it to the boom. He was about half a mile off shore, so he fished around in his kit for the pair of field glasses he had taken off the body of a dead German officer in 1943. He wanted a close look at an outcropping of rock that climbed up from the surf like a wall. It was late afternoon and he hadn't more than an hour of daylight left. He didn't want to waste it.

The boat had an auxiliary motor, but there had been a good breeze blowing straight down the coast so he hadn't felt the need to use it. Besides, the sail was quieter and attracted less attention. It was the irresistible prejudice of the machine age that sailboats were the province of harmless cranks. None of Hagemann's army of sentries would be made nervous by a tiny triangle of white canvas bobbing up and down on the horizon.

He was reasonably sure this was the right place.

He couldn't see a house, but the cliff faces matched Hirsch's description and there didn't seem to be anyplace like it near enough that he could have made a mistake. Burriana itself was only about a mile and a half farther up the coast, its low whitewashed buildings twinkling in the sun. He could have pulled in there and asked, but that probably wouldn't have been very bright.

The cold waves lapped against the sides of the boat, and it rocked slightly with every move Christiansen made—it was only about twelve feet long. There was something strangely comforting about being out alone on the open water. As almost nowhere else, one really was alone.

Christiansen scanned the cliff face through his field glasses, and, yes, it looked almost as formidable as Hirsch had warned. There were no tides to speak of in the Mediterranean, and the rock dropped straight down into the sea. There was no beach, no firm ground from which to mount an assault. And along the south wall, where the sunlight hit it, the face glistened. It was oozing wet, probably slippery as the sides of a fish. It could be climbed—anything could be climbed— but it would take time. Nobody was getting up there in a quick three minutes.

Everything, of course, would depend on how heavily the crest was patrolled.

He wondered what sort of a life Hagemann was leading up there in his seaside fastness—did he feel safe or were his nights tormented by dreams of retribution? It would have been nice to think so, but it wasn't likely. There wasn't much evidence that he had either the conscience or the imagination for anything like that. An intelligent man within certain limits, Egon Hagemann was otherwise your standard Nazi thug.

It was all there in the Allied War Crimes Commission dossiers—quite a typical career for the sort of man who ends up running a death camp. Born February 3, 1899, in Günzburg, son of a primary-school teacher. Drafted into the German army in July, 1917, and saw the war at close quarters as an infantryman along the Ardennes front. Wounded twice, received the Iron Cross, Second Class, mustered out as a sergeant in January of 1919. Briefly attended the university at Munich.

Then Egon Hagemann seemed to find himself. He discovered politics—or at least that side of politics concerned with breaking people's noses and throwing bricks through plate-glass windows. Membership in various *Freikorps*. Joined the Nazi Party and the SA in 1927. Transferred to the SS in 1930. From there the only direction was up.

And now he was living in splendor because he had convinced the Syrians that he could deliver the formula for a nerve gas that would finish the work of the Final Solution.

And just to be sure he survived to see it, he had talked his Arab sponsors into buying him this fortress by the briny deep.

It was wonderful, the confidence the Germans placed in such things. When they had overrun Norway in 1940, one of the prizes that interested them most was the heavy water facility at Vemork—they wanted the stuff for their atomic weapons research, and Vemork was almost the only large-scale producer in Europe. Anyone would have supposed they would have taken adequate precautions against sabotage.

The plant itself was located on a little notch in the rock face of a mountain. The workers had to cross over a suspension bridge from town and, for the rest, the place was considered impregnable. After all, you could guard a bridge easily enough, and who in his right mind would try scaling a six-hundred-foot rock face?

Nevertheless, four Norwegian commandos, some of them men Christiansen had trained with, had climbed straight up from the frozen riverbed with enough plastic explosives to put the place out of business for months. They even got out alive, which just went to prove that anything was possible.

Perhaps not anything. There was one crucial difference: the Vemork team had merely to reach its target, plant a few charges, and run, while in this instance it would be necessary to capture Hagemann and take him out, alive. Further, at Vemork the Germans had been so sure of themselves they hadn't even bothered to patrol the cliffs. Hagemann was unlikely to make the same mistake.

But one mustn't complain. At least the cliffs weren't six hundred feet high.

The wind was beginning to pick up as the sunlight faded. Christiansen's little boat began to buck slightly against the restraint of the anchor rope, and he was glad he had thought to bring his rain parka. He slipped his arms into the sleeves, lit a cigarette, and had another look through the field glasses to see if anyone was moving up there.

At twenty before five he saw his first sentry, just a man in a checkered coat walking along with a rifle slung over his shoulder. No uniform, of course. Sometimes one becomes conscious of an expectation only after it has been disappointed. Needless to say, Hagemann wasn't going to call attention to his people by dressing them up in SS black.

Christiansen would wait and see how long the fellow took to make his circuit. It would provide some idea of the size of the property, and also of how much time an assault team would have to get up that rock face to level ground. One could hardly start the second he turned his back.

The man wandered by, his eyes down on the ground and his hands in his pockets. If he was thinking about anything it was probably his dinner. He wasn't really expecting anything to happen—he was bored. After a few seconds he disappeared behind a clump of trees.

It all seemed so straightforward now. Hagemann was up there; all that was required was to go get him. It wasn't a matter of success or failure—Christiansen expected that he would probably be killed—it was simply that now everything was very clear.

He had even written what was in effect his will, disposing of the only piece of property he had that could be said to have any genuine value. When they had stopped off in Bern for a day and a night, Christiansen had left Esther behind in their hotel room and had gone to visit his old composition teacher, who, with the war over, had returned to Europe and was teaching at the conservatory. They had spent an hour together, drinking tea and talking about New York and what everyone was doing now and whether there was any future in this serial music that was such a hot item just then with the avant-garde, and at the end of it Christiansen had left behind his cello, along with a letter to be opened in three weeks' time. If he wasn't back to claim it by then it was a safe bet he would be dead somewhere, and the cello would go to Juilliard. They would find someone to do it justice.

That only left Esther. He couldn't give her anything except the cello, which she wouldn't want and which wasn't really his anyway—a great instrument like that, a work of art in its own right, is never more than out on loan. Perhaps the only thing he could do for Esther was to find some way of getting to Hagemann, so she wouldn't have to be the bait in their trap. The bait—that had been his idea to begin with. Poor little Esther, who said she loved him. He didn't have a lot to be proud of on that side.

Hagemann was up there, waiting for her.

At a few minutes after five, two men appeared at the top of the cliff. Neither of them was the sentry, who hadn't returned. They weren't part of the troops.

They both were wearing expensive-looking overcoats. The taller man's was a double-breasted camel's hair, quite stylish with a wide turned-up collar, and the other man's was blue. The shorter man was wearing a hat, which shaded his face, but he seemed a dark-complected sort anyway. They stood together talking—perhaps they had come outside expressly for that purpose, to be away from everyone.

It was impossible, at that distance, to make out their features. They were just two men, tall and short, light and dark, watching the sea. They could have been anyone.

And then the sentry came by again, and stopped to give the taller man a crisp straight-arm salute, and Christiansen knew at once.

Hagemann returned the man's salute, raising his hand and then opening it so that the gesture appeared to be nothing more than a friendly wave. He disliked performing these little military ceremonies in front of Faraj, who seemed to find them somehow rather humorous. Faraj was a civilian, without any great respect for the soldier's view of the world.

Of course, given the current state of the Syrian army, that wasn't really such an unreasonable attitude.

They waited in silence until the sentry had disappeared out of earshot, and then Faraj turned to him and smiled his tranquil, maddeningly diplomatic smile.

"You must understand our impatience, Colonel," he said soothingly—it was almost as if the man fancied himself in a boudoir. "The best estimates are that, even after you have provided us with the formula, it will require at least two weeks before we can begin generating tactically useful quantities of the gas. We must have results soon if we are to justify the very considerable expense . . ."

"Yes, my friend, all in good time. The girl arrived by train less than two hours ago. Do you see how the Mossad delivers her into my hands?"

Hagemann allowed his eyes to rest on the cold Mediterranean horizon. He hated Faraj. The man was always at his elbow; it was almost like being under arrest. He hated the constant reminders that time was running out—as if he needed reminding. Faraj was like an omen of failure.

There was a single boat out on the water, its slim mast sticking up like a needle. Most likely it was some silly English tourist out dragging the bottom for a few muddy-smelling turbot. The Spanish fishermen were all comfortably back in their berths by this hour.

"Perhaps it is the Norwegian," Faraj broke in suddenly. His unreadable smile was still in place when Hagemann turned to look at him. He could even have been joking after his macabre fashion. "Perhaps his intention is to climb up these cliffs and murder you in your sleep."

"That he plans to murder me I have no doubt, but I'm sure Christiansen can think of some easier method of approach." Hagemann smiled in his turn—it was necessary constantly to be reassuring the lesser races that one was not afraid. "After all, he is an economical man."

Nevertheless, Hagemann rather wished he had thought to bring his field glasses with him.

He had had no indication of Christiansen's whereabouts for over a week, not since the news of Pilsner's death in Vienna. It had not been necessary to inquire into the circumstances of that event.

One's old sins came back to haunt one. Hagemann did not have to ask himself why this Norwegian was hunting him. Kirstenstad had been a turning point in both their lives.

Of course it was possible that Christiansen was in Spain. It was even possible that he was collaborating with the Jews, although that was not a conclusion that Hagemann rushed to embrace about an enemy whom he had come to respect. Anything was possible, but there was no immediate cause for alarm. Everything would sort itself out now very quickly.

Yes, very quickly. Christiansen might hang him in a broom closet, or the Syrians might lose patience and

leave him in a shallow grave somewhere with a bullet
hole in the base of his skull. Those were the alternatives to success, and he was not quite as confident
of success as he led Faraj to imagine. But it was none
of Faraj's business if a cold, sick feeling settled in the
pit of his stomach every time he thought of . . .

"You should come to the Café Pícaro with me this
evening," he went on, turning back to contemplate
once more the presence of that lone sailboat on the
horizon. "You will be able to see our Miss Rosensaft
with your own eyes—along with her new 'husband.'
It will confirm for you how agreeably things are pro-
gressing."

"She is surrounded by an army of Jewish agents—
you said as much yourself."

"That is perhaps overstating the case. All we can
say with conviction is that Leivick has been in Burriana for several days now. If he brought anything like
an army with him, I'm sure my own people would
have detected them by now."

The tops of the waves had long since been dyed
a smoky red, and it was growing cold. After so many
months in Damascus, Hagemann was glad to have
returned to the chill dampness of Europe, even as
that was represented by Spain. Syria was a kind of
hell, fly-ridden and suffocating, unbearable winter or
summer. But the Syrians needed him. They had given
him back his rank and a reason for living.

Still, he hated them. The Syrians were all like
Faraj—corrupt and effeminate. The Jews, who were
at least Europeans, were a thousand times superior
in every way. Leivick was a man it was possible to
respect, at least. But Faraj . . .

But Europe had been a dead world for him since

1945, a place that had forgotten how to listen to the voice of its own heart. It would not do to grow too contented here, where the fascist police merely tolerated his presence for reasons of sentiment. Syria commanded his loyalty now, and history had seen to it that the Jews were his implacable enemies. One had to learn to deal with the world as it was.

And now Esther had come back. What a shock it had been when that shabby lawyer of von Goltz's had turned up in Beirut. Hagemann had fancied himself hidden from the whole world, but the General had known precisely where to send his final message: "Find Esther if you need something to trade for your next meal. If you have an ear to listen with, she can tell you where to find the process book." Only those few sentences and a brass key, the sort that might have fit a post office box or, much more probably, a bank safe-deposit vault. What a delicious joke he must have thought it, writing that note on a piece of stationery with "U.S. Army, Provost Marshal's Office" embossed on the letterhead.

Of course, he had hardly needed von Goltz to remind him of Esther.

Only an imbecile would mention the word "love" within the context of a slave labor camp, but Esther had meant something to him nevertheless.

What had there been about the war that could have made him into what he had become? Nothing, except its terrible cruelty—and the need to keep from going mad. He had known enough men who had finally had enough, walked quietly to their tents, and shot themselves through the roof of the mouth. He had decided very early that he would not be among the ones who ended that way.

But Esther had defeated him. One could embrace cruelty, making it into the religion of a cruel age, but finally a girl hardly into her teens turns to one with dark, frightened eyes and all resolution simply fades into nothing.

All the great conquering nations of history had included women in their booty. From Achilles to Genghis Khan the victorious warrior had carried off the wives and daughters of his slaughtered enemies. It was a traditional right. Esther had been no different; she was part of the spoils of war, and he had felt himself free to do with her as he liked. There had been others before her. There was nothing different about Esther.

Except, of course, that in the end he had accepted with relief when the General had said, "Don't distress yourself about the girl. Leave her to me, and I shall see to everything. There will be nothing left for the Russians." Except, of course, that von Goltz hadn't had any intentions of killing her.

Had she ever understood the power she exercised over him? Was that something a woman was born knowing? Of course, she had hardly been a woman. She had hardly been more than a girl, but she might have seen him with a woman's eyes. When she had pretended to be so afraid, had she merely been playing on his vanity?

The war had left him with many such questions. The war had been like fire from heaven, a mad time.

Before—and in all the time since, hiding from what had become the law—he had never thought to do such things, think such things, as the war had made seem so natural, the accustomed pattern of human life. It had been like no other time, and he both missed it and was glad it would never come again. The war had been such freedom as perhaps no man should have.

In May of 1918, Hagemann had come home from the Ardennes on his one and only leave, and everything had been as he had left it. His mother was still alive then, still keeping up the tiny house in which he had been raised. By then he had already killed four men in combat, one of them with a broken bayonet, but she still treated him like a child home from school. *"It will be all right,"* she had told him, over and over, stroking the side of his shaven head with her soft, warm hand. *"I'm sure your officers look out for you and wouldn't allow such a young boy to come to harm."* Behind the lines, Germany was unchanged, unchangeable.

And then, of course, it had changed. Defeat had brought with it the moral chaos of socialist governments and revolutions and soldiers who had to beg for bread. Hagemann could remember how, straight after demobilization, still in his sergeant's uniform, he had wandered around the streets of Munich, his heart black with anger. All the suffering and death of the Great War, and this was how it had ended. How he had hated Germany then.

"It will all come right of its own—you'll see," his mother had told him while she struggled to keep them both alive on his mustering-out pay, money suddenly worth next to nothing. *"Only they shouldn't have sent the Kaiser away like that. It wasn't respectful of them."*

And she would watch him as he drank his *ersatz* coffee, feeling his rage without understanding it. For her, somehow, the world still made sense—that world of Sunday services, her little home, her son somehow mercifully spared from the war. She felt no need to go searching after something to light the darkness inside.

"Believe, Obey, Fight!" Hitler had told him. What more did he need? What more was there? It had filled the vacuum in his soul. It had given him back his honor and his reason for living. It had led him, step by step, to his terrible awakening, to this place and this web in which he found himself tangled.

From September of 1939 until the very last, he had never been out of his uniform. Germany was a place he traveled across in a troop train. The war had been the whole of life. France, Norway, Russia, Poland—and, finally, Waldenburg. He had been a different person.

And now he was working for the Syrians, quite an ordinary military commander. He ordered men killed and sent others to their deaths, but that was no more than every commander did. He carried everywhere the knowledge of what was possible for him, but he was once more a man like other men.

And now Esther was back. It would be strange to see her.

"You will see," he said, almost as if to himself. Faraj had to crane his fat, nimble little neck to hear. "I will have the girl back within twenty-four hours, and then, very soon, we will know everything."

"Will we? You were always most convincing in Damascus, but some of us have come to wonder if perhaps you weren't depending too much on a scribbled note from a man about to be condemned to death. Von Goltz might have been playing with us all—what would he have to lose or gain?"

Faraj looked up at him, smiling like a cat. One

might have supposed he was merely posing a hypothetical question, of no real interest to anyone.

"You did not know him, so how could you possibly understand?"

The sun was almost gone now. In a few minutes it would be dark. It was time to go back to the house, but Hagemann found that he was unable to bring himself to move. The white mast of the little sailboat caught the last of the light and glistened as it pitched to and fro.

"The General was a curious man," he went on, forcing himself to look away from that distant patch of water. He returned Faraj's smile, hating him. "He has set us a riddle, but by his understanding of the rules the riddle must have an answer. He no doubt expected that I should fail—he always underestimated me. But if I solve it—when I solve it—then it shall be as he said. When we have the girl, you shall have gained your victory over the Jews."

"But at this moment it is the Jews who have this Miss . . . What did you say her name was?"

"Rosensaft. Esther Rosensaft. But, of course, she is only part of the answer."

"What? You mean she can't tell you after all?"

Faraj took off his hat and wiped his brow against his coat sleeve. When he was excited or panicky, his eyes bulged and his neck had a way of swelling, as if it might burst any second.

"Consider, my friend." Hagemann put his hand on the man's shoulder, giving the impression he expected he might otherwise topple over, like a plank of wood. "Would the Jews put this girl so easily within my reach if the answer were really hers to give with a word? I told you, we are in the presence of a riddle."

Yes. *"If you have an ear to listen with, she can tell you . . ."* Poor Esther—one could not simply wring the answer out of her, like water from a damp rag. The General had been too clever for that.

But Faraj couldn't appreciate the charm of the situation. Faraj could only stand there, rubbing his hands together, his throat puckering in distress.

"When we have her, we shall have to exercise a little intelligence, that is all. She is important—more important, I think, than even an old fox like Mordecai Leivick appreciates—but in herself she is hardly more than a medium. I doubt if von Goltz ever actually told her anything."

"Colonel, if you have led us this far and she is . . ." Faraj returned his hat to his head and allowed the implied threat to hover wordlessly between them, like an uninvited guest. The sentry was coming back. Even Faraj understood the necessity of not arguing in front of a subordinate.

Hagemann stood with his back turned. He could hear the sentry's footfalls on the pine needles behind him. He wanted to ignore his existence.

The sentry already had his flashlight on.

"Leave these matters to me, Faraj. I won't fail." The words seemed to come from between clenched teeth.

As if the sentry's flashlight had been a signal, the sound of an outboard motor insinuated itself across the water. The little sailboat wheeled about and began making its busy way back to the harbor at Burriana.

Well, of course. He wouldn't have lingered so long if he had to depend upon the wind to get him home.

"Come with me tonight." Hagemann turned around—he could hardly see Faraj's face, the light had grown so dim. "Come and enjoy the cabaret. Forget your Moslem principles for a single evening and we shall drink a bottle of champagne together, and you can see for yourself how the net closes around your hated Jews."

16

"He may not come this evening. Don't let yourself expect him. Don't look for him. Plan nothing. Let him make all the moves, solve all the difficulties. Pretend nothing. Above all else, we must do nothing to make him suspect that he is not in perfect control of events."

Herr Leivick sat on the bed beside her, his hands pressed down against his lap, speaking in a calm, almost monotonous voice that still somehow managed to communicate a sense of irresistible urgency. They seemed to have been there together for hours, but it had been only the four or five minutes since Itzhak left the room to buy a pack of cigarettes in the hotel lobby. The cigarettes were for Herr Leivick, who seemed to smoke them more or less continuously now, but Esther felt reasonably sure they had only provided the excuse for these few moments of private conversation.

"How are the two of you getting along?"

"Fine."

Esther smiled, gasping out one voiceless syllable

of embarrassed laughter. What was she supposed to say? She and Itzhak were registered here as man and wife. They must somehow contrive to spend the night together in this room, and yet on the train ride down from Barcelona they had hardly spoken. It was necessary that they appear to be lovers, yet how could they?

"It has to be made to work, you know." Herr Leivick took off his rimless glasses, which were clouded with moisture, and wiped the lenses against the lapel of his jacket. "This is supposed to be a honeymoon you're on, my dear. Itzhak's quite taken with you—play on that."

"I can't. I . . ."

"You don't want to hurt his feelings? Hurt his feelings. He's a big boy—you won't kill him. Esther, this is more important than Itzhak's feelings."

"Does he know that?"

"Yes, he knows it."

And did Inar? She would have liked to ask Herr Leivick that as well, but how could he have told her? Inar had left the train in Barcelona. Inar understood everything that was expected of her, but he had left the train. She had been a whore for so long—she wondered when she would be entitled to stop. What would Inar say? After this was over? Yes, after this was over.

"I'll do whatever you tell me," she said finally. "It's not as if I have anything to lose, is it?"

"You're a good girl, Esther, so don't talk like that."

"Am I?"

He never had a chance to answer, because that was the moment Itzhak chose to come back with the cigarettes.

"It isn't Inar's brand." Herr Leivick opened the package and, with a slight ironical nod that meant *With your permission, madame,* allowed Itzhak to hold a match for him. "That man is introducing us all to bad habits."

Itzhak stood in front of the dresser, tying his tie in the mirror. The expression on his face was concentrated, as if he were prey to uncomfortable thoughts. He always seemed to look that way when they were alone together.

"We'll go down to dinner in about half an hour," he said, his reflection peering at her with evident suspicion. "Mordecai says we should be there by nine, but that gives us plenty of time. He says we should be seen in the hotel together, just in case Hagemann sends someone around to check. The club is only a five-minute walk from here."

"I wish it could be finished already."

"What? What did you say?"

He turned around and stared. She could have been some local curiosity, some odd little animal that had wandered into their room by mistake, the way he was looking at her.

"I'm frightened, Itzhak—can't you understand that? You can't know how that man frightens me."

There were tears streaming down her face. It didn't matter to her. She was a coward, and she didn't care whether anyone knew it or not.

"I just wish you would sit down here and put your arms around me, Itzhak. Could you do that for me? I won't tell anybody."

And he did sit down and pull her to him. She had wondered what it would be like, but she didn't feel

anything. Inar's body had a warmth she could feel
even through his clothes. Inar made her feel safe, as
if it might matter that . . . But this was just a man
holding her in his arms. She could smell the cologne
he used and feel the slight scratch of his beard, but
she was just as alone. There was no comfort.

In that way at least, Itzhak was not so very different
from Hagemann. Very well then, so much the easier.

His head rested on her shoulder. She took it between her hands and pushed him away, just enough
to let her kiss him on the face, touching the corner
of his mouth with her own. Herr Leivick had said . . .

He was surprised, of course. She could see that
in his eyes—Itzhak hardly knew what had happened.
He was about to speak when she covered his lips with
her fingers.

"It doesn't matter what you think of me, Itzhak.
It's better if you don't like me. I'm the kind of girl
men use, and you have to learn to use me the way
the others have."

"The way Inar does? Does he use you?"

"Forget about Inar—this doesn't have anything to
do with Inar."

She wanted to strike him, to make a fist and hammer his face. She hated him for reminding her, for
trying to make her weak. But instead she took hold
of his hands, which were gripping her shoulders, and
brought them down so that the palms were pressing
against her breasts.

"You have to learn to touch me. I'm not like the
nice girls you knew in Tel Aviv, so I won't pull away.
You can do anything you want to me. You have to
learn to treat me the way a man treats a new wife, a
woman with a past—like something you own."

He didn't know—she could read everything in his face. He was just a little frightened, like the younger men, hardly more than boys, hardly older than she had been herself, in the barracks at Waldenburg. They had known she wouldn't stop them, that they could beat her if she tried, that they could do anything they wanted. Still, they had been frightened. Afraid of what she might think, as if what she thought could possibly matter. For some of them, probably, it had been the first time.

It was all there in his face—she could see everything. Of course he was afraid of Inar. He was afraid of her. But he wanted her, and that was all that mattered.

They were all the same, just the same. The fear was always there, even in Hagemann. That was why there was no comfort in them. Only in Inar, who feared nothing, not even death.

But she didn't want to think about Inar.

"Go ahead—what are you waiting for? I won't tell anyone."

She couldn't seem to feel anything. His hands were there, cupped over her breasts. She had only to glance down to see. But it was as if she had turned to dough. He could dig his fingers into her, twist the flesh, press the nipple down to nothing with his thumb. It didn't make any difference.

Except that Itzhak was helpless. He simply sat there, holding her breasts, staring into her face. With a certain surprised relief she realized that he could go no further unless . . .

And she wouldn't. She didn't have to now.

"You'll wrinkle the dress," she said, pushing his hands away. "Do you want me, or not?"

He didn't answer immediately, but his eyes burned with pain.

It doesn't matter, she kept telling herself. *I have nothing to lose, so it doesn't matter.*

The thing had to be made to work. Then Inar would have his revenge, and it would make him whole again. And nothing would ever make her whole. This would be all she would ever be able to give him.

The street was dark and noisy. Lights flickered yellow and demonic through tiny windows, and people pushed past one another on the cobblestones. She was wearing high-heeled shoes, and the uneven path and the darkness made her feel less than steady, so she held Itzhak's arm.

He had become a little drunk from the wine at dinner—just a little, but it made him sullen. He was almost violently possessive; he would run his hand over her shoulder and down to her arm, and he would reach across the table to do it. She closed her mind and let him. This is what she had wanted. This was what would make Hagemann believe everything.

Itzhak was a nice boy, but he should never drink because he wasn't nice then. It wasn't his fault. He felt she had cheated him, and he was right.

"Is it always this way with you?" he had asked, standing by the dresser as they waited for the moment when they could go downstairs to the dining room. "Are you always so—businesslike? I would have been all right if you just hadn't been . . . Hell, you act as if it were a field exercise or something."

"You can't expect romance, Itzhak. It isn't always that important. Don't you have any whores in Pal-

estine? Haven't you ever known any girls who trade
it for money?"

"Is that what you're like?"

"Maybe." Even as she spoke, she could feel her
throat tightening. "At least I'm not going to die of
shame if some man wants to put his hands on me."

He stood with his back to her as he adjusted the
knot in his tie, and the hunch of his shoulders revealed
how deeply his vanity had been wounded.

But at least he wasn't afraid anymore.

"Don't be mad at me, Itzhak. Try to understand."
With her left hand she brushed a few wisps of hair
away from her face, feeling once again quite calm.
"We have a part to play, and we have to be ready to
play it. We can't go there and sit at a table and be
polite to one another—Hagemann is no fool. Now you
won't have to act at all. You can treat me just like a
whore you've picked up to spend the evening with."

"Will Hagemann believe that? You're supposed to
be my wife."

"He'll believe it."

"The only whores in Tel Aviv are the Arab women."

"Not even you believe that."

So Itzhak had gotten a little drunk at dinner and
had started pawing her. And as they walked along the
narrow, crowded, treacherous Spanish streets, and he
began to grow sober again, he was finally able to put
his arm around her, quite as if he had forgotten that
sort of thing had ever been a problem. They would
do very well together.

The club was smaller than she had expected, hardly
larger than one of the tiny shops, selling everything
from embroidery to newspapers to wine by the glass,
that lined both sides of the street. The outer walls

were whitewashed, like those of every other building in town, and covered with huge, brilliantly colored posters announcing bicycle races and soccer matches. A surprising number of small children were standing around, taking turns opening the club door for patrons and holding out their hands for tips.

"Give them something," she whispered. The sight of them made her throat tighten. "A man on his honeymoon is expected to be generous. Give them all something."

"The world is full of begging children—what difference does it make to you?"

"Never mind. Just give them something."

He did. He reached into his pocket and took out a handful of silver coins, dropping them into eager palms that snapped closed around them like traps. It turned into a kind of game.

"Come on, Esther. Let's go inside before they mob us."

It was not quite eight-thirty. Somehow the place seemed larger from the inside, but perhaps that was only because it was still half empty. In one corner by the stage, which was itself little more than a long table against one wall, was a band consisting of a piano player, a drummer, and a boy of about fifteen with a trumpet polished up so bright it hurt one's eyes to look at it. The floor manager, in a tuxedo with a gleaming display of shirt front, guided them to a table in almost the precise center of the room. No one would have any trouble seeing them.

Itzhak ordered a bottle of champagne and the waiter brought it over in a silver bucket, wiping the outsides of the glasses before positioning them with elaborate ceremony on the table. Esther tasted hers and then set it back down again. The band was playing an American dance tune. She couldn't rid herself of the idea that everyone was watching her.

"He isn't here," Itzhak said, almost as if he could read her mind. "His table over there in the back is still empty. It's early yet."

"Don't imagine I'm looking forward to it. I can wait."

"What's he like?"

"He's the devil."

"I mean, what does he look like?"

She turned her head slightly and let her eyes rest on him, smiling the way she imagined new brides to smile, wondering what he could be talking about.

"There aren't any photographs—at least, none that we have—and Mordecai hasn't let me near this place. I just wondered."

"He looks quite ordinary. Perhaps he is quite ordinary. Light brown hair, a little taller than average, nice looking without actually being handsome. In his late forties by this time. You could meet him in the street and never notice him. That is, of course, unless you were at Waldenburg."

"Drink your champagne. You look as if you've seen a ghost."

"Perhaps I will, tonight."

But she did drink the champagne. She drained the glass, and then Itzhak poured her another. He didn't touch his own—he was working now.

At a quarter to nine there was a little drum flourish and a man in checkered coat and black-and-white saddle shoes came onto the stage. His whole manner announced that he was there to be a comedian—he grinned and swayed at the shoulders and recited a

few jokes. At least one assumed from the expectant
silence that followed each of them that they must be
jokes. Esther and Itzhak didn't laugh because neither
of them understood any Spanish. No one else laughed
either. No one seemed even to notice that he was
there. After he was finished, a woman obviously in
middle age but still quite handsome came out and, to
the accompaniment of the piano, sang a sad and beautiful song in a language that was probably Catalan.
When the song was over, she stood quietly and received the audience's fierce applause with the resignation of a martyr. Nothing, it seemed, could induce
her to sing another, and when she left the waiters
suddenly became very busy taking people's orders.
One gathered that the first phase of the entertainment
was over.

"According to Hirsch, the girls don't come on until
after nine, so Hagemann never bothers to come until
then. He says it's a pretty tame show. I wonder why
your friend is such a fan."

Itzhak filled her champagne glass again, studying
her face as if he really expected her to know. Perhaps
he was only having his revenge, for which she couldn't
blame him.

"Don't make it any harder for me, Itzhak—please?"
She smiled and reached across to place her hand on
his arm. They couldn't know who at that moment
might be watching them. Itzhak covered her hand
with his own. He was smiling too. Yes, he was having
his revenge.

"I don't know what you're worried about. This is
a public place and the war's over. He can't touch you.
I wouldn't let him touch you."

Esther could only laugh. She realized she must

have gotten a little drunk, but that was just as well. She felt as if her heart had frozen shut, but the laugh still sounded pleasantly girlish. No one turned to stare at her.

"If he decides he wants to touch me, he will simply kill you, Itzhak. 'The war is over. I wouldn't let him touch you.' How would you stop him, would you tell me? Do you really imagine this is just anyone?"

Suddenly she was sick with dread. She wanted to get up and run, and knowing that she couldn't, that she might be running straight into Hagemann's arms, only increased her rising sense of panic.

Oh God, where was Inar? If she could know only that he was somewhere around, she would feel safe again. But perhaps she had forfeited her small claim to his protection. Yes, of course she had. She had given up even her right to love him, except that she couldn't help herself.

Poor Itzhak, he was all at sea. He looked so uncomfortable, almost ashamed. They weren't having a very pleasant honeymoon.

Another flourish of the drums and three girls tumbled on stage, almost as if they had been pushed. The trumpet blared out one of those throbbing tunes that everyone knows but that don't seem to have any name, and the girls swayed back and forth in a parody of dance, swinging their hands and behinds, like mechanical toys. Their costumes were bright yellow, edged with ruffles, and no less modest than the sort of thing one saw every day on any beach in Europe, but the whole performance still managed an impressive lewdness. After a few moments the comedian returned and stood at one corner of the stage shouting jokes as the girls continued to dance. Now everyone laughed.

In the barracks at Waldenburg they had laughed like that. Esther could remember, almost as if it were happening that instant, how they had made her dance naked up and down the little corridor between the rows of beds, how they had beat time against the floor with their boot heels and how they had laughed. As she danced by, some of them would try to grab at her, or strike her on the buttocks with the flats of their hands. They wouldn't allow her to stop, not even when she fell down weeping with exhaustion. When she couldn't get up again, they had made her crawl on her hands and knees.

But the girls on stage, with their fixed grins, safe up there from their tormenters, was it any different for them? Did they think so? Their eyes, hunted and weary-looking, said not. It was no wonder Hagemann liked to come here.

"It's pretty silly, isn't it," Itzhak said finally, having almost to shout over the laughter and the screaming trumpet.

But Esther couldn't answer. She could only draw back her lips into what she hoped would be taken for a smile as she listened in her mind to the stamping of boot heels.

Hagemann's car was a long gray Mercedes that had once, he was assured, belonged to a member of the Spanish royal family. He hardly cared which member, since he had bought it less to please his vanity than for the steel shields that turned the back seat into a bullet-proof cocoon. In case of attack, if he had time to throw himself to the floor, to get down below the window line, he would be safe enough. It seemed a reasonable precaution, even in General Franco's Spain.

The drive from his villa to the club took less than twenty minutes, along a road that swept by Burriana's harbor. The bay was too shallow for ships of any size, so all one saw there were the pleasure boats of wealthy tourists and fishing craft belonging to the local peasants. They made a picturesque sight, clustering around the sides of the long wooden piers like swarming bees.

Hagemann kept his own boat anchored closer to home, at a private wharf just beyond the fence surrounding his property. All he needed to do was to climb down a narrow metal stairway—so cunningly concealed by the undergrowth that one could look straight at it and never know it was there—walk across the narrow beach, and there it was. He kept the wharf guarded, of course. The sea was his avenue of escape.

But tonight he had no thought of escape. Two of his bodyguards were sitting in the front while he rode behind with Faraj. The others followed in a separate car. He was on his way to one of the more important moments in his invisible career.

"You see, my friend, we reach our goal not all at once but by a logical progression. We could not succeed in getting the girl out of her prison, but the Jews did that for us and now deliver her over into our power. What clearer proof could you demand that history is on our side?"

But Faraj was not in a temper to be consoled. Faraj was a nervous little man with none of the gambler's confidence in his luck.

"They are preparing a trap for us," he said. It was a sentence he had repeated at intervals throughout the evening.

"Of course they are. What of it? Wouldn't you, in

their place? Like us, they are fighting for their survival."

"I wish you were a little less confident you will win, Colonel. Such self-assurance seems almost like tempting providence."

"It is that. To be a German and alive after 1945 is to tempt providence. I have grown used to it."

After that, and until the car began to make its slow, careful way through the narrow streets of the central town, they did not speak again. Hagemann was grateful. It was politic to bring Faraj this evening, but he would have preferred to be alone. He wanted to think, and to remember. He wanted to be alone with Esther.

It had been Becker who had first told him about "the *Herr General*'s new girlfriend—a skinny little thing, not your type at all. We picked her up on the way, in one of those glue factories in northern Poland. The General practically snatched her from before the doors of the crematorium. You should have seen her— messy little bitch! We've all had her, almost everyone in the camp, so she's kneaded soft enough that she won't be too demanding on our commander's energies. By now you could push that little lady's thighs apart with a feather. Hah, hah, hah!"

Yes, it had been a marvelous joke, in the best tradition of refined military humor. At the time, Hagemann had hardly even been listening.

Because, of course, he had been away—in Berlin, for conversations with the bright young things on Reichsführer Himmler's personal staff who were concerned that "Project Loki" might not come to fruition quickly enough to turn back the American and British armies in France.

Well, they had been right to be concerned.

So he had not arrived at Waldenburg until nearly
a month after the main force, under General von Goltz,
had established themselves. The Berlin trip had been
a great secret—he had not even employed a driver—
so he alone had not been in on the great good fun of
the little Jewish bitch who was keeping the General
amused of an evening. At the time, it hadn't seemed
a very important omission.

The next morning he had gone to report. He and
the General sat drinking captured Russian tea together, and the door to the bedroom was slightly ajar.
There she was, sitting on the bed, a blanket wrapped
around her shoulders, staring out at him through huge,
liquid brown eyes that seemed to see straight through
him. Probably von Goltz had planned it that way—he
took a curious pride in his little acquisitions, the way
another man might in the bottles of wine that lined his
cellar walls. The half-open door was a kind of boast.

Even then, while he and his commander drank
tea together and discussed the politics of their mission
in this peculiarly godforsaken place, Hagemann had
known—yes, it was not too much to say he had known—
that it was the shaping destiny of his life who stared
at him with those frightened, hollow eyes.

So it was more than merely the answer to von
Goltz's riddle that drew him to the Café Pícaro this
night. After all this time, he wanted to know what he
would see in her eyes now.

When his car pulled up in front of the entrance,
Hagemann saw that Lutz was already standing in the
doorway, his arms crossed over his chest, waiting. The
usual crowds of begging children were nowhere in
sight—they were all deathly afraid of Lutz.

"She is already here, *Herr Oberst,*" he said, open-

ing the car door for Hagemann. For a moment he
stared at Faraj with what appeared to be astonished
contempt and then, seemingly, dismissed him from
his mind. "She is sitting at table fourteen, where you
will have a good view."

"You have done well, Ernst. And is her husband
with her? What is he like?"

Lutz merely spat on the pavement—it was answer
enough. He was a big man, with muscles that bulged
visibly under his black dinner jacket. His hair was
cropped so close that it was impossible to say precisely
what color it might have been, and his massive head
was seamed with leathery folds, like old wounds. The
wound that had invalided him out of the SS in early
1944 did not show, but it kept him from ever raising
his right arm above his shoulder. He was an old-line
fighter, and he hated Jews worse than death.

"Of course—I quite understand. I suppose I shall
see for myself. Have you arranged the distraction?"

"*Ja, Herr Oberst.*"

He glanced once more at Faraj and then gave Hagemann an inquiring look, as if to ask, *Must I have
this greasy little carpet peddler in my club as well?*

"Come, Faraj." Hagemann slid his arm over the
Syrian's narrow, chubby shoulders. "We'll drink
champagne and look at the girls. If you see one you
particularly fancy, I'm sure Ernst can arrange something for you. Can't you, Ernst?"

"*Ja, Herr Oberst.*"

The club was crowded. Hagemann went in behind
his bodyguards, along the rear wall, and sat down at
the table that was always kept for him. He had not
yet seen Esther, and he was sure she had not seen
him.

There was a great deal of noise—the band, and that idiot of a comedian shouting into his microphone, and everyone laughing and whistling and calling to the girls. The girls, in their high-heeled shoes and their tiny swimsuit costumes that made them look all leg and bosom, the girls were dancing with frantic energy, as if caught up in some clumsy ecstasy of motion. It would be like this until the small hours of the morning.

Hagemann liked the club. The show was exactly the same, night after night, but he came as often as he could. He liked it because it was all vulgar nonsense. He let it wash over him like warm water. He liked it because it left room for nothing else. There were no dark thoughts at the Café Pícaro.

Lutz was very obliging, and none of the girls was averse to entertaining gentlemen, but Hagemann wasn't interested in looking for that sort of pleasure here. Smiling chorus girls were not what he wanted, and Spain was full enough of dark Madonnas. He preferred women who understood the pain of life.

The woman he wanted tonight had no place at the Café Pícaro, and yet she was sitting, quite calmly, not ten meters away from him, watching the performance with an expression of uneasy pleasure frozen on her lips. Hagemann found it necessary to close his eyes for a moment, as if the light bothered them. He was not sure that he could bear the longing that was almost a surge of physical pain.

Of course she knew he was there. She gave no sign, but she knew. The time had been when he and Esther had understood each other very well, so it was impossible to hide against the wall of a crowded room and pretend not to be there. She would always know.

The Jew who was pretending to be her husband was slight, with curly hair, and much too young. He watched the show with a nervous intensity and now and then turned to Esther, spoke a few words, and gave his attention back to the stage, which, from the expression on his face, might have been the scene of his personal drama. Esther would never have married a man with eyes which had seen so little of life.

Hagemann did not regard himself as, at least in the theoretical sense, an anti-Semite. During the time of National Socialism, he had killed Jews on the orders of his superiors, but without conviction. They were harmless enough people, and the Zionist Conspiracy was a paranoid delusion—he knew that. Even the greatest of men can have their eccentricities, and Himler had played upon that side of the Führer's nature to create a foolish disaster. The whole policy had been a catastrophic waste. Only fools like Joachim believed anything else.

"Haven't I told you often enough to read the *Protocols of the Elders of Zion*?" he would rave. "Isn't it all there, how they plan to take over the world? Isn't that just what they are doing this very moment? Look at Russia. Look at the Near East. Look at America!"

Nothing, of course, could convince Joachim that Truman and Stalin weren't Jews and that any Zionist plot afoot in the world was merely a conspiracy of survival forced on them by the events of 1933 to 1945. Hagemann was a soldier, not a political philosopher, but even he could grasp as much as that.

For Joachim the theoretician and for Lutz the street brawler it was all so obvious, so straightforward. He envied them the clarity with which they saw the world.

But, for all that, he was committed now. When

once one begins with the annihilation of a people, there can be no turning back. He, Egon Hagemann, through no particular wish of his own, found himself locked into a vendetta: the Jews and their allies would hound him to his death if he did not strike first. One could hardly blame them. There was no right or wrong in the matter. Those were simply the terms of engagement.

So the Jews must not have their nation. As one of their own had said, let them be blown about forever by the cruel winds of history. This Israel they longed for was not going to be his death, so let it be theirs.

All, perhaps, save one.

She was not precisely beautiful. Esther had never been beautiful—her particular charm had resided in nothing so superficial. As she sat near the stage, her face turned away so that all he could see was the line of her cheek and, occasionally, the bright glimmer of her left eye, she still made something inside his chest contract with a peculiar mingling of cruelty and tenderness. She was the child who had lived long enough to see everything, who understood him as no one else did in the wide world. Even when he had tormented her until she wept with fear, it had been like an act of mercy, a concession to his weakness, a contemptuous admission of what a nature such as his seemed to require.

And now she held von Goltz's secret in her tiny hand, and his life, and such heart as the world had left him.

And in five or six minutes, as soon as there was an intermission and enough quiet for a few words between old friends . . .

Ernst managed these things very well. He had been a good lieutenant—no originality as a commander, but strong on the details—and he had found his natural place in life as the owner of a sleazy Spanish night spot. He was on excellent terms with the local police. There was nothing within these four walls that he could not manage, including the temporary removal of an unwelcome husband.

The music died away. The stage was empty. Hagemann glanced toward the door, saw Ernst standing there with a corporal in the Civil Guard beside him, and nodded. It was time for the real performance to begin.

Ernst went down to Esther's table. He was perfect. He leaned down with the confidential air of a good waiter troubled about a problem with the bill, and whispered something into the Jew's ear.

"I am very sorry, *Señor*, but there is a gentleman here from the police who wishes a few words—something about an irregularity in your passport."

It wasn't necessary to hear. Hagemann could read it all in Ernst's face, and the way that boy's head snapped around to the entrance, where Ernst's tame constable was waiting with such a show of refined, professional patience. It was delicious.

Of course, the Jew's reaction would tell everything.

And, yes, he did precisely what Hagemann had expected. He rose from his chair, touched Esther on the shoulder—that was important, the little sign that she was to stay behind and wait for him—and left with Ernst. In a moment the policeman had taken him outside, where a car was waiting. This was not a prob-

lem that could be settled there in the street; it was
official and required the Jew's presence at headquarters. They would be gone for at least an hour.

Hagemann could only shake his head. How stupid
did they imagine him to be? They had, of course,
expected that he would use some device to maneuver
the husband out of everyone's way, but did they have
to fall in with it quite so readily? The fool didn't have
to be so very willing to leave his bride behind. They
might as well have written him a note and sent it
around to his table: "We are setting a trap for you,
and there is the bait. Please respond." It was all so
painfully obvious.

But, of course, what did he care? He was willing
to go along with them, up to a point.

Esther did not look around. She did not let her
eyes follow her husband away. Her face was turned
resolutely toward the stage. She gave the impression
she was waiting for something to happen.

Hagemann's bodyguards, thick-necked men chosen for loyalty and a certain cruel dexterity rather than
intelligence, watched his face, waiting for a sign. Instead he turned to Faraj, putting his hand on the man's
arm, as if to hold him in place.

"Now, my friend, you will have perhaps a more
entertaining performance to witness. It is a pity you
won't be able to listen. I expect my little Scheherazade
will have a fascinating tale to tell this night."

And he smiled, hating the waxy little Semite for
whom all this was merely politics and war, for whom
he had to make speeches that masked the longing that
ached in his chest like a bruise.

Even when he sat down at Esther's table, almost

touching her left arm with the sleeve of his coat, she
didn't so much as glance at him.

"So. You were expecting me then?"

"Yes."

"You saw me when I came in?"

"Yes."

At last, as if with great effort, she managed to turn
her head to look in his direction, although whether
she saw him through her clouded eyes was another
matter. She was coiled as tightly as a spring; she seemed
about to fly at him with her nails, or perhaps merely
to run away. Or perhaps, in some dark place in her
mind, she took a kind of pleasure in this reunion. She
had always been just that way with him, poised between fear and temptation, as if fear were as necessary
to her as breath.

"You could have denounced me to your husband,
Esther. He would, I'm sure, have been glad of this
chance to play the protector, the avenging knight.
Why did you miss the opportunity?"

"Because you would have killed him."

"Would I have? Yes, perhaps I would." He smiled
and picked up the champagne glass that stood next to
her tiny beaded evening bag. His mouth was dry—it
was a sensation not unlike the fear that precedes a
battle, the fear of the unknown. Why should that be?
What was there he didn't know about Esther, except
how it was she always seemed to . . . But the champagne tasted like stale beer, and he felt no better for
it. "Or perhaps you had another reason for your re-
luctance. This young man of yours, he doesn't have
the look of one who has ever been behind barbed
wire. Perhaps he wouldn't have understood?"

The man who played the piano came back and sat at his instrument, setting a large, heavy-looking glass of red wine down on the bench beside him as he began leafing through the pages of a score. A few of the patrons watched him expectantly, but he was not about to touch the keys before the end of intermission. There was all the time in the world.

"No, I thought perhaps you hadn't told him about me."

She dropped her tear-laden eyes and her hands drew together in her lap, where they were almost hidden from view below the table. She had always been a remarkable actress.

"Leave me alone, Colonel," she said finally, her voice thick and slightly blurred. "I have a chance for a new life. I'm married, and I want to live like everyone else. Can't you find it in you to leave me where I am?"

"No I can't, Esther. I couldn't possibly do that, not once I've seen you again. You couldn't really expect it of me."

He wanted to touch her. More than almost anything, he wanted to feel his hands on her thin, young shoulders. She was young—she couldn't be more than twenty, probably not even that. He hadn't realized until that moment how he had yearned for her, but it was not to be, not now. This was not Waldenburg.

"What have you done with my husband?" It was merely a question—she asked it in the calmest voice.

"He is with the police. Presently they will discover that there has been a terrible misunderstanding, and they will drive him back here and return him to you with a handsome apology. How did you happen to come to this place, Esther?"

Yes, she was very good. There was no tiny start of surprise; for a moment she seemed not even to have heard the question. And then she looked up at him with a painful smile.

"It was close to the hotel—I'm on my honeymoon, you know, and he wanted a bit of nightlife. Where else could we possibly have gone?"

"Yes, of course. Where else?"

The boy who played the trumpet was threading his way among the tables, exchanging a word here and there with the regular customers, careful not to spill the tapered beer glass he carried. The intermission was nearly over.

"I could take you back to your hotel myself, Esther. Where are you staying?"

No, the first panic was over now. She merely shook her head.

"I don't like your husband, Esther. I don't like the way he touches you."

"Is that surprising? He is my husband and, like me, a Jew. Why should you like him? He'll survive without your good opinion."

"Will he?"

"You wouldn't dare. You wouldn't . . ."

"Wouldn't I?" He smiled. They were playing an old game and they were both perfectly familiar with the rules. He allowed himself the luxury of drawing a shade closer to her. She didn't pull back. "What have I ever not dared, Esther? Shall I kill your husband? Or shall I simply tell him why he had so little difficulty with your maidenhead?"

"You are a bastard!"

Yes, it was just like the old times now. She was cornered and full of hate. Her eyes burned. Now she no longer had the burden of choice.

"I won't be happy until I've seen you again, Esther." He allowed his hand to come to rest over her arm. "In fact, I must insist on it. Tomorrow night, I think—at your hotel room. Don't trouble yourself with the details. I'll see to it that your young husband is safely out of the way."

The Café Pícaro was very proud of its theatrical effects. Sometimes the dancers would perform bathed in pink light, or the curtain in the rear would be a swirl of golden flecks. It was all achieved with the aid of a few colored lenses and an arc lamp worked from a cramped little space under the roof, where the ceiling dropped about three feet directly behind the stage. A man would sit up there, watching through a tiny window no one even noticed was there.

"Just change the lens every so often, *Señor*, and everyone will be quite satisfied. It makes no difference—one must simply keep the eye from becoming bored."

That was what the man said. The space was entered through a door above the stage. There was a stairway. The man had a key to the building and came so early and left so late that hardly anyone even remembered what he looked like. For a consideration, he was perfectly willing to disappear for an evening and allow another to fill his place. One of Ernst Lutz's waiters, a Spaniard of carefully concealed Republican sympathies, had told Christiansen all about him.

So, with the exchange of a few hundred pesetas, Christiansen found himself in possession of the best seat in the house. It wasn't the show that interested him, however; it was the audience.

From the moment of his arrival, at about ten minutes after nine, Egon Hagemann, former colonel in the Waffen-SS, former commander of the Fifth Brigade, was within easy pistol reach. All that would have been necessary was to break out the little window and start firing with the revolver Christiansen carried in the pocket of his coveralls. It would have been a dead cinch.

Of course, Hagemann had his bodyguards, and the minute they saw the holes starting to pop open all over their leader's shirt front they probably would make it pretty hot for the man locked up in a space not much larger than a packing case. Still, he might conceivably survive. It wasn't the fear of death that restrained him. For one thing, Esther was down there. Hagemann's goons, realizing the boss had been set up, would certainly see to her as well. And then there was the fact that he had, after a fashion, given his word.

So he crouched up there, sweating, miserable and unseen, for close to two hours. He had come to observe, to confirm his worst fears or, just maybe, to learn something useful, not to settle his private score.

Besides, something new had entered into the equation. He was discovering that Hagemann had to share his hostility with, of all people, Itzhak Dessauer.

For close to half an hour before Hagemann even arrived, they sat at their little table, in plain view of the whole room, and drank champagne. Esther, cold as ice, as if she were waiting in line at the post office, and Itzhak, with his face full of longing and his damn hands all over her.

He had left them at the Barcelona station only this morning—had it really been so short a time?—like a couple of children in a dancing class, the introductions barely over, uneasy in their new clothes, uncertain about the steps, embarrassed, hating the whole business and each other into the bargain. Itzhak particularly—the boy had acted as if he was made out of wood. And now, only a few hours later, they had that indefinable air of people who understood each other's secrets.

Nobody had to draw Christiansen a diagram.

What he couldn't understand was why he was taking it so hard. It didn't matter, after all. It wasn't as if Esther were his property, or even, for that matter, his girl. They had had a little interlude, which now, it seemed, was over. What of it?

The little bitch.

Of course, it wasn't as if she hadn't warned him. *"I will do what is necessary—no more. . . . Would it offend you?"* She had understood what was coming. He could have stopped her with a word, but he hadn't thought to speak it. *"Would it offend you?"*

The little bitch.

It was hot up there with the arc lamp. There was hardly enough room to sit, and nobody seemed to have done any cleaning up in this little hole any time in the last several months. There was a thin coat of dust over the window, which was probably just as well—nobody could have seen in anyway, but camouflage was always nice. What would Esther have thought if she could have looked up and seen him scowling down at her. Christiansen decided he wasn't having a very entertaining time.

And then, after a while—after he had had a moment to recover from his self-pity—he figured out that neither was she.

She was allowing herself to be handled, like a woman in a doctor's office. It was Itzhak who had changed, not Esther. She just didn't seem to care, poor little bitch.

She was used to this. Men had been pressing their fingers into her flesh for years—probably she just didn't care anymore. She was dead inside. It was sad, but there it was.

God, he felt rotten. He felt like a man coming off a long drunk. The dust seemed to have settled over his eyeballs, over the whole fucking world: *". . . yet my soul drew back, / Guilty of dust and sin."* What was that from? He couldn't remember.

And then Hagemann had arrived, behind his wall of bodyguards. Yes, that was the man from the cliff.

It was the first time Christiansen had ever seen him close up, this man who had murdered his parents. As he sat down at his table, and the waiter came to stand by his chair, bowing and smirking, he looked straight up at the window above the stage, almost as if he knew he was being watched. Possibly the small, dark man beside him had made some sort of joke. Hagemann stared at the window and smiled, as if he understood everything.

And then, when the fellow in the tuxedo, who was probably Lutz, had lured Itzhak away, Hagemann came and sat down beside Esther. And then it was Christiansen's turn to read the truth in her face.

Yes, darling, he thought to himself, *yes, I can see*

now. It was my fault, and I'm the one to ask for pardon.

He took out his revolver, pointing it at the pane of glass, lining up the sights on the handkerchief in Hagemann's breast pocket, wondering if he would have the nerve not to pull the trigger.

✠ 17 ✠

It was part of the plan that Christiansen at some time or another should provide a distraction, something to keep Herr Hagemann's mind occupied while Mordecai and his boys crept up with their butterfly nets. After all, he seemed to know all about Christiansen—enough, at any rate, to be sending all kinds of unpleasant types out to kill him.

So it was time to let Hagemann know that he wasn't being neglected. If he wasn't going to kill him—not right away, not this minute—Christiansen figured he could at least allow himself the consolation of throwing a good scare into him.

He waited until there was something agreeably noisy going on out front, then he gave them all a shower of pink snowflakes on the back curtain to look at and crept down the rickety little stairway, left his coveralls neatly folded on a packing case, and let himself out through the stage door. In about five minutes he had circled around and found a nice dark alleyway where he could be sure of his back and had an unobstructed view of the café entrance. He would wait until Esther and her escort had left.

That happened almost as soon as the police brought Itzhak back and, with a great show of politeness, escorted him inside. Five minutes later the door opened again and Itzhak came back out with Esther on his arm. They were walking fast and Esther, even from a distance of some twenty-five yards, looked not so much frightened as haunted, as if she had already seen the worst and was trying to accustom herself to it.

Almost as soon as they were gone, swallowed up in the darkness, another man came out of the café, looked around warily, and then set off after them. That was to be expected—Hagemann would have them tailed back to their hotel just as a precaution. The man wasn't rushing. He wasn't even trying to catch up with them, so it didn't seem very likely he was part of any plan to waylay the young couple before they reached home. Anyway, Mordecai had doubtless taken a few precautions of his own. They'd both be safe enough.

So that just left Hagemann, sitting at his special table with his bodyguards and the little Arab gentleman for company, considering what a clever fellow he was and what he ought to do next to amaze the world. He probably felt invulnerable.

The Colonel had had a lovely time this evening. Poor little Esther, perched there alone in the midst of strangers, and who comes to help her finish off the champagne? Just like old times back at Waldenburg, and he had enjoyed every second of it, the son of a bitch.

Christiansen stepped out of the darkness and crossed the street to the entrance of the Café Pícaro, where he pushed open the door and went inside.

"*Una mesa, Señor?*"

Lutz smiled primly at him but his eyes had a worried look, as if he realized this was a face he should know from somewhere. He glanced behind the bar, where the man in the white jacket polishing glasses put down his dish towel and started to reach for something in his back pocket.

"I don't have a reservation, but I'm expected," Christiansen said in German. He was standing no more than eight or ten inches from Lutz. He let his left hand drop down, allowing the fingers to sweep open his jacket so that the pistol in his waistband was out in plain sight. "And if I don't see your friend's hands on the bar this minute you're dressed for your funeral, understand?"

Lutz looked at the butt of Christiansen's revolver, and then at the bartender, and shook his head. He was the reasonable sort. He wanted to stay alive to enjoy his prosperity.

"I quite understand, sir. We are at your service."

"We're going to have a chat with Colonel Hagemann, and you're going to make the introductions. How does that sound?"

It sounded fine. The smile on Lutz's face went suddenly crafty—it had something to do with the lines around his mouth. And, yes, by then he had made the connection. The big Norwegian with the private grudge could be left to the Colonel's bodyguards, who were experts. All Lutz had to do was to contrive to stay out of the way.

"But not out here in the open—I'm not that stupid. We'll go to your office, and then you'll pick up your phone and tell whoever's listening that your patron has a call."

The office was next door to the men's room, along

the same wall as the bar. It was well screened from Hagemann's table, so there wasn't any particular reason to suppose his thugs had spotted them yet. Lutz opened the door with his key, standing aside to let Christiansen pass through first—how dumb did he think the opposition came? Christiansen took a handful of his tuxedo jacket, just at the armhole, and shoved him inside.

It was a small room, poorly furnished, almost military. A metal desk, a couple of filing cabinets, two chairs—that was it. There was one window, with metal shutters that locked from the inside. They opened onto a courtyard lined around all four sides by trash barrels, but Christiansen already knew that. The stage door was just around the corner of the building. Narrow alleyways led off in four different directions. You couldn't ask for anything more.

"Sit down."

Lutz did as he was told. He had lost some of his sparkle. Christiansen did a quick body search and came up with a tiny Mauser automatic in a shoulder holster. It was almost like a Humphrey Bogart movie.

He unlocked the shutters and took a look outside. There was no one waiting. He pushed open the two halves of the window and listened. Nothing.

He took the coil of catgut out of his pocket and dropped it on the desk, where Lutz could look at it.

"Are you going to kill me?"

"Could be. I haven't decided. Will the Colonel have to come to the bar for his call, or can the phone be brought to him?"

"It can be brought to him. I have had an outlet installed there. He insisted."

"Good—then that's just how we'll do it. Put your hands behind your back, would you?"

Lutz was only too glad. His eyes hadn't once wandered from the coil of catgut. He had heard all the stories. He would rather have the stuff around his wrists than around his neck.

"If you are going to kill me, I would take it as a kindness if you would use the pistol. It's more dignified."

"We'll see."

When he had finished making sure that Lutz wouldn't go wandering off, Christiansen picked up the telephone and held it up close to Lutz's head.

"No tricks, or I'll shoot three or four holes in your guts and let you die the hard way. Is that clear?"

"No tricks."

"Tell your man at the bar to bring a phone over to Hagemann's table."

Lutz nodded stiffly and murmured something in Spanish into the receiver. His voice sounded as if it hadn't been used in a week.

All that remained was to wait.

"What do you say we give him something to listen to, hmm?" Christiansen touched him on the back of his head with the muzzle of the pistol, and Lutz jerked to a kind of attention, sucking in a short, sharp breath through his nostrils. He wasn't thinking about his dignity anymore.

Well, and why not? Once in a while a little self-indulgence was good for one, and Lutz wouldn't be any great loss to the human family. He had all the right credentials to have earned getting his brains scattered around the room. And it was the sort of thing likely to make an impression on Hagemann the way a few whispered threats over the phone never would.

"Yes? What is it, Ernst?"

Christiansen didn't have to be told whose voice it was. He had never seen Hagemann before today, and had never heard him speak a word, but there was a certain intimacy to that kind of hatred. He would have known the commander of the Kirstenstad operation in a thousand.

"It isn't Ernst, Colonel. It's Inar Christiansen. I'm going to kill you pretty soon—not just this second, but soon—and I thought you'd appreciate knowing that you've finally run out of places to hide."

For a moment there was no answer, only silence. Hagemann probably had his hand over the mouthpiece. He was probably telling his goons to get moving, to make sure that nobody named Christiansen came out of that office alive. He knew no one was kidding, and he wasn't a man to miss an opportunity.

"I don't think I understand, Herr Christiansen. What reason could you have for wanting to kill me?"

That settled it. He was stalling, the son of a bitch. He was trying to give his boys time to get into position.

Christiansen glanced back toward the window, making a rough calculation as to how long it would take someone in a hurry to find his way around the building and into that back courtyard. He was willing to play along for the odd few seconds, but he didn't relish the prospect of really letting himself be taken by surprise.

"You must pardon me, Herr Christiansen, since I am not sure what purpose you could have had in telephoning me."

"I'm in your friend Lutz's office, Colonel—as if

you didn't know. I'm not fifty meters from where you're sitting." He swung the Mauser around so that the front sight was almost touching Lutz's earlobe. "I want you to appreciate how close you have been to death this evening. I want you to sweat a little before you die. Listen to this."

He set the telephone receiver down on the desktop. Lutz twisted his head around, saw the gun muzzle out of the corner of his eye, and looked away again, breathing in short little gasps.

"*Auf Wiedersehen,* Lutz."

But he couldn't do it. For some reason he couldn't even begin to guess, he couldn't bring himself to kill this man in cold blood. He had made the decision to do it; Lutz deserved to die, and it was the right move. Everything was there except the will.

"Aw, shit!"

Christiansen turned the barrel about an inch and fired. The bullet hit the wall, hurting no one, but Lutz made a faint gurgling sound and pitched forward face first onto the desk. He was alive unless the shock had killed him, but he was out cold, his eyes half open and staring at nothing.

At almost the same instant, the office door sprang open with a sound of splintering wood and a man in a dark blue suit pushed his way inside. Christiansen seemed to have all the time in the world—the man had pale blond hair, he noticed, and the knot in his tie was pulled a little loose. There was a Luger in his right hand, but apparently it hadn't occurred to him yet that he would be needing it. He seemed surprised to see Christiansen, as if they had known each other somewhere else and he hadn't expected to run into him in a place like Burriana.

With something like relief, Christiansen realized that there would be no problem this time. The man was armed, and everyone was playing for keeps now. It was open season. He brought the Mauser up and fired twice. Both slugs went into the man's face, one just below the left eye and the other almost square in the middle of the upper lip, popping open his mouth so that he seemed to scream, but there was no sound, only a thick rush of blood. The man was dead, even as he reached back to brace himself against the door frame. The Luger dropped harmlessly to the floor.

There was a lot of racket now, and Christiansen could look through the open doorway and see people staring at the body. It seemed to be causing quite a sensation. So far, apparently, no one had noticed him—the sound of gunshots and the sight of a corpse were distraction enough.

It wasn't going to last—he needed to get out of there. He let the Mauser slip through his fingers and started climbing out through the open window. He was already well outside and crouching in the shadowy courtyard before the first man came around the corner of the building.

This one wouldn't be alone. The other one, the fellow who was lying dead inside, had simply made a mistake. He had gotten flustered by the sound of shooting and had rushed inside without thinking. No one would make that mistake again.

Hagemann had had five bodyguards sitting at the table with him—unless you counted the little Arab, and Christiansen had a feeling that Hagemann didn't. One was already blown away, one was following Esther and Itzhak back to their hotel, and Hagemann would certainly want to keep at least one with him, so that left two.

They would come from opposite directions. Let them.

The first man was simply a shadow, an outline against the pale yellow light from the street. Christiansen took the big British revolver from under his belt, aimed carefully, and fired. One shot was all it took—there just wasn't anything there anymore.

There was a sound of footsteps behind him as Christiansen turned. He sprang to one side and rolled, and a bullet careened off the cobblestones with an ugly whine. Number Two had seen the flash of his revolver, but any number could play at that game. Settling for an approximate target, Christiansen fired off three quick rounds, giving them a good spread. He rolled away again, but this time no one fired at him. The courtyard was still echoing with the noise of shooting before he heard the low wail that told him why.

All he saw was a shape, and that only for a second. A man bent over at an odd angle, holding his side as he limped around the corner and out of sight. That one just wanted to get away. Let him. Let him live to tell Hagemann all about it.

Christiansen got to his feet and ran. He just picked an alleyway and ran. He didn't stop until he was sure there was no one behind him.

The Casa General Moscardó was conveniently located for mischief. It was a four-story structure sandwiched in between a furniture factory and a building housing a noisy little restaurant on the ground floor and the offices of a maritime insurance company above. The street in front stretched right down to the docks, and there was an alleyway behind that was wide enough to allow the garbage trucks to get through. The view from the roof took in everything for half a mile in any direction.

Christiansen had taken the long way, just to be certain he hadn't been followed. He hadn't seen a sign of life in forty minutes.

He didn't have any trouble breaking in. There was a fire escape on the side facing the alley where, on hot summer nights, the patrons of the hotel probably laid out their mattresses on the landings to take advantage of the sea breezes. Mordecai had left a window on the third floor unlatched for him.

In the dark of the morning, after the curfew had blackened out even the nightclubs, when even the whores were asleep in their innocence, you couldn't see so much as your feet.

On the third-floor landing there were a few slivers of light visible behind one of the window shades. That was all the invitation he needed. He pressed his fingers into the narrow gap between the two halves of the window and pulled them toward him. He hadn't managed to get them open more than three or four inches before the shade popped up and he found himself staring through the window into the muzzle of a British 9-millimeter.

"We were beginning to think you had gotten lost," Hirsch said, helping him through with his free hand— he seemed reluctant to put the pistol away, as if he thought he might still need it. Christiansen merely grunted as he pulled the window closed again, latched it, and lowered the shade. They were all there, almost.

"Where's Itzhak?"

"He's in the room across the hall, getting his beauty rest." Hirsch grinned at him slyly. "I didn't get the impression he was real eager to welcome you back."

Esther was sitting on a couch, her face in profile as she studied the joints of her fingers. Every so often she would glance at him out of the corner of her eye, but that was all.

"Have you had a productive day?" Mordecai asked from the armchair where, pinched between two fingers, he was holding a brown paper cigarette that produced the bluest smoke Christiansen had ever seen. His shirt sleeves were rolled up over his heavy forearms. He raised his eyebrows expectantly, prepared to ignore everything else.

"Yes, I've learned a good deal. Where would you like me to start?"

In the difficult silence that followed, Faglin handed him a cup of coffee. The instant he tasted it, Christiansen realized how tired he was. He sat down on the sofa beside Esther, put his arm over her shoulder, and felt her elbow pressing against his rib cage. He had his woman back and his coffee, and they both felt comfortably warm. That was all he really cared about.

"I took a look at the seaward side of Hagemann's little bungalow," he said finally, as if the matter were of indifferent interest. "The guard makes his circuit about once every twenty-two minutes. He carries a flashlight but doesn't use it except to light his way. They aren't expecting trouble from that direction."

He turned to Esther and smiled, giving her a small squeeze. There was a look of wordless, incredulous gratitude in her eyes, and something like fear. Well, yes, of course. Why shouldn't there be?

"There isn't any reason why they should. What's the matter, Christiansen? Didn't you get a load of those cliffs? They're slick as gooseberry jam and seventy feet high if they're an inch."

"Probably higher—so what?"

He was enjoying himself. Hirsch looked like he was ready to pop his cork. So let him.

"It can't be done, that's what." Hirsch, who was now the only person in the room still standing, looked toward Mordecai and made an exasperated gesture with his right arm, as if he were trying to shake water from his fingers. "We've already gone into all this. It's impossible."

"What's the matter, didn't you ever do any climbing when you were a kid? It's practically the Norwegian national sport. Except I keep forgetting—you grew up on Ninth Avenue. That probably explains it."

"Stop trying to provoke a quarrel, Inar. What is it you want to say?"

Christiansen looked over at Mordecai, who seemed to be studying his face like a map of hostile territory.

"What I want to say is that the reviews are in and your little melodrama has been panned. I saw Hagemann tonight when he came to the café—he looked at the back of Esther's head as he sat down at his table and he smiled. Don't you understand? He smiled. He wasn't even pretending to be surprised to see her. She was expected."

They all knew what he was talking about.

"It's my fault," Esther said quietly, almost as if to herself alone. "It was all for nothing then. It's my fault. If I—"

"No, it isn't. He saw it coming, kid. You were blown before you even walked into the room."

Christiansen's eyes felt hot and dried out, as if he hadn't closed them in hours. When he tried they burned.

"He's just trying to keep his girlfriend's neck out of the noose," Hirsch said suddenly. He still hadn't been able to bring himself to sit down, so he leaned back against the window sill, his arms locked across his chest, glaring at some object only he could see. He didn't even believe what he was saying himself.

Faglin, who had hardly spoken at all, who seemed to wish he were somewhere else entirely, picked up the coffee cup on the floor between his feet and rose from the corner of the bed into which he seemed to be trying to disappear.

"Does anybody want some?" he asked, in all innocence. Hirsch merely scowled at him.

"It's true, isn't it?" With a kind of savage petulance, Hirsch pushed himself away from the window. "All he wants is to take care of himself. If we help him get close enough to kill Hagemann, that's fine with him—just so long as we don't do anything to interfere with his love life. Well, I've got a flash for you, pal—"

"That will be enough, Jerry."

Mordecai let his gaze drift from Hirsch's face to Christiansen's and, finally, to Esther's. He smiled at Esther, as if the sight of her alone gave him a twinge of pleasure.

"And you can rest yourself as well, Inar," he went on, the smile disappearing from his lips. "I won't ask the two of you to kiss and make up, but you'll have to continue your argument some other time. Let us keep to the point."

"What is the point?" Hirsch snapped.

"The point is that your plan isn't going to work." Christiansen was almost insultingly calm. "The point is that if you want Hagemann dead or alive you're going to have to go right up that cliff face and get him."

"It can't be done. It's impossible."

"No, it's only difficult. Nothing is impossible."

As if on signal, Mordecai stood up, pushing himself out of the chair with his arms. He looked around him with a certain distaste.

"I think we've discussed it enough for now," he said, principally to Christiansen it seemed. "Jerry, remember you're supposed to be working in this place, so get downstairs and sit behind the night desk like a good boy. You come with me, Amos. I want to talk to you."

There was some grumbling, but Mordecai could still make himself be obeyed. In a moment, after the shuffling exodus was over and the door had closed, Christiansen found himself alone in the room with Esther, who still sat at her end of the couch, her hands pressed into her lap. She looked as if she had been dreading this very moment.

"I can't understand why Hirsch is so down on me all of a sudden," he said, switching off the ceiling fixture so that only a standing lamp in the corner near the chest of drawers bathed the room in soft, white, shadowy light. "I haven't set eyes on him in nearly two weeks, and all day long he's been riding me."

"He doesn't like that you're sleeping with a Jewish woman."

"What's the matter? Does he want to keep them all for himself?"

He grinned. It was supposed to have been a harmless joke, but already he wished he hadn't said it. Esther only stared at him with dark, sad eyes and then turned her face away.

"I didn't go to bed with Itzhak," she began, almost whispering. What made her want to go into all that now, he wondered. "But I think you should—"

"No, I really don't want to hear anything about it. No confessions, is that all right? There's not much you could tell me I don't already know, and it's a little late in the day."

He sat down on the couch beside her, and she threw herself at him, burying her face in his lap and weeping out of control. He cradled her head in his arms and let her cry. There were things about her that never ceased to astonish him.

"I love you," he said quietly. He hadn't meant to say it—he hadn't meant to say anything. It had just slipped out. He wondered if there was any chance it could be true and then decided that, yes, it probably was. So much the worse for both of them.

Fortunately, she didn't seem to have heard him. Or perhaps it wasn't something she wanted to hear.

"Finished?"

She looked up at him and nodded, wiping away the tears with the palm of her hand. She was smiling now.

"Fine. Then I'd like to take a shower and then maybe get some sleep. It's been a long day, and I'd just as soon get it over with."

She was waiting for him when he got out of the shower. He couldn't see her—he couldn't even see the bed once he had turned off the bathroom light— but she was there nevertheless.

They didn't say anything. He crawled into the narrow bed, and when he put his arm around her, and touched her bare shoulder, he could feel her toes brushing against his legs, just below the kneecaps. She was wearing a thin blue cotton nightdress. He liked that nightdress; it was better than if she was wearing nothing at all. It was gathered up around her waist; he slipped his hand in underneath and let his fingers glide up the curve of her back. When he kissed her she opened her lips as if she wanted to bite him, and he could feel her warm, moist breath and hear the tiny whimper of longing that seemed to come of its own. By the time she guided him into her, she was already breathing in short, ragged sobs and her forehead, pressed against his chest, just below the collarbone, felt hot and damp. She made him feel pleasure through his whole body. It was as if they really did become one flesh.

No, he didn't require any explanations. She still loved him. She belonged to him. She would never have betrayed him in anything, and what had to be done had to be done.

It was nearly morning, and he had the impression he had been asleep for something like half an hour, when he heard the tapping on the hotel room door. He tried to get out of bed without waking Esther, but she had her arms around his neck and, besides, she had heard the tapping too.

"It's one of the good guys," he said, slipping his arms into the sleeves of his bathrobe. "Go back to sleep."

It was Faglin. He was still in his suit and looked as if he hadn't been near a bed in days.

"Mordecai wants to talk to you. Can you come right down?"

"Sure. Just let me get dressed. Come inside—you can babysit until I get back."

"Sure."

It was the off season for seaside resorts, and three quarters of the hotel's rooms were empty. Mordecai had installed himself in the front of the building, where he could watch the street. Still, it was an ugly little box he had chosen, with a cold linoleum floor and paper that threatened to come peeling off the walls in great sheets. But it was next door to the stairwell— probably you could hear people through the wall. From a practical point of view, Mordecai had chosen well.

"We had a policeman here about half an hour ago," he said. He was in the bathroom, standing over the sink, shaving. His voice seemed to come from nowhere. "He had your description. He even had your name. It was only with some difficulty that Jerry was able to keep him from searching the hotel. He said you had killed three men at the Café Pícaro."

"The third man died? I'm glad."

Mordecai stepped into the bathroom doorway and looked at him almost as if he had to confirm for himself that there really was someone else in the room. He was in his undershirt, and his face was still half covered with lather. Christiansen grinned at him.

"It was dangerous, Inar. And it draws official attention to us, and we don't need that."

"I was supposed to provide the distraction—that was the idea, wasn't it? Hagemann will have something to think about now besides where all the trip wires and trap doors are in this thing you've set up for him. He's frightened now. He knows that I'll kill him if he hangs around much longer. There's a time limit now. It'll make him careless."

"That's a good reason, but is it the real reason?"

"No."

"You feel like telling me what is?"

Christiansen sat down on a peculiarly ugly wooden chair with a circular seat, took the pack of cigarettes out of his shirt pocket, and lit one. He felt like a schoolboy called into the headmaster's office to explain why he had been found scratching his name into the top of his desk.

"I told you, I was there tonight." He crossed his legs and stared up at the ceiling. The cigarette smoke drifted up and then seemed to lose energy, flattening out like a layer of silt. "I sat up in the little box from where they run the lights, and I watched Hagemann playing the great man for close to three hours. I had my gun—it would have been the easiest thing in the world to blow the back of his head out, to make such a mess of him they wouldn't even have bothered to bury him, just feed him to the dogs. But I didn't do that. I remembered you, and General von Goltz's nerve gas, and the Jewish homeland. Why the hell am I supposed to do my bit for the Jewish homeland, I might think to inquire? So don't ask me why I felt the need to burn down a few of Hagemann's soldiers."

"All right. I won't ask."

Mordecai had wiped his face clean by the time he came out of the bathroom. He looked quite bright, as if someone had gone over him with metal polish. Mordecai was one of those men who could wash his face and make a brand new start in life. It was a gift.

"Would it be still all right if I asked you something else?"

"Ask."

"This business about going up the cliffs behind Hagemann's villa, is that because you want to keep Esther out of his way? I have to know."

"I don't want her used as bait, but the cliffs are still the only way to reach him. He knows all about the bait. Use her like that and he'll steal her right off your hook."

"And are you sure you can make it up the cliffs without being found out?"

Christiansen wanted to laugh, but he couldn't. He felt rotten and his nerves were played out, and half an hour's sleep and a little sex hadn't worked their magic. He wasn't up to being sardonic.

"I'm not an idiot, Mordecai—I'm not sure of anything." He took another drag on his cigarette, but it tasted so dead in his lungs that he put it out. "All I know is that some chance is better than none at all."

"Then talk to Faglin. He can help, and he'll know enough not to say anything to Hirsch. Tell him you're going climbing."

* 18 *

Burriana, Spain: March 18, 1948

He didn't know exactly what had happened last night.
He might even have decided to dismiss the whole
subject from his mind, except there was still substantial evidence that Inar Christiansen was not the for-
giving type. On that basis, Mordecai Leivick decided
that it would probably be best to keep Itzhak out of
the way for a while.

In any case, the boy had served his turn, and
Hagemann knew him by sight now and had made
certain threats. There was nothing wrong with his
nerve, but he had a mother who worried and Leivick
would just as soon keep him out of harm's way. What
he needed was something to keep him pleasantly busy—
too busy to think about Esther Rosensaft.

Because Esther Rosensaft seemed to be gnawing
at his insides like the Spartan fox.

"Forget about her, boy. She's not for you. Anyway,
she's not the sort of girl you could bring home to meet
the family, is she."

They were having breakfast together in a little restaurant about half a mile from the hotel, just the two of them. Leivick wanted to have a talk, and it wouldn't do for one of Hagemann's thugs to see them together—their cover story was threadbare enough as it was. They were seated across from each other at a long table, at the end nearest the stove because it was a cold morning, and Itzhak was in a sulky sort of mood.

"I don't know what you mean by that," he said, in a voice that told Leivick he knew perfectly well what he meant. He had hardly touched his fried eggs. He was in a bad way.

"She has a past, Itzikel. Your mother is a nice lady, but she knows even less about the world than you do. She wouldn't understand about a girl who's been an SS prostitute and God knows what else."

"In Israel no one will care about the past—we'll only think about the future."

"That's a good speech, but it isn't so. When we forget our past in that brave new world we're making, we'll be finished. We'll disappear, like morning mist. That girl isn't ever going to forget, and neither would you. Leave her to Inar, boy. He's been through enough to entitle him to forget for the both of them."

Leivick drank his coffee, wishing he had a cigarette—wishing that just once, sometime or other, life could work itself out to everyone's satisfaction. He was tired of the mess and the trouble. If, God willing, they ever got their homeland, he thought perhaps he would retire to a kibbutz somewhere and spend the rest of his life picking oranges.

"If you're not hungry, let's get out of here," he said. As he rose from the table he dropped a handful of coins beside his plate. They clattered against the wood with enough noise to rouse the waiter from his slumbers.

Outside, there was hardly any traffic. Women in heavy shawls carried their shopping home in net bags, and here and there one saw men in felt hats and business suits, their collars high and heavily starched. It was the middle of the morning, perhaps the quietest time in the day.

Itzhak had a thick knitted scarf that went around his neck God alone knew how many times. Some female relative had made it for him, and it was his only concession to the time of year. He seemed positively to be enjoying his misery.

They had walked nearly two blocks before Leivick found a tiny stall where he could buy a pack of cigarettes—not American cigarettes, but one had to learn to compromise. The girl behind the counter, who was probably every day of seventeen and looked at Itzhak as though she would have liked to make a meal of him, counted out his change and gave them both— Leivick found himself included, probably out of pure, simple-hearted generosity—a smile that should have set any man's shirt buttons smoking. Itzhak hardly even noticed. It was a bad sign. That sort of self-absorption could mean real trouble in their business.

"Why don't you spend the day at the movies, It-zikel?" he said as he tried lighting a wooden match in the faint stirrings of the morning breeze. He finally had to take shelter against the corner of a building, almost burning his fingers in the process. Even with the first puff, he could feel his chest loosening. It was a lovely thing to have rediscovered a lost vice. "Take a seat in the last row, just so that no one can put an ice pick in your ear. You'll be around people, so Hagemann's thugs won't feel free to kill you just to stay in practice. They can watch you—it will make them feel safe. Young husbands do sometimes spend the whole day at the movies when they've been fighting with their brides. Just make sure we know where to find you."

"Am I supposed to stay away so that Hagemann can have his chance with Esther?"

"More or less—yes."

"I thought you told Inar to get ready to go after Hagemann in his villa."

"I did. We're doing it both ways. It never hurts to have two plans."

Itzhak gave him a funny sidewise glance, as if he thought that somehow the thing wasn't quite honest but was too polite to say so out loud.

"We'll see how it goes," Leivick went on. The wind had stilled quite suddenly and he was surprised at how quiet everything was. In a week he had grown used to the Spanish street noises, but just at that moment there seemed to be nothing, not even the ever-present sound of a baby crying. It made him feel nervous for some reason. "We'll set our trap as planned. Perhaps Inar is mistaken. If he is not, then we can do as he suggests. If the years have taught me nothing else, I have at least learned not to depend upon anything."

"Do you think he is mistaken?"

"I don't know. He might be—he has an interest to protect now. He isn't the same, not like he was in Vienna. Perhaps you haven't noticed it, but there's a change. A man like that, who has been alone a long time, he meets a young girl . . . I'm not sure we can rely on his judgment anymore. Do you understand?"

Did he? Who could say? Itzhak buried his hands in his trouser pockets, staring at the paving stones as they walked along together. It was perhaps only his sexual vanity that had been wounded, but did that matter, at his age? If Inar Christiansen could no longer be trusted, how could he?

"That goddamn bitch, what's she doing to us, Mordecai?" His face had tightened into a mask. He looked, poor boy, as if he might actually begin to cry. "Last night she . . . Oh, shit."

"That's what some women are like. That's why we went to so much trouble to bring this one here. Let's just hope and pray the poison works as well on Colonel Hagemann."

It did the job, after a fashion. At least Itzhak no longer seemed on the verge of tears, which was not a good place for a nice boy from Tel Aviv to be. He didn't look any happier, and his hands were still curled into fists in his pockets as he walked—perhaps he was merely cold—but now he had a little fiction he could believe, something more intelligible and less painful than the truth. Esther, that pathetic, abused little waif, could be his Theda Bara, the Siren to whom he must now learn to shut his heart. It was a story fitted to his capacities.

And as for Mordecai Leivick, the Ibsen of comfortable lies, he had, as usual, eaten too much breakfast and was experiencing that intestinal melancholy that felt so much like a bad conscience. Or perhaps it really was a bad conscience. As he had so grandly informed Itzhak, he had learned enough of life to give up the idea of being sure.

Did he really, for even a moment, believe that

Hagemann would fall into their arms, rendered helpless by some twisted passion for little Esther Rosensaft? Yes, sometimes, just for a moment. But not as a working hypothesis. If Hagemann kept his appointment it would be for hard, pragmatic reasons—he knew Esther was the key to more than just his own happy fantasies of pain and humiliation and death. Hagemann was an adult, so, unlike Itzhak, he did not believe in love.

Yes, they were both adults. Both of them, antagonists ever since the forests of Poland, growing more alike every hour. Mordecai refused to jolly himself along—he lied to Itzhak about Esther and used them both because that was what the builders of nations did. That was how politics on the grand scale was played, which was precisely what men like Hagemann have been telling themselves for the past thirty years, and doubtless even longer than that. He wondered if Hagemann ever felt this way after breakfast, but then Hagemann was probably more hardened to it.

In the next cross street a dark green car of a make Leivick had never seen before slowed almost to nothing as it approached the center of the intersection and then shot away, almost as if the driver had been frightened.

"Itzhak, go over to the other side of the road and lose yourself in a doorway. Go on, be a good boy. I think we're beginning to attract someone's interest."

"What do you want me to do if we have?" he asked. He really was a good boy—all business when it came to it.

"If they're just looking, find your way home. Forget you know me. If they want you, play the injured tourist, but I'm afraid you'll have to let them have you. If they want me, don't be heroic—just disappear."

It was the standard drill, and Itzhak had been trained. He ducked his head in a quick nod and cut across the street. Within a few seconds not even Leivick knew where he had hidden himself.

It was probably nothing, probably just someone looking for a street number, a stranger like himself. Probably, in the tail end of his middle years, he was simply becoming paranoid. The decades wither you up, and you lose your courage. It was a common enough phenomenon.

Leivick lit another cigarette, wondering if he would have the opportunity to finish it in peace. He wished he had brought his revolver and then was glad he had left it behind in his suitcase. He might have been tempted to use it, and they had had enough publicity of that kind lately. He was a docile old Jewish gentleman, taking the sea air for his health. If they wanted to kill him there was very little he could do about it.

No, he wasn't paranoid. The stillness was almost deafening. After ten years of fascist rule, the Spaniards had learned about avoiding trouble. If it was the police, or possibly even Hagemann's people, who seemed to enjoy something like the same status, probably the whole neighborhood knew about them and had simply retired behind their locked shutters.

He didn't turn around when he heard the sound of automobile tires hissing on the wet street. He just kept walking.

It was one of those rare moments when experience takes on a peculiar, almost painful clarity. The pale, paper-colored wall of the building next to him, with its water stains and its peeling plaster. The damp air with its smells of cooking and engine grease and sea salt. The scrap of newsprint that jigged down the sidewalk, driven on by currents of wind too subtle to make themselves noticed any other way. It was like the time at Treblinka, the instant after the grenades had gone off, the gasoline fires winding up the watchtowers—it was like that. The heart stops. Only the senses live. These few seconds, perhaps all that remains.

A car door slammed. Then another. They were very close. Leivick turned around now—it was permitted. Even old Jewish gentlemen interested in the sea air have a right to look.

"Señor . . ."

They were big men, in dark blue overcoats, clean shaven, with the hollow, uncaring eyes of professionals. They moved toward him together, shoulder to shoulder, as if it was something in which they had been schooled.

One of them grabbed for Leivick's arm. He pulled away, which turned out to have been a mistake. The second man, with remarkable dexterity, caught him on the point of the elbow with a small truncheon, hardly bigger than an after-dinner cigar. The pain was exquisite, paralyzing. Leivick could feel it all the way into his chest, so that he could hardly breathe.

A short, sharp blow to the abdomen—he had no idea who had hit him this time—and he was helpless. He hardly noticed when a handkerchief was held over his mouth and nose, its sickly sweet smell blending in with a blunt, nauseating ache that seemed to fill him up. He was slipping away. It was almost a relief.

Itzhak, get the hell away from here. Go tell them—
Inar was smarter than any of us. Inar was . . .

He hadn't really expected to wake up. He had
assumed they were murdering him, but that didn't
seem to be the case. He was alive. He was conscious
of that, merely that, even before he began the excru-
ciatingly painful process of opening his eyes. He began
to wish they had murdered him.

He was lying down, which was probably just as
well. He was quite sure he would die if he tried to
move, so there was no temptation to be anything else.
They must have given him something like chloroform,
probably without being too terribly precise about the
dosage. It had left him with an appalling headache
that seemed to take up his entire body. When he
finally did manage to open his eyes he had to close
them again immediately. The light was blinding.

He could wait on finding out where they had taken
him. Just then it didn't seem so very important.

And the worst of it was that he felt such an idiot.
Hadn't he been warned? Now the trap had been sprung,
but only on himself.

After about five minutes he was able to nerve himself up to an attempt at moving. His right arm, for
some reason, wouldn't respond. He could bring the
hand up only a few inches, up to about his waist, and
then something stopped it. It was as if someone were
holding him by the wrist.

The left arm was better. Finally he managed to
shade his eyes with his hand, and then it became
possible to open them. When at last he was able to
focus, he wondered why he should have gone to the
trouble.

He was in a prison cell—brick walls, an iron door, gray tile flooring. The war had made him an expert on prisons. He knew all about them.

He was alone. It was a large room—the Germans would have had thirty men in a cell this size. There was no one else. Somewhere he could hear the drip, drip, drip of water, but not another sound. It occurred to him that perhaps he ought to feel flattered.

It was a plank bed they had him on. Just boards, chained to the wall—an antique. Perhaps it hadn't been Hagemann at all. Perhaps he had run afoul of the Inquisition.

Enough games. It was time to do something about sitting up. The idea itself was enough to floor him with nausea.

It was while he was trying to sit up that he discovered that his right hand was manacled, riveted by a short chain to the end of the bed.

When finally he made it, he felt better. The sum of his indispositions had reduced themselves to the sickening throb in his head. Otherwise, he felt weak but intact. Time to consider his position.

He couldn't understand why he wasn't dead. Did Hagemann expect him to betray their plans for capturing him? It seemed unlikely.

Anyone could be broken. No one dies with his secrets inviolate, not if his interrogators care to go to the trouble of digging them out. Leivick had seen enough people questioned under torture to have lost his trust in heroism. But that sort of thing took time. A determined man can't be made to talk with threats, and torture is a tedious process. Time was something that Hagemann had very little of.

At any rate, he would have all the answers he

wanted soon enough. There was nothing to do in the meantime except to wait, and gather strength against whatever was to come.

They had taken his wristwatch. That was a bad sign. Did they want to disorient him, to make him lose his sense of continuity? No—there was a window in his cell. All he had to do was look outside; the chain was long enough for that. Perhaps someone had stolen it. Perhaps they were afraid he might break the crystal and use the pieces to cut his wrists.

He was considering the implications of this when he heard the sharp click of a key in the door lock. The door swung open and Colonel Egon Hagemann himself walked in, just as if it were something he did every day. Leivick had to control the impulse to snap to attention.

"I trust you are feeling better, Herr Leivick?" He smiled. He was a resplendent figure in his white suit, tall and rather cruelly majestic. His face was tanned and hardly lined by age. He was what every man wishes to be in the middle of his life and hardly ever is: untouched. In his right hand he was carefully balancing a heavy clay mug.

"I have been better. How long have I—?"

"Only about forty minutes. I was here when you arrived and have only been waiting until you came round. Drink some of this—it will take away some of the grogginess." He held out the mug, which contained what appeared to be very strong tea. "Go ahead. There's nothing in it except two spoonfuls of sugar."

"Thank you."

Leivick took the mug and drank from it. Certainly if Hagemann planned to drug him again he had no need of so roundabout an approach. And, yes, it did seem to be nothing except sweetened tea.

"Do you mind if I sit down?"

Perhaps it was only the lingering effects of the anesthetic, but Leivick found himself empty of all the emotions he might have expected to feel at this moment. Outrage, fear, unreasoning hatred—they simply were not there. All the misery this man had caused, this evil presence spreading back and forward in time, this monster who had profaned and destroyed everything that came in his way, who still might destroy the ragged remnants of a nation before it was even born, all that was an abstraction. Only the individual was real, standing here in the center of a prison cell floor, asking permission to sit down. A man like other men.

Very well then, let him sit down. Leivick shifted himself to make room on the plank bed.

"Thank you."

As if to establish a recognized border they could both respect, Hagemann took the tan felt hat he had been carrying and dropped it on the space between them. It was the sort of gesture that established his humanity—no, he was not the god of wickedness. There were no demons.

"I have been looking forward to this meeting," he went on.

"I can imagine. What is this place?"

"This?" Hagemann looked around appraisingly at the brick cell. "This is the Burriana town jail. You were arrested by the Spanish authorities—didn't you know? You are being held on a passport violation; they expect very shortly to be able to prove that your documents are forgeries, since certainly the British would never have issued travel papers to someone of your reputation. In the meantime you can expect to be treated decently."

"And what happens when the authorities have completed their inquiries?"

"You will be deported—to Syria."

Hagemann had a way of reaching behind his jacket lapel to smooth down his necktie that was expressive of extreme uneasiness. To Syria, to the very door of one's enemies. And yet it was possible to wonder whose victory this was.

"We will be leaving rather quickly. Early tomorrow morning, I should think."

"Is there some particular hurry?"

Leivick forced himself to smile, and the effort had an unpleasant effect on him. It compelled him to realize that it was still possible, in the ordinary way of human beings, to hate this man.

"Inar Christiansen is in town." He said it quite matter-of-factly, but anyone with eyes could see that Colonel Hagemann was not pleased. His right hand slid inside his jacket and the fabric of his necktie pulled smooth and straight. "But, of course, I'm forgetting you must know that."

"As it happens, I did not. I've never met the formidable Mr. Christiansen." Leivick found it easier to smile now, pleased with his facility at lying. "But I can understand now why you're suddenly so unwilling to linger here. I imagine you really would feel safer in Damascus."

Hagemann glanced away suddenly, wiping his hand on the knee of his trouser leg. He had a hunted look. It was possible to know exactly how he must have felt.

"He has always been the wild card, hasn't he, Leivick," he said, in a tone that suggested he wished to be understood—that claimed that, after all, the two of them shared at least a common appreciation of each other's aims. "If he killed me, would it simplify matters for you? At the moment, yes, probably—but if you were not here in this cell? Perhaps not? You and I have political objectives which give a certain clarity to our actions, but what of Mr. Christiansen? Can I be sure you haven't brought him over to your side?"

"I doubt if you can be sure of anything."

For just an instant the phantom of a smile played across Hagemann's lips. Leivick took his point.

"You are on the verge of reminding me who is the prisoner here?" he asked. He raised his free hand a little and then let it fall dejectedly back into his lap. "No doubt you are right, but I was not attempting to bargain with you—only to point out the obvious fact that no matter what becomes of me, and even if you and your Syrian masters win your war, this will not help you against Christiansen. I think that, in the end, he will kill you."

He set the tea mug down on the cell floor, and when he straightened up again and glanced at Hagemann he could see easily enough that the man was struggling with the urge to confess something. It was not to be, however.

"It shocks you that I am afraid of him," Hagemann announced finally—in place, it would seem, of saying something else.

"No. It is only reasonable to be afraid of him. Only a fool would be anything else."

"Just so."

Out of force of habit, Leivick checked his shirt

pocket for the pack of cigarettes he had bought less than an hour ago, but of course they were not there. Someone must have stolen them. Someone always stole one's cigarettes in a prison.

"Are you looking for these?" Hagemann asked, taking the pack from his right jacket pocket. He even had the box of matches.

Leivick took them and lit one. The smoke made his headache worse, but he felt more tranquil.

"Were you in the war, Herr Leivick? I mean, of course, the 1914–18 war."

"Yes. I was a corporal of artillery in the Austrian army."

"Did you see much of the fighting?"

"No. One doesn't in artillery."

"I was in the infantry."

He said this as if it were meant to explain something, turning his head to see what impression it made. Yes, of course. The Western Front in its full savagery.

"I was in Treblinka. These things cannot be made to constitute an excuse."

"You are a Czech, are you not, Herr Leivick?"

"I was a Czech, yes."

The irony did not escape Hagemann's notice. He raised his eyebrows and made a short gesture with his left hand, as if to concede the point.

"Very well then, you *were* a Czech. It amounts to the same thing. For you the great war's end meant national liberation—freedom from Austria. For us it meant nothing except defeat."

"So you followed Hitler?"

"Yes. Hitler wanted to recast the world, and we both know it needed recasting. He wanted a real revolution, not just in politics but in the way people thought and acted and lived. You don't do that unless you are prepared to be ruthless."

"So you were ruthless? I have heard this argument before, Colonel."

"And you will hear it again, provided you Jews ever manage to achieve your utopia in the desert."

"Which you are determined to prevent."

"Yes, which I am determined to prevent. You see, this war will not end. The logic of the conflict perpetuates itself forever. It will go on and on, however any of us may feel, until we are all dead."

"Which is, it would seem, something Christiansen understands as well as you."

"Yes." Hagemann smiled, nodding his head, almost as if this were the conclusion he had hoped they would reach. "Yes, for him too there is no turning back. The old war was over when it was over, but not this one. This one, never. I knew it that morning in June, 1942. I rather suspect I had known it all along, but Kirstenstad forced it upon me."

"Then you know why he means to kill you?"

"Yes. Of course. He is a Norwegian, isn't he? Who could blame him? Would I act any differently in his place? He has a right to kill me—provided he can."

"And so do we."

"Who? You mean the Jews? Yes, of course. We have all behaved just as we ought, all along."

Leivick had finished his cigarette. He ground it out under his heel, feeling not the least bit tranquil. The tea had grown quite cold, but he picked the mug up from the floor and moistened the inside of his mouth with it. Hagemann was mad, of course.

"You have been responsible for the deaths of thousands of innocent people, and now you prepare for the murder of countless thousands more, and you claim we have all behaved as we ought? You astonish me, Colonel. Even coming from an SS man, that is simple insanity."

"On the contrary, Herr Leivick, it is the only antidote for insanity. Do you know what they taught us in the SS? 'Believe, Obey, Fight!' We are soldiers in the Waffen-SS, not bureaucrats or policemen or politicians—soldiers. That is the logic of the military life: 'Believe, Obey, Fight!' We have nothing else to keep us sane. To doubt is to perish—to die inwardly and, finally, to die in earnest. Do you know what my orders were concerning Kirstenstad? 'You will destroy the village with the utmost ferocity.' Those were General von Goltz's very words: 'with the utmost ferocity.' It was to be a reprisal. Such operations were being carried out everywhere in Europe to avenge the assassination of Reinhard Heydrich, and everywhere the orders were the same: 'with the utmost ferocity.' I was a soldier—I did my duty. The great trick is to do one's duty and not go mad."

Leivick wanted to hide his face in his hands. His head was pounding again and he was filled with despair. No, Hagemann had not gone mad—except in the sense that the whole world had gone mad in this maddest of times. Everything Hagemann said made perfect sense. He was not a raving lunatic. And that was what Leivick's despair consisted of, the consciousness that he understood everything, that, like Hagemann, he had always understood.

"You do evil, knowing it to be evil, and you do not go mad. Tell me, Colonel, what is your secret? I am not joking—I would like to know."

"You know already, Herr Leivick. Tell me, when

you were a corporal of artillery, and you sent your
explosive shells whistling off into the enemy trenches,
didn't you do evil and know it? Have you ever seen
what artillery shells do to men? I was in the trenches
in France. I can tell you. I've seen men, still alive,
with their guts torn out, or wandering around half
mad from the pounding of the guns. To be a soldier
is the condition of life in our time. You may wish to
draw distinctions, to say that the things I did in Norway and in the East were somehow different, but I
do not. Horror is horror, suffering is suffering, death
is death. If we wish to live—and perhaps, I grant,
under such circumstances it is better not to live—but
if life is what we want, then we submit to evil. We
surrender to it. We embrace it. I embraced it, and
not without cost to myself, but I lived. We are none
of us any different, not you nor myself nor Christiansen. For all of us it is the same. Triumph or perish,
and the cost of that triumph is wickedness."

He had become quite excited, whether from some
private despair or out of a cruel delight in his own
words it was impossible to say. When he stopped
speaking he stared straight ahead for several seconds,
as if waiting to return to himself.

"Good." Leivick smiled and lit himself another
cigarette. "You might try explaining all of this to Christiansen, provided there is time before the catgut chokes
off your windpipe."

"Do you hope to frighten me, Herr Leivick?"

"No. Only to remind you that there is still something of which to be frightened."

"Oh, I knew that already."

"You really have gone mad, Colonel."

"No, I have merely discovered freedom."

He turned to Leivick as if he expected to be understood, as if that was why he had come—to be understood. He had not been disappointed.

Yes, of course. Leivick knew all about freedom. It was part of war, that freedom. One's government released one from moral responsibility. Mercy became nothing except a species of intellectual weakness. It happened even in the death camps, to the prisoners themselves, whose very powerlessness became a liberation of sorts. One will do anything to survive, just as in the SS one could do anything and survive. They all went mad. And none of them would ever recover. Nothing would ever be the same for them again.

"You will only be free until Christiansen kills you."

"Yes, I know. But the fates of individuals don't matter so very much, do they. That was something else we both learned in the war."

He seemed to derive some sort of satisfaction from the idea, almost like the comfort of a religious faith—people didn't matter. But that, of course, was his freedom.

"And am I to be allowed to know what my fate will be?"

"You will die—in Syria. After you have told me where I can find the late General von Goltz's legacy."

"You seem surprised. Did you imagine, Herr Leivick, that I was really so naive? Didn't you think I would realize that if you were willing to bait your trap with Fräulein Rosensaft you must already have learned from her everything she could tell you? And who would know if not you?"

Leivick was glad to be sitting down. He felt weak and shaky and full of anguish, and he had no idea whether it was still the drug or merely the consciousness of his own failure. His eyes burned and were damp with sweat. He took a handkerchief from his pocket and wiped them dry, but it hardly seemed to make any difference. Hagemann, who, it seemed, had deliberately chosen to be a mad brute and hardly a man at all, was still watching him with something like resentment.

"So you never wanted her at all then?"

"Yes, I wanted her. And I will have her, within a matter of hours. But it will be you and not she who is put to the question in Damascus. That will be better."

"Better for who?"

"Better for her, and better for me."

It was not until he had been alone for several minutes that Leivick could bring himself to take the handkerchef out of his pocket once more, to wipe his face, and to consider calmly—in the sense of a rational progression of ideas, of propositions expressible in words, not simply images of horror—where his miscalculation had led him. Emotion and appetite, they were the province of a creature like Hagemann. Any animal could feel, but it was the special gift of men to think. And now, in his extremity, Leivick wanted most particularly to be a man.

He was in possession of a terrible secret, a secret that could lead to the destruction of many lives, of a nation, a people's last hope. And now, through his own stupidity and blindness, he had been delivered into the hands of one certain to turn that secret to the most appalling ends. If he could have died, simply by willing it—if he could just . . .

They had taken his watch, and of course his necktie

and belt, all of the more obvious methods of suicide. But sometimes living and dying were nothing more than questions of fortitude. A man could run his head against a wall, crushing it like an eggshell, if he had but the will.

Except that Hagemann had thought of that, and had ordered him chained to the plank bed. It was unlikely, under the circumstances, that he would end by doing more than knocking himself into a stupor and thus making matters that much easier for Hagemann and his allies.

So, after all, there was nothing to do except, once more, to wait upon events. The next few moves were up to Hagemann—and, perhaps, Hirsch and Faglin. Perhaps they might furnish the means of defeating the interrogators in Damascus.

There was strength in hope—and in the knowledge that it was not the Angel of Death they were fighting, only a weak and frightened man who might, in another life, have been just another in the faceless innocence of the human race but whom instead history had made its victim. Villainy in itself was nothing. It had no strength of its own; it needed the support of a uniform and a gun and a mandate of its own devising. That was how it had murdered its six million Jews.

Hagemann was mortal, though, and could be killed. Perhaps finally Inar Christiansen really would kill him, but perhaps it would be better for Inar Christiansen to learn that Egon Hagemann wasn't worthy of such intensity of hatred.

Still, please God let him kill him. Let him do it before Egon Hagemann has his chance to murder another six million.

❖ *19* ❖

The distance between the hotel and the spot where Dessauer hid while he watched Mordecai being taken was only a little more than a quarter of a mile, yet it took him nearly half an hour to cover it. He had never been more frightened in his life—every shadow seemed to conceal an enemy with a gun; at every intersection he expected to be run down by a speeding car that would come out of nowhere. Until that morning they had all been embarked upon what he had somehow taken to be an adventure, one of those slightly unreal conflicts between good and evil that men talk about after dinner, when the women have left the room. Now, suddenly, this was actual life.

Mordecai was unconscious when they put him into the back of the car. Two men carried him, and his head hung at a strange angle. He might even have been dead except that then they wouldn't have bothered to make off with his corpse. Before they got in the car themselves, the men looked around, searching the neighborhood, scowling as if surprised and annoyed to have found Mordecai alone. Then they drove off. They weren't in any hurry. They had a lifetime and nothing to be afraid of.

I have to find a telephone, Dessauer thought. *I've got to warn them—and then I've got to get back.*

A grocery store in the next block had a telephone. Dessauer dialed the hotel and gave the desk clerk his room number. Esther was the one who answered. When he was finished he managed to fumble a five-peseta note out of his billfold—he didn't seem to have any change—and handed it to the grocer, who stared at him with undisguised astonishment before hurriedly stuffing the money into the pocket of his apron.

He made his way through back yards and over fences. Every so often he would stop and listen. He was full of fear. There was nothing except himself, and a nameless menace, and the next few hundred meters.

When he reached the hotel he didn't go near the front entrance. If they weren't afraid to pull Mordecai off a city street in full daylight, they wouldn't worry about doing the same for him in the lobby of a hotel. He slipped in through the employees' entrance and made his way up by the back stairs. No one tried to stop him.

It was Faglin who opened the door. They were all there, even Christiansen, who was supposed to be in hiding from the police. He could have done without seeing Christiansen, who looked at him through the same cold blue eyes, as if nothing had changed. Maybe he didn't know about last night. Maybe he didn't care. Esther, of course, seemed unwilling to look at him at all. Her hand kept reaching up to touch Christiansen on the arm, as if to steady herself.

"Was it Hagemann's boys or the Spanish police?" Hirsch asked. He seemed impatient, even angry, as he stood by the dresser drinking coffee out of a tin cup. He was the only man there still in his shirt sleeves.

"I don't know—Spanish, I guess. They called him 'Señor.' "

"That doesn't make them the police," Faglin noted calmly. As usual, he was sitting in a corner, as inconspicuous as a piece of furniture. "Our friend might prefer to use local talent for a job like this—it might create fewer problems for him with the authorities."

"And the logical extension of that reasoning is that he would use the local police to cart off Mordecai. He's got that kind of drag. Didn't he get them to decoy Itzhak out of his friend's club last night?"

It was Christiansen—huge, impassive as granite. He glanced at Faglin and the two men exchanged a nod.

"The fact is, if the police don't have him we've got a real problem. We can't make a move on Hagemann's villa in daylight—we can't expect his patrols to be blind—and Mordecai knows Esther's part in the code. He and I are the only ones who do. Hagemann can wring it out of him in an afternoon. He's good at that sort of thing. Our only chance is if Hagemann has a few qualms about wearing thin his host country's tolerance and he's keeping Mordecai in a Spanish jail cell. He can do what he likes in Syria, but maybe not here."

"Let's hope you're right. Then maybe we can find out where Mordecai is being held and kill him before he has a chance to talk."

The silence that Hirsch had created seemed to hold everything suspended, like amber. No one moved.

No one even appeared to live. Finally Christiansen reached into his shirt pocket and brought out a pack of cigarettes.

"Where did you learn to be such a bloodthirsty little bastard?" he asked, almost as if he were inquiring directions to the men's room. His hands were busy lighting the cigarette. He hardly seemed to notice Hirsch. "Murder and apostasy—I thought those were the two great sins for a Jew. Better to die than to deny God or man."

"I'm not real big on the Tradition. The Tradition is part of what got us Yids into Auschwitz. But since when are you so heavy on the Jewish law? How 'bout it, Christiansen?"

He put his stress on that first syllable of the name, and a thin little smile tightened Hirsch's mouth. He was having a good time.

"We find him and we kill him," he went on, his voice strained and angry. "Believe me, Mordecai would understand."

"You do what you like, but I think maybe I'll just go looking for him on my own. I think you'd be wise, however, not to get in my way, Hirsch."

Everybody knew that Hirsch carried a small, flat automatic tucked into the waistband of his trousers. They all waited to see if now his hand would slip down toward his belt. It appeared, crazily enough, that it might actually come to that.

But it didn't. He picked up his coffee cup from where he had left it on top of the dresser, and the crisis seemed to pass away.

Faglin stood up from his chair, looking slightly embarrassed, as if someone had mentioned a family scandal. He was only about a meter away from Hirsch. He gave the impression he would have liked to reach out and touch him on the sleeve but couldn't quite muster the courage.

"Really, Jerry, I think maybe we should talk about this. There's room for compromise."

"Yeah, Jerry. You know, maybe Inar—"

"You keep your mouth shut, Itzikel. You know the rules." Hirsch looked as if he was ready to hit someone. "Mossad discipline—you know that goddamned well. With Mordecai gone, I'm in command, and I give orders."

"You give any orders you like," Christiansen said suddenly. He rose from his seat, seeming to fill the room. His voice was cold and quiet, like falling snow. "Just see to it you don't give any orders to me, pal, since I plan to make my own arrangements. My understanding was with Mordecai. It still is."

"You fucking *goyish* bastard! Who do you think you are, you—"

He never had a chance to finish, because Faglin's fist caught him just under the floating ribs, causing the wind to gush out of him in a noisy wheeze. Before Hirsch had a chance to react, Faglin reached in under his belt and took out the automatic, throwing it across the room to Christiansen, who caught it with his left hand. Hirsch's legs seemed ready to buckle under him until Faglin put an arm around his back to hold him up. He looked at Hirsch for a moment, as if to make sure he was really all right, and then turned his gaze toward Christiansen. He was smiling, but without much conviction.

"What was it you had in mind?"

"What is in your mind, Colonel?"

The smile on Faraj's heavy, subtle face betrayed a certain uneasiness. Faraj had not enjoyed last night's unscheduled performance at the Café Pícaro. Faraj was a weak and pathetic creature, the product of a decaying race, who hated all displays of violence, particularly public violence. The agile Herr Christiansen had made a profound impression on him.

Hagemann took a sip of the ice water that was an accompaniment to all his meals and sighed, wondering whatever had possessed him to come back to the villa for lunch, since he could so easily have avoided this kind of close examination had he been content with a little wine and a plateful of greasy meat in town.

But the fact was that he felt safer at the villa. Christiansen had made an impression on him as well.

"Would it please you to go back to Damascus, Faraj? Yes, I rather imagined it would." He refolded his napkin and set it down next to the plate in a way his Spanish servant understood to mean that he was finished. As the dishes were taken away, he studied Faraj's reactions—or, more accurately, his lack of them—wondering to himself which would finally come to seem the more dangerous, Christiansen with his pistols and his strangling cords or this pudgy, effete little politician. Yes, of course it would please Faraj to go back to Damascus.

"Might I know when your excellency plans for us to depart—and, if it is not too much to ask, why?"

"Because I have what I came here to obtain. Or very nearly. I think you will agree that Leivick can be more conveniently interrogated in Syria."

"Will the young lady be accompanying us?"

"Yes."

"Then you are within reach of your solution?"

"Yes."

After lunch Hagemann took a walk around the grounds. It was a chance to be alone, since Faraj liked to lie down as soon as he had eaten—he said that exercise didn't agree with him. Hagemann was just as pleased.

His mother would have liked this place—the gentleman's house overlooking the sea. She had never wanted her son to be a soldier. She had never understood that this was a decision taken not by him but by history. *The war is over*," she had said. "*You can go on to the university now, just as you always planned. You can study to be a lawyer.*" So merely to please her, and because he had felt himself adrift, he had begun to attend the lectures in jurisprudence. The world was falling to pieces—what conceivable difference could the law make?—but he had had nothing else to do. And now the soldier's life had brought him to a villa overlooking the Mediterranean.

"*Stay away from those men. What are they except hooligans?*" "*They are right, and they will remake the world.*" "*What is so bad about the world as it is?*" How could he have expected that good, simple woman to understand his answer?

Within six months she was dead; her heart simply stopped beating. She had been Hagemann's last attachment to the orderly old world of his boyhood, and the day following her funeral he resigned from the university to give himself over full time to the Party.

And in the end nothing had turned out as they expected, so perhaps his mother had not been so simple after all.

He was tired—that was it. He had been living too long on nerve alone. But it would all be over soon, and then there would be time to rest and think idle thoughts. But not now.

He wanted to go over the plans in his mind, looking for flaws. A perfect plan led to a perfect result. It was a law of nature.

Except, of course, for the inevitable imponderables. Leivick was now safely locked away in a cell at the Civil Guard station, but Leivick most certainly had not come to Burriana alone. A general must have his soldiers.

Leivick was a cunning old badger, content to rest in his hole until the darkness came. Like Hagemann himself, he would have others to deal with the uglier side of affairs. The difficulty was that, aside from that boy, that little Jewish pimp who had so conspicuously served as Esther's "husband"—did she let him sleep with her, the bitch?—all the rest of Leivick's troops had so far managed not to be detected.

Unless, of course, one could count Christiansen. Could one? It was a distasteful idea. Christiansen was of the right sort, an Aryan and a soldier. It was unpleasant to think of him hunting with the Mossad. Nevertheless, it was a possibility that could not be discounted.

Hagemann had seen the bodies of his men last night. After the nightclub had been cleared the three corpses had been lined up beside the bar, covered with tablecloths until the ambulances came to carry them to the police morgue. Weichbrodt, the idiot, had had most of his head shot away. Imagine rushing into the office like that. It had served him right. And poor Ernst. It had been several hours before he could

be brought even to speak. They had fed him straight
gin by the tumblerful until he calmed down, and it
required a great deal to frighten Ernst.

Three men dead, and Hagemann could have been
among them except that Inar Christiansen had decided to wait. When would he decide he had waited
long enough?

Hagemann was tired of pretending not to be frightened. He was glad he was alone, even if the cold,
strangely impersonal terror washed through his chest
like ice water. It was almost a relief. Yes, of course
he was afraid. Leivick had been right—it was only
reasonable to be afraid. Christiansen was going to kill
him, and he wanted him to know that there was no
safety.

The wind had dropped. In the afternoon stillness,
among the pine trees that fronted on the cliffs so that
one could look in any direction and hardly know whether
one faced the sea or the land, Hagemann walked along,
listening to the scraping sounds of his footsteps against
the soft, sandy ground. A dozen yards behind him
followed a pair of bodyguards, rifles slung casually
over their shoulders as they kept pace. He had grown
so used to their constant presence that he couldn't
even have said what they looked like.

Hagemann felt in the pocket of his overcoat for
one of the thin cigars he had taken to smoking lately,
usually after a large meal or before going to bed. In
the SS and as a serving officer in wartime, he had
scorned all such petty vices, but he was growing soft
now, middle-aged and soft. He knew it perfectly well.
There seemed to be nothing he could do about it. He
put the cigar between his lips and lit it with a Ronson
lighter, made in America, that someone had given

him—he couldn't remember who. He was turning into jelly, like Faraj. And, like Faraj, he had learned to be wily. Perhaps it was a form of compensation. As strength and courage and youth all deteriorated together, cunning increased.

Five years ago he wouldn't have been so afraid of Christiansen. He would have welcomed the challenge. Five years ago, death had seemed neither so terrible nor so near.

But five years filled with defeat, then flight, then a slow gathering of strength had taught Hagemann to think more, to look inside himself, and that sort of reflection was no friend to the martial virtues. So now he smoked thin cigars and worried about fat Arab politicians and was frightened of a man like Christiansen.

Well, then, perhaps that meant that he would survive them all. Warriors should die young, their ideals intact, and since he had been denied that fate perhaps he would be spared to live to a ripe age, having buried all his enemies.

There was a house outside of Damascus, beside a grove of date palms, belonging to a lieutenant colonel posted to the war ministry, a paper soldier from an influential family, the sort of man who was easily moved aside. Hagemann had had his eye on the house for a long time. It would serve as his place of honorable retirement after he had provided the Syrians with the means of annihilating their Zionist enemies. In their gratitude they would give it to him. They would give him whatever he wanted.

He would live there with Esther. Now that Leivick was a prisoner, her part in this affair was merely incidental. At the right moment, she would do as she

was told and that would be all that would be required
of her. She would not have to be tortured for information—Leivick would serve very well in her place.
She would come through without a mark on her.

Would she consent to stay with him? At first, perhaps not. He would not allow her consent to matter,
not at first. But Esther had always been a reasonable
sort of girl. In the end she would even come to forgive
him. In the end she would remain of her own free
will.

Yes, he had missed her. He hadn't realized how
badly, not until last night. And now, in another few
hours, she would be here, and they would never be
parted again. She probably hated him and, excepting
his mother, he had never loved any woman, but that
was unimportant. Esther and he had no need to concern themselves with love. Each of them found something in the other without which they stood incomplete.

Tonight then. There would be a Syrian merchant
ship waiting forty kilometers off shore. In the small
hours of the morning they would join her. Then everything would be as it had been before the defeat.
Everything.

There was a break in the trees, a small clearing
where one could stand by the sheer stone cliffs and
look out at the Mediterranean, as calm as any lake.
Hagemann always stopped here—he had no idea why,
since the view always made him feel uncomfortable.
The sea was his avenue of escape—it had been in 1945
and would be again tonight—but somehow, looking
down on it from this height, it seemed shrouded in
menace. He would stand there, sometimes for several
minutes at a time, feeling the dread crawl through
him like maggots.

"Herr Oberst."

He turned around and saw with some slight sensation of relief that it was Gerstein, the captain of his bodyguard.

"Yes, Rudi, what is it?"

"It is almost time to go into town, *Herr Oberst.*"

Gerstein kept his face rigid and unsmiling. He was a tall, wide-shouldered boy with hair the color of butter, almost unchanged from the day in 1942 when, at the age of seventeen, he had been assigned to the Fifth Brigade as a private. He was a good soldier, brave and cruel, but somehow he had never stopped being that boy of seventeen. Hagemann always felt more at ease around Rudi.

"And are we quite prepared here, Rudi? You know, even after we bring the thing off there will still be danger. We shall have to wait here until just before the rendezvous, and they are bound to try hitting back at us before then."

"You mean the Jews, *Herr Oberst*?" Gerstein allowed himself to smile, as if his commander had made a joke he was bound to acknowledge. "We will be ready for them. We are always ready for them."

"Good. I am glad to hear you say so."

Hagemann turned his eyes back toward the sea. It was almost as if he couldn't help himself. What was he looking for? He hardly even knew.

And then he remembered the little sailboat of yesterday afternoon.

"Perhaps it is the Norwegian," Faraj had said. *"Perhaps his intention is to climb these cliffs and murder you in your sleep."* Sleeping or waking, what difference would it make to Christiansen?

And, of course, it would be impossible to scale these cliffs without being detected. Nevertheless . . .

He glanced at his trusted subordinate, whom he had trained, whom he had rescued from the insignificance and boredom of a conquered Germany, and he watched the smile die on those youthful lips. He meant to make it understood that there must be no miscalculation, no concession to arrogance. And, yes, Gerstein understood all that.

"Rudi, I think it would be well if we doubled the patrols tonight, just as a precaution. And now perhaps we can go down to the car?"

✠ 20 ✠

It was a three-story brick building that looked as if it dated from the time of the Republic. Even for a small-town Civil Guard station it wasn't much, and Franco had inherited the old monarchy's obsession with the grandeur of its public edifices. The only windows that were barred were on the top story, so that had to be where the holding cells were located.

"It isn't very wide," Faglin said, cocking his head a little to one side, like a painter considering a landscape. "There's probably only one big cage up there, somewhere to store the drunks of a Saturday night. What more would they need in a little fishing town like this?"

"Nevertheless, we will have to know."

Christiansen's cold blue eyes played nervously over the street, as if he were looking for someone. They, of course, were looking for him. Probably every policeman in Burriana had his name and description by then.

"You think maybe one of us should go in there and ask them?"

"Don't make jokes, Itzikel."

"He's right. That's precisely what one of us is going to have to do."

The icy gaze settled on Faglin. No, there was no chance that Christiansen was making a joke. Christiansen looked as if he had never made a joke in his life.

"If Mordecai is in there, we'll have to find a way of communicating with him, and I'm the one they're so eager to lock up. I'll just turn myself in."

"You can't do that! It's crazy—it's . . ."

But Faglin made an impatient gesture with his left hand and Dessauer fell silent.

"Once you get inside, how will you let us know where you are?"

"It's not a problem. There are only two barred windows, one on each side of the building. You take one and Itzhak takes the other. If you see my left hand clutching one of the bars, I'm in the same cell with Mordecai. Are your eyes good enough to see my scar from that distance?"

He held out his hand for them to look at. It was a huge scar, covering the width of all four fingers and reaching back almost to the wrist.

"Yes," Dessauer said. For some reason the sight of it awed him. "No trouble."

"And if you're not in the same cell?"

"Then I'll throw down a shirt button or something. If I can't make contact, if I don't think he's being held up there at all, I'll just give a shout and the pair of you can lose yourselves and live to try again another day."

"Don't you think we'd try to get you out then?"

From the way Christiansen's eyes narrowed, Dessauer knew at once he had said something stupid. The silence of those few seconds was almost unbearable. Then Christiansen smiled faintly.

"You might, but Faglin's been around longer. No hard feelings."

Faglin shrugged his thin shoulders. "No, no hard feelings. I think it would be a good idea if we took another look around before you go pay your courtesy call."

The three of them were standing together in the shadow of a shop awning diagonally across the intersection from the Guard station's front entrance. It was the lunch hour—sacred in all Latin countries—so the shop was closed. The streets were nearly deserted. Everything was quiet, which meant that any bored policeman who happened to glance out the window because he had nothing better to do would be sure to notice them. In Christiansen's case, this could present difficulties.

"I'll wait for you here," he said, lighting another cigarette. It was his third in not quite twenty minutes.

"That might be best."

The other two men stepped out into the sunshine of the quiet, wind-still street. They didn't look behind them, but Dessauer could feel Christiansen's eyes on the back of his head. It wasn't until they had passed around the front of the Guard station and turned the corner onto the next street that he lost that sense of being watched.

"What will we really do if they don't put him in the same cell with Mordecai?"

Faglin only glanced at him for a moment and then

went back to his study of the building directly behind the Guard station.

"We'll go through on the other side and hope we find Mordecai there. What choice do we have?"

"And leave Christiansen behind?"

"Yes. There won't be time to get him out as well."

"And he knows that?"

"Yes."

"Shit."

"Nobody ever said he didn't have guts. Not even Hirsch."

There was a large dog with a heavy, matted coat, brown with black patches, lying on a doorstep, stretched out to make the most of the sun's heat. He lifted his head to watch them as they went by and then turned back to lay it between his paws again. The sight of them seemed to depress him.

"What are you going to do about Hirsch?"

"Nothing."

Faglin stopped and looked up at a third-story window framed in shutters that had been painted a bright blue. He smiled, as if at something funny.

"If I planned to do anything about Jerry I would have done it before we left the hotel," he went on. "Jerry's all right—he's the practical type. He'll stay in his room and sulk for a while and then it'll be business as usual.

"We'll go in through there. Let's hope everyone is having lunch out, unlikely as that is."

He hadn't taken his eyes off the window with the blue shutters.

They went around the next corner and found the entrance to the apartment building. It really wasn't anything more than a tenement, with an outside stair-

way and only one door per story. They had rented a
car and had it parked just out of sight, not half a block
away, but they still had to get to it. The stairway was
completely exposed—it would be a problem if the
police came around fast enough to catch them before
they made it down to the street. That was the sort of
thing they would have to worry about when the time
came. You couldn't expect to have everything.

Christiansen was still under the awning when they
got back. He still had a cigarette between his lips,
and the remains of four others were on the sidewalk
in front of him, each rubbed out with the toe of his
shoe so that they looked like squashed insects. He
reached down and picked up a knapsack that had been
resting against the outside wall of the shop, handing
it to Faglin. Then he took the revolver from under
his belt and gave it to Dessauer.

"Keep it warm for me," he said. In the shade, his
eyes looked as if he were already dead.

"Sure."

He walked across the street and, without a pause,
as if it were the sort of thing he did every day, opened
the left side of the double doorway to the Guard station, letting it swing closed behind him when he disappeared inside.

"Just like that," Dessauer said under his breath.

"That's right, kid. Just like that."

Faglin made a gesture to indicate that he would
take this side of the building and that Dessauer should
go around and watch at the other window.

The dog was still there. This time he didn't even
trouble to look up as Dessauer took a station on the
sidewalk in front of him. Dessauer glanced at his watch.
It was three minutes after one.

He tried to imagine what was going on inside the station. What would Christiansen do, just walk up to the front desk and announce, "I understand you gentlemen have been looking for me"? He might, come to think of it.

And what would the police do? At this hour, all the senior officers were probably off home, enjoying a little nap after lunch—Christiansen would be counting on that. The desk sergeant wouldn't dare risk trying to interrogate him; he would leave that to his superiors, so they could take the credit. He would content himself with a body search, which was why Christiansen had given Dessauer his gun, and then he would toss him in a cell and settle back to wait. The rough stuff would come later, when they could all feel themselves on safer ground.

How long would all that take? Ten minutes? Fifteen? Dessauer looked at his watch again and found that exactly two minutes had passed.

He thought he could hear a telephone ringing somewhere, but he couldn't be sure. The sweat was collecting under his armpits. His hands were cold, so he slipped them inside his overcoat pockets. It was seven minutes past one.

No, he couldn't blame Esther for liking Christiansen better. Dessauer wasn't at all sure he would have had the nerve to walk into that place—in Spain they punished murderers with the garrote. They strapped you down in a chair, put a loop of rope around your neck, and twisted it with an iron bar until it crushed your windpipe and you strangled.

At sixteen minutes after one, a hand appeared in the cell window and the fingers closed around the middle bar. It was a left hand, and the pale winter sunlight made the scar on the back glisten like silver.

Dessauer had to force himself to keep from running. This time he went around the back of the building. As soon as he reached the other side he saw Faglin standing on the opposite sidewalk, looking up at the barred third-story window like a man in love. When he noticed Dessauer, he hoisted the knapsack to his shoulder and came over.

"Well? Hand or button?"

"Hand. Lucky for Christiansen."

"Lucky for us too. We'll need him to help cover our escape."

The tenement had been built probably at around the same time as the Civil Guard station, but the brick was a slightly different color. The Republic had favored brick; brick was more "proletarian." The back of one building was flush up against the back of the other; you couldn't have fit a business card in the space between them. Faglin and Dessauer trudged up the stairway together to the landing on the third floor. There was no bell, so Faglin knocked at the door. When there was no answer right away, he knocked again.

Finally the door opened. The man inside was perhaps thirty years old, with a stubble of beard and uncombed black hair that had a tendency to fall forward into his eyes. He was wearing an undershirt that showed off his heavy arms and shoulders, and there was a napkin in his right hand. He looked annoyed.

"*Si?*"

Faglin only smiled at him, swung the knapsack down from his shoulder, and pulled a revolver out from beneath the flap. He rested the barrel against the man's chest and pushed. The man stepped back, the door opened wider, and everyone was inside. Dessauer closed the door behind him.

The whole family was there—mama, grandma, a boy of perhaps five with long, thin legs, a baby in a highchair. They were sitting around a table covered with the remains of the midday meal. Papa, the one in the undershirt, had retreated back to his wife's chair, where he stood with his hand resting on the wooden backrest. They were all staring at Faglin's gun—enchanted, like mice before a cobra.

"Any of you speak English?" Faglin asked. He almost seemed to be pleading.

"Yes," the wife answered. "I work at Gibraltar two year."

She smiled tentatively, as if afraid she might be thought to boast. She had a round, brown face and remarkably large eyes.

"Then tell your family that we have no wish to hurt anyone, that if everyone behaves himself we'll be gone from here in just a few minutes. Just do as you're told and everything will be fine. Understand?"

"Si—yes."

She nodded emphatically two or three times and then translated for her husband, who seemed less than convinced. He looked first at Dessauer, and then at Faglin, and then turned back to his wife, to whom he spoke in a low, anxious voice.

"He wishes to know what you plan to do." Again the tentative, apologetic little smile.

"We have a couple of friends in the Guard station. We're going to get them out. There will probably be shooting, so let's see if we can't find somewhere you and your family will be out of the way."

They were Spanish, and old enough to have vivid memories of their civil war. They knew all about the virtues of being out of the way.

"Please, then, will you tie us up?" the woman asked. She held up her hands, the wrists together, as if to explain what she meant. "The Guards, you must understand . . ."

Faglin nodded. They all knew all about reprisals.

There seemed to be three rooms in the apartment. In the front was the main living area, with a few chairs, a sofa covered in worn rose-colored fabric, a dining table and, crowded into one end, a kitchen. The two bedrooms were shallow and wide and opened directly out into the main room, and both of them had tiny windows. Faglin made a gesture toward the one on the left.

"You'll all be much safer in there—with the door open. Just remember, the only way anyone can get hurt is if he tries to be a hero. Keep your heads down, and in half an hour you can get back to your lunch."

The little boy got down from his chair and took a few steps toward Faglin before his grandmother seized him and held him to her. From the protection of her arms he continued to regard the intruders with large, curious eyes he had obviously inherited from his mother. When Faglin smiled at him he found no difficulty in smiling back.

"Itzikel, take them in and tie them up—and don't make a big production of it. Let's keep everybody comfortable."

Faglin took a coil of clothesline out of his knapsack and watched through the door as Dessauer did his work. The little boy seemed to think it was all great fun and could hardly wait until it was his turn.

The other bedroom was apparently mama and papa's. There was a crib for the baby, a four-drawer dresser, and a double bed, all crowded together in a space hardly twice the size of the bed alone.

"Our flat in Haifa isn't much bigger than this," Faglin said as they stood together just inside the doorway. "One bedroom for the wife and me and one for the girls. At least we don't have to have mama out on the couch."

He grinned, but in a way that suggested the thought of his family caused him some pain.

"Come on. Let's get to it."

He crouched by the wall that adjoined the Guard station, resting his hand against the plaster as if trying to feel a pulse. Then he used the knuckle of his middle finger to tap the surface.

"I'll bet the builder saved himself a little money," he said finally. "I'll bet this is a single layer of faced-over brick, and he counted on the adjoining wall for insulation and support. I'll bet we can punch straight through, like poking a hole in a loaf of bread with your thumb."

"What are you going to use?"

Faglin ran his fingers down the wall once more in a loving gesture. It was obvious he was enjoying this.

"A shaped charge. I'll draw myself a little circle with plastic explosives and bevel the edges so the broadest side is flat against the wall. When she goes off, the force of the blast will all go in that direction—right on through to the cell next door. Nothing to it."

He dumped out the contents of his knapsack on the bed. There was a knife with a flat point, a battery pack with two bare wires protruding and what looked like an egg timer attached to it with black electrical tape, and about four meters of something resembling window putty, a tube of the stuff, wrapped in what might have been waxed paper. Faglin began peeling away the wrapping. It was like watching a snake shed its skin.

"Do you know what you're doing?" Dessauer asked, the fingers of one hand nervously tracing the crease in his trousers. "I mean, isn't there a chance the explosion will kill them on the other side?"

Faglin looked up from where he was sitting on the bed. His face was masklike, and his fingers never stopped stripping away the paper wrapper.

"Christiansen knows what's going to happen," he said. "Let's hope he's smart enough not to belly up to this particular wall. Beyond that, we just have to trust to luck."

In about five minutes he had most of the explosive free from its wrapping and coiled up in a pile on his knees.

"That should do it—we don't have to blow a hole they can walk through."

He twisted off the last piece and threw it back into his knapsack. Then he stood up, stepped over to the wall, and began pressing the long strip of explosive, as soft as modeling clay, up against the plaster with his first finger and thumb. When he had described a circle and blended the two ends together, he took the knife and used the flat point to shape the edges. When he was finished, the circle was about three fingers wide against the wall and its spine narrowed to a right angle. Faglin attached the timer by the simple expedient of pushing the bare tips of the two wires into the explosive near the bottom, so the battery pack could rest on the floor.

"We'll give it fifteen seconds," he said. "All the time in the world considering we only have to step into the next room."

He twisted the dial around a quarter of a turn and took his hand away, just as if the thing had become white hot. Dessauer thought the ticking it made was perhaps the loudest noise he had ever heard.

"Let's move it—fifteen seconds isn't that long."

They went outside and closed the door. Faglin took the pistol out of his belt and held it at the ready, the muzzle pointing toward the ceiling. Both of them seemed to have stopped breathing.

Was it really only fifteen seconds? Whole minutes seemed to go by, and still nothing happened. Dessauer could feel the blood pounding in his neck. He tried to count—one, two, three—but his heart was going too fast.

"Itzikel, give me Christiansen's gun."

Faglin held out his hand and Dessauer put the revolver down on the palm, where it looked awkwardly large and out of balance.

"I suppose we—"

The explosion was not so much a sound as a physical shock, like being struck in the chest with the points of someone's fingers. The whole room, in one instant, seemed to start forward—plates, spoons, picture frames, a pair of silver candlesticks that might have been a wedding present, all sorts of loose objects suddenly dashed to the floor as if of their own volition. And then, of course, when you had almost decided that it would never come at all, the ghastly, tearing boom of the explosion, like the sound of a giant clearing his throat, made you want to clap your hands over your ears and sent a painful stab to your eyes. The

door to the bedroom flew off its hinges and hit the
table before bouncing to the floor.

Faglin didn't waste any time. The bedroom wasn't
a room anymore—it was simply the space that held
a heavy cloud of white plaster dust. But he threw
himself inside, his body cutting a slot through the
chalky haze.

Dessauer followed him and in a few seconds, after
he had wiped his eyes, he could see what looked like
the mouth of a tunnel. The explosives had done their
work. Bars of light were shining through from the
holding cell in the next building.

"Christiansen, catch this!" Faglin shouted. His
arm went through a low arc and Dessauer heard something land with a thud inside the hole. It was the
revolver. Almost at once there was the sound of a
single shot.

A few seconds later, Mordecai's head and shoulders became visible as he crawled through from the
other side on his hands and knees. He looked up at
Dessauer's face, blinked in the dusty light, and smiled.
Dessauer reached out to take his hand and pull him
through. There was a handcuff around his wrist, but
the chain had been broken.

At almost the same moment there were several
more shots fired inside the cell, this time from more
than one weapon. One bullet came through and buried itself with a thud in the plaster wall not a handspan
from Dessauer's right knee.

And then there was silence.

And then the light from inside the tunnel went
dark and Christiansen pushed the upper half of his
huge body through, his shoulders scraping against the
ragged sides of the hole. He threw out his arms.

"Help me out," he shouted. "I don't fancy getting shot in the ass."

As soon as they were all through, and Christiansen had stood up from his crouch, Faglin made a gesture toward the door. Surely by then the Guards must have figured out what had happened, and the four of them still had two flights of stairs to get down before they even reached the street.

"You lead," Christiansen said, putting his hand on Faglin's arm. "Then Mordecai, then Itzhak. I'll pull up the rear."

Faglin nodded. It was almost as if they had agreed on everything in advance. As he pushed through the door to the outside landing, Dessauer thought he could hear the baby crying.

They spaced themselves about five meters apart as they started down. Christiansen waited by the open door, his revolver already cocked, still watching the bedroom door to see if any more Guards would have the nerve to come through from the cell. The stairway shook under their weight, and the sound of their footsteps on the wooden risers was a sullen roar.

Dessauer had already made the second landing when a Guard with a rifle came around the edge of the building. He brought his weapon up to his shoulders—it was aimed square at Faglin—then there was a short, high-pitched bark of gunfire and the Guard toppled over, dead before he hit the ground. Christiansen had shot him from above, and the bullet had gone right through the top of his head.

"That way!"

Pointing toward where they had left the car, Dessauer looked up at Christiansen. But Christiansen waved him on, as though he didn't care. Two more Guards—

men were already on the street, running for the cover
of an alleyway. One of them lost his hat, and it bounced
against the cobblestones with a click. He was carrying
what looked like a machine gun.

Faglin and Christiansen both turned to fire. The
Guardsman who had dropped his hat went down,
twisting around as if he had been pulled from behind.
Even as he died he clutched the machine gun to
him.

His friend had better luck. A final sprint carried
him to the mouth of the alley, where he found cover
behind a trash barrel. There was no time to worry
about him. There was only time to run. Christiansen,
who was standing in the middle of the street, the
biggest target anyone could ask for, emptied his pistol
to give the others some cover, but it was too late.
Within two meters of safety, Mordecai suddenly collapsed.

There was no time for anything. Dessauer, who
was directly behind him, nearly stumbled over Mordecai's body. As soon as he caught himself, he reached
down and took the old man under the armpits and
began trying to drag him out of the line of fire. It was
then that he saw the bullet hole in his side, just under
the elbow. The blood was welling out in a thick, heavy
stream. Dessauer looked back over his shoulder, hoping to see Christiansen, hoping for help. He hadn't a
doubt that Mordecai was dying. What he saw he
wouldn't have believed.

The man was crazy. Christiansen, his hands empty,
was charging down the cobbled street, straight at the
Guardsman and his trash barrel and his gun. Suddenly
he started to yell—not a word, just a sound, the sound
of an animal in a blind rage. He had maybe twelve

meters to cover. He would never make it. The Guardsman would kill him for sure.

But he didn't. He never even fired. He even stood up. He was in plain sight now; he looked as if he wanted to know which way to run. He never had a chance to do even that.

Christiansen hit him hard, using everything—head, shoulders, arms, everything. The Guardsman went over backwards. They both disappeared into the alleyway and, a few seconds later, Christiansen came out, carrying the rifle. It hung in his hand like a club. He glanced around, his face dark. He seemed to be looking for someone else to kill.

But there was no one—at least, no one else came running at them from the direction of the Guard station. Christiansen walked over, threw the rifle to Dessauer without even troubling to look at him, and scooped up Mordecai in his arms.

"Let's get out of here."

Faglin was already backing the car up toward them. Dessauer opened one of the rear doors, stepping out of the way so that Christiansen and his burden could get inside. Then he went around to the front. In a second the car lurched forward.

"Don't try to talk, Mordecai. You'll be fine. We'll get you to a doctor, and you'll be fine."

Christiansen was crouching over the rear seat, cradling Mordecai's head in the crook of his arm. There was a quality of pleading in his voice.

"No time." Mordecai licked his lips. He seemed to be struggling to keep his eyes open. "Stop the car. Finished with me. Listen. Stop the car."

"Do what he says, dammit! Faglin, pull over somewhere."

They had gone no more than half a dozen blocks, but no one was following them—it seemed they had killed every Guardsman with the misfortune to be on duty that afternoon. Faglin found the driveway behind a store marked *Ferretería* in flaking green paint. It didn't seem to be very busy. Even before the sound of their engine had died away, Mordecai was looking up at the front seat, at Faglin, and making a vague beckoning gesture with his right hand. In that tiny space he had everyone's complete attention.

"Thanks," he murmured, casting his eyes around to the three of them and smiling faintly. "I didn't want to die in Syria."

He took a deep breath—at least his chest heaved, but he seemed to take very little benefit from it. There was a faint gurgling sound from his windpipe.

"Amos, I saw him." An excited look came into his eyes. He was looking at Faglin, but he put his hand on Christiansen's arm. "He's scared good—of our friend here. Our friend was right, all along. Do it his way now."

"It's okay, Mordecai." Faglin reached over the backrest and touched him on the face. "We'll get you patched up. We'll—"

"No. No time. They've killed me, Amos."

His gaze appeared to wander for a moment, and then he turned his head a few degrees and looked for Christiansen.

"He'll try for the girl now. No choice. He told me . . . He's mad, Inar. Crazy. You'll know what to do. You'll know . . ."

It wasn't until his hand slipped from Christiansen's arm that they knew for certain he was dead. For a long time no one said anything, and then Christiansen reached across with his right hand and closed Mordecai's eyes. When he spoke, his voice was thick but calm.

"Take care of the body," he said. "Find somewhere quiet and bury it. You'll know what's needed. Don't let the Guards . . ."

"Where will you go?" Dessauer asked. There were tears in his eyes, but he couldn't help himself.

There was a pistol lying on the floor in front of the back seat. Christiansen picked it up and hid it under his coat. He didn't look at anybody.

"I'll be at the hotel, with Esther. Hagemann can come for us there."

* 21 *

As soon as the car was out of sight, Christiansen started on his way back to the hotel. It wasn't far—nothing was far in this little town—but he had to be careful. He had killed probably half the Civil Guard contingent for the whole of Burriana, and they could hardly be expected to take a thing like that in stride. They would be looking for him.

But he had to get back to the hotel and Esther because now Hagemann would be looking for her. Right now there was no one keeping watch on her except Hirsch, and Hirsch might have all kinds of other things on his mind.

In an hour and a half, two at the outside—how long did it take to get rid of a corpse?—Faglin and Itzhak would be back, and then they would decide what to do next. They would have to decide. There was no more Mordecai to call the shots for them, just a corpse in the back of a borrowed car.

Christiansen decided he would just as soon not

think along those lines anymore. He would confine himself to the problem at hand and save the regrets for later. Mordecai was dead. For the time being they would all be better off simply to leave it at that.

Hagemann would have to make his try for Esther now. Mordecai had said so and it was the logical, even the necessary move. Hagemann was running out of time, just like the rest of them.

He would kill Hagemann now. He promised himself that. He would kill the bastard twenty times over and it still wouldn't be enough. But he would try to make it enough. He would square things the best way he could.

But first he had to get back to the hotel, and avoid being arrested—if there was still anyone left alive to arrest him.

Would that guy in the alley be one of the ones who haunted him? If the poor son of a bitch hadn't panicked . . . Why hadn't he fired? What had he seen that had made him want to run? Christiansen didn't know—he had hardly realized what was happening until he found himself on his knees, his hands around the Guardsman's neck, staring into those wide-open, dead eyes. The poor monkey was as limp as a rag doll. He didn't even know how he had killed him.

But for dumb luck, it would have been the other way round. Christiansen figured he had probably used up that day's supply of dumb luck.

He had to get this business settled today—tonight at the latest. He would probably be able to keep from getting arrested or killed that long, but not any longer. Tomorrow the whole area would be crawling with police. Four, maybe five more hours of daylight, and then the covering darkness, and it had to be finished. Either Hagemann died or he did. There wasn't any third choice.

Esther was taken to Jerry Hirsch's room for lunch, which was delivered on a covered tray by a waiter in a starched white jacket. Since Jerry was an employee of the hotel, as well as a foreigner who spoke English, could talk to the guests on more or less equal terms, and was not required by his position to touch money, he was treated with some deference by the rest of the staff, and the meal was quite good. There was even wine, but it did nothing to improve the atmosphere. Esther was to regard herself as no more than a pampered prisoner—a role, it was implied, to which she should long ago have grown accustomed. It might be protective custody, but Jerry Hirsch was still her jailer.

They were on a first-name basis. He was one of those men who always called women and children by their first names. He wasn't being friendly; it was merely habit. He wasn't in the least friendly.

"What will you do when all this is over," he asked, a faint, contemptuous smile on his lips, as if he already knew the answer. "Are you expecting Christiansen to take you back to Norway with him? Do you think you can get him to marry you? Do you plan to turn into an Aryan?"

"He will never go back to Norway."

"No?"

"No."

She didn't smile at him. She discovered she had the power to look him straight in the face without feeling either ashamed or frightened. It was something new for her. She didn't care what Jerry Hirsch thought of her—it simply wasn't important.

"Then what is your plan?"

"I've given up having plans. I'll do whatever Inar wants. I'll trust to that."

"Maybe you should have stuck with Itzikel. You could have been sure he'd marry you. That's the way his mind works."

He set down his coffee cup and picked up the pack of cigarettes that was lying on the table next to his plate. There was something almost satirical in the way his fingers managed the book of matches, cupping around the tip of the cigarette as he lit it, almost as if he were parodying someone.

"Itzikel would take you to Israel—and it will be Israel, very soon. You could be a Jew there."

All at once Esther had an impulse to laugh. She couldn't help herself. She put her hands in front of her face and laughed.

"Oh yes," she said finally. She still had to laugh a little, because it was all so funny. "I could be a Jew there, but what else? Do you know when I found out I was a Jew? When the Nazis told me. Suddenly it was the most important fact about me: I was a Jew. You're just like them, Jerry. You despise me, and not because I've led a bad life but because I'm Jewish and have led a bad life. I'm a little Jewish tramp, and you feel insulted because Jewish women aren't supposed to be like that. Is that what would happen to me in Israel? Would I become so Jewish that there wouldn't be room for anything else? If it's just the same to you, I'll stick with Inar. I don't know whether he cares for me or not, but at least it's a woman he takes to bed with him and not a cause."

"Are you finished?"

Yes, he really did despise her—she could see that in his eyes, and in the tight little lines around his mouth. With another man it might have been merely an amused contempt, as if she were some kind of incarnate dirty joke, but it went deeper than that with Hirsch.

"Is it so bad if I just want to live like other people?" she asked. She really wanted to know.

"Yes. For us, yes. I don't believe in God—to hell with God. But we're the Chosen People anyway. They chose us—the *goyim,* people like Hagemann and your friend Inar. You're a little fool if you think you can ever make yourself into one of them. You'll always be a Jew, whether you like it or not."

"So maybe it's enough that Inar doesn't care that I'm a Jew. Maybe I can be a Jew and he can love me anyway. You think maybe that's possible, Jerry? You think maybe they're all just like Hagemann, without any heart?"

She stood up, the tears brimming in her eyes. She wouldn't cry—she would force herself not to cry.

"I'll go back to my room now," she said, her voice only a little choked. "Inar will be back soon."

"Inar and all the rest of them are very probably dead by now, don't you know that?"

"Don't say it! Don't you ever say it!"

"Have everything just your own way, Missy."

He smiled again, this time an uncomfortable, unhappy smile. No, he wouldn't be glad if they all died. He didn't wish for that.

Jerry Hirsch's room was on the first floor, so he took her up the stairway to the third-floor landing and then brought her to her door.

"I'd better wait with you," he said. It was part of the routine.

"No. I'll be fine by myself. All I need do is pick up the telephone."

That was even true. Jerry's room was next to the switchboard—if he left his door open he could hear the ringing, and there were little red lights to indicate the room. She would be safe enough, and she really did want to be alone for a while.

"Okay. Fine."

It was the room she had shared with Inar last night. One of his shirts was hanging in the closet, and his shaving things were still resting on the shelf above the sink. No one had been in yet to make the bed, and when she sat down on it she passed her hand in under the sheets, as if to see if she could still feel the heat of his body. There was nothing, of course. All at once she felt terribly lonely.

It had been easier when she had had no one. Her loneliness then had been something of an abstraction, a window between her and the world. It was one thing to miss the parents who had died at Chelmno five years ago, but it was quite another, she was discovering, to miss a man who might come back in ten minutes or never. The luxury of that uncertainty made her heart seem to twist inside her.

Inar was strong and hard—the muscles in his arms were directly under the skin and were just as smooth and unyielding as steel. But he was a man and any man could be killed by any other man. Inar knew it, she knew it, even Hagemann knew it. It was the great lesson that the war had taught each of them, the reasonableness of fear. But if Inar was ever afraid he never let it show. That was his armor—his massive indifference to death. That was why they were all just a little afraid of him, even Hagemann. Even Jerry Hirsch.

And she was more afraid than any of them because she loved him. Inar made her feel as if the war had never happened—with him everything was innocent, as if it were for the first time.

If he died, she had no idea how she would support it.

But she would not cry. She had had all done with tears a long time ago. Even if she could love, she had not yet learned how to grieve.

The room was cold. Someone had left the window slightly open, and the damp cold had gotten inside. She rose from the bed and closed the window, still feeling half numb after her conversation with Jerry Hirsch. He was so brutally sure of himself that she—

The bed was unmade. No one had been in to attend to the room. So who had left the window open?

All at once fear rushed at her like darkness. She couldn't think at all, and then she could only think of escape.

Then she remembered the telephone. All she had to do was to pick up the telephone.

It stood on the night table beside the bed, two steps away. She almost stumbled as she crossed over to it. She picked up the receiver and pressed it against her ear, listening for the familiar crackling buzz, but there was nothing. The line seemed to be dead.

No. It wasn't that. Someone had anchored down the cradle prongs with heavy black tape so they couldn't spring up when she lifted the receiver.

She mustn't panic. She kept telling herself that she mustn't panic. She had to do something. She could try pulling the tape up, but there was too much of it to manage easily and her hands were shaking. She might even drop something and make a noise. She had to try to get out of the room as quietly as possible.

She put the receiver back on its cradle, trying to remember the plan of the room. Had the bathroom door been open when she came in? Yes, it had—no one could be hiding in there. Perhaps they were out in the corridor. Perhaps she had been wrong about the bathroom. There was nothing except to try to run away. Even if they caught her in the hallway, perhaps if she screamed loud enough someone would hear.

"No, Esther, it wouldn't do you any good to scream."

She spun around so fast that if she hadn't caught herself on the edge of the night table she probably would have fallen down. A man had stepped out of the closet. He had been waiting there the whole time. He was wearing a pair of blue worker's coveralls, and there was a pistol in his right hand. He was tall and slender and smiled at her. He was Hagemann.

The door that the hotel's kitchen help used was off a side alley, almost hidden behind a row of huge trash barrels that smelled like the devil and were emptied only once a week, winter or summer. But one couldn't very well use the fire escapes in broad daylight, and at least Christiansen could come in this way without having to worry about the police. No one would notice him. Delivery men, the fellow who repaired the pipes, and one or another kind of crook or huckster were always streaming through here. Besides, it was the short cut to Hirsch's room and Christiansen wanted a word with him before he saw Esther. There were a few things to get settled.

It was the last of the big lunchtime rush, when everybody was too busy with their sinks full of dirty dishes to notice an unfamiliar face or two. No one even looked at him as he brushed through to the staff quarters. Hirsch was at the desk in his room, sorting through a stack of registration cards.

"It didn't go very well. We got him out, but he took a bullet along the way. He didn't make it."

"Anyone else killed?"

Hirsch looked up at him with blank eyes, as if they were discussing the laundry count. His manner suggested nothing except a certain impatience.

"Everyone else is fine. I was under the impression Mordecai was a friend of yours."

"He was. I've worked with him for nearly three years. So what? Is it any of your business?"

"No. Sorry."

"Forget it."

Christiansen sat down on one of the flimsy little wicker chairs that one found everywhere in the hotel. He lit a cigarette, realizing for the first time how tired he was. He felt like hell. He didn't blame Hirsch a bit for not liking him.

"Hagemann will make his try at Esther now," he said, watching the smoke curl upward from his hand— the sight of it depressed him. "He doesn't have any choice now that Mordecai's dead. But if he doesn't come by, say, midnight, then I'm going after him. One way or the other, we nail him."

Hirsch merely smiled. "What's the matter, Christiansen? You feeling guilty because you couldn't get the old boy out?"

"I just want to know if you're coming along."

It was a long silence. The two of them sat there,

hardly moving, almost within arm's reach of each other. It could have ended any way at all.

Finally Hirsch stood up and went over to a small wooden cabinet on the wall beside his bed. There was a bottle inside. He grabbed it by the neck and carried it and two glasses back over to his desk.

"I think we could both use a drink," he said, pouring the clear liquid into first one glass and then the other. "White Moroccan rum—not at all bad once it burns away the nerve endings."

It tasted exactly like nail polish remover, but by the time he had finished half the glass Christiansen discovered he was no longer so sick of life.

"I take it the others are ready to go along with you in this piece of foolishness. Yes? I thought so." Hirsch, who apparently was more used to the stuff, poured himself a second glass of rum. "I think you're all crazy, but I'm prepared to be practical. If you'll wait until midnight, you can count me in. I still think he'll come here."

"I hope you're right. Those cliffs scare the hell out of me."

The both laughed, perhaps a trifle uneasily.

"Okay. Now tell me about what happened to Mordecai."

It was only by chance that Christiansen happened to see him. The passageway that led from the staff quarters to the back stairway happened to have a door that opened onto the lobby, and that door happened to have a small triangular pane of glass in it, and Christiansen happened to look out through it as he passed. The man was sitting at one end of a sofa, in his overcoat, pretending to read the newspaper. His face was partially obscured by a frond of one of the potted palms, but it was him. The night before he had been sitting at Hagemann's table at the Café Pícaro.

He was a big man in his early twenties, with yellowish-blond hair. His face had a deceptive look of innocence, which only meant, if he was one of Hagemann's bodyguards, that he hadn't learned anything from experience. He was keeping his overcoat on so the outline of the Luger he carried under his left armpit wouldn't show through the jacket.

And if this lug was around, that could only mean that Hagemann was somewhere in the building, way ahead of schedule.

Christiansen felt his throat tighten as he fought off the temptation simply to push through the door, gun in hand, and start shaking the big dumb thug down. Except, of course, that he might not be a big dumb thug, and there was nothing to be gained by starting a fight at this stage. Esther was upstairs in her little third-floor room and, for all anybody knew, Hagemann might be up there with her. It was a time for walking on tiptoes.

He had to find Hagemann first.

The man was showing signs of getting ready to leave. He pulled back the sleeve of his overcoat to look at his wristwatch and then refolded his newspaper and set it down on the table beside him. His right hand crept up and pressed briefly against his chest and arm, as if he sought to be reassured that he hadn't left his Luger at home.

Christiansen forced himself to begin climbing the stairs. He dreaded what was coming next.

The stairwell was narrow and opened onto every floor through a fire door. It was the perfect place for an ambush, but Christiansen managed to get all the way to the third story without running into any more of Hagemann's bodyguards. Perhaps he felt sure enough of himself that the one man downstairs was deemed sufficient.

It was a question of waiting and seeing. If Hagemann was in the room with Esther he couldn't leave without Christiansen knowing about it. There was always the fire escape, of course, but Esther's room faced the front of the building and Hagemann would be unlikely to attempt an escape with an unwilling hostage where he could be seen by anybody who happened to be walking by on the street. Besides, what was the goon for unless he planned to come back down through the building?

And if the goon came up to the third floor, then that was where Hagemann had to be. And it was necessary to take care of the goon first—it wouldn't do to make a move on Hagemann unless one knew one's back was safe.

He hated it. He hated the very idea of leaving Esther alone in there with a creep like Hagemann. But there was nothing to do except to wait and see.

Christiansen listened for the sound of footsteps on the carpeted stairs. He didn't have to listen long.

This kid had never learned that he wasn't invincible. The Reich might fall, the Fatherland might lie in ruins, but this particular son of Germany seemed to think he had nothing to worry about. He wasn't expecting any trouble. Who the hell could give him any trouble? He didn't care how much noise he made.

A smart man knows how to deal with people who hide behind doors. He just pushes the door all the way open and squashes the poor bastard flat. This didn't seem like a very smart man, but Christiansen wasn't taking any chances. He stood with his back to the wall, on the same side as the hinges but far enough away that the door couldn't catch him as it swung around. He kept his gun under his coat. This was not the time for guns.

The door opened, only about three feet—so much for precautions—and when it closed again Hagemann's trained dog was looking around, trying to figure out which way the room numbers ran. By the time he saw Christiansen it was already too late.

It all happened in a blink and a half. The man turned a little to his left and something in his face changed as he realized he didn't have the place to himself. He was too surprised to know what to do— he never even got his right hand out of his overcoat pocket. Christiansen gave him a push on the shoulder, just enough to turn him a little so they faced each other straighter, then he caught him with a good, solid jab to the floating ribs. This was a big boy, so he gave it everything he had.

It seemed to be enough. The wind shot out of him in a rush and almost at once he blushed bright pink, all the way up to the hairline. He wouldn't be shouting for help any time soon—and he wasn't going to live any longer than that. Christiansen hit him again, just for insurance, and then, while the man sank quietly to his knees, reached into his coat pocket and took out the coiled length of catgut that was his constant companion.

As soon as he had made a noose he slipped it over the man's head and pulled it tight. They tear at the air and they fight—you have to give them "A" for effort—but there's nothing they can do. There was a faint gurgling sound, cut off sharp, and the man's legs kicked out wildly as Christiansen dragged him down the hall toward a storage closet that someone had left with the door ajar.

Good. Let the son of a bitch enjoy himself.

It was a distance of no more than eighteen or twenty feet, but Hagemann's boy had already stopped struggling by the time they got there. He might even have been dead already, but in any case it wouldn't be long. Christiansen made a second loop, tied it, took out his pocketknife to cut away the slack—he was running short and might need the rest of it for later—and hung the fellow up from a coat hook. The next person to come in here for a couple of rolls of toilet paper was going to be in for a nasty surprise.

The pistol was a Luger sure enough. Christiansen left it right where it was, in the inevitable shoulder holster under the man's left armpit. The fewer complications the better.

The hallway down to Esther's room seemed to go on forever. Christiansen walked as quietly as he could, listening for the slightest sound. It was the middle of the afternoon— who would be in his room at this hour?

But someone must have been listening for him as well—or, perhaps, just listening—because quite suddenly, as if it had been planned as a surprise, the door to Esther's room staggered open. No one came out. Christiansen took the pistol from his waistline and waited.

"Rudi, is that you?"

So much for the element of surprise. Christiansen decided there was nothing to be gained from playing it coy—after all, the man was in there waiting for trouble and there was no point in panicking him into anything drastic.

"No, Colonel, it isn't Rudi. Rudi isn't coming."

There was silence. Christiansen didn't move—he simply took his pistol in both hands and pointed it toward the open door—and apparently Hagemann didn't move either. It was a stalemate.

"It's you, isn't it, Mr. Christiansen."

"Yes, it's me."

"Yes, of course, it would be. I thought you would still be off with your Jewish friends."

In the pause that followed, Christiansen could hear what sounded like a struggle, with the advantage all on one side, of course. There was movement—the noise clothing makes as it brushes against furniture— and, at intervals, a few tiny female gasps. At least he hadn't killed her.

"Tell me, Mr. Christiansen, did you get Leivick out?"

They were talking now not to be polite, but to keep track of each other's position. It was a kind of unspoken truce that would last until Hagemann decided it was time for him to come through that door.

"Yes, we got him out."

"You did? Mr. Christiansen, you never cease to astonish me. It will serve to remind me that I'm dealing with one of my own kind now. I'll have to be more careful—the Jews don't have your sort of enterprise."

That was the moment he chose to step out into the corridor. Christiansen was ready to drop him at the first little flurry of movement, and then he saw that what he would be shooting at wasn't Hagemann, but Esther. He had his arm around her, just at the rib cage so he could hold her arms down, and the muzzle of his Luger was pressing against her neck.

"As you see, it's a difficult position." Hagemann grinned at him over the girl's shoulder. Yes, Mordecai had been right—the man was insane. "If you shoot, I'll shoot. Even if your bullet kills me instantly, my finger will still contact on the trigger, a reflex action of my dying nervous system, and Miss Rosensaft's brains will be scattered all over the corridor wall. Of course, I'm assuming you do care something about the state of Miss Rosensaft's brains, but perhaps the evidence of your presence in her room last night is nothing from which to draw hope. Perhaps a man like you takes a more dispassionate view of our little melodrama, and the sight of her head split open and gushing blood wouldn't disturb you so very much after all."

He was smiling. He actually found the idea amusing.

Christiansen lined up on a spot just a quarter of an inch or so below the inside corner of Hagemann's right eye. He didn't look at his gun—he didn't have to—and the last thing he wanted to look at was the expression on Esther's face. He concentrated on Hagemann. All Hagemann had to do was to move the muzzle of his pistol so much as two inches and he would be a dead man. He would never feel a thing or even hear the sound of the shot that killed him. He would simply die.

"Take it easy," Christiansen murmured. "Just relax, Esther, don't try to fight him. Don't struggle at all. Just be a limp weight."

He didn't want to look into her eyes. He didn't want to see them huge with fear. He could just imagine . . .

Her feet weren't even touching the floor—Hagemann was carrying her under his arm like a child's doll, but then she didn't weigh very much.

"I'm going to the stairwell, Mr. Christiansen." The smile on Hagemann's face had taken on a fixed quality. He wasn't fooling anybody—he was just as scared as everybody else. "You are going to back away to let me pass."

"And suppose I just stay right where I am."

"Then I shall know there is no way out for me and I shall kill Miss Rosensaft here and now. Why not? Why shouldn't I? Are you going to start backing up, Mr. Christiansen, or do we end it this second?"

Christiansen took a tentative step backward. It didn't commit him to anything, but it bought a little bargaining time.

"So what if you make it to the stairwell? You've got two flights to go down, and then there's the lobby. And you'll be all alone. Would you like to see Rudi before you go? I've got him hanging around in that broom closet just down the hall. He makes a picturesque sight. Perhaps you'd like to say goodbye."

The light changed in Hagemann's eyes—whether it was fear or anger was impossible to know. But something had reached him. He took a step forward, pressing the muzzle of his gun deeper against the side of Esther's throat. She gave a little gasp of pain.

"You shouldn't have killed Rudi like that, Mr. Christiansen. Did you strangle him with your little cord? He was a soldier—he had a right to be shot."

"He was a butcher, just like you."

The two men were no more than fifteen feet apart, so there was no room for error. Christíansen took another step backward, and then another.

"I'll get you," he said quietly. "Somewhere between here and the street, I'll nail you. Kill the girl and I'll see to it that you take hours and hours to die. I'll gut-shoot you, Hagemann, and let you roll around on the floor, praying that you'll bleed to death quickly. You'll have plenty of time to remember how you murdered my parents at Kirstenstad. But either way, easy or hard, you'll never make it out of this hotel."

"Won't I? Won't I really?"

And then, of course, Christiansen understood. The stairway—yes, the windowless stairway. Once Hagemann was inside, and had let the door swing closed behind him, he could make it a condition of trade that if the door opened again, if Christiansen tried to follow him there, Esther would be shot at once.

"I didn't come here with just Rudi, you know." Hagemann shook his head slowly, and as he did so the gun muzzle wobbled against Esther's throat in a way appalling to see. "My driver is downstairs now. He has his orders, to come inside the moment he sees Rudi start upstairs and to wait in the lobby. Don't come along with me to the stairwell, Mr. Christiansen. You would make me very nervous in that enclosed space, and no one could tell what foolish thing I might do."

Like partners at a dance, they moved down the corridor, one careful step at a time. It seemed to take hours, and then, suddenly, they were almost beside the stairwell door.

"You might open it for me, Mr. Christiansen."

"No, Inar—don't!"

It was Esther, in a voice that sounded like a scream of pain. He had to look at her now, and her face was ravaged. The suffering of years had been etched into her in those few minutes. There were tear stains on her cheeks, unheeded and left to dry. Her eyes pleaded with him.

"Don't let him take me with him, Inar. Don't do that to me, not if you care at all. Kill him!"

She tried to tear herself free, knowing that if she succeeded it would mean nothing except her own death. She fought against this man she hated and feared so desperately, but he was too strong. Hagemann simply clamped her more tightly under his arm until it seemed she would not be able to breathe.

"Go ahead, Mr. Christiansen. Now is the time, if you want to."

"Please, Inar! Don't let him have me alive."

It was a done thing. In his mind's eye he could already see it happening—the way Hagemann's head would snap back when the bullet hit him, his arms and legs flailing out, the fine spray of blood as his skull split in two . . . The man was already dead, dead meat bleeding into the carpet. All it would take was that one little squeeze on the trigger. Except that he couldn't bring himself . . .

Except that it would all happen to Esther too. She would die in the same instant—Hagemann wasn't kidding about that. That was what Christiansen saw in his mind, the split second when she too would be turned into garbage. And he just couldn't. Hagemann had won.

With his left hand he reached across his body to touch the wall, feeling his way until his fingers brushed against the door handle.

"My God, Inar—please!"

"He doesn't have any choice, my dear. It would seem that once more you have worked your magic. You've made Mr. Christiansen love you even more than he does his revenge."

The sound of Hagemann's laughter filled the corridor. It was all a great mad joke, you see. He had been right all along.

As Christiansen moved backward he carried the door with him until finally it was all the way open. The arm at the top locked into place—the entrance to the stairs yawned open. He stepped away. He would give Hagemann all the room he wanted. There wasn't any choice.

Hagemann stepped over the threshold, still carrying Esther in front of him like a shield.

"Close it behind us like a good fellow," he said. "And don't follow us. Don't do anything except wait up here and stay out of trouble. I don't have to explain what will happen if you decide on something desperate."

The look in Esther's eyes pleaded with him. There were many things worse than death, and this surely was one of them.

It was still possible. Christiansen willed himself to fire, but he couldn't. The nerves in his arm simply wouldn't obey. Hagemann was grinning at him—he knew what was in his mind. He was daring him to do it.

With painful, sluggish deliberation the door swung closed.

The muzzle of Christiansen's pistol sank slowly down—he couldn't seem to hold it up anymore. There was a pressure in his chest and neck, a feeling that something inside him would burst any second. He could feel his heart pounding in his ears and he wanted to weep with simple rage.

Do something, you stupid bastard, he thought to himself. *Do something before you die of indecision.*

And then he remembered Hirsch.

A telephone, God damn it. All he needed in the whole stinking world was to pick up a goddamned telephone and call the goddamned desk. Hagemann wasn't going to walk through the whole fucking lobby with that filthy Luger screwed into Esther's ear. Hirsch could still burn him down before he got to the front door.

He ran back to Esther's empty room. Maybe it would have been quicker just to kick in the first door he came to, but that never even crossed his mind. All he could think about was the phone in Esther's room.

He picked up the receiver and for perhaps as long as three seconds couldn't understand why he didn't hear it buzzing. Then he glanced down and saw the tape over the cradle.

The clever bastard. The god damned, fucking clever bastard.

He took the knife from his pocket, glad he still had sufficient presence of mind not to start just clawing at the stuff with his fingernails, and within a few seconds he had the cradle loose. How much time was that wasted? Where the hell was Hagemann now?

"Yeah?"

It was Hirsch—he had picked up the phone in the middle of the second ring. He sounded almost as if he had guessed how much had gone wrong.

"Hagemann's coming down the stairs—yes, right now! He's got Esther with him, so have a care. He'll kill her in a second if you give him that long. And he's got another man down there waiting for him. His driver."

"Anything else? What are you doing upstairs then? Jesus, Christiansen, what is—?"

"Just stop him, dammit."

Christiansen hung up—he couldn't stand it. He just couldn't stand it another second. What *was* he doing up here? He didn't have the remotest idea.

He had to get downstairs.

The fire escapes—the fucking fire escapes. He would have to use the back one, or Hagemann would see him coming and leave Esther on the curb with her brains blown out.

This time he did break down doors. He got a running start on the one directly opposite Esther's and went through it as if it had been made out of paper. There was a middle-aged woman asleep on the bed, fully dressed with just a blanket over her legs. The scream she let out when she started awake and saw Christiansen striding through her room, glaring at her as if he would have liked to break her neck, could have been heard in Saragossa.

"Shut up, you old bitch!" he cried savagely. He hated the damn woman and didn't even know why.

He threw open the window, crawled outside to the fire escape landing, and began clambering down the metal stairs that swayed under his weight and his urgency. When he reached the second landing he lost patience and jumped over the rail, hitting the cobbled alleyway with a jolt that nearly sent him sprawling. He could already hear the sounds of pistol shots.

Oh God, he thought—the idea ached in his brain like a wound—*oh God, if he's killed her . . .*

As he reached the mouth of the alleyway, where it opened up behind the hotel, he could see a huge gray Mercedes as it drew away down the main street.

He was too late. He was already too late.

In the lobby of the hotel, just inside the main entrance, lay the body of a man who had been shot through the heart by someone who knew what he was doing. He had just died, from one instant to the next, with no trouble to anyone. He was curled up like a baby, sleeping the sleep of innocence on the polished wooden floor. He was nobody Christiansen had ever seen before, but it didn't take a degree in logic to figure out how he had got there.

Otherwise, the place was nearly empty. In Spain, people had enough sense not to hang around when the fireworks started.

Except, of course, for Hirsch.

He was on his knees beside the main desk. His gun was on the floor in front of him, and he was bent over at the waist trying to keep from toppling onto his face. He was holding his left arm just above the elbow. There was a lot of blood leaking out between his fingers. When he saw Christiansen, he looked up and grinned.

"Sorry, pal. Close but no cigar."

"Did he take Esther with him? Is she still alive?"

"Yeah. I got the driver, but then I ran out of luck. I don't know why Hagemann didn't finish me off, except maybe he didn't feel he had the time."

"How bad are you?"

Hirsch laughed softly. All right, it had been a stupid question.

"I'll have some trouble with my golf for a while,

but I'll mend. Not soon enough to go up that cliff with you, but I'll mend. You'd better get out of here."

He had a point. Christiansen had been pushing his luck with the police all day.

"He diddled us, pal." The expression on Hirsch's face was pained, and not only from the hole in his arm. "You think maybe that's why he grabbed Mordecai, to decoy us away from here so he could take the girl? He suckered us good."

What was there to say? Christiansen didn't pretend to know how the man's mind worked, but it was possible—more than possible. Hagemann was a clever, devious bastard.

"I'll call here tonight—seven o'clock. Try to be stitched up and finished answering official questions by then."

"Don't worry about me—is it my fault if unknown persons start firing guns in my hotel? Hey, Christiansen . . ."

"What?"

"You really are a son of a bitch."

"Take care of yourself."

Already, even as he walked down the sidewalk away from the hotel, Christiansen could hear the high-pitched tinkle of the police siren—so perhaps he hadn't killed them all after all. He ducked under the shade of a shop awning and waited for the car to pass by.

There was nothing to do now—nothing to do until it had grown dark.

✠ 22 ✠

It was a large room. The bed stood in the center of a thick white rug, almost like the skin of an animal. Otherwise the floor was covered with small square tiles the color of brick and polished so they seemed to glow. They were like ice. Esther took off her shoes so she could feel the cold. It reminded her that she was still alive.

Hagemann had left her completely alone. He was so sure of himself that he hadn't even bothered to lock the door.

Why shouldn't he be? Where was there to go? This house was a prison, with armed guards patrolling the grounds. She wasn't even sure where it was. She might as well have been back at Waldenburg.

She sat down on the cold tile floor, wrapped her arms about her knees, and let her despair overcome her. She could feel the tears running down her face, but otherwise she had no sensation of crying. She felt dead. She would never get away from Hagemann. He would keep hold of her until he grew bored, and then he would kill her. There was nothing to look forward to except death. She would never see Inar again. She might as well be dead. She almost was.

Why hadn't Inar saved her from this? Why hadn't he killed Hagemann when he had had the chance? Why hadn't he taken his revenge and let her die where she could still see his face?

"You won't mind it so much, my dear," Hagemann had said. "After all, we've grown accustomed to each other."

He had thrust her in through the driver's door of his car and, with his hand still clamped around her wrist, had driven them away from the hotel. One of his men had been waiting for them in the lobby, and when Hirsch killed him Hagemann had stepped over his dead body almost as if it hadn't been there. He had shot Hirsch—had he killed him? Esther didn't know.

He had driven fast, all the way back here. She should have had the courage to open the door and throw herself out. She shouldn't have been so very afraid of a little pain.

Because now she would never get away.

"You will have to tell me everything you know, Esther. You must tell me the truth if I am to keep you alive and unhurt. I have to know where von Goltz hid the formula, and you are the key. I shall get the truth out of you one way or the other."

"I don't know anything. The General never told me anything. I tell you I don't know about any formula!"

And he had merely smiled. He was looking forward to hurting her. He knew all about how to hurt her.

And then he had left her in this cold room.

At Chelmno, sometimes, when someone in the women's barracks had had enough, she would find a way to kill herself. She would make a run for the fence and the guards would shoot her or she would die on the electrified wires. It had happened almost regularly. Once the girl who had slept next to Esther had stuffed strips of her dress down her throat until she had strangled. They had found her in the morning, cold and stiff. She hadn't uttered so much as a sound.

The means of death were everywhere. She couldn't stuff pieces of cloth down her throat—she hadn't the courage for that; a person had to be half mad with despair to do a thing like that—but she could find something.

All she had to do was to get up and look for it.

Was she such a coward that she couldn't even get off the floor to find the means of saving herself? No, she was not such a coward as that.

It was a bare room. There was a fireplace, blackened and cold, as if it hadn't been used in years. There was the bed. She opened a closet and discovered that it was empty. Nothing else. Why was the bed there? Surely no one could have slept in this room. She looked out one of the windows and saw that she was on the second story. Hagemann must have brought her up a flight of stairs. Why couldn't she remember that?

There was nothing. She couldn't help feeling a certain shamefaced sense of relief, as if she had been reprieved at the last second. And then she remembered the glass in the windows.

Suddenly there was no air in her lungs. Her hands were sweating, and the pounding of her heart seemed to course through her whole body like a throb of pain. She didn't want to die. She was a coward, but she didn't care—it was too much to think of. She didn't want to lie there in a sticky little pool of her own blood, her eyes still open, staring out at nothing, feeling nothing, something to be cleaned away and buried in a hole. To be nothing—it was awful.

Still, she would do it. The windows were barred on the outside, but that wouldn't prevent her from escaping. She would put her fist through one of the panes—what did she care if she cut herself; wasn't that precisely the point?—and she would pull loose a piece with a sharp enough edge . . . She had heard once that you should cut vertically along the wrist if you meant it—one deep slash and it would all be over.

It shouldn't be painful. After the first shock, why should there be any pain? It couldn't take very long to bleed to death. In an hour, or two, they would find her . . .

She walked over to the window and looked outside again. A man with a rifle over his shoulder was passing by on the lawn outside. He would be the last human being she ever saw. She doubled up her fist, wondering how hard she would have to hit the glass before it would break.

No—this wasn't the way. She would never have the nerve to do a thing like that twice. Better to save every last little scrap of courage until she really needed it. There were some old fireplace implements lying around the empty grate; she went back and got an ash shovel. She would use the knobby handle—it would do very well.

As soon as she struck it against the pane, and the

glass splintered, an alarm bell went off, so loud and so suddenly that she almost screamed.

There was no time now. Pulling with her fingers, feverish to have it done with before anyone could come to stop her, she worked a thin, slightly curved piece loose from the window frame. It looked as if it had been waiting just for this moment.

She got down on her knees—somehow it was too much to do the thing standing up—bunched the skirt of her dress up around her waist, and used the hem to wrap one end of the long sliver of glass. She pressed her left forearm down on her thigh so that the back of her hand was against the knee and raised the glass to strike. One deep cut—she was ready. She . . .

At first it was only the shock—no pain, no sound, nothing more definite than the sense of having been violently transformed. Was this what it was like to begin dying?

No. She glanced down at her arm, and there was no blood. Something else had happened. She didn't know what it was.

And then she felt it. First the pain—in her head, a sense of being crushed, a throb of suffering—and then the white flash of light that made everything seem sharp and hard, and then the weakness. Her hand let go of the sliver of glass. She didn't have any choice about it; the hand simply opened and the glass fell into her lap. And then she felt herself falling forward. The floor was coming up at her. It would strike her in the face, and she found herself hoping that it wouldn't hurt too much.

It didn't. It never happened. The floor simply dissolved, turning first red and then black and then disappearing into oblivion.

When she woke up she didn't know where she was. Her face hurt—that was the one certainty. With her eyes still closed she tried to turn her head, but the pain was so bad it made her feel as if she would have to vomit. She lay still for a moment and the sensation passed away.

And then she opened her eyes and saw Hagemann. He was sitting beside her. She was lying on the bed in the room with the tiled floor, and now she remembered everything.

The feeling of shame was even worse than the aching in her head. *You stupid, cowardly, worthless little slut,* she thought to herself, *you couldn't even succeed in cutting open your veins.*

Hagemann was watching her in an odd, speculative way. It was almost as if he had only just discovered her existence. She didn't like it—it filled her with unfocused dread. She had thought she would always know what to expect from him, but she had never seen that expression on his face before.

"You set off the alarm," he said, and then his lips shaped themselves into a thin smile. "All the windows in this house have been wired. The guard thought you were trying to escape—that was why he hit you."

"He hit me?"

"Yes, with the butt of his rifle. I expect it hurts."

Yes, of course it hurt, but she didn't care to say so. She turned her face away from him and discovered, after she had done it, that she could move her head without feeling sick. So she would recover after all.

"But you weren't trying to escape, were you—at least, not in the sense my guard imagined. I would have thought you were the last . . ."

There was something in his voice, something almost like uncertainty, as if suddenly he found himself no longer quite the master. Yes, she would look at him now. Yes, it was there—whatever it was.

"Would you really have killed yourself, Esther?"

"I don't know." It was the truth. Now, having spoken it, she would never know.

"It wouldn't have worked. It takes a long time to bleed to death through a slashed vein. Hours, in fact. You were wasting your effort."

But even if he was right, it didn't matter. Anyone could have seen that in his face. Somehow, she had won something from him.

"Esther," he said, reaching out and, with the tips of his fingers, delicately brushing a strand of hair out of her face, "Esther, it won't be like Waldenburg this time. I've changed—everything has changed. You needn't be frightened. You won't try to harm yourself again, will you?"

"I don't know. Yes, if I can find the courage."

"Then you've changed as well. It used to be that nothing was more important to you than staying alive, but not anymore, it would seem."

"I guess not."

"Then we must make very certain that you never have another opportunity," he said, the thin artificial smile disappearing. "I cannot allow you to throw yourself away, Esther. There is much more involved here than merely your one wretched little life, precious as that is to me. I shall have to take steps to see that you behave yourself."

"What is it that you want from me, Colonel? What is it?"

"My dear, do you really mean to tell me that you don't know?"

Suddenly she was tired beyond bearing. She wanted nothing more than to be left alone—to die if that was possible, but if not, merely to sleep. Hagemann's voice was just a buzzing in her ears, something that kept her awake. What was it all about? No one had told her. She had never wanted to know. She didn't want to know now.

"Shall I tell you then?"

"No. Don't."

"Yes, I rather think I ought to tell you." He smiled again. He was the old Hagemann once more, and nothing had changed since Waldenburg. "I shall need you now. Perhaps you have the answer without knowing it. At any rate, I don't suppose you'll be of any use at all if you don't understand at least in a general way what I want you to tell me."

He reached into his jacket pocket and pulled something out, holding it up between first finger and thumb for her to look at. It was a little circle of thin gold chain, a loop hardly big enough to go round his thumb. And from the chain dangled a key.

"There's a box, Esther. A safe-deposit box in a bank somewhere. This is one key, and you're the other. Von Goltz had this sent to me after he was arrested, along with a cryptic little note about you. You see, he knew they were going to hang him. He didn't care anymore how the world would go on without him—he wasn't choosing sides. He didn't care about anything except his little joke."

He put the key back into his pocket. He was so sure of himself. He was so convinced he had won.

"Do you see my situation now?" he asked, shrugging his shoulders, as if he couldn't understand how such a thing could happen to a man like himself. "I had only the one key before, but now I have both. I don't know the name of the bank—I don't even know where it is. But you do. Somehow, in some way I'll come to understand, von Goltz made you the vehicle of that information. And you're going to give it to me."

He seemed for a moment to be looking at nothing, and then Esther realized that he was looking at her arm, her right arm, where the scar was still fresh from when the doctor in Vienna had removed her tattoo. He took her by the hand, as if for a closer inspection, and then let it drop back down to her side.

"What is that, another suicide attempt?"

"No—they rescued me from a Russian prison in Vienna. I was wounded."

It was only at that moment that she realized why Herr Leivick had insisted that the number be removed. Yes, of course. It was the second key.

She could feel her heart pounding. Could Hagemann see anything in her face? Did he know now? Oh, God . . .

It seemed not. His eyes darkened for an instant, but not with recognition.

"Good. I should hate to think . . . Well, it doesn't matter. Your life will be quite safe with me, Esther. You see, in addition to everything else, the safe-deposit box, wherever it is, is in your name. You shall have to be the one to open it for me."

"What's in it?"

"You wouldn't want to know."

He smiled again, the old smile that said it was something more terrible than she could imagine.

"Then you will never have it. You will never persuade me to open that box for you—never, no matter what you do."

"Never, my dear? Oh, I think so."

He had left her alone again. He had even given her something to help her headache.

"It's very good," he said, picking up a half-full bottle of brandy from where it had been resting on the floor beside the bed, "very old and smooth as cream, and there's nothing in it except brandy, so you needn't worry. A little will settle your stomach and ease your head. More will help you to see your situation with greater clarity. You need to relax, Esther. Don't be afraid of anything. We'll talk again later."

He laid the bottle on its side, cradled between her arm and her body, and got up to go.

After a while she sat up and, when she remembered it was there, picked up the bottle, read the label, and pulled the cork. She had hardly tasted the stuff in three years, not since Waldenburg.

The General had been a brandy drinker. Perhaps Hagemann had acquired the taste from him, or perhaps it was simply that more men drank brandy than Esther had realized. Did Inar? She hoped not. No—it was unimaginable.

She raised the bottle to her lips and tipped it up, swallowing as fast as she could so that the liquor ran down her throat like water. It burned, and when she stopped she had to cough several times. She hated it, but that didn't matter. Hagemann was right—she needed something to bring her back to herself. If Hagemann wouldn't allow her to die, then she would stay more than just alive. She couldn't run on nothing but nervous energy forever.

So she would drink brandy, and stay calm, and think.

She took two more short swallows and set the bottle down on the floor beside the bed. It was hardly any time at all before her headache had almost disappeared. She could still feel the lump on her scalp where the rifle butt had hit her—it felt as if someone had burned it with a hot iron—but that was nothing. It didn't prevent her mind from functioning.

How could she keep from telling Hagemann about the tattoo? Eventually she would have to tell him something—with a man like that, one was better off not having any illusions. She could tell him anything except about the tattoo. She had to keep that buried within her, so deep that she would forget about it herself.

But she would have to tell him something.

And he would have to be allowed to extract it from her by torture. It was the way his mind worked—if he didn't have to take it, he wouldn't believe it. She would have to think of something, something she could give him when in the last moment her strength failed her. Perhaps it would even be necessary to think of two lies. Perhaps he wouldn't believe the first, thinking that he hadn't yet reduced her to the point where she would abandon such little stratagems, where all she would want was for the pain to stop. Yes, she would need two stories. Anything—it didn't matter what they were—so long as she forgot about the tattoo.

Why hadn't she guessed before? That night in Vienna, when Inar had looked at her arm so strangely and had sent her off in tears to find Herr Leivick, why hadn't she seen it then? Because she had been too busy being in love with Inar, that was why.

And that was why she had tried to kill herself, and why she would tell Hagemann lies as he burned away her fingertips. At Waldenburg she had belonged to herself, so her only purpose had been to survive— she had had a right to do anything she had to if it would keep her alive. But it was different now. Now she belonged to Inar.

It was better this way. When life was its own purpose it became simply a burden, a thing heavy with accumulated shame. This way she could hate death without believing that it was the worst.

She lay down again, feeling strangely tranquil. Perhaps it was merely the effect of the brandy, but for the first time in as long as she could remember, fear had become something that didn't fill her up, like the air in her lungs. She could be afraid. It was all right to be afraid. It didn't matter. She could turn her mind to something else. She would find the lies to tell Hagemann.

✠ 23 ✠

"We'll need to do something about him before we get on with the rest of it. If we let him stay there, he's bound to hear us."

"Can we be so sure it's even Hagemann's?"

"Of course it's Hagemann's," Faglin snapped impatiently. "God damn it, Itzikel, who else around here is going to put an armed man to looking after his boat?"

Christiansen merely shrugged. "I don't think we can ignore him."

"It's just as well. Who likes leaving Hagemann with an escape hatch? While you settle things with the guard, I can wire the boat."

Faglin grinned. That was very much his line of country.

They were perhaps three hundred yards off shore, in Christiansen's rented sailboat—whispering because sound carries well over water, and because the guard who stood with his back to them at the foot of Hagemann's private wharf, bathed in the half-light that filtered down from the compound above, was paid to listen.

"We'll have to land farther up." Christiansen raised his arm and pointed out at the invisible shoreline. "Just you and me. Itzhak can bring the boat back down to provide a little distraction."

"How about it, Itzikel? You think you can sail her a quarter of a mile without piling up on the rocks?"

Itzhak didn't seem to think he was being the least funny, so Faglin patted him on the arm.

"It's okay, kid—just a little joke to break the tension."

"You don't have to worry yourselves about me."

"Fine. Then we won't."

Christiansen smiled at him in the darkness. There was only the palest sliver of a moon, which was fine except that they could hardly see each other. He was being as nice as he could to Itzhak. The kid seemed to think he was planning to murder him over that business with Esther—it seemed to be the translation of every look and word and gesture that passed between them, as if that was all they had to think about—and tonight of all nights they needed their minds clear. So Christiansen was being as nice as he knew how. If they both got out of this alive, which seemed a remote enough possibility, all was forgiven.

Hagemann's dock was just about the worst place imaginable for trying to jump someone. The beach, if you could call it that, was nothing but a narrow apron of loose rock—no sand, nothing to cover the sound of footsteps. The only possible approach was directly under the cliff face, where enough loose dirt had fallen down to provide a little path a man could walk on without raising the alarm as surely as if he had brought along a full symphony orchestra just to keep from feeling lonely. When Christiansen had seen it yesterday in daylight, he had nearly decided that Hirsch was right and the place was impregnable. Nearly.

There was a fair breeze this night, coming straight down the shore, which was both good and bad. Even Itzhak, who had learned everything he knew about sailing in the last hour and a half, wouldn't have any trouble steering for Hagemann's dock once Christiansen and Faglin had been landed farther up. But the wind also carried sound, so the kid was going to have to put on one hell of a show if that guard wasn't going to hear them coming.

Christiansen raised his sail—a dark red one, since he didn't particularly care to have it pick up the reflection of anyone's searchlights—and headed the little boat's nose as close into the wind as he could. She bucked a trace, but before long they were a good three hundred yards up the coast.

When he and Faglin jumped into the water it was only chest deep, which was cutting it a bit fine for the keel.

"Take her out a bit," he said to Itzhak, who was peering over the side at them, precisely as if they were a couple of mermaids. "Come in on him from the sea, and try not to be too subtle about it."

By the time the water had dropped to their waists they could no longer see the boat at all. When they came up on shore they might as well have been alone in the world.

"Good God, I'm cold," Faglin muttered. And he was too. His teeth were chattering. Anyone would have been cold.

"Count your blessings, and hope you live long enough to die of pneumonia."

"Very funny. Doesn't it bother you at all?"

"Yes, but I'm used to it. You fought your war in the desert, I fought mine in northern Europe. We used to say, if water doesn't have ice floating in it that means it's warm enough to make tea. Now, not another word until we've seen to the guard."

As they stood by the shoreline they could hear the waves dragging the shingle back and forth. It was a melancholy sound, suggestive of life's final futility. Clackity, clackity, clickity, clack, on and on, like a death rattle.

When they reached the cliff face and were a little sheltered from the wind, they took off their trousers and sweaters, wrung them out as best they could, and put them back on. There was nothing they could do about their shoes except empty them.

They crept along, trying not to stumble—they could hardly see each other, let alone the path in front of them. There was absolutely no light until they were almost level with the dock. When they could see that, they crouched down and waited for Itzhak and the boat.

It was only a floating pier, running twenty feet or so out from the shore and anchored to a couple of massive posts. Hagemann's motorboat was just visible at the end, a ghostly white shape bobbing slightly in rhythm with the waves from the almost tideless Mediterranean. She was sleek and luxurious-looking, the kind of boat that had never been intended for anything except the amusement of people with too much money. It would have been interesting to know how Hagemann got the Syrians to pay for her.

The guard was nothing but a shape huddled against one of the posts. He was smoking a cigarette—they could just make out the plumes of smoke—and he was huddled up after the fashion of soldiers who have grown weary and bored with sentry duty. He wasn't looking at anything. His thoughts were somewhere else.

It was perhaps a quarter of an hour before they had any sign of Itzhak, and they heard him before they saw anything.

He was singing, the little bastard: "Sixteen men on a dead man's che-est, yo ho ho and a bottle of rum." And then the sound of slurred laughter drifted across the churning water.

"Hi there! Anybody home? I can't get my fuckin' motor started again."

The guard reacted quicker than one would have expected. He brought the rifle down from his shoulder and glanced around, as if he couldn't make up his mind where all the noise was coming from. He must have had a flashlight in his pocket, because very quickly there was a thin beam of light playing over the sand. If he pointed it toward the cliffs they were all finished.

"Come on, pal. Give us a han', will ya?"

That settled everything. Now he knew where it was. The flashlight caught the side of Christiansen's boat in its beam and ran down the mast until it encountered Itzhak's smiling, innocent face. The guard raised his rifle.

The kid had maneuvered in to the side of the dock, close enough that he could almost have reached out and touched the hull of Hagemann's gigantic pleasure craft. He was sitting on the stern, not even trying to steer, not more than fifteen feet from where the guard was peering at him over the sights of his rifle. It was a bad moment.

And then Itzhak raised the thermos bottle he had been holding between his knees, which turned it into something of a standoff.

"Be a sport, pal. I been flounderin' aroun' all night, God damn it. Give us a han', an' we'll have a li'l drinkie, jus' you an' me."

If he was scared—and who the hell wouldn't have been scared?—he didn't look it. What he looked like was just another damn fool of a tourist, out on a little toot that had gone ever so slightly wrong. He was a good boy. He was doing great.

And the guard seemed to be buying it, at least to the degree that he wasn't going to shoot anybody out of hand. He lowered his rifle just a little and took a few tentative steps toward the dock. He wasn't quite fool enough to go out onto that spit of creaking, heaving wood, not just yet, not until he was a shade clearer about what was going on. But, for the moment, at least, he wasn't going to kill anybody either.

And maybe, just maybe, the supposed contents of that thermos were not without interest. There wasn't anything in it except coffee, but he didn't know that.

"Come on, be a sport—you know anythin' 'bout engines?"

The guard was watching Itzhak now. He was all attention, and his back was to the cliffs. Christiansen didn't wait any longer. Keeping a hand on Faglin's shoulder, he stood up. He didn't want any help—this sort of thing was supposed to be his specialty.

It was distance of perhaps sixty feet—not very far, except that the rocky shore crunched like a cement mixer with every step he took. There were no covering noises except the clicking of the stones as the waves drew them back and forth and the sound of Itzhak's voice. It was to be hoped he wouldn't run out of things to say.

Christiansen paced himself. Every time the waves rushed up the shoreline he stood still, waiting. When they receded he would risk a few carefully placed steps. He had to be so cautious—all that loose rock could sound like an avalanche, and there was always the risk of tripping in the darkness. Out the water would go. One, two, three, four paces closer. Then wait. Fifty feet, then forty, then thirty . . .

"How 'bout I throw you a line—you tie me up? You got a phone around here I could use? Come ON, sport. Be a sport."

It was an open question whether Hagemann's guard understood one word of this singular monologue. He hadn't spoken. He was merely watching, waiting, listening . . .

Christiansen was only about twenty-five feet behind him now—standing there, waiting for the waves to fall back. He could rush the guard now. Even if he were discovered, he would have at least a fifty-fifty chance of reaching him before he could take aim.

It wasn't good enough. If the guard fired the rifle at all, the game was up and they were all dead.

He reached into his pocket and took out his coil of catgut. It was the only way.

The guard was getting restless. In a second or two he would make up his mind about what to do. If he shot Itzhak, they were finished. If he stepped onto the pier, Christiansen would never reach him.

The waves slid back down, and the sound of the

clicking stones returned. A few more paces. Now just fifteen feet.

"Look, pal, I'm tired of waitin'." Itzhak climbed down from the prow of his boat, stumbling as his feet landed on the pier. It gave the guard something new to think about. It was perfect timing.

Ten feet, now seven, now five . . .

Itzhak started down the pier toward them. At the last possible moment he caught Christiansen's eye. Did the guard notice?

But it was too late for him. Christiansen dropped the noose over his head and pulled tight.

In the first second the guard went rigid. They all did that. The only thing he could think about was that cord around his neck, cutting into his flesh, choking him as it closed around his windpipe. His hands flew up to his throat—it was a reflex; he couldn't have helped himself. Itzhak rushed forward to take the rifle from him before he remembered to fire it.

Christiansen just hung on. There was nothing else to do. The man was clawing at the cord, fighting, trying at least to turn around, but Christiansen yanked him down to the ground, put a foot on his shoulder, and kept pulling. The guard's head was turned away—there was always that saving mercy; at least you didn't have to watch their eyes while they died—but he could still see it, the whole death agony. It was mirrored in Itzhak's face.

Finally it was over. It was always surprising, and just a little sickening, to realize how long it took a man to strangle. The body had been limp for a long while, and then some subtle change took place, that strange thing that marked the difference between mere uncon-

sciousness and death. Christiansen, when he was sure,
allowed himself to let go. As he loosened the cord, the
last breath the man had ever taken rushed from his
lungs in a drawn-out, mechanical wheeze, and Itzhak,
wheeling around, supported himself against the closer
of the two posts and retched loudly. Christiansen didn't
blame him a bit.

"What should we do with the body?"

It was Faglin, who had probably seen worse things.
He was standing beside Christiansen, his eyes darting
between the guard's corpse and Itzhak, who was still
busy being sick.

"Drop him in the drink and let the current carry
him off. If somebody looks down and sees he isn't
there, maybe they'll just think he's off somewhere
taking a leak. Better that than somebody stumbles over
a stiff."

"Right. You take care of that. I'll see to my own
business."

He stepped up on the pier and climbed aboard the
sailboat to pick up the knapsack he had brought with
him from his hotel room. Then he disappeared up a
short steel gangway and into Hagemann's boat.

"I'm sorry. I didn't mean to . . . It's just, I've never
seen anybody die like that before."

Itzhak was sitting at the foot of the pier, wiping his
mouth, trying hard not to look at the dead body that
was curled up almost at his feet.

"Don't worry about it. You played that scene very
well, by the way."

Christiansen had been through it all himself. He
knew what the kid was feeling, that mixture of gratitude and appalled consciousness that, yes, he had
helped to kill a man. Like a lot of other kids, not that

many years ago, who had suddenly found themselves in uniform to fight the great war, Itzhak was fast coming of age in a world where manhood was indistinguishable from the taste of blood, and he was entitled not to be too crazy about it.

When Faglin came back out onto the dock, he was still carrying the knapsack. He looked very pleased with himself.

"She must be carrying a hundred gallons of petrol," he said. "I rigged a small charge directly under the fuel tank and wired it to the starter. She'll go up like a Roman candle the first time anybody tries to take her anywhere."

"Is there enough left over for your other job?"

"Plenty." Faglin hefted the knapsack to show how heavy it still was and then dropped it into the stern of the sailboat. It gave Christiansen the fantods to watch how carelessly the man handled enough plastic explosive to send them all to glory, but one had to assume that he knew what he was doing.

"Then let's get out of here—the night won't last forever."

Christiansen and Itzhak carried the dead guard out to the end of the pier and pitched him into the water, where he landed with a loud splash. Then they all climbed back into the sailboat and cast off. Within a few minutes they could hardly even see the shore. Christiansen steered them well out and finally dropped anchor about half a mile from the deserted cliff face that he had chosen for the assault.

He checked the luminous dial of his watch. It was five minutes after two.

"We'll wait here for a while," he said, "just to get the sentry's rhythm. I could use some of that coffee."

Faglin handed him the thermos, and he unscrewed the top and carefully poured himself about three ounces. It was still extremely hot and as bitter as death. Three ounces was about all anyone would want.

He looked up at the cliff face, which in that darkness he could not even see, and he felt his heart twist inside him. He had sounded confident in front of the others—he had had to, otherwise they would never have agreed to such a lunatic idea—but in the quiet of his own soul he was not at all sure he could pull it off. He would have to get a line up to the top of those bluffs, and then he would have to pull himself up on it, and all in the pitch dark. He didn't have any clear idea how high the cliffs were—seventy feet was nothing more than a hopeful guess—and the highest he had ever had to climb on a rope was about two thirds of that. And this time he would be working against a time limit and, to top it all off, with a left hand that couldn't even bear to work the strings of a cello for longer than twenty minutes at a stretch. No, he wasn't sure he could pull it off.

Esther was up there, alone with that maniac. She had been more afraid of that than of death itself, and he had handed her over to him. If he ever got her out, it would take him a lifetime to make it up to her.

And, quite suddenly, it occurred to him that that was precisely what he wanted. With Esther it was possible, for the first time in years, to consider what the future might be like. He wouldn't have to be alone anymore, the prisoner of this obsession with revenge. The world was wider than that, something Mordecai had understood and had tried to make him understand.

Well, by now it was all somewhat academic. In a

few hours either he would be dead or Hagemann would be dead, and then revenge would be put to rest.

"What will you do when it's over?"

It was Faglin—he was sitting right next to him on the prow. Christiansen hadn't realized he was so close.

"I don't know. Go back to America, I guess. Get a job somewhere teaching music. I hadn't thought about it much."

"You won't go home—to Norway, I mean?"

"No. You?"

"Take a couple of weeks off and see if my wife and children still recognize me." He laughed, but not very convincingly. "If we don't get Hagemann, I've decided I'll try to move them to safety. I couldn't just leave them there, not if the Syrians . . ."

"If we live long enough for you to get home you won't have to worry about the Syrians, and if we don't there won't be anything you can do about it."

"No, I suppose not."

"You're damned right. So the only sensible thing to do is to succeed. We'll kill Hagemann, and lay this secret weapon of his to rest, and then you can go home and I can spend my remaining days teaching the cello to juvenile delinquents. How does that sound for a program?"

Faglin smiled thinly. He didn't believe it either.

"I think I need a cigarette."

"They might see the light from up there."

"No." Christiansen shook his head. "Not at this distance. And, besides, we'll know when they're up there when we see their flashlights."

He lit the cigarette, cupping the match behind his hands, and drew the smoke into his lungs. As usual, it didn't make him feel any better. That was something else he would do if he survived until daylight: he would give up smoking. He would give up all the vices of wartime.

When he saw the first pale flickers of light up on the cliffs, he dropped the cigarette into the water and heard it go out with a sound like the clicking shut of a door lock. He looked at his watch. It was two-twenty.

"Now we'll see how long it takes for him to make the circuit."

The light grew clearer and then died away as the sentry retreated back into the surrounding woods—there was a stretch of only a few yards there where he would have an unobstructed view of the sea. From the way the beam had remained steady, it was clear the man was only using his flashlight to keep from stumbling in the darkness. Hagemann's men, obviously, did not regard themselves as being under siege.

Christiansen found himself wishing that he had brought a change of dry clothes. It was goddamn cold out here on the water, but one couldn't think of everything. He wouldn't die of discomfort. He tried some more of the coffee, but it didn't make him feel any warmer.

"We'll establish an order for going up the rope—first me, then Itzhak, then the equipment, then Faglin. Itzhak, if it comes to that, have you got a weapon on you—something silent?"

"No."

Faglin reached into his pocket and, when he brought his hand back out into the moonlight, a vicious-looking blade, about seven inches long, shot out of his fist with a sound like splintering glass.

"Be my guest," he said, handing the knife to It-zhak, hilt first. That seemed to solve the weapons problem.

"Have either of you guys ever done any of this sort of climbing?" They both shook their heads, and Christiansen experienced a certain sinking feeling. "Well, there's not much to it. You just wrap the rope around your chest clockwise and let it hang down between your legs. Then, when you cross the right foot over the left, you've locked it in place and you can just hang there for a bit. You don't have to be pulling with your arms the whole time, but when you do, use both arms together and pull straight down."

"And you expect a couple of city Jews like us to go up seventy feet of rope like that, in the dark?"

"Yes."

"Okay."

They all laughed. They were all scared, but it was all right to be scared. Everything was permitted except failure.

"How long are we going to wait out here?" Itzhak asked. He was getting impatient—that was good.

"Until we know how long it takes the sentry to make one round, remember?"

"Well, there he is."

"No, that's not him. That's—"

Christiansen looked at his watch. It was twenty-eight minutes to three. Twelve minutes. Yesterday evening, all those ages ago, the sentry circuit had been slightly more than twenty-five minutes. Either he had taken to running it, or . . .

"I've got some bad news, fellas. They've doubled the guard."

✠ 24 ✠

They waited forty-five minutes, just to be certain. The sentries were passing every twelve or thirteen minutes, so it was reasonable to assume that there were two of them, rotating around Hagemann's compound like moons.

That meant that he would have less than twelve minutes—more like eight or nine—to set the rope, shinny up seventy feet of cliff, and be there to meet the next one when he came by on his rounds. There would be no room for error or human frailty. If any one of them messed up, they would all be dead in a matter of minutes.

Christiansen brought the boat in almost straight up to the cliff face. He couldn't use any lights, of course, and if he tore her belly out on a rock it was bound to be awkward. But the water was fairly deep just there and he got within about fifteen feet before he felt the keel scraping against the sandy bottom. He dropped anchor—it was almost unnecessary—and fetched up the grappling hook and line he had purchased in Barcelona. It weighed about three pounds, which was the perfect weight for a long throw, and this was going to be the longest throw Christiansen had ever made in his life. He just hoped that if he actually did manage to get it up there, the goddamn thing didn't ring like a gong against some rock or other. The sentries had the odds heavily enough in their favor as it was.

It was nearly four when they could look up and see the sentry's light flickering overhead. Morning came early that time of year—they were running out of time, along with everything else.

Christiansen stood on the prow of the boat, the grappling hook in his hand and its line uncoiled and lying loose so that it wouldn't hang up. He let the hook slide through his hand until it hung down nearly to the deck and then, very slowly, began swinging it around so that it described a circle almost parallel with his body. He was just limbering up. The first one had to be right because there wouldn't be time for a second.

The light overhead disappeared. He would give the man two—no, two and a half—minutes to get far enough away that he wouldn't be likely to hear anything, or make much of it if he did. There were no guarantees, however; when he got to the top—if he got to the top—he might find the son of a bitch up there waiting for him.

He was swinging out over the water now, wider and wider. His arc was probably close to ten feet across, and he could hear the tearing sound the hook made as it swept through the air. One chance, only one. He had to put everything in him behind the throw, and he had to know when to let go.

Finally, with one last sharp twist of his body, he released the line and it shot up into the darkness. He waited—it seemed to take forever. He imagined the hook coming straight back down on him. It would probably kill him. It would be just as well.

But there was nothing. No impact, no splash, just silence. The rope hung in the air, disappearing into the vacant night. He gave it a gentle tug and then another, harder. It was holding. The hook had found something to get its teeth into. God damn him, he had done it.

Itzhak and Faglin were standing in the back, just trying to stay out of the way. He waved them over.

"Okay. This is your one and only lesson," he murmured, pulling on a pair of canvas work gloves. He felt as if the whole world were up there on that bluff, peering down at them. "The line goes around the chest, like this, and then one foot straight over the other. You clamp it with your right foot and when you want to climb you let go, just a little. See? Wrap your right arm around the line and pull with both hands. Got it?"

Neither of them said anything. What was there to say? Christiansen locked his hands together over his head and pulled up. He had about six minutes to make the bluff.

It was all right for about the first forty feet. You did this sort of work with your back muscles more than with your arms, and Christiansen had never let himself slide after the war. After all, his war wasn't over yet.

But then, at forty feet, his left hand began to bother him—just a little at first, but then more and more—until he felt as if he didn't have the strength left to hold a pencil. By fifty feet he hurt everywhere and his lungs ached. His back, where he had taken Pilsner's bullet, felt ready to tear open, and he could hardly feel his hand at all. If the top was up there, he hadn't seen it yet. He would give himself a fifteen-second rest, he decided. He clamped the line between his feet and let his arms down.

It was a mistake. He had to catch himself to keep from toppling over, and the instant the strain was off his arms they felt as if they were made of stone. He thought perhaps he had never lifted anything in his life as heavy as his own hands.

He couldn't go on. There was just no way he could go on. He would hang there for maybe another minute and then he would fall. He was as good as dead, and he hardly minded at all.

When the fifteen seconds—or what felt like fifteen seconds—were over, he reached back up, his arms breaking, and took the line again. One more pull. What the hell, he wouldn't be any deader for falling that extra foot and a half. One more pull.

And then another, and another after that. He no longer tried to open his left hand; he just let it slide up the rope. It seemed to slip just a little more each time. One more pull.

Finally, when he was finished for good, when there was nothing more inside him, he saw where the line seemed to dig into the cliff face and then vanish. It was the top. It had to be the top.

One more pull. Just one more.

With his left hand he reached up and felt the flat surface of the bluff. A few more feet, just that, no more, and he could rest.

One more pull.

Christiansen lay there, his face buried in the fallen pine needles, trying to catch his breath and summon up the courage to move. He pulled his arm down toward his head and looked at his watch. It was two minutes after four—he had made the climb in eight minutes. The sentry would be walking straight over him in another minute and a half.

Get up. Get up, get up. Get up or they'll kill you while you lie there with your nose in the mud, feeling sorry for yourself. Get up.

He got up. First to his knees—one doesn't rush these things—and then, finally, to his actual and authentic feet.

The grappling hook had landed almost ten feet back from the edge of the cliff and had caught on a tree root. Christiansen just had time to pick it up and to press his back against the tree when he saw the first tentative jabs of yellow light from the sentry's flashlight. Within a few seconds he could hear the sound of the man's boot breaking a fallen twig. He held the grappling iron in both hands and waited. There wasn't any time and he was just too fucking tired to try anything fancy.

Almost at once the little trail was as well lit as the back terrace at an evening party. The sentry would come right by Christiansen's tree—they would practically brush shoulders. Christiansen held his breath and waited.

The man was muttering to himself, something about the goddamned sergeant and missing his tea. Just a word or two. Just enough to make him human. He was just out for a night's forced patrol. He carried his Mauser over his shoulder like a parcel.

Christiansen let him pass, waiting one heartbeat,

and then stepped out into the trail and swung down on him. One of the grappling iron's prongs caught the man square in the side of the head and just tore it away.

The sentry was dead at once. He didn't even stiffen. He just fell straight down. There was blood everywhere, spattered around like paint. It was gushing out just over the dead man's right ear, from a trench you could have stuck your whole hand into. Christiansen was wet to the elbows—he even had to wipe some of it out of his eyes.

But there was no time for horror. There was no time for anything. The sentry's flashlight was lying on the ground, still on. He picked it up, switched it off, and dropped it into his pocket. Then he grabbed the corpse by the arms and dragged it into the bushes and out of sight.

The grappling hook was lying on the ground, right where Christiansen had dropped it. He picked it up again and dug it into the tree root. He took the line and shook it wildly. That would be Itzhak's signal to start up.

When the line went tight, Christiansen sat down with his back against the tree and closed his eyes. For a few minutes at least there was nothing he could do about anything. And he couldn't remember when he had been so tired. He had been in Spain less than forty-eight hours. He had killed nine, maybe ten men—he couldn't even remember. It was all beginning to seem just a little pointless. What could be worth all this? What had he done with his life that he was sitting under a tree, trying to clean a total stranger's blood off his face?

Finally he decided he was weary of his own low

spirits, so he went over to the cliff edge to see how Itzhak was doing on the line. He wasn't doing very well.

"Give me a hand, can you?"

Itzhak was stuck about twenty feet from the top. If he rested a bit he would be able to make it, but there wasn't any time for resting. Christiansen took the line in both hands and began pulling him in. At the end, he held the line in his right hand and reached down for Itzhak with his left.

"Grab the wrist, not the hand. The hand isn't much good anymore."

When they were both up, Christiansen lay down on the soft ground, spent. He would never get up again. He was sure of it.

And then he remembered the second sentry.

"Do you know what it means to 'make your bones,'" he asked. No, Itzhak hadn't a clue what he was talking about. "Well, you're going to make your bones tonight, kid. Go hide yourself by the trail and kill our friend when he comes by on his watch. Did they teach you how to do that?"

"Yes." Itzhak swallowed hard. "But couldn't you—?"

"No, I couldn't. The way I am right now, I'd buff it. He's all yours."

He made a vague gesture with his left arm. He really was exhausted.

Itzhak took the knife Faglin had given him out of his pocket and pressed the little lever on the hasp. The blade shot out with a snap so that the thing nearly jumped from his hand. He really didn't seem to like the look of it.

"Fine—if you can't you can't. I'll—"

"No, you're right. I suppose I have to learn some-time." The forced grin in Itzhak's face wasn't fooling anyone.

"Not if you really don't want to."

"I really don't want to, but I think I'd better."

Christiansen nodded. "Okay. Go for the heart. And don't even try to be sporting, all right?"

"Sure."

He disappeared—it wasn't hard up there, where you could stand shaded from the moonlight by a tree limb and be shrouded in impenetrable black. But the Mossad must have taught him something because Christiansen couldn't even hear him moving. It was a noiseless winter night, and he didn't make a sound. After a while, Christiansen went back over to the edge of the cliff and began hauling up the equipment, which was about all he was good for.

There was a slight scuffle, that was all. You might not even have known it was going on if you weren't listening for it. And then Itzhak came back into the little clearing by the cliff face and sat down. He didn't have the knife with him anymore, and there was a dazed look in his eyes.

"Any trouble?"

"No. Nothing. It's just . . . Is it always like this?"

"Yes, it's always like this. Not so bad after the first time, but always just like this."

The line pulled tight, which meant that Faglin was on his way up. There was nothing for either of them to do except to wait.

"My God! I won't ever want to do that again."

Christiansen reached down over the edge, grabbed

Faglin by the arms, and dragged him up. They waited while Faglin lay there on his face, trying to recover. They knew just how he felt.

Finally he rolled over. He wasn't ready to do much more, but he wasn't just waiting to die either.

"What do we do now?" he asked.

"We see if you were bright enough to remember to bring the coffee."

Christiansen opened the knapsack, and there it was. He unscrewed the thermos cap and filled it about half full. The sides of the cap felt deliciously warm against his palms. Then he decided that Itzhak probably needed it worse than he did and passed it over to him.

Faglin was busy with the rest of their gear. He took out the sections of a Sten gun and fitted them together. There were also two pistols. The rest he left in the knapsack.

"Where's my knife?" he asked, looking at Itzhak. Itzhak only stared at him. He was still too engrossed in his own private nightmare to be able to provide an answer. It had been a heavy few hours for him.

"I imagine it's sticking in a dead German," Christiansen said. "You might go have a look—the trail is back there. Itzhak blooded himself tonight."

Faglin got up to have his look. When he came back he was carrying two Mauser rifles. Christiansen had forgotten all about the rifles.

"I found my knife," he said. "What happened to the one with his head torn open?"

"The grappling hook. It was at hand."

"Oh my God."

When Itzhak was finished with the cup, Faglin

and Christiansen each had some coffee. It was almost like a picnic, except they all knew there was very little time before one or another of the sentries was missed.

"Let's go find the barracks," Faglin said.

They had the flashlights, and there really wasn't any reason why they shouldn't use them. Anyone who saw would just think it was one of the sentries making his rounds. They followed the trail, and pretty soon it led out of the woods and into a clearing. From there they could see Hagemann's villa, its white walls gleaming in the cold, hostile light of a series of flood-lamps—Hagemann wasn't taking any chances. Across a lawn was a squat little building that had one light on over the door but was otherwise dark. This was where the guards slept. For the rest there was only a chain-link fence that stretched off into the darkness in both directions.

They didn't like the clearing very much. There was too much light—all somebody would have to do was look out through a window. The woods were safer, so they went back there.

The minute they were protected behind the shadowy line of trees, Faglin squatted down over his knapsack and pulled out something that looked for all the world like a bratwurst. It had wires coming out of either end, and he attached these to a device shaped like a clock face except that it was the approximate size of a tea saucer and in place of hands it had a single dial.

"This will detonate ten seconds after impact," he said, twisting the dial around with a precise movement that indicated a certain gingerly respect for the thing's destructive power. "Or if someone attempts to fiddle with it—whichever happens first. I'll toss it through the barracks window. Believe me, we won't have to worry about any interference from those boys."

There were probably ten or twelve men asleep in that darkened building, and Faglin was proposing to kill them all in one go. It would be abstract—he wouldn't have to look into their faces while they died. He wouldn't have to have much of anything to do with it, and it wouldn't bother him a bit. That was how murder was achieved in the modern world. Hagemann's soldiers would be no loss to the human race and, God knows, if Faglin didn't have a right to kill them they could live forever. Christiansen wasn't offering any criticism. He was just glad, for the state of his soul, that he performed his homicides directly. He would rather put up with the bad dreams.

"That will only leave whoever is in the main house," he said, trying not to remember that Esther was one of them. "We'll have to flush them out somehow. Do you suppose you'd have enough of your modeling clay left over to start the right sort of fire? Something with lots of smoke? Just for the sake of a little excitement?"

"I don't see why not."

Christiansen avoided Faglin's eyes—he didn't want to see what was there. Everything was settled. For good or ill they had their plan, and now events would roll forward with a momentum that would make everyone its victim.

If it came to it, and there was no other way of keeping Esther out of Hagemann's hands, Christiansen had decided that he was going to kill her. If he didn't, Faglin would—the Mossad simply couldn't afford to let the secret she carried get away from them.

Not a second time. And if it had to be done it was better it be done by someone who loved her.

All he could do was hope that it wouldn't come to that.

He knew now why he was here, and that it had nothing to do with events in Kirstenstad all those years ago—at any rate, almost nothing. He wanted to kill Egon Hagemann, but that was not what had brought him. He wanted to get Esther back. He wanted the chance to go on with his life.

There were propane tanks outside the villa's kitchen. Faglin was that very minute huddled beside one in the darkness, fixing a charge to the underside. It would cause one hell of a fire.

First they would blow up the barracks, then the villa—one right after the other. And then it was hunting season, with every man for himself. Itzhak would cover the back of the villa with his rifle, and Faglin and Christiansen would go in the front from opposite sides. There was no knowing how everything, in the end, would turn out.

Christiansen looked up at one of the windows on the second story—still lit up, even at this hour of the morning.

It had been several hours since Esther had tasted any of the brandy, but she still carried the bottle around with her, holding it by the neck in her right hand, hardly remembering it existed.

It had done its work. Her headache was gone and she felt almost calm. Everything seemed very simple now. She had decided that she would kill Colonel Hagemann herself. It was only a question of hitting on the means.

Provided they had no fear of death, anyone could kill anyone. The strong were helpless against the weak—all she had to do was decide how.

She glanced down at the brandy bottle, a little surprised to discover it actually existed, and then she smiled.

"Am I interrupting something?"

It was Hagemann. He had opened the door and stepped inside so quietly that she hadn't imagined he was there, but she managed to smother the sudden rush of fear and turned around to meet him tolerably composed.

She hated him—"hate" was hardly even adequate—but she managed to smile after a fashion.

"I'm glad to find you in better spirits, Esther. Are you prepared to live now, and listen to reason?"

The smile on his own lips seemed to mock at her, as if he understood everything that was in her mind, had always understood and would never be taken in. He was a superior being, a member of the race of masters. What could she hope to achieve against him? He took a few tentative steps toward her and raised his hand, as if offering to take hers, and then he stopped and the smile died.

She was standing beside the bed, just at the edge of the white carpet beneath it, and suddenly she knelt down and smashed the brandy bottle against the tile floor. The bottom broke cleanly away, leaving the upper half a series of vicious, jagged points. As she got up she took a lunge toward Hagemann and the broken bottle raked across the palm of his open hand.

He looked down at it with surprise, as if he hardly knew what to make of the blood that was suddenly pouring out over his fingers. It didn't last long, but for that moment he didn't seem to have the will to defend himself. Esther got ready to lunge at him again— this time she would cut his throat.

But she was just too late. As she swung her arm around toward him, his own came up to block it and the shock of pain that reached all the way to her shoulder caused her to let go of the bottle. But not before one edge of it touched lightly against Hagemann's cheek, leaving behind a thick trail of blood. It was the best she could do.

The bottle struck the floor and smashed, and at almost the same instant Esther felt a blow to the side of the head that sent her reeling. A second had her down on her hands and knees, and when she tried to get up Hagemann kicked her in the ribs, using the whole top of his shoe so that the toe caught her in the left breast.

She couldn't breathe anymore. All she could hold in her mind was the hope that he wouldn't kick her again, that she would have those few seconds to find a breath of air before he killed her. And of course he would kill her—at Waldenburg once she had seen him hack a man to death with a shovel merely for daring to look him directly in the face.

But instead he was kneeling beside her, his hands on her shoulders, lifting her up. He had wrapped a handkerchief around his cut hand, but otherwise he hardly seemed to notice. The wound on his face was bleeding so freely that it had soaked the front of his shirt and his clean white jacket.

"What's happened to you, Esther? Do you hear me? What's taken possession of you—have you gone mad?"

She was all right now. All she felt was pain.

"I wanted to kill you," she said. Merely to speak the words, and to see the expression on Hagemann's face, gave her an intense, almost sensual pleasure. Yes, this was worth dying for.

Hagemann pushed her away and rose to his feet. He hardly seemed to know what to do.

And then, quite suddenly, his confidence returned. He looked down at her with his old smile.

"So I was right—more right than I could have guessed. This time it won't be anything like Waldenburg, will it, my dear. No. Perhaps that's just as well."

He took the handkerchief from around his hand and used it to make some attempt at wiping the blood off his face.

"At Waldenburg you were a reasonable creature and afraid of me, and you survived that place—you survived longer than any of my other women. But you should have learned in the camps what happens to those who hang on to the illusion of being human. They are trampled into the mud."

"Do you think I care if you kill me?" she shouted. "Do you think I care?"

She struggled to rise from her knees. She didn't want to meet death like that. Just for once, not like that.

"No, perhaps you don't. But you will when the moment comes. When I've decided to kill you, I'll make it my business to make you care."

He began to take off his belt. He was excited—she could see that clearly enough. He had plans.

No, he hadn't changed at all.

"It will be interesting to see how your newfound dignity holds up, Esther. And this, of course, will only be the merest taste of what's to come. Before we're finished you'll give me everything, my dear. You'll tell me all your little secrets. You'll beg me—just as you used to—to do whatever I like with you."

As she staggered to her feet he reached out and took the front of her dress in his hand, pulling it away and yanking her back down to the floor. She hit her elbow against the tiles, and as she reached up to cover her naked breast she felt Hagemann's belt cut her across the face.

Yes, let him kill her. There wouldn't be anything to hold him back now. She wanted him to kill her. She would force him to kill her.

"He'll kill you," she whispered. She could hardly even do that—it felt as if the buckle had torn her mouth. "He'll kill you, no matter what you do to me. How will you feel then?"

Yes, this was the moment. He wouldn't be able to help himself—she could read it in his face. He raised his hand . . .

She felt the tremor before she heard anything. It was something that passed through the room like a shudder. And then she looked up at Hagemann and realized it wasn't what she had expected. Hagemann wasn't even looking at her. He had forgotten her completely as he stared into empty space. The belt dropped from his hand.

He said something, but it was lost in the sound of the explosion.

* 25 *

Christiansen walked around to the front of the villa, carrying a pistol. He had left his rifle behind—this was going to be a night for close work. Anyone who looked out a window could have seen him, but it was too late now for that to make any difference.

He never saw Faglin throw his incendiary. The explosion was terrific, and thick black-red columns of fire licked out of the broken windows. One man got out through the front door. He was screaming and the whole back of his body was on fire. He only managed six or seven steps before he collapsed and lay quite still on the ground, still burning. No one else came out. No one else was ever coming out.

The kitchen fire started only a few seconds later. Christiansen couldn't see it, but he heard the blast. Now it was time to do something.

The front door gave way with a kick, and he found himself in a large entrance hall with a tiled floor. There was a stairway, made of massive dark wood and carpeted with a Persian runner, a couple of doors at either

end of the hall, and two arched entryways to what
were obviously reception rooms, side by side against
the rear of the building. What impressed him in that
first instant was the stillness. No one was anywhere
to be seen, and there wasn't a sound.

He stepped into one of the reception rooms and
snicked on a light switch. It was a beautiful room—
the floor was dark, polished hardwood covered with
a Persian carpet that could have been worth any amount
of money. The furniture was old, heavy and well cared
for. There was no one there, nor in the other reception
room, with which it connected. It was almost as if no
one was coming to their party. The only sound was
the muted roar of flames and the crackling of burning
timber. In just a few minutes this place would be an
inferno.

There was a door leading off the second reception
room. It was open just a few inches, and Christiansen
pushed against it with the palm of his hand. Inside,
standing behind a desk as if he were looking for something, was a man in what was obviously an old SS
uniform but with the identifying badges removed. He
had thin hair, almost white and carefully combed back
from his forehead, and he wore a pair of rimless spec-
tacles. The desk drawer was open. When he saw
Christiansen he reached inside. Christiansen shot him
through the eye and the man pitched over backward,
hitting his head against the wall behind him and leaving a wide smear of blood. He was quite still when
Christiansen came over to look at him. There was a
Luger lying in the desk drawer, but that didn't make
any difference. Christiansen would have killed him
anyway.

There was the noise of shooting from the entrance

hall—Faglin's Sten gun from the sound of it. Christiansen ran back and found a fat Arab in a pair of red and white striped silk pajamas lying at the foot of the stairway, his chest cut open by a burst of machine-gun fire. It was the man Christiansen had seen sitting beside Hagemann at the Café Pícaro the night before. It seemed like a thousand years ago.

Faglin was there too. His face was streaked with smoke and he looked excited, the way men always do in battle.

"Do you know who that was?" he asked, gesturing toward the dead Arab with the muzzle of his gun. He didn't wait for an answer. "That was Mustafa Faraj, the head of the Syrian Foreign Office's Department of Jewish Affairs. These people meant business."

"Where is Hagemann?"

"What?"

You could smell the fire by then, the thick smell of burning varnish. And the air was hot and hard to breathe. They had perhaps two or three minutes before everything within those walls would be as dead as the house itself, but still Faglin didn't seem to know what he was talking about.

"Dammit—have you been upstairs?"

"No." Faglin looked down once more at the corpse of the fat little Arab, and then he seemed to return to himself. "There hasn't been time."

Christiansen stepped over the body and started up the stairs, three at a time. And Faglin was right behind him.

"Esther!" he heard himself shouting, "Esther, are you there?"

The second floor was a long corridor with doors on both sides. Some of them were open, as if people had left in a hurry. Christiansen kicked in the first one he came to, but the room was empty—there was just time to notice that it smelled strongly of violet water. The window was open. Outside there were two shots from a rifle, the reports just far enough apart to indicate that they had been very carefully placed. There was the crack of a pistol firing out in the corridor, overwhelmed at once by another burst of machine-gun fire.

Christiansen went to the next bedroom, and the next. In one he found another man in his pajamas who looked as if he had shot himself in the heart, God alone knew why. His pistol was on the floor beside him. But he didn't find Esther, and he didn't find Hagemann. When he came back out to the landing, Faglin was waiting for him.

"Let's get out of here while we still have the chance. Everyone's dead anyway. Come on."

"He's got Esther! He's here and I'll find him. He's—"

"He's not here. Nobody's here but the dead." Faglin was beginning to look a little wild. "Come on, Christiansen—let's go!"

They could already feel the fire on the second story, and as they went down the staircase it was like descending into a furnace. Some of the walls were already in flames, and almost every second there was the sound of breaking glass. The smoke was so thick they had to cover their faces to breathe. There was nowhere to go but outside.

They came onto the lawn just in time to see the great chain-link gate slide open and a car shoot by on the driveway. Faglin raised his Sten gun and fired after it, but he wasn't really trying.

A few seconds later there was the hollow sound of something Christiansen hadn't heard since the war. He could see the explosion almost at once. He found himself wondering where the hell Hirsch had ever found a grenade launcher.

"Do you think that could have been Hagemann in the car?" Faglin asked. Christiansen shook his head.

"No. Hagemann isn't stupid. He would know we'd have something as obvious as the front gate covered."

But, of course, he didn't know for sure. Could Esther have been in that car? Could that be her, right this instant, burning to death because she couldn't get the doors open fast enough? If it were so, he would kill Hirsch. He would . . .

"He suckered us good, pal." That was what Hirsch had said, only that afternoon. Hagemann, that bastard, what was he—?

Suddenly it was all made clear for him. It was as if he could see into the man's mind, as if they had had the same thought together. Down there on the road into town, probably not fifty yards from the front gates, a car full of Hagemann's men was burning like a tar ball, sending smoke and dark red flames into the night sky. It wasn't a way anyone would want to die.

Hagemann had sent them, or at least allowed them to go, to take what he must have known was a fool-hardy risk. Neither Hagemann nor anything that Hagemann cared about was in that car, but they had served his purposes just the same. It was Mordecai in the slammer, all over again.

"He suckered us good, pal." Yes, he had. But maybe not this time.

"They were a decoy." Christiansen put his hand around the barrel of Faglin's Sten gun—if he was right, he was going to need more to bargain with than just a pistol. "Those guys in the car, they were sent out to die so Hagemann could have a running start."

Faglin was looking at him as if he had grown another head.

"Give me the grease gun. Everyone else is dead—you won't need it. Let go, dammit!"

As if his fingers were operated by springs, Faglin released his grasp on the weapon. Christiansen took it and handed him his pistol. He didn't say anything more. There was no time now for formalities.

There was a narrow iron ladder that could be let down the cliff face to the beach and Hagemann's private dock. Christiansen had seen it through his field glasses that first evening. It looked as if it probably worked like a fire escape—you released a catch at the top and the ladder came down in sections, one telescoped inside the other. That was how the sentries got up and down and that was how Hagemann would reach his boat.

That side of the bluff was heavily wooded, so Christiansen had only the most approximate idea where Hagemann was headed. It was simply a question of choosing your direction and going as straight as the screen of trees and undergrowth would let you. If there was a path, Hagemann was the only one left who knew where it was.

And, of course, there was always the chance that he had left behind a couple of his boys to cover his escape.

But Christiansen wasn't thinking about Hagemann's boys. He just ran. He kept his head down so the tree limbs he couldn't even see wouldn't catch him quite so often in the face, and for the rest he only thought about one thing—getting there. He wasn't even carrying a flashlight, but no one was going to stop him. He didn't give a damn what they had.

And then, of course, his foot caught on a tree root and he found himself suddenly rolling through the bushes like a hedgehog. The palms of his hands were scaped raw when he stood up again and he had to hunt around for the Sten gun. It gave him a chance to listen. There was someone out there, trying just as hard as he was to keep still.

Hagemann? Could it be Hagemann? Then he heard the rasp of metal against metal and he knew whoever was out there, waiting for a shot at him, definitely wasn't Hagemann. Hagemann was already lowering his escape ladder.

Which meant that he had found some poor boob who was enough of a fanatic and a damn fool to hide in the bushes and protect his retreat.

Okay, if he wanted to die for the cause, that was his business.

Christiansen peered into the darkness, looking for the shadow that wasn't supposed to be there. He was a big target, so why didn't the stupid bastard take a shot at him? Come on, buddy, what's the—

There was a sharp little cough, like someone with an iron windpipe clearing his throat, and a tiny flash of light. Then another, and Christiansen felt something strike his leg, just an inch or two below the hip. He didn't wait. He turned and fired, and the burst from his machine gun was answered almost at once by a high-pitched scream.

It was only when he took his first step that he realized in any concrete way that he had taken a bullet himself. Well, so what? It wouldn't kill him anytime soon.

The poor chump was still screaming. Christiansen walked up to him and found him lying on his side, his back against a tree. Something on the ground beside him reflected a dull gleam of moonlight. Christiansen reached down and picked it up. It was a flashlight. When he turned it on he saw that the man's insides were leaking out through his fingers. His pistol was there beside him, but he had forgotten all about it. He was a goner; all that was left to him now was fear and pain and, finally, death. Christiansen took the pistol, put the muzzle against the man's temple, and pulled the trigger.

Now it was strictly between the two of them. There was just himself and Hagemann, with Esther as the prize.

He didn't have any trouble finding the ladder after that. Hagemann had turned the floodlights on. Apparently he didn't fancy breaking his neck as he climbed down seventy feet of slippery iron rungs.

And Hagemann had one other problem. As he stood at the edge of the bluff, looking down at the struggle that was going on beneath him, Christiansen could see quite clearly why Hagemann hadn't made good on his escape yet. Because Hagemann was carrying baggage. He had Esther between himself and the ladder, with one arm around her waist, and he was finding it tough going.

They were almost to the bottom. They never looked up, either one of them, but Christiansen had no doubt that Hagemann knew he was there.

There wasn't any time to lose—he had to get down

there, and the ladder was the only way. And he could only use the ladder as long as Hagemann was still on it and had both his hands full.

He transferred the Sten gun to his left hand and started down, two or three feet at a time, using his arm to lower himself and letting his feet catch on the rungs when he needed to brace himself. And all the time all he could think about was getting shot in the ass when Hagemann reached the bottom and had a hand free again.

But by then Esther knew he was there. He could look down and see her face as she stared up at him. At least she knew she wasn't alone.

And when he felt the shudder of release when Hagemann jumped off and onto the stony beach, he knew she was down there trying to keep him alive. He could hear the brawl.

And suddenly there they were, hardly more than fifteen feet apart, almost where they had left off the afternoon before. Hagemann had his arm across Esther's throat, and he was struggling to free the Luger from his belt, shaking her viciously, like a dog with a dead rat, while he fought off her hands. It was a battle he was destined to win.

But not for a few seconds yet. Christiansen was perhaps twelve feet from the ground—he let himself come down one more time against the ladder and then pushed himself free. He could feel himself falling through the cold air, seemingly adrift, and then he hit the stony beach with a scraping sound and a jolt violent enough to buckle his legs underneath him like the magician's collapsing hat. He lurched to one side and landed on his left arm, but he had Hagemann in his sights the whole time. Once more, they had achieved a stalemate.

Finally Hagemann got his pistol free. For a wild moment he seemed ready to point it at Christiansen, but then he thought better of the idea. After all, how could he hope to win against a gun that sprayed bullets like a goddamn garden hose? He wasn't such a fool as that—no, the pistol came up until, once more, it rested lightly against Esther's throat.

"You see?" he said. "Once more I have the girl. And I will shoot her just as quickly now as yesterday. How can you win, Christiansen? Tell me. How can you hope to win now?"

There was a cut on his face. It was fresh enough to be bleeding heavily, coating his cheek. His white jacket had blood on it too and was streaked with smoke and dirt. It looked as if Hagemann had been having a rough time of it just lately.

And, finally, it could be he was just pushed too far in his mind—his eyes said that. He looked half crazy with that mixture of fear and exultation that comes to men who almost don't give a damn anymore whether they live or not, who are ready to stake everything on one last gamble. He was crazy like that. And he didn't care who died with him.

"Are you really demented enough to think you can play the same game with me twice?" Christiansen forced himself to laugh. The sound of it shocked even him—it was a hollow, cruel laugh, almost a mad laugh. Almost inhuman. "Take one step backward, just one, and I'll blow you to smithereens. The girl will just have take her chances."

Hagemann might be loose from his moorings, but

he wasn't stupid. And he was never rash. A strange, speculative look came into his mad eyes—he was calculating the chances that Christiansen was bluffing.

And all Christiansen could do was to wait while he made up his mind. Because he wasn't bluffing. It wasn't a situation in which he would dare a bluff. If Hagemann so much as stirred, he would open fire. He would aim high—he would take the top of Hagemann's head off and hope for the best—but he would have to fire. You didn't bluff a man like Hagemann.

And it was possible Esther might make it. People had survived some pretty terrible bullet wounds—they did it all the time. But if he let her go with that lunatic . . .

But Hagemann didn't attempt to move. It seemed he wasn't going to commit that particular mistake.

"Where are your friends the Jews?" he asked. He was smiling. He was a man who knew all there was to know about the Jews.

"They're up on the bluff, killing what's left of your Praetorian Guard. But they'll be along directly. They don't like you much, you know that, Hagemann? You haven't made yourself popular."

Something very odd was going on. While they had been talking—and it was part of the reason Christiansen was bothering to talk at all—Esther had slipped her hand down to the opening of Hagemann's right jacket pocket. She never took her eyes from Christiansen's face, and her eyes were damp and large and frightened, and all the time he had the feeling that she was trying to make him understand something. She wasn't pleading with him to save her—it was something else. Something she obviously thought was more important.

And this while the muzzle of Hagemann's Luger pressed against the side of her throat. She was braver than any twenty men.

What the hell did Hagemann have in his pocket?

"Then why not?" Hagemann's smile turned into a demonic grin. "I would as soon you killed me as they—sooner. After all, you and I are at least of the same blood, and you are a real soldier, not some ragged partisan. I have no inclination to be butchered like a kosher steer."

"Does it matter to you so much then how you die, Hagemann? If it was such a matter of honor with you, you might have blown your brains out like your friend back up at the house."

"Who—Joachim? You mean he actually did it? He'd been looking for an excuse to restage *Götterdämmerung* since the end of the war. No thank you. I am not so mad as that."

"Then maybe it's just possible that you and I could cut a deal."

Christiansen tried very hard not to look at Esther as he spoke. He didn't want to think about her, about what she might or might not want or feel. He could worry about all that later—if there was a later—and then he would make it the business of his life, but not now. Now there were only two people on that beach, himself and Colonel Egon Hagemann. That was enough.

Oh how he hated that man. It was as if he was experiencing it all for the first time, as if he had never known about Kirstenstad and all the rest of it until that very minute. What a pleasure it would be to kill this one—preferably slowly, an inch at a time.

"My friends the Jews will be down here in about

three minutes, I figure. And they aren't the least sentimental about Miss Rosensaft. So if we're going to reach an understanding I suggest we don't waste any time. I'll trade you your life for the girl, Hagemann. Take it or leave it."

"How? To be led away from here in chains?" Hagemann shook his head, and the muzzle of his pistol dug a little deeper into Esther's neck. "How long would I live? An hour? A week? Until an Allied war crimes tribunal could put a noose around my neck? No thank you, Mr. Christiansen—I would just as soon die here and now."

He seemed to be waiting. It was a test of resolve, and there wasn't any doubt that Hagemann was ready to die. The only hope was that he might still be prepared to live, if the terms were right. Christiansen lowered the barrel of his Sten gun a foot or two, just to show his good intentions.

"I said your life, Hagemann. This is the deal. You let the girl go, and you throw down your pistol. In exchange for that I'll give you sixty seconds. No more, no less. What you do with them is your business."

For just an instant, Hagemann's eyes glanced toward his boat, which was still tied up at the end of the pier, white as a marble tomb in the light from the floods. Like a sensible man, he was considering his chances. It was sixty feet across the beach, then perhaps twenty-five feet to the end of the dock—considering the surface, a distance a man could cover in, say, ten to twelve seconds. Then up into the boat, which he could have started and moving within another fifteen to twenty seconds. Given that it was Hagemann's, there was probably an arsenal on board anyway, so he wouldn't have to worry so much about time. Yes, sixty seconds would be all he needed. But, of course, he wasn't so stupid . . .

"And what possible guarantee would I have that you wouldn't simply kill me, Christiansen? Why should I believe that you are prepared to be so sporting?"

But he was smiling again. Every man has his give-away, and that was his. That tight little smile that said he felt himself to be master of the world.

"You haven't any choice, do you. You can believe me, or you can die."

"And if I accept your offer, do I have your word that you will stop hunting me down like an animal, Mr. Christiansen? I'm getting tired of spending my life waiting for you to turn up. Will you call it square between us?"

"You heard the offer—sixty seconds. Just sixty seconds."

Hagemann's soft laughter pulsed through the air, fading out into the growl of the waves.

"I wouldn't have believed you, Mr. Christiansen—I would have known you were lying to me. You'll never stop, will you."

"No. I'll never stop."

They stood there, facing each other on the edge of the land, the blind sea murmuring in their ears, filled with their hatred for one another. It was a moment when each felt he understood the other's heart. It was a moment that had become almost unbearable.

And then Christiansen allowed himself one furtive glance at Esther, and what he saw in her face made him understand. Yes, of course.

"First the gun—throw it well away. And then the girl. Make up your mind, Hagemann. There isn't any more time."

Things might have gone either way in the pause that followed. Hagemann seemed not to know what he dared believe.

"On your word as an Aryan, Christiansen?" he asked finally.

"Yes, if that's what it takes. On my word as an Aryan."

It must have been the hardest decision he had ever made in his life, but finally Hagemann did ease the barrel of his pistol away from Esther's throat. He held it up, as if to show it off to Christiansen, and then, very gently, he tossed it to one side. For another instant he stood there holding her, as if he couldn't bear to be parted from her, as if he were waiting to see if he was about to die.

Quite suddenly, he pushed her away, starting back from her like a man who had been bitten by a snake. Her hand was still clenched around the opening of his jacket pocket, and as she fell she ripped it away with her, the pocket simply coming off in her grasp, the contents spilling out onto the beach, tinkling as they struck the stones.

And, of course, Hagemann understood. He stood staring at her, his face dark with hatred.

"Run, Hagemann. Sixty seconds—don't push your luck."

And that was what he did. His eyes dropped to the muzzle of Christiansen's Sten gun, and then widened with terror, and then he ran. His footsteps ground against the pebbles.

And Esther was down on her hands and knees, searching among the loose stones.

"He had it in his . . . I know it's here. I know . . ."

"Come away, Esther. There's no time."

"But it's here." She looked up at his face, pleading but determined. Nothing would move her. "It's here . . . It's— Yes, I found it! See? I . . ."

There really was no time now. Hagemann was already climbing the gangway to his boat. Christiansen took Esther in his arms, giving her the only protection he had left to offer. He covered her with his body and lay down on the beach.

It sounded like the end of everything. The noise of the explosion seemed to reach them in waves, one after the other. It was terrible. They could feel the fire. The last day would be like this.

And when they turned to look, the boat at the end of the pier had simply ceased to exist. In its place was an inferno, black and red, shooting out in every direction, mirrored in the black water until it seemed to fill the world, burning their eyes so that they couldn't bear to look at it.

"What is it—what HAPPENED?" Esther screamed, burying her face in Christiansen's chest. All he could do was put his hand on her hair.

"It's Mordecai's Roman candle," he said.

26

Linz, Austria: March 25, 1948

Esther never relinquished the key she had picked up on the beach that night. The next afternoon, in Marseilles, Inar bought her a thin gold chain for it so she could wear it around her neck. She thought perhaps she might wear it the rest of her life.

They all left together, by sea. Inar had a little boat. He disappeared for a few minutes and then suddenly there it was, at the end of what remained of the pier. They all had to wade out into the water to get aboard—even Jerry Hirsch, who was alive after all but whose left arm was in a cast up to the shoulder—and they got away just as the first sirens were sounding. None of them had been hurt except Inar, who had been shot in the leg. The bullet had gone straight through, so he cleaned out the wound himself. It was a gruesome process and must have been terribly painful, but from the calm deliberation of his manner one might have supposed he was merely oiling a bicycle chain.

They said their goodbyes in Valencia, early that morning. They would see Jerry again in Munich, but Itzhak and Amos were going home. Inar bought two tickets on the train to France. They stayed in Marseilles for two days, and on the night before they left Inar took her to hear a concert—a string quartet, but they didn't play anything by Bartók. "You'll have to get used to this sort of thing," Inar told her. It made her feel as if they shared a delicious secret. After the performance Inar took her backstage to meet the violist, who turned out to be a friend from a place called "Juilliard."

The next day they stopped off in Bern for three hours. Inar left her to wait in the train station, and when he came back he was carrying his cello. He was smiling—it was the first time she had ever seen him really happy, and he was like a different person. It made her believe that the past might really be over.

They had to wait a day before Jerry showed up at their hotel in Munich, and then Inar hired a car and they drove to Linz. It was evening by the time they arrived, too late for anything except dinner. The expression on Jerry's face when he bid them goodnight at the door of the restaurant was strained and uncertain, as if he were embarrassed to be seen with them.

"Why is he like that?" she asked as they walked back to the pension where they had taken a room. It had rained that evening and the sidewalks were still wet. "Why does he act as if he didn't trust us?"

"Because he doesn't. Palestine will be partitioned in three weeks, and that's all Hirsch can think about. Everyone who isn't his friend is his enemy—that's just the way his mind works."

"After all this, aren't you his friend?"

"No."

"But he has what he wants. It's over, isn't it?"

"No. It won't be over until tomorrow."

That night she sat on their bed in her nightdress, her arms wrapped around her knees, listening to Inar play the cello. She felt she could very happily spend the rest of her life just this way, in a tiny room with him, watching the way his strong fingers moved over the strings. She wondered how long it would take for her to learn to recognize all of the music he played, or if there was too much of it for that. Inar said there wasn't a lot written for the solo cello, but she didn't think she had ever heard him play the same thing twice. Sometimes he would even play something he had written himself, and then smile and ask her how she liked it. When she didn't know how to answer he would just laugh.

Tonight he played Bach, slow and tragic so that she wanted to cry. He could do that, make the music into something almost like a state of soul. He could make her believe he understood everything about her. She loved him so much it was like being in pain.

And when he came to bed, and ran his hand down her back in a way that made her tremble, it was as if the music were still playing somewhere. It was as if they never would have another tomorrow. She felt helpless against his great strength, and that helplessness itself was a kind of ecstasy. But, no, the past was not over yet.

In the morning Inar telephoned down for their breakfast. He seemed unwilling to let go of their little moment, almost as if he were afraid it would never come again.

"What do I have to do?" she asked.

"Nothing much. We'll drive you to the Österrei-chischer Bankverein, and you'll go inside and clean out your safe-deposit box. It's all perfectly legal—they must have your signature on file. Did von Goltz ever ask you to sign anything?"

"Yes. A little yellow card the night we escaped from Waldenburg. He made a joke about wanting it for his memory book." Suddenly she felt ashamed, unable to look him in the face. "Inar, do you mind so very much about the General and—the rest of it."

"Let's not worry about what I mind and don't mind. After today it'll be as if it never happened."

"Do you promise?"

"I promise."

There was a knock at the door and a woman wearing an apron over her black dress brought in their tray. Inar had nothing except a cup of coffee, and while he sat in his chair and drank it he talked about his family in New York—it seemed he had an old aunt he liked very much, and cousins—and a place called "Broadway" where he had worked before the war.

"Could you still work there? I mean, if you went back?"

"Maybe as a bass player. I could pick up jobs as an arranger, or maybe even take up conducting. I could go into teaching—find a little ivy-covered university and give lessons on the cello and spend the weekends writing quartets. I might even like that. Don't worry. We wouldn't starve."

It was the first time he had spoken as if he assumed they would always be together. But when he smiled he made it seem like nothing but a wistful dream.

When they went downstairs Jerry Hirsch was already waiting for them on a bench in the entrance hall. He was looking at a newspaper, which he quickly folded up and put away when he saw them.

"I was reading the news from home," he said. "The Syrian foreign minister is making lots of vague threats. I wonder if that means he hasn't heard about Hagemann yet."

"I rather imagine it means he has. He must assume you're in full production by now."

The look that passed between the two men suggested a division so old and so clearly understood by each of them that they hardly even needed to mention it. Their care with each other was a symptom of respect across an unbridgeable divide that had nothing to do with personal feelings. It simply didn't matter whether they liked each other or not. They could never even pretend to be friends. It always made Esther profoundly uneasy to be around both of them together.

"The woman who runs this place promised our car would be perfectly safe parked outside overnight. Was it still there when you came in?"

Hirsch nodded. "This place is a long way from New York, isn't it."

"Yes, it's a long way. My leg is bothering me a little this morning, so why don't you drive. Can you manage all right with your arm?"

"Sure. It can use the exercise."

The bank was perhaps two kilometers into the center of the city. Nothing they saw on their drive suggested that Linz had sustained any war damage, but the people, if not actually ragged, were at least shabbily dressed, as they were everywhere in the occupied territories. It was a clear, bright morning, a proof that spring was really upon them. Inar sat with Esther on the rear seat and held her hand. He seemed far away.

When they stopped the car, Inar got out and held the door open for her. He remained standing on the sidewalk, and when she turned around to look for him, just before stepping inside the bank, he smiled and waved in encouragement.

The clerk who took care of the safe-deposit customers sat on a stool inside a tiny cage. Why this was necessary was unclear, since he didn't look particularly ferocious and there was nothing in the cage with him except half a dozen registry books and a large metal card file. He was about fifty, thin and pinched. His hair was light brown and carefully combed and his skin seemed a little too large for him. He peered at Esther without smiling, as if unsure what she could possibly want in such a place.

"Yes?" he said at last. "May I help you?"

Esther pulled up the chain from underneath the collar of her dress and showed him the key.

"I have a box here. My name is Fräulein Esther Rosensaft."

The clerk took down one of his books and looked something up. It seemed to take him a long time.

"The number, please?"

"3454641."

"Yes—would you sign this, please?" He pushed a yellow card toward her through the opening in his cage, and Esther wrote her name on it. He checked it against another card in his file. Nothing in his face betrayed whether or not he was pleased they were a match.

"Yes. Now if you would please give me your key?"

They went back into the vault together and the
clerk took out a key of his own, which he kept tethered
to a long silver chain that ran from a loop around one
of his suspender buttons into his left-hand trousers
pocket, and opened a small metal door from which he
extracted a black box, also metal, the approximate size
and shape of a kitchen drawer. He handed it to her
with all the ceremony of someone ridding himself of
a public trust.

"I expect you would prefer to examine the contents
in private?"

Esther was shown into a room not much larger
than a shower stall, where nevertheless there was a
desk and a chair. She sat down and the clerk closed
the door on her. It was a relief, she discovered, to be
alone.

The box contained nothing except a large manila
envelope, strangely bulky. When she opened it she
understood why. Inside was a set of papers, perhaps
an inch thick and held together between stiff back
covers, and a 9-millimeter Luger, standard Wehrmacht issue. There was also a note.

Dearest Esther,
    If you are reading this you have survived
in spite of everything, for which I am thankful.
I leave you the pistol in case Hagemann is
waiting for you outside, since you will have to
kill him or he will certainly kill you. Be sure
to disengage the safety catch and then, when
first you see him and before your courage has
a chance to fail, shoot him. Keep pulling the
trigger until the magazine clicks empty.
    No one would ever think to punish you for

ending the life of so wicked a man, so you will
be safe. I would have given much to see his
face when he sees what you have brought him
from this dark vault. Please don't fail me in
this. I have a right to my little joke.

Ulrich

Yes, the General would have to have his little joke.
In the first few minutes, as she struggled with the
impulse to weep, she hardly knew what in her confusion of feeling took the first place. There was fear
at the narrowness of her escape, and there was a bitter
loathing. Had they all gone through so much for so
little? It seemed so.

No, this she would not show to Inar. They both
had enough to forget without this. There was a waste-
paper basket under the desk; she tore the note into
the smallest pieces she could manage before she threw
them in. She would have burned them if she could.
She would leave the pistol behind.

The clerk was waiting for her outside. They put
the metal box back into the vault, and the clerk handed
her back her key. That was all there was to it.

Outside, Inar and Jerry Hirsch were both standing
on the sidewalk, the sun on their faces. They looked
as if neither of them had spoken in several minutes.

"Is that it?" Jerry asked, not even trying to conceal
his eagerness. He held out his hand and, without
thinking, Esther gave him the papers. He opened the
front cover and began flipping through the pages so
that they crackled in the windless air. "I'm no tech-
nician, but it sure looks like the real thing. Holy
Moses—wait 'til the boys back in Tel Aviv get a load
of this!"

Inar's face went tight for just an instant and then he glanced at Esther and smiled, opening the door to the rear seat for her. When they were both inside, Jerry came out of his trance enough to walk around the front of the car and get behind the wheel, tossing the papers on the seat beside him.

It wasn't until he had started the car that he noticed the revolver in Inar's hand, the same one he always carried. Esther had grown so used to the sight of it that she hadn't even noticed he had it with him. The butt was resting on the top of the backrest and it was pointed directly at Jerry's head.

"Just drive," Inar said quietly. His voice sounded tired. He leaned back against his seat, cradling the pistol on his lap. Perhaps as a precaution he reached across and took both of Esther's hands in his scarred left hand, holding them gently but firmly. He didn't look at her. "Stay where I can see you and don't even think about playing the hero. You of all people know what a mess one of these things makes at close range. Let's go."

"Jesus Christ, I should have known." Jerry turned around to look at Inar, but he kept his hands up on the steering wheel. "Okay, pal, where to?"

"I'll let you know along the way. For now, just drive."

Jerry put the car into gear and headed slowly out into the traffic.

What was going on? Esther was afraid even to ask. She searched Inar's face for an answer, but he had retreated into a stony sullenness that revealed nothing. As he had so often in the past, he wore a mask behind which only his eyes seemed alive. She would have to wait and see, the same as Jerry. She would have to find out why he had ceased to trust her.

They drove away from the center of the city. Every so often Inar would issue a brief command and they would turn off into another street. The people on the sidewalks paid them no attention. This drama seemed to concern only themselves.

In ten minutes they were outside of Linz entirely. In fifteen minutes they were in the countryside. Inar directed them to a dirt road that led off into fields covered with yellow stubble.

"Stop the car," he said. When the engine was still he let go of Esther's hands and reached across the backrest to the front seat to take the keys out of the ignition. "We get out here, Jerry. Bring the goods with you."

Outside it felt colder than it had in the city. There was even a breath of wind, enough to make Esther bury her hands in the pockets of her coat. She felt a strange excitement. No fear—what did she have to be afraid of, except perhaps that Inar no longer cared for her? Inar was not dangerous, not to her. Inar was not Hagemann.

And yet the expression on Jerry Hirsch's face said something quite different. As he stood there at the edge of the dusty little strip of road he was in the presence of his enemy. And he knew all about enemies.

"Shall I give them to you now, or do you want to wait until after you've killed me?" he asked, holding the papers in their stiff black cover under his arm. "Who are we waiting for out here? I can just imagine."

There was a small stand of trees some sixty or

seventy meters away, where the ground seemed to slope down as if to meet an irrigation canal or perhaps even a river. Inar held up his arm and pointed toward it.

"Let's go over there," he said. "We'll be out of the wind."

"Anything you say, pal. You're the one with the gun."

The fields were hard, crusted mud, broken into patches like the surface of an old oil painting. Jerry stayed in front, and Esther and Inar walked behind. There was nothing to suggest his wounded leg was bothering him.

Inar held his gun in one hand and Esther's hand in the other. He was no longer worried about her interference, if that was what it had been; he simply held her hand the way any man might have, to let her know that he hadn't forgotten that she belonged to him. It was the only way she could have known, because he never looked at her.

They were almost to the trees before she saw the little stream, hardly two meters wide, that seemed to form some sort of natural barrier. The field on the other side was already tractored into neat little furrows, ready for the spring planting.

"We can stop here," Inar said. He let go of Esther's hand and leaned against the thick trunk of a tree that looked ageless. It hadn't regained its leaves yet and its roots were partially exposed on the side nearest the stream, which added to the impression. For the first time, Inar showed that he was tired.

Jerry Hirsch stood waiting, tense and expectant. He seemed to be trying to decide who was absent, as if he looked for them to show up at any moment. When his eyes fell on Inar they were filled with resentment.

"I haven't sold out, if that's what you're thinking." Inar pushed himself a little away from the tree trunk, as if to draw notice to his independence. "We're not out here to meet anyone from the Syrian foreign office. This is strictly between you and me."

"Really, Christiansen? You amaze me. Then why here? Any business you have with me could have been settled in town over a couple of drinks."

"Not any business. They don't like fires in hotel rooms. You're going to burn that file."

"The hell I am!"

Inar brought up the muzzle of his revolver and pulled back the hammer with his thumb. It was pointed at a spot just an inch or so below Jerry's right eye.

"Jerry, use your head. Why do you suppose I waited for you in Munich? I could have taken care of this three days ago. You're here as my witness, so your bosses in Tel Aviv can sleep at night and I don't have to spend the rest of my life waiting for you or someone just like you to show up wanting to know what I did with von Goltz's recipe book. You're here so that it can all end today. Burn the file."

He reached into his coat pocket and took out his cigarette lighter, holding it up for Jerry to see and then throwing it to him. It landed on the ground at his feet.

"Burn the file, Jerry. It isn't going to solve anything if I have to shoot you and then burn it myself. At least if you do it you won't imagine there's been some sort of conjuring trick played on you. Come on, burn it."

"God damn it, Christiansen, you're out of your

fuckin' mind!" Jerry was almost beside himself. He held the papers in his good hand, shaking them threateningly as if they were a weapon. "God damn it, don't you know we'll have a war on our hands in just three goddamn weeks? *Burn* it!?"

"Burn it. You can fight your war without using nerve gas, Jerry. The Syrians won't know any better— bluff them. I'm not going to let you make it easy for yourself at the price of committing a wholesale massacre. You'll have to find some other way."

"It isn't your decision to make, Christiansen. Jesus Christ, it isn't any of your damn business!"

"It's my business. If I turn my back on this, and you use this junk to murder innocent people, there's no way I can avoid the responsibility. I will have handed this to you."

"You made a deal, Christiansen. And now you're welching on it."

The two men stood staring at each other in silence, Jerry's accusation hanging in the air like a pall. Finally Inar shrugged his shoulders, as if abandoning the attempt to make himself understood.

"My 'deal,' as you call it, was with Mordecai. Not with the Mossad, and not with you—with Mordecai. I have the impression I'm keeping faith with that." He lowered the muzzle of his pistol and let the hammer back down. "We got Hagemann, Jerry. He and his friends butchered half of Europe, but we finally got them. That's all finished. If you and your brand-new country want to grow up to be just like them, that's up to you. I don't think that's what Mordecai would have wanted, but he's dead so it's up to you. Just don't expect any help."

"You really mean it."

"Yes, I really mean it. I have enough blood on my conscience."

Jerry reached down and picked up the cigarette lighter. Then, holding the file by one of its stiff covers, he lit the last page at the corner. They stood there watching while, one by one, the sheets began to burn. Finally Jerry had to let it drop. It lay spine up on the ground until finally even the covers had caught fire. In all, it took about five minutes before the flames disappeared and there was nothing left except smoke and ash.

"The ultimate weapon," Jerry said at last. "The little country's atomic bomb, and I burned it. I can't believe this."

"There's just one more thing."

Inar tossed his pistol into the air and then caught it again so that he was holding it by the barrel. Then he took two steps forward and offered it to Jerry Hirsch, who took it probably without thinking.

"Now or later, you'll want to settle up for this. It might as well be now."

"No, Inar, please . . ." She took his arm and buried her face in it. There had been enough now. She would never forgive him for this. "Please, Inar—please think of me a little."

But he only stood his ground, hardly even breathing. He really was prepared to die.

And Jerry Hirsch was just as ready to kill him. He raised the pistol, taking careful aim at Inar's heart. The process seemed to take forever.

"You have this coming," he said. "If ever anybody earned it, you sure as hell . . . Aw, shit!"

And then, suddenly, he pulled back his arm and threw. The pistol hit Inar square in the chest and bounced off. He hardly seemed to notice it.

"You goddamn sentimental *goyish* bastard. You've ruined everything."

Inar reached over and picked up the pistol, putting it out of sight under his coat.

"What will you tell your bosses back home?" he asked.

"I don't know." There was real anguish in Jerry's face. "I guess it'll have to be that we both agreed to this, and I decided not to take the chance of soiling the Jewish national honor with possession of a genocidal weapon. Anything would be better than confessing I was dumb enough to let myself get jumped like a goddamn schoolkid. Isn't that a choice phrase, 'Jewish national honor'? Tel Aviv is filled with bleeding hearts, so maybe they'll even buy it."

"It was the right thing to do."

"Like hell it was." He swallowed hard and made a disgusted gesture with his right hand. "This won't be a nice war, Christiansen. A lot of raw things will get themselves done, and just once, just once, I'd have liked to see the atrocities happen to somebody else besides the Jews. Of course you wouldn't be able to understand that, would you."

"Maybe not."

"You weren't in the camps," Esther found herself saying. No one could have been more surprised than she, but the words seemed to come of themselves. "I was, and so I have a right to care what is done in my name. I think Herr Leivick would have agreed. It is a blasphemy to invoke the dead to justify such things.

Jews of all people should know the value of clean hands."

As they walked back to the car, Inar put his arm over her shoulder and drew her to him. He smiled in that way she had seen only a few times, the way that meant he was really happy.

"You didn't tell me," she said, trying to sound angry. "You didn't trust me."

"I didn't want you to have to decide between one loyalty and another. It didn't have anything to do with trust—you might have thought I was doing the wrong thing."

"I don't think you did the wrong thing."

"But now you won't ever have to question your part in it. Nobody gave you a choice, so you're off the hook. It's better this way."

They continued on in silence. Esther was almost too happy to talk. It really was over now. The past was dead. She felt as if she had just turned sixteen, as if Inar were the first man to come into her life. Perhaps in a way he really was. At any rate, she felt free. That was love, to feel free.

And then something occurred to her. She had seen the little announcement in the Munich newspapers, so she didn't know why it suddenly came as such a surprise.

"Inar," she said, "did you know that today is Purim?"

"Now how would I have known that?"

Catalog

If you are interested in a list of fine Paperback
books, covering a wide range of subjects
and interests, send your name and address,
requesting your free catalog, to:

McGraw-Hill Paperbacks
1221 Avenue of Americas
New York, N. Y. 10020